The Storms of Fate

Also by Cynthia S. Roberts

The Running Tide
Upon Stormy Downs
A Wind from the Sea
A Seagull Crying
The Fox-Red Hills

The Storms of Fate

Cynthia S. Roberts

This title first published in Great Britain 1992 by
SEVERN HOUSE PUBLISHERS LTD of
35 Manor Road, Wallington, Surrey SM6 0BW
First published in the U.S.A. 1992 by
SEVERN HOUSE PUBLISHERS INC of
475 Fifth Avenue, New York, NY 10017–6220.

British Library Cataloguing in Publication Data
Roberts, Cynthia S.
  The storms of fate.
  I. Title
  823.914 [F]

  ISBN 0-7278-4337-0

Typeset by Hewer Text Composition Services, Edinburgh
Printed and bound in Great Britain by
Billings & Sons Ltd, Worcester

To Mary Sheila Gammon,
for loyal and valued friendship.

Part One

FRANCE 17

'A brave man struggling in the storms of fate'

(Pope – Prologue to Addison's 'Cato')

CHAPTER 1

Jean-Luc, Vicomte de Saint Hilaire, knew that whatever happened he must not betray fear . . . It was the mark, Papa had told him, of cowards and men ill-bred. The blood of their family had been spilled over many centuries in the cause of France, and always with valour and nobility. Jean-Luc was nine years old, and did not want his blood to be spilled. Once he had seen a wild boar killed in a hunt in the forest, and the violence and the blood and the cries of the dying creature had stayed with him, filling him with pity, so that he could scarce move for sickness that burned in his throat. He had not shown Papa, for he knew that it would anger him. Yet, sometimes, at night, he dreamed of it. It was always the same, save that now he was the hunted, and the fear and blood and the savage faces crowding upon him were the faces of wild boars, tusked and vicious. He felt the pain as they tore at his flesh, small eyes cruel, teeth sharp. He would scream aloud, and awaken, face wet with sweat and tears, hoping that none had heard him . . . No. It would not do to confess it to Papa, or that his greatest terror lay in the confusion which clouded his mind, for the men's faces and the wild boars' were one and the same, and of people he recognised and trusted.

Jean-Luc did not want to leave the chateau, for he had been born within it and, until now, had felt safe and protected by its grey walls. He regretted every moment spent away from it, whether in the house in Paris or Mama's childhood home in Brittany, which she loved so deeply, and where Grandmère and Grandpère, although so very old, still lived.

But now, all of France was in such a turmoil, Papa had explained to him gravely, and the lives of all those who, like themselves, owned estates and were of old and privileged families, were in danger of death . . . The mobs were

11

murderous and baying for blood, and none was safe from their vengeance.

"But are we not safe here, at Valandré, Papa?" he asked, puzzled . . . "The servants and villagers upon the estate are friends. Why should they hurt us?"

"When there is hatred and discontent, my son," the Comte de Valandré had explained, "it kills all reason, as it kills compassion . . . It is the law of the mass, the brute . . . God knows, there have been cruelties and excesses enough by those in power. They have practised every kind of villainy and infamy, caring for nothing and no-one but their own indulgence. They have sown the seeds of rebellion in their contempt for the poor and starving, and reap in return a harvest of death . . ."

"But, Papa," Jean-Luc had protested vehemently, "They cannot think that *you* are cruel! No man could believe it of you . . ."

The Comte de Valandré put a gentle hand upon his son's shoulder as Jean-Luc continued passionately, "You have always told me we were responsible for them. Our tenants and workers are our inherited family, and it is our duty and our privilege to serve them, as they serve us . . . Is that not true?"

"Yes, Jean-Luc," answered the comte, feeling a surge of helpless affection for this earnest, grave-faced boy who had learnt, too soon, the duties of his name . . . "It is true."

"Then there is nothing to fear . . ." Jean-Luc's childish face cleared, grew confident. "Only fools or imbeciles would seek us out and kill us for the . . . cruelties of others, or the name we bear. They will see that you are a good man, Papa, and brave. I will stay with you, whoever comes."

A small hand reached out reassuringly to touch his father's. The Comte de Valandré was not a man given to emotion. He had been well schooled to control it, for it made a man vulnerable to his enemies, but he saw in Jean-Luc the promise of the man he would become, and was glad.

"You had best return to your lessons," he said, more brusquely than he had intended. "It would not be fitting if the future Comte de Valandré were a dolt and a dullard."

"Yes, Papa."

He watched Jean-Luc leave obediently with a smile and a careful bend of the knee, and bowed his head in return. Soon,

12

he thought, he must be told of what he must face, should all else fail . . . Paris was already a charnel house, it was said, with the mobs whipped to ever greater violence and bloodlust . . . There were guillotines at every street corner, the gutters fouled with blood and with putrefying corpses, a stench upon the air . . . None was safe from the depravity of the mass. It had become a brutish, mindless beast with a lust to kill . . . uncontrollable, insatiable. Families were torn apart as callously as their flesh, the screams unheard in the roaring, drunken bloodiness of the crowds. One corruption had simply given place to another. He sighed despairingly. Vengeance grew by feeding upon itself, like a starving animal, gnawing at its own flesh, devouring its own blood, until it weakened and perished . . . But how many others must perish first, innocent and guilty? His wife, the comtesse, had begged that Jean-Luc should not be told of the horrors he might face, "He is too young. A child. Sufficient unto the hour!" He must send them away to safety with Raoul, the old seneschal, for he could be trusted, and, if there were need, would certainly die beside them rather than betray them . . . No, Jean-Luc was not too young to learn of death. It would come, and soon, and he could only pray that it would be swift, for it was never easy . . .

Hélène, Comtesse de Valandré, was restless and afraid. She had warned Jean-Luc that he must, on no account, stray farther than the parterre and lawns, and remain within calling distance at all times, never venturing beyond the curve of the carriage-way. He was an adventurous boy, with a lively intelligence and curiosity and a deep love of forest and stream. Yet she had no doubt that he would do as she bade, for he was always obedient. Soon they would be gone from here, and the knowledge brought her a depth of pain which she had never expected to experience. She had always, in the past, thought of Brittany as her home, with its savagery of rock and shore, the high clifftops ablaze with sulphurous broom, and tufted cushions of sea-pinks and heather . . . She had missed the cries of the sea birds, and wept for them, as she had wept for herself and the need to return to those wild places, pungent with the sharpness of tide and sand, and softened with wind-borne thyme.

It had been a marriage of convenience, as was the custom; a

joining of two families, each complementing and renewing the blood of the other . . . Now that blood was the birthright of Jean-Luc . . . How strange that such a marriage should grow into love . . . like those sea-plants growing upon rock which seemed barren, yet clinging to the thin soil until they take firm root, and blossom with vivid, unexpected power . . . A flowering of love for Armand de Valandré, felt now in their son. A flowering too late for this alien countryside, and even this great, impersonal chateau which had so filled her with terror and foreboding as a young bride, its darkness reflecting her own fears . . . She would grieve its loss, and dream of returning . . . It had stood for so long, its walls stout, its turrets crowned with sharp, conical roofs, as if sheltering those within from storm and deluge . . . No shelter now.

She glanced apprehensively from the window of the petit-salon, as she had so many times of late, reassuring herself that Jean-Luc was safe . . . an outwardly elegant, assured woman, hair immaculately coiffed in the high powdered wig with its pretty fall of ringlets. Her skin was porcelain-fine, and barely had need of powdered haresfoot or rouge pot for cheek and lips, so gently natural was her own pretty colouring. Her eyes were wide, blue, and long lashed, her unusual slenderness enhanced by the hooped skirts of her rose-silk dress, trimmed with panels of delicate Valenciennes lace, repeated in the fichu about her pale shoulders. There was a parure of dark sapphires at her throat and ears, and matching gemstones set into the heels of her pretty slippers . . . Yet there was a restless agitation in her movements which could not be hid. She would summon Raoul to ride beside Jean-Luc into the countryside and woods. It was too cruel to incarcerate the child here. He grew oppressed and troubled, unable even to find stability in the familiar discipline of lessons, for his tutor, Monsieur Deferre, had left, simply disappeared, without the courtesy of a reason, or notice of his intention. It seemed to her that the wound that affected Paris, festering and obscene, grew ever wider and deeper, spreading its putrefaction . . . Was it her own fear which bedevilled her, or were the servants infected with it too, growing more resentful and surly with each passing day? All save Raoul, whom she would trust with Jean-Luc's life . . .

14

Jean-Luc and his protector rode out in high good spirits, for they were at ease in each other's company, and the day was as warm as their pleasure in being free . . . Raoul was careful to lead them only upon the narrow, little-known by-ways, for it would not do to meet a band of vicious, unknown rabble, seeking sport at the young vicomte's expense. He had served the Comte de Valandré, and his father, the old comte, before him, but, to his sorrow, it seemed that he would not now serve a third generation . . . The Ancien Régime was already dying, and those, such as he, who had known its true paternalism, would regret its passing. He was an old man, and did not care for change, and who could foretell what rabble and filth might be spawned to replace it and the elegance of its ways?

The old man and Jean-Luc rode companionably together for an hour and more, until the old seneschal, hearing some alien sound, paused, alert and ready to bid the boy take flight . . . No, he had not been mistaken; there was the sound upon the highway of an ill-disciplined crowd, their cries and shouts as yet indistinguishable, but inexorably drawing nearer.

He grasped the bridle of the vicomte's horse, and, urging the boy to silence, rode back swiftly with him upon the sheltered way they had ventured. When they had come to a forest clearing, and the way was safe it seemed, a woodcutter upon the estate, a brawny, uncouth youth of low intelligence emerged from the shelter of some trees bearing a scythe . . . Jean-Luc had no fear of him, or any in the comte's service. He had known and greeted them from early childhood, but Raoul's heart was pounding harshly in his breast, for he knew he was no match for the other's quickness and savage strength, should he attack . . . In a swift movement, the woodcutter grasped at the bridle of Jean-Luc's horse, and raised the scythe high, its honed steel bright in the sunlight.

When it seemed that the blade must fall, slashing through flesh, some shamed remembrance of past good halted the man's arm, and the weapon dropped uselessly to his side . . . Then, with an oath, the youth screwed up his lips and spat full in the vicomte's face, and, with a smile of contemptuousness, strode off into the trees. Jean-Luc, outraged beyond fear of danger, would have ridden after him, had not the servant put a restraining hand upon the bridle of his mount. The old

15

man's skin was ashen and moist, and his lips so blue-tinged that Jean-Luc was fearful that he would not be strong enough to ride back upon the way. He dismounted, awkward with concern, to murmur, "Raoul, you must rest awhile, then I will lead you home." He hesitated, only to add more firmly, "I beg that you will tell no-one of what has occurred . . . It is best that I let him go, and make nothing of it. I would not wish to add dignity to his actions, nor lose my own . . ." Raoul nodded, his eyes warm with pride,

"If that is your wish, Monsieur le Vicomte," he said, "it shall be as you command . . ."

When they finally returned to the chateau, Jean-Luc led the horses to the stable block, bidding Raoul rest within the house, for, although the old man's colour had returned, his breathing remained harsh and pained . . . There was an unnatural quietness pervading buildings and yard, the only discernible sounds those of the animals as they fidgetted and pawed, making small restless noises of unease. Although he called out loudly with growing impatience, and searched the harness-rooms and barns, there was no sign of stable-boys or grooms. The outbuildings were deserted, as were their living quarters, and all their possessions carefully removed, as if they had been coaxed away, rather than fled in terrified haste . . .

Jean-Luc approached the chateau with a feeling of apprehension and chill, not knowing what changes awaited him. There were none. The graciously curved symmetry of the twin staircases of stone, their sculpted balustrades, its pointed turrets, the elegance of its high-windowed facade remained unaltered. All was the same . . . Yet, was there not something ominous about such silence? What it lacked was movement, life. None laboured upon the flower beds of the parterre or upon the lawns and carriageway. No footman advanced within the hall; no servant scurried about her duties, or hurried from sight into the dark caverns below stairs.

Jean-Luc, afraid to call out, ascended the great staircase. The portraits of his ancestors, stern and forbidding, stared down at him sombrely from their gilded frames, their haughty features arrogantly dismissing such an ignoble sprig. The scion in whom the mingled blood of all faltered and grew thin.

"Jean-Luc!" It was Raoul's voice from above, urgent and commanding. "Jean-Luc! At once!"

Jean-Luc, hand gripping the baluster, mounted in haste. Raoul led him towards the turret room where the Comte de Valandré sometimes withdrew for solace from the affairs of the estate, and where none dare disturb him nor enter uninvited . . . He stood now before the marble chimney-piece, the two great hunting hounds lolling at his feet, unchained, and with collars of thick leather studded with protectors of brass . . . Jean-Luc could only stare at them in amazement and disbelief, because never were they allowed beyond the base of the staircase, in case they should damage the fragile porcelain, and trample the pale Aubusson carpets under their great muddied paws, or shed hairs upon the silk of sofas and chairs. Papa had even instructed the iron-smith to craft replicas of the entrance gates to the chateau, miniatures, perfect in every fine-wrought detail, and had them secured across the staircase. His 'hound-gates', he had christened them, to Mama's amusement, and all, whether servants or family, were required to see that they were kept firmly closed, on pain of incurring his displeasure. The unlikely sight of the chiens-de-chasse sprawling unhindered at his father's feet disturbed Jean-Luc's sense of the order of things more than the emptiness of the stables and yard, or the open case of pistols and shot and the musket upon the desk.

"Papa?" he said, puzzled, awaiting explanation.

The comte glanced first towards Raoul, as if in some way signalling wordlessly for his help, then said to Jean-Luc,

"I must ask you . . . No, I must command you to do exactly as I instruct, Jean-Luc, without question or hesitation, you understand?"

Jean-Luc did not understand, but the gravity in his father's face disturbed him.

"Yes, Papa," he said obediently.

"As soon as it begins to grow dark, you will leave the chateau with Mama and Raoul."

Jean-Luc looked towards Raoul for enlightenment, but the old man's face was carefully expressionless.

"Raoul will provide you with clothing suitable for a farm-boy, and you will spend the night in the forest in a hut which he has prepared . . ."

"But Papa . . ."

"You will do as Raoul says at all times, and immediately!" the comte continued implacably. "You will no longer be the Vicomte de Saint Hilaire, but Luc Nolais, Raoul's grandson. You will remain silent when he bids you; do whatever he orders, without hesitation. Blind obedience might well save your life, for he has only your safety, and Mama's, in mind, whatever he demands . . . He has my authority, you understand? His word will be mine."

"But will you not be coming with us, Papa?"

Again the comte glanced at Raoul with a wry smile, then said, more gently,

"There are matters which will keep me here at the chateau for a little while . . . but, if it is possible, then I will follow, soon . . ."

"The servants, Papa . . . there is no-one to serve you."

"No. I have sent them away, for their own safety. It would not be . . . just, or fitting, that they should remain."

"Then they are coming here, Papa, to the chateau? Those people you spoke of . . . the murderers . . . from Paris?" His voice was rising childishly, despite all his efforts to keep it firm . . . "Those who seek revenge . . .?"

"Raoul has heard rumour of some . . . mob approaching . . . bent only upon drunkenness and mischief, perhaps . . . We cannot be sure. Yet, even if they prove harmless, I would not have Maman subjected to their foul-mouthed blasphemy, their insults . . . I trust her to your protection . . . You understand?"

"Yes, Papa . . ." Jean-Luc's face was as fiercely earnest as his tone as he blurted, "You may trust me and speak to me as a man . . ."

"Indeed, my son." Despite the comte's gravity, he could not altogether suppress a smile. "What would you have me say?"

"The truth, sir," replied the vicomte simply. "I know that you would not have dismissed the servants, nor arranged for our flight from the chateau, unless you faced the greatest danger . . . Unless we all faced death . . ." he amended accusingly. "Is that not so?"

"Yes. I cannot deny it."

"Then I will stand beside you. It is my duty as a de Valandré . . ."

18

The comte's eyes met Raoul's above the young vicomte's head, and although neither of them spoke, no word was necessary, for they were in perfect accord.

"You are a brave . . ." the comte paused, "a brave man," he said firmly, "and honest . . . I will be honest, as you ask, and speak the truth. I have your mother's safety at heart, for she is dear to me, and even without you, Raoul would not fail to protect her and deliver her from harm . . . But you, too, are dear to me, and you are the last . . . will be the last living and bearing the de Valandré name . . . You, as I, must place duty above all other things . . . It is what we have been bred to expect, is it not?"

"Yes, Papa . . ." Jean-Luc's voice was low, uncertain. "But I would not be afraid to stand beside you."

They stared at each other in silence for a moment, but the comte made no movement to embrace Jean-Luc, but said,

"Since I acknowledge you to be a man, I have no need to remind you of what you have known from your earliest days; that your loyalty and allegiance are to God, France, the king, and the good name of your family, and those who serve it . . . It is a sacred trust, and cannot be forsworn . . . You will act upon it always . . ."

"Yes, Papa . . . I will act upon it, always."

The tears were running soundlessly down Jean-Luc's face, although he was unaware of them.

"And will I be allowed to return, Papa? When all is finished here . . . ?"

"Yes. I pray that it may, one day, be possible . . . when reason holds sway over bloodshed . . . The castellan has orders to save whatever can be taken and stored, for there are cellars and passage ways unknown to any, save those I trust . . . Raoul has a plan of them in his safekeeping, which he will, one day, deliver to you or destroy, should there be need . . ."

"And the animals, Papa; the horses and the dogs . . .?" the child's voice broke helplessly.

"The servants have orders to take for their own those beasts which may be of use to them . . . the horses have been left simply because they are too distinctive for common usage, and would serve to identify those in sympathy with us . . . The castellan will see that they are shot . . . Death will be

19

swift and humane, I promise. The dogs will remain here with me . . ."

"But, Papa . . ." the cry was torn out of him as Jean-Luc, abandoning all that he had been taught, ran to fling his arms about the elegantly clad figure of the comte. "Oh, Papa . . ." he wept, "they will kill you, and the dogs too, and burn the chateau . . . I will never wish to return . . . What will be left for me . . .?"

"Your name, my son," said the comte, touching the fair head and, with an ache of tenderness, feeling the child's thin body shaken with grief. "Your name, my son," he repeated gently, "and life itself . . . It is all a man may ask of God."

CHAPTER 2

With the slow beginnings of darkness, the air grew chill, and the chateau became a cold, silent place, as if its walls and turrets, like those within, were oppressed by some terror which could be neither named nor imagined.

Hélène, Comtesse de Valandré, divested of all her finery, had dressed herself in the coarse homespun garments of a peasant woman. The clothing was ugly and much stained, and reeked of human sweat and the stale odours of cooking. The undergarments were stiff with dirt and wear, and had taken on the feel, and even the shape, of their previous wearer. The comtesse was a fastidious woman, but she did not shirk from wearing it, nor thrusting the crude, misshapen sabots upon her feet, for she knew they might well be the means of saving her from violation or death itself. She stared at herself in the looking-glass, taking in the unkempt hair, so crudely disarranged, and the pale face which, save for the wide blue eyes undeniably frightened now, was scarce recognisable as her own. The few jewels she was able to take with her, and the precious Louis d'or, were stitched into a cloth bag and tied about her waist under the coarse petticoat . . . the rest taken to the cellars by the castellan for safekeeping . . . Now, even he had left. The comte had paid him handsomely, but, despite his protestations, would not permit him to remain, for he valued him as a friend and would not set his life at peril.

Despite her resolution to stay calm and keep her dignity for Armand's sake and the boy's, a single tear spilled and ran through the dirt Hélène was streaking now upon her face, upon Raoul's insistence.

"You must disguise your face and your hands, Madame la Comtesse," he had urged quietly. "They are the hands and

21

skin of an aristocrat, and will betray you all too soon to those who search for such signs."

"I will do as you say, Raoul," she had replied, "for it is not some game we play, some masque or charade."

"No, Madame la Comtesse. It is truly a matter of life and death," he agreed soberly, "as is the need for me to call you Hélène, and no other name, lest it betray you . . . I ask most humbly that you will believe that I hold you in no less respect . . ."

She had patted his shoulder, declaring with a sincerity which had touched the old man deeply, "I have come to think of you as a friend, Raoul. A member of the de Valandré family . . . You are the equal of any in courage and loyalty. It will be fitting that you call me 'daughter' . . . You have earned that right . . ."

The comtesse was still staring, unseeing, into the ornate looking-glass when the Comte de Valandré entered, but she had wiped away that one stubborn tear which had betrayed her wretchedness. The comte was dressed in his most lavish costume; the coat of embroidered cloth-of-gold which he had last worn so proudly at the Court at Versailles . . . His small clothes were of creamy brocade to match the silken stockings, and his shoes wore buckles of chased silver . . . His cravat was of ruffled lace, with a diamond sunburst to hold it, and a froth of lace erupted into elegance at the cuffs of his coat. His well powdered hair was tied with an embroidered band, and decorating his breast the riband and order he so prized blazed defiance 'neath the candlelight of the heavy chandelier. "It is time, Hélène, my little peasant . . ." There was a smile upon his lips as he studied her, yet it did not reach his eyes. She saw in them only an anguish of loss deep as her own.

"I am sorry, sir," she said, only half in jest, "that this will be your last remembrance of me . . . I could have wished it otherwise."

"My dear . . . My love . . ." he said, drawing her to him, "I regret no moment of my time with you, not even this. You have been the joy of my life and its fulfilment . . . If I have never truly told you of my love for you, then I tell you now, humbly, and with gratitude . . . I have loved you with all my soul from that first moment I saw you . . ." The words, begun but not completed, were a sorrow between them. He kissed her most tenderly, then gently disengaged the soft arms which clung insistently about his neck. "Come, my dear . . ." He took her hand, turning over her palm, smiling at the softness under the careful coating of grime. Then he put it to his lips and kissed it reverently, and with regret. "Were you comtesse or peasant, Hélène, I swear that I would have found you . . . and taken no other, for without you I am incomplete . . . In life, or in death, I shall go on loving you . . ."

"And I you, Armand. I thank God for every moment I have been granted with you . . . It has been so short, but with so much happiness . . . Memories to fill the whole of my life, and after . . ." She could speak no more for the thickness in her throat and the tears which flowed, now, unchecked through the dirt upon her face. This, she thought, is the beginning of a death . . . If he dies, I shall surely die too . . .

He wiped her eyes patiently with the silken handkerchief at his cuff, the tightness of pain in his breast too fierce for the healing release of tears. He had talked to his son of courage and manliness. Now he had bitter need of his own.

Jean-Luc, waiting impatiently with Raoul in the dungeons below the chateau for his parents' coming, shivered, more from the dank, cold atmosphere than from fear. The moisture seemed to seep from the walls and stone pavours as the dampness of the earth bled through. He would not think of those who had suffered and perished here . . . perhaps upon the very place where he stood, their tortured cries of hunger and pain unheard . . . Perhaps this icy dampness was born of their tears, weeping still from the stones themselves . . . "You are cold, Monsieur le Vicomte? Tiens! I must learn to address you as 'Luc!'" the old man corrected himself irritably, aloud. "You are cold?" he repeated solicitously.

"No, I thank you, Raoul. It is the chafing of these clothes I wear . . . their harshness . . ." he lied. He glanced down before admitting with wry amusement, "I have often envied the freedom of others to dress so . . . with no thought that their discomfort might be greater than my own! I have much to learn . . ."

"Indeed!" And all of it more painful to endure than the mere roughness of clothing, Raoul thought compassionately. Yet,

God willing, the boy would survive, for he had courage and humour as well as the blood of the de Valandré's to sustain him. The comte had ordered that the iron flambeaux set into the walls be extinguished, and only lantern light used, lest the mob be alerted to the way of escape. In its thin light the child looked tense and ill-at-ease. Despite the pale hair streaked with filth, the dirt grimed face and limbs, and his foul-smelling clothes, the boy retained a curious dignity. A sense of his own identity. It had been bred into him, and might well be his undoing.

The old man and Jean-Luc heard at the same moment the iron gates to the cell grinding open, and the entry of the comte and comtesse. Beyond rose the muffled shouts and cries of those who had already scaled the walls and the sounds of pistol fire, mercifully diminished by distance, yet oppressively close . . .

The comte urged quietly, "There is little time, Raoul . . . help me to release the door to the tunnels."

Raoul bade Jean-Luc hold the lantern still and high as, with the comte, he grappled fiercely to prise away the loose stone which concealed the mechanism. It took but minutes, although, to those who watched as to those who laboured, it seemed an eternity before the wall itself swung outwards with a grinding slowness to reveal the foetid cavern beyond.

"Raoul," the comte commanded. "Take them now! Do not hesitate, I beg of you . . . Go, else it will be too late!"

Jean-Luc had clung to him, weeping, and declaring stubbornly, "No, Papa! I will not leave! I will stay with you . . . Please do not cast me away!"

But the comte, deaf to his pleas, and filled with terror lest they be discovered by the encroaching mob, thrust the boy with savagery into the blackness, shouting, "If you love me, I beg of you, go!"

Then, with an effort which brought the blood painfully throbbing and surging through his veins and a burning to his flesh, he wrenched the door closed . . . Then, with a greater effort, he bent low to lift the vast stone, the muscles and sinews standing proud upon his neck, a cry escaping him involuntarily as he thrust it into place, tearing nails and skin in his fury to be gone.

When all was secure, he took the one lantern remaining, and, returning through the passageway, mounted the stone staircase which led to the servants' quarters, and then emerged into the great hall . . . At once the two hounds awaiting his return ran to his side. He doused the lantern flame in his fingers. The flambeaux burning fiercely upon the walls filled the great hall with flickering torchlight, casting shadows upon the empty spaces where the portraits of his ancestors had once hung.

Surprisingly, Armand de Valandré felt no fear; he felt nothing save a great joy and release that those he loved would not stand beside him at the end, for he could not have borne to witness the pain and degradation of those he most dearly loved . . .

There was a sudden violence of ripping metal which told him that the great iron gates had been torn from their hinges and hurled aside by the mob . . . The dogs barked harshly, terror raising their hackles, a wildness of hysteria sharpening their voices, making them shrill . . . Armand de Valandré spoke to them quietly, reassuring them, bidding them be calm . . . The sounds of cries and shouts grew nearer, with a shattering of glass and a thunderous banging at the massive oaken doors . . . Then the relentless thudding of a battering ram; with screams and oaths of triumph, the doors flew open and the fierce bodies surged within, staves, guns, weapons and stones within their grasp.

Strangely, there was a silence before the crowd struck. The hounds leapt, snarling, tearing savagely at the throats of those who threatened. With a wild cry, the youth who had spat his contempt at the young vicomte in the forest raised his scythe and slashed it across the neck of a hound, severing flesh and bone. The remaining hound gave a shrill howl of pain and terror as the scythe descended once more; the comte raised his pistol and fired . . . The face of the woodcutter showed surprise and disbelief as blood slowly crimsoned his shirt front, then he fell beneath the trampling, careless feet of the mob.

Armand de Valandré knew for a moment the horror of Jean-Luc's nightmares as the cruel bestial faces closed for the kill. The knives and bare hands ripped and tore at his clothing and flesh, until the blood from his wounds blinded his eyes, and he knew only the all-devouring pain that came before death . . .

May God forgive them . . . he thought. May God prove more merciful than they . . .

The comtesse, fleeing with Raoul and her son through the dark passageways, felt a pain and terror which almost stilled her heart, and she could not, at first, believe that she had not screamed aloud. In the guttering light of the lantern, Raoul, who had been urging her onwards, saw the tears upon her cheeks, then a calm finality of loss . . . It told him, as surely as if he had seen him fall, that Armand de Valandré was dead.

The journey through the darkness of the forest was a halting and uneasy one, despite Raoul's sure knowledge of its safest tracks. In the thin lantern light the trees loomed high and menacing, their gnarled and twisted roots a trap for the unwary. Low branches and the raking stems of brambles tore at clothing and flesh, while all about, the scurrying of unseen things and the harsh screech of an owl with some small trapped creature fast in its talons reflected their own cruel plight . . . They, too, were fugitives, prey to the unknown dark and predators unseen. Hunted. Dispossessed. Yet to each the greatest anguish had come when Raoul first bade them halt, and rest. Behind them the sky had been licked with red and orange flame; a glowing sunset fire, from which the towers and pinnacles of the chateau rose stark as burned-out coals . . . Spent . . . Lifeless.

Waiting only to crumble into useless ash . . . They would not think of what might be within.

"The chateau will last a thousand years . . ." Raoul's voice had been rough with hurt; the voice of a tired old man grown halting and unsure . . . "The stones will stand for ever . . . The fire is in the courtyard beyond . . . They are burning useless, valueless things . . . All that is of worth has already been saved . . ."

Dear God, he thought, I speak like a madman, an imbecile! A fool in his dotage . . . What comfort is it to them, or me? Seven hundred years, and more, of stone and history! It has been all of my life . . . and theirs. Yet, I would willingly forgo every last stone, and my own poor flesh with them, for the life of Armand de Valandré. Tears made his voice harsh as he ordered,

"We must move on, at once! Lest the light be seen . . . They will surely come seeking us . . ."

Clumsily, awkwardly, he had stumbled upon his way, bidding

them follow, but the comtesse's hand fell gently upon his shoulder, halting him.

"Raoul . . . I know that your grief and suffering are as ours . . . If I am unable to speak of it again, for any reason . . .", she hesitated, searching for words, "Whatever befalls, I beg you will believe that my love and thankfulness for your loyalty are as deep as . . . Armand's . . ."

Her voice faltered and fell silent upon her husband's name. Raoul lifted his lantern high before him, that she might not see his ravaged face, saying in return,

"I will do my best to protect you, Madame la Comtesse, I promise . . . although I could have wished myself younger, and with greater strength . . ."

"You have strength of spirit, Raoul."

"When the cause is just, a man has God's strength to uphold him . . ." The voice was the young vicomte's, but the words those of his father, the comte, stirring within the boy some childhood memory long buried. Neither Raoul nor the comtesse made reply, but it was, to each of them, as if Armand de Valandré came to them, not as one dead, but in the warm and living flesh, to walk beside them, keeping trust, urging them on . . .

For hour after weary hour Raoul forced himself onward, and the comtesse and Jean-Luc with him, hurrying, goading, sometime dragging them into obedience, allowing neither fatigue nor compassion to halt him . . . He ached in every sinew and nerve; his heart beat with such harshness at his ribs that he feared they too must be aware of it . . . There was a rawness in his throat and at his breastbone . . . Exhaustion and pain rendered his eyes so dim that he could not be sure what lay ahead . . . The darkness and failing lantern light cast shadows, real and imagined, so that he grew confused, awkwardly stumbling, and once falling hard upon the pathway. Somehow he had struggled to his feet, scarce able to feel his limbs for weakness and fear, his only thought for the lantern, lest it be shattered, and their journey halted.

When the first light of dawn came seeping through the trees, and the lantern dimmed, he could not, at first, believe that the hunting lodge lay before him. It was, he feared, some figment of his tired imagining, but Jean-Luc's voice was real, and raw with relief.

27

"We are here, Raoul! Maman . . . we are here . . . and safe!"

Despite his fatigue, the boy ran forward and joyously flung open the door, all else forgotten.

The light which pierced the bleak tracery of branches briefly illuminated the comtesse's face. It was a face, Raoul thought with pity, familiar with grief, and as filthy and wearied as his own, yet her voice betrayed nothing of it.

"Yes, Jean-Luc, we are safe . . ." she agreed gently. Then she turned towards Raoul, her eyes dark with such pain that it scarred his spirit, and murmured, so that the boy should not hear, "It has been a long, harsh journey, and a beginning . . . Were it not for Jean-Luc, I would have gladly ended it at Armand's side . . ."

"And I, Madame . . ." he said with truth, "but the boy lives through his father's courage . . . and has need now of yours, and his own . . ." "Then help me, Raoul," she begged humbly, "for without Armand, I have no will to survive on my own account . . ."

"Today is over," the old seneschal said gravely, taking her hand and leading her forward reassuringly, as if she were a young child. "It is all we can be sure of, Madame la Comtesse . . . One day at a time . . . One day at a time," he repeated. "It is all we can learn to bear . . ."

The shooting lodge was barely more than a timbered hut, but, although primitive and cold, it at least provided the fugitives with shelter and a place to rest. Raoul had laid his plans well, and soon there were bread, cheese, apples and wine set upon the rough trestle table. Hélène de Valandré and the old seneschal had little enthusiasm for eating, weariness and apprehension dulling their appetites. Jean-Luc however, with that natural resilience of the young, made an excellent meal, and his mother and Raoul, exchanging glances of amused affection over his eagerly lowered head, found consolation in such normality.

Already it was growing lighter, the gnarled tree-trunks around the small clearing in the forest showing first an intricate pattern of branches, their scabbed bark pitted with dark boles. Raoul cautioned,

"You must sleep in snatches, as and when you can, because

when it grows light enough, we must be upon our way . . . It will not be possible to move in darkness, and even by day we must take the greatest care, guarding our tongues and our actions, for the rabble who call themselves 'The Citizens' Army' will be constantly vigilant . . ."

"You believe, Raoul, that we will be safe at my parents' house in Riberac?"

The comtesse's voice was thin with exhaustion and the rigours of the day.

"I believe, Madame, that . . . we shall have a greater chance of being hidden there . . ." he said carefully. "Brittany is far removed from Paris, and the peasantry upon the large estates are more loyal to those they serve . . . Like Madame la Comtesse, I am a Breton by birth . . . and know the people to be devout and staunchly independent . . . They are an insular race, segregated by language and custom . . . their loyalty to their own rather than the mobs from the gutters and alleys of Paris . . ."

"I hope that you are right, Raoul . . ." He saw the gleam of tears upon her lashes as she lay her hand upon Jean-Luc's matted hair. "It has always been my son's desire to live as a peasant," she said wrily. "At least he has achieved that small ambition . . ."

Raoul nodded and watched her guide Jean-Luc towards the raised straw palliasse, edged in wood, and set upon the timber bench which served as a bed . . . She watched him settle under a blanket of rough sacking, then gently kissed his cheek.

"Bonne nuit, Maman. Bonne nuit, Raoul . . ." the child's voice was soft with weariness and the beginnings of sleep.

"Bonne nuit, Jean-Luc . . ."

No longer may I think of him as le Vicomte de Saint Hilaire . . . thought the old man, for I know, as surely as Madame la Comtesse that he is le Comte de Valandré . . . He sighed as he took his position at the small window of the hut, standing guard over them. It was an irony that Jean-Luc had, in the hour of his becoming le Comte, achieved his childhood ambition of living like a peasant . . . It would be a savage irony indeed if he were expected to die like an aristocrat . . . Yet, should God demand it, Raoul thought, He would give him the spirit and courage to face even that . . .

Raoul watched over them for an hour or more, his gaze shifting restlessly between the window and their slumbering forms . . . In sleep, their faces were relaxed, drained of emotions and fatigue, the young comtesse's face absurdly childlike. "May God protect us all!" he prayed silently. How alike were mother and son; their fine-boned oval faces, the wide gentle mouths, the high proud cheekbones . . . Despite the dirt smeared upon their cheeks, and their filthy peasant clothing, they were unlikely daughter and grandson for an old peasant such as he . . . Still, there were many upon the estates and villages who bore the unmistakeable likeness of their noble lord . . . 'Droit de Seigneur' . . . The right of the aristocrat to take that which he owned . . . to procreate . . . to live on, in another. It was, in Jean-Luc, what Armand de Valandré had thought vital enough to die for . . . Raoul was tired and confused, and felt very old. He could scarce keep his eyes from closing, for there was a weariness of spirit plaguing him, as well as of blood and bone.

Was it for the de Valandrés Monsieur le Comte had died? he wondered bleakly, or for the child sleeping quietly in the narrow bed? His head ached and he could no longer think clearly. Perhaps they were, after all, one and the same. What did it profit him to dwell upon it? Armand de Valandré was dead. The child was alive. . . .

He recalled the words he had used to comfort la comtesse.

"One day at a time . . . One day at a time . . ."

He found that he was muttering them aloud, and hoped that they had brought her more comfort than they had brought him.

Raoul, finally overcome by age and inertia, dozed as he stood, despite his resolution to stay watchfully alert. He awoke with a jarring start as his chin struck against his breast, then glanced about him guiltily. Jean-Luc and the comtesse slumbered undisturbed, for which he was grateful . . . Then, hearing the creak and rattle of an approaching cart, Raoul quietly slipped without, closing the door silently behind him. He had neither pistol nor sword to defend himself, nor those within, for they were not the accoutrements of a simple peasant upon the road. Yet he had taken the precaution of arming himself with a stout woodcarving knife with a good, sharp blade, and, having

levered it open, held it extended in his palm in readiness . . .
The peasant cart which entered the clearing was cumbersome
and crudely fashioned from split logs; its wheels absurdly
irregular . . . The mule which dragged it was as wretchedly
unprepossessing as the cart, its ribs clearly visible beneath
its mangy hide. A poor, starved creature, contrasting oddly
with its well-fed owner. The man leapt to the ground with
surprising lightness, obese, self-satisfied, his jowls shuddering
as his feet struck earth.

"Well, Raoul, my friend!" He slapped the seneschal heartily
upon the shoulder, "I have brought your fine carriage, as
you requested. It is not as fine, perhaps, as your companions
have been used to, yet, preferable, without doubt, to a
tumbril . . .?"

Raoul hushed him irritably into silence, replying brusquely,

"I hope, Jean, that you keep a closer guard upon your
tongue elsewhere!" The cart's owner had the grace to look
ashamed, saying resentfully, "I risk my own life as much as
theirs and yours . . . It is proof enough that I am here, as
you asked!"

Raoul stood rebuked, thrusting his arm about his companion's
shoulder to urge,

"I ask that you forgive me, Jean . . . I am old . . . and
unfitted for the task ahead, and the sorrow which this day has
brought . . ."

"Monsieur le Comte de Valandré?"

Raoul glanced quickly towards the hut.

"The boy sleeps within . . ."

"Ah, it is finished then! I had feared as much . . ." There
was sadness and deep regret in his eyes and voice. "It is an
end to the old regime . . . the good sacrificed with the bad.
God alone knows what bloodshed and horrors lie in wait . . .
The 'sans culottes' who struggle from gutters awash with their
own filth and the blood of others may yet drag all France
down to their brutish level . . . it is certain that none is fitted
to lead . . ."

The two men stood in silent agreement for a time.

"Cometh the hour, cometh the man," quoted Raoul, "But I
have lost so fine a master and friend in Armand de Valandré
today as can never be replaced . . ."

He wiped a tired hand across his eyes; an old man's hand, gnarled and blemished, veins bruised under the loosened skin.

"You will need to take great care, Raoul. Keep to the by-ways only, for the towns are no longer safe . . . Trust no-one. The rabble from Paris spread their vileness everywhere, and men will sacrifice their beliefs, and even their own souls, for gold, or for fear for their own miserable hides . . . "He glanced apologetically towards the mule, then smiled wrily, saying with disarming candour," A miserable enough hide, I do not pretend otherwise, but, despite his looks, he is sturdy enough to bear you upon your way, and the cart too . . . 'tis better if you appear to be as poor and ill-favoured, Raoul, as he . . . Here . . ." Jean set his hand into his pocket and produced a small compass, saying awkwardly, "A gift from a friend, Raoul . . . one who appreciates your worth. I do not know from whence it came, stolen or looted perhaps, I did not enquire too deeply, but bought it for a few centimes . . . and a hen. 'Twas a scrawny, ancient bird, argumentative and tough-fleshed, like you . . ."

As Raoul smiled his appreciation, Jean added, "You must follow the sun . . . advancing always towards the west, if you make for the sea . . ."

"We go to . . . But already Jean's hand had reached out, grasping the old man's wrist, bidding him be silent.

"Tell me nothing of your route, or where you hope to find safety, my old friend. I am not the bravest of men, and what I do not know I cannot disclose, even upon pain of torture . . ."

His smile did not quite reach his eyes.

"Yes, it is better so," agreed Raoul, "but you are already a man of courage, and I shall not soon forget your kindness . . ." He motioned towards the hut, "Nor shall they . . ."

He took a coin pouch from his pocket and pressed two gold Louis into Jean's hand, and, despite his friend's protestations, closed his fist upon them with finality.

"Then I thank you, Raoul . . ." he said gratefully, "although the payment you make is too great for the little I provide . . . You will find victuals and food enough for several days in the bottom of the cart . . . I have added some baskets of eggs and vegetables so that you might barter with others upon the way. It will give reason for your journeying . . . I have also mixed cow dung and other animal filth with the straw, lest others be tempted to halt or threaten you upon the paths . . . The stench will deter them! I wish you a strong stomach and a safe journey . . ."

The two men embraced briefly, but with real warmth, not knowing when, or if, they might meet again. Raoul watched Jean walk past the mule and cart and into the heart of the forest. His plump face had been wreathed in smiles and his salute jaunty and extravagant, but as he had turned away, Raoul had glimpsed the bleakness in Jean's eyes, then the drooping of his broad shoulders.

There was a rush of sound from the hut as the door flew open, and Jean-Luc, blinking the sleep from his eyes, ran to his side.

"Maman! Maman!" he called excitedly, "See . . . Raoul has found a mule and a cart for us! Tell me that I may drive, Raoul . . ." he begged, "and Maman shall sit in the straw . . ."

The comtesse nodded above Jean-Luc's head, and Raoul bade him hold the reins as he assisted Hélène de Valandré to clamber aboard.

"It smells!" declared Jean-Luc, making a mock-pained face. "Oh, how it smells!"

"It is a good clean smell. The smell of the country . . ." rebuked his mother equably, settling herself unconcernedly upon the straw. "Besides, we smell much worse . . . What is one more stench amongst so many? Do you not agree, Grandpère Nolais?"

Raoul smiled and nodded, then climbed upon the cart to sit beside Jean-Luc, declaring,

"You are right, Hélène, my daughter . . ."

"Where shall I drive, Grandpère?" asked Jean-Luc expectantly.

"Towards the sun, my child," said Raoul as the mule cried out and kicked its heels, and the shadows of the forest fell behind them.

CHAPTER 3

As the mule cart and its occupants began their long journey to the house of Hélène de Valandré's parents at Riberac, sunrise raked the sky with flame. It held no beauty for them; no promise. Each saw in its glow only the starkness of the abandoned chateau; the ashes of the past.

They travelled, unspeaking, and when the light paled to lavender and rose, Raoul turned the cart towards the west and the ill-frequented byways which skirted Chartres . . . The city would be alive with violence and danger, he feared, and no man able to trust another. Even the holy sanctuary of Chartres itself would offer no refuge, for those who murder and plunder in their own name have scant respect for God's . . . No priest, no man, woman or child would be safe from their blood-letting. Theirs was the feral savagery of the brute. Like scavenging foxes, they would kill with neither pity nor remorse, without need or reason.

Hour upon hour they rode, the only sounds the grating of wheels and cart, the grunting sighs of the mule, and the cries of unseen animals and birds. Finally Raoul, bones aching and eyes raw with the need for sleep, had allowed Jean-Luc to take over the reins. Hélène de Valandré had made room for the old man beside her upon the floor of the cart, shifting the baskets of eggs and scattering the mounds of vegetables. The stench of the straw and animal ordure clung oppressively, and their own unwashed bodies added stale odours of sweat and filthy clothing. The over-ripe vegetables, soured by the heat of the sun, mingled with the sulphurous rottenness of spilled eggs . . . Yet Raoul was so exhausted by emotion and age that he slept soundly as soon as he was curled up on this foetid bed, and even the deep cart ruts and potholes upon the way and the occasional honking bray of protest from the mule did not awaken him.

Always there was fear. Fear of the silence and fear of speech. Fear of all that was seen and unseen; real and imagined . . . of the future as of the past. It rode with them, a silent companion, menacing and unacknowledged.

Hélène de Valandré made no complaint nor shed a tear, allowing Jean-Luc to take a turn at the reins or to leap from the cart and run alongside. She smiled, chided, bade her son move quietly lest Raoul be awakened . . . The lice and vermin in clothing and straw went unheeded and unremarked. The cart's clumsy progress bore the unreality of a dream. She was surprised that the hands upon the reins were flesh and blood, and her own, and alive. Surely she had died with Armand de Valandré . . .? Jean-Luc took the reins from his mother's unresisting hands, and she smiled, laying her head upon his shoulder, falling asleep instantly, like a tired child. Jean-Luc's grief was a soreness within him. He was glad that the others slept. This desolation of loss was all that remained to him of Armand de Valandré, and he hugged his hurt to him, jealous of sharing it. The reins and the landscape blurred, and he bit his lip fiercely, tasting the salt of blood, relishing the pain, forbidding his tears to fall. The mule trotted on uncaring, and, envying it and hating it, he slapped savagely upon the reins, its forlorn cry adding shame and guilt to his wretchedness. Hélène, wrenched from sleep by its cry, looked about her, bewildered.

The wide, flat plain stretched all about them, serene and unchanging; in the far distance, fine as needle points, the tapering spires of Chartres cathedral, distorted by sunlight and misted heat. It was there that I made my marriage vows, Hélène de Valandré thought. In the cool, shadowy solace of the nave, the sun through its rose window patterning light upon the white silk of my gown. A moment in time, like the window itself, jewelled, many-splendoured. She felt the sudden pain of memory piercing, drawing blood . . . recalling her unwillingly to life. There could only be a deeper pain and loss, she knew, were she ever to forget.

"Maman?" Jean-Luc's voice was high and frightened despite his efforts to control it, and her hand went instinctively to cover his upon the reins, comforting, reassuring, as of old; a promise of love that need not be spoken. He was all that remained to her now.

"When we reach Grandmère's house at Riberac," she said, "we will be safe. There will be welcome and shelter for us there . . . Nothing will be changed . . ."

And she knew, even as she spoke the words, their foolishness.

Once beyond the city they had been unexpectedly halted by a mob of ruffians, and Jean-Luc had hastily shaken Raoul awake. The old man had rubbed the sleep from his eyes, regaining his wits, wiping his mouth and nose with his fist before spitting contemptuously upon the dust of the roadside.

"Death to all aristocrats," he sneered with conviction. "They are scum! Vermin! May their filthy carcases rot in hell!"

There was a murmur of agreement from the rabble surrounding them, and Jean-Luc, incensed beyond reason at the old man's betrayal, would have leapt from the cart had not Hélène's nails dug deep into his flesh, silencing him. Raoul's hands were trembling uncontrollably, face flushed, saliva flecking his lips.

"The old man is palsied," called out one of their number, laughing drunkenly, "See how he rages!"

"And his cart smells worse than a dunghill!" jeered another, cracking his stick against the side of the cart, so that the mule retreated, giving anguished voice.

"He is as much an aristocrat as the old man," cried their leader, "and as skinny and ill-tempered!"

"I would sooner bed the mule than that stinking wretch beside him!" sneered another. "She reeks of cow filth and farmyards. Give me the women of the gutters, for the stench is their own . . ." His pock-marked face was pushed close to Hélène's, and she forced herself not to betray her revulsion, gazing at him unflinchingly, a hand bearing down fiercely upon Jean-Luc's arm lest he be tempted to rashness. The gorge rose into her throat, and she tasted its sourness, before, with a last spate of drunken insults, they were upon their way, bawdy and undisciplined, to wreak mischief elsewhere . . .

Jean-Luc gazed straight ahead and flicked at the reins, back rigid with anger, sick with disgust and self-loathing. Hélène made to put an arm about his shoulders, but he shrugged away as though her touch burned him. At her glance of mute appeal, Raoul shook his head in warning. Neither spoke as the boy took out his impotent fury upon the path ahead, the mule hurtling, the cart jarring and swaying upon the uneven track . . . It was no rougher than the way they had come, the old man thought, and God alone knew what evils lay ahead . . .

Hours lengthened into days, indistinguishable one from the other save for the changing landscape. They arose with the sun and halted with darkness. They slept fitfully upon the fetid straw of the cart or in the shelter of walls and ditches. They bartered for food at farms and small villages, regarded always with unease and suspicion. They begged, stole, were cheated. They washed in streams and dewponds, relieved themselves amidst thorn and bracken. They became stripped of all false modesty, sometimes despairing, always hungry, obsessed now only with the need to survive.

At one bleak hovel, an old woman had emptied a chamber pot of slops upon Raoul's head, crying,

"Be off with you! Beggar! Scum! Filthy old scarecrow!" Her cracked laughter had pursued him shrilly across the cobbles of the yard as he had stumbled to escape the stinking deluge. Viscous slime ran from his hairline, and its stench all but suffocated him. Breath raw, he would have paused to ease the hurt in his ribs, but the snarling of the yard dog and the clanking of its chain sent him clambering feverishly over the gate, to drop, enraged, upon the track. "Dolt! Cretin! Imbecile!" he had called back impotently from the foot of the waggon as the crone appeared threateningly in the yard. "Do you not recognise quality? Breeding?"

"There is more breeding in my old sow!" called out the woman contemptuously as she gathered the cur's chain, "and she, too, is past her prime and useful days!"

Jean-Luc struggled hard to suppress his hilarity, but laughter bubbled up, loud and irrepressible, and soon his mother and Raoul were laughing helplessly with him in a fierce release of tension and hurt . . . Smiling, Jean-Luc descended, and helped the old man to climb aboard, wrinkling his nose expressively at the odour.

"She did not take us for aristocrats, Raoul?" Hélène de Valandré's voice carried clear and filled with mirth.

"No, Madame la Comtesse . . ." Raoul struggled to his feet amidst the straw and delivered the harridan in the yard a

37

grotesque bow. "Fools! Peasants!" muttered the woman sourly to the dog.

After a while Raoul had halted the mule and cart beside a small stream to bathe the filth from himself, and to water and feed the mule. Jean-Luc's spontaneous laughter at the mule's droll antics, and the comfort of food and rest, so uplifted his elders that they set off in rare good spirits. Lulled into a sense of security, they relaxed, and Jean-Luc even drifted into snatches of nursery songs which Raoul and the comtesse enlivened with impromptu verses, so bizarre that they all broke into uncontrollable laughter, and were unable to continue the game . . . It was as they were nearing the main road from Alençon to Paris, and approaching a crossroads, that the reality of their danger returned. At the very centre of the cross, a high spirited, expectant crowd of countryfolk was gathered, barring their way. They were armed with pitchforks, scythes and other implements of toil, their cries wild and vociferous as one of the younger, brawnier men ran forward to clutch the mule's reins, halting them.

"What ails you?" Raoul cried anxiously. "We are harmless farmfolk upon our way to the markets . . . We have no quarrel with you . . ." "Nor we with you!" called a toothless crone from the fringe of the crowd. "Calm yourself, grandfather! You will bring on a fit, and miss the fun we are expecting . . ."

"Fun?" Raoul's voice was irritable. "I have no time to waste upon amusement. Like you, I work to earn a poor pittance that I might live!"

There was a shouting and jeering from the Alençon road which briefly diverted the countryman at the mule's head, but so fiercely thronging was the crowd that Jean-Luc did not dare to flick the mule onward lest someone be crushed beneath the wheels. Trembling and silent, he allowed the cart to be pulled bodily to the grassy verge beside the road.

The filthy, motley citizens' army which came into view were screaming and shouting obscenities at two figures standing upright on a cart as dilapidated as their own . . . An aged man in the reviled garments of an aristocrat was half-supporting, half-lifting the gentlewoman beside him. Their faces were smeared with blood, clothing torn and foul with excrement hurled by the mob which ran beside them, jeering and mimicking their

38

expressions and stance . . . The old man's sparse hair was matted and blood-caked, like that of the woman he supported, as if trying to force some of his own strength into her weakening spirit. A man amid the rabble was prancing grotesquely in the nobleman's powdered wig, and a fat, coarse-featured harpy, blowsy and foul-mouthed, had perched the gentlewoman's wig upon her own filthy locks as she postured beside him . . . All the time, as they were dragged along in the crude cart by the spitting, contemptuous crowd, they were being assailed by stones and blows, yet the old gentleman's face retained its expression of dignified remoteness, as if he were already beyond reach of their taunts and violence . . . Most pitiful of all was the sight of the woman's thin-boned hand, bare of all ornament, clutching at the fragments of her bodice which had been cruelly ripped aside to reveal the flattened, pendulous breasts and the deep hollows of her neck . . . skin hanging wrinkled and loose.

"Grandmère! Grandpère!" Jean-Luc's voice rang out, harsh with anguish. He would have leapt from the cart, but Raoul dragged him backwards from his perch and to the floor of the cart. As he struggled to rise, the old man's fist struck him hard across the mouth, sending him sprawling at his feet. The crowd had stopped, confused by the boy's cry, suspicious, and ready to drag him from Raoul's side. "Fool! Imbecile!" the old servant's voice rang out, clear, and filled with contempt. Another stinging blow sent the child reeling, face down, into the filthy dung-laden straw, and Raoul ground him lower with his boot, to the jeers of the mob. Then, tapping his own forehead with a forefinger, and gesturing towards the boy, he intimated that Jean-Luc was a poor, unhappy idiot.

"Cretin! Numbskull!" he cried as the crowd roared its approval. "Would you think yourself an aristo . . .?"

The mob screamed their derision, convulsed with helpless laughter at the sight of the child weeping, bewildered, his face and mouth stained with straw and ordure . . . Jean-Luc tried to speak, but horror and despair choked him. He stared back at the Chevalier de Riberac, and the old nobleman stared back at him without recognition, standing expressionless and unmoving, save for the almost imperceptible twitching of a raw nerve at the edge of his mouth. The old gentlewoman beside him now stood as erect as he, motionless save for the tears which ran soundlessly down her face, splashing from mouth and chin. The chevalier's gaze rested briefly upon Jean-Luc, and then upon the ravaged face of his daughter, Hélène, his eyes begging her wordlessly not to betray herself.

"Paysan!" he spat the words arrogantly at Jean-Luc. "Do you dare to call yourself a de Valandré? Return to the farmyard where you belong!"

There was a wild howl of rage from the rabble surrounding his cart, and a renewed hail of blows upon the Chevalier as he set his arms protectively about his wife to ward off the sticks and stones of the incensed peasantry . . . A lout, wielding a knife, leapt upon the cart, and slashed at the nobleman's coat, and blood spurted from an arm and soaked his sleeve, dripping below the lace of his shirt cuffs . . . Then, furiously, without ceremony, the cart upon which he stood was dragged away, pushed and hustled by the chanting mob, and hauled upon the road to Paris.

"Madame la Guillotine will silence him!" cackled the toothless crone from the midst of the rabble. "He will boast no more! He will lie in the gutter where he belongs . . . deep in his own blood!" "Then the stones themselves will cry out!" The words were so loud in Hélène de Valandré's brain that, at first, she thought that she had spoken them as, half fainting with grief and terror, she saw her parents being dragged along in the heaving, surging mass of bodies . . . Briefly, as they passed, the chevalier's eyes met hers, and in them was all the love and tenderness he could not hide. Then Raoul was urging the mule into life, and the cart and its occupants were upon the by-way to La Loupe.

It was almost a kilometre upon the road before Raoul bade the mule halt, while all the way the anguished cries of Jean-Luc and his mother's quiet sobbing tore at his heart, "I had to strike you, Jean-Luc," the old man's voice was unsteady as, harsh with pity, he placed his hand tenderly upon the boy's head. "It was all I could do . . . Forgive me."

"It saved his life, Raoul." Hélène de Valandré's voice was weary as that of an old woman, and her eyes bleak with unendurable pain. "You are a good man, and Jean-Luc will learn to thank you for it . . . ."

The boy's harsh sobbing ceased as he rubbed his swollen eyes with his fists, saying stiffly,

"I thank you, Raoul, for, as Maman has said, you saved my life. There is nothing upon this whole earth to forgive . . ."

Raoul held the boy to him awkwardly, in pity and in love, until Jean-Luc pulled away.

"But I shall never forgive *them!*" he said bitterly, "that filth and rabble, for what they have done today, to grandmère and grandpère . . . I hope they rot in hell! They are pigs! Animals! I will be revenged, I swear it, even if it takes me all of my life! I will search for them, and deal them blow for blow, wound for wound!" The rage and fury in his face made Hélène de Valandré cry out,

"No, Jean-Luc! You must learn to forgive . . . else you will be no better than they. The deaths of those who truly loved you will be valueless, for you will have learned nothing! Only a hatred which will cripple and devour you . . ."

"Do you forgive, Maman?" His eyes looked steadily into hers, and she turned away, unable to give him that assurance.

"One day, Jean-Luc," she promised helplessly. "One day . . . God willing . . . I shall find the strength to forgive . . ."

"I do not think I shall ever be able to forgive, Maman . . ." It was a cry from his very soul, "And even should I learn to forgive, I will never be able to forget what I have seen . . ."

"No-one would want you to, my son," Hélène de Valandré said gently. "It is right and just that you should remember . . ."

Raoul nodded, and returned abruptly to take the reins. He could not, at first, see the road before him, for, although his back was straight and his head held high, his eyes were blinded with tears that he was unwilling to let fall.

CHAPTER 4

They passed that night huddled together in a hollow alongside the cart. Hélène was granted the luxury of an old apple sack for warmth, while Raoul and Jean-Luc made do with heapings of straw . . . Only Jean-Luc slept, the old man hearing the stifled anguish of Hélène's tears could find no words to comfort her, or himself. By early dawn their limbs, so cramped by day upon the cart, were chilled by a heavy dew and a keen wind, which had sprung up in the darkness, adding to their stiffness and unease. The mule's restlessness and occasional cries, startling in the silence, had made their nerves as raw as their flesh, and it was with little enthusiasm that they climbed back upon the cart to set out in near darkness.

They rode through the sleeping village of Logny, its silence eerie and strangely unreal . . . Another world, another place, Hélène de Valandré thought. She was no more a part of it than of the world she had known . . . That world lay in ruins about her now, her childhood and all her growing days perished with those she had loved, as though they had never been.

"You are ill, my dear . . . would you have me halt the cart?" Raoul's voice was anxious, concerned.

"I was thinking how good it will be to reach the sea at Cap Frehel . . ." she said. "There will be the clean, fresh smell of salt upon the wind, and the scent of heather and wild thyme, and I shall feel young again . . ." Her mouth so easily formed the lies she spoke aloud. The truth throbbed in her head. Fierce. Insistent. Drowning out all else . . . No Valandré. No Riberac. No parents. No husband. No future. No past. The rough wheels of the cart echoed and re-echoed it until she feared her heart must break with the weight of sorrow . . . but it did not break, nor she.

Raoul, watching her covertly as Jean-Luc took the reins, was

42

alarmed by her increasing silence and apathy. She seemed, sometimes, so remote that he feared not only for her physical survival, but for her reason itself. Surely no-one could be called upon to bear more suffering than Hélène de Valandré already knew? The good God could not demand it . . . He realised, too late, that he had been staring at her, the pity he felt for her clear upon his face. She stretched out a hand and took his own, saying quietly, so that Jean-Luc could not overhear the words,

"We must all work out our own salvation, Raoul . . . in our own way . . . There is no help for it. It is a cruel and lonely path . . ."

"Indeed, Hélène . . ."

"I thank you for remaining here beside me, my dear friend . . . and for saving Jean-Luc . . . and beg you will not take my silence for ingratitude. Sometimes there is so great a hurt I am unable to speak . . ."

She lifted the old man's hand and held it tenderly against her cheek.

Raoul, much moved, said, as to a small child,

"It will get better . . . I promise . . . If I could take upon myself your pain, then, I swear, I would do so, and gladly . . ."

She nodded.

"It is all I have of them, Raoul . . . and would not forgo even that, for then I would be bereft of all, even memory. It would be too great a price . . ."

It was Raoul's tears which fell helplessly then, and she who offered comfort.

Gently, almost imperceptibly, the plain gave way to leafy copses, wide tranquil étangs, and woods and softly rolling hills. A Breton landscape, fertile and familiar.

"We are nearly home . . ." Hélène de Valandré had spoken the words aloud, not knowing that she had uttered them.

"Yes, Hélène. We are among friends . . . our own people. Yet, even here there is danger . . ." he warned. "Strangers, ever-watchful, intent upon harm . . . You must trust me to find those of your parents' household who are still loyal, you understand?"

"But I may return to Riberac?" Her voice was low, pleading.

"No. It is better not." He could not know if it lay in ruins, and others, as the Chevalier, brutalised or slaughtered by the mob. "I will travel alone," he said firmly. "You, Jean-Luc, have a care for your mother. You will be safe here until I return."

"But if they harm you?" The boy's voice was raw with fear, face sharpened with anxiety.

"I will be safe. My family and friends are here . . . None will betray us . . ." Raoul's calm certainty reassured Jean-Luc, and he nodded, the tenseness leaving him. Raoul could have wished his own forebodings as swiftly eased.

At the inn where he had been drinking alone while awaiting his friend, the landlord had warned him quietly of the stranger seated near the door,

"Guard your tongue . . ." he had whispered to Raoul when gathering up the tankards from his table, "he is an informer . . . one of the so-called citizens' army. Say nothing which will alert him to your purpose."

So it was that Raoul had arisen and ostentatiously set a gold Louis upon the bar, declaring boastfully,

"Citizen brothers . . . I give you a toast! And I shall pay for it with the one remaining Louis which I stripped from the dead body of Armand, Comte de Valandré! Death to all those like him . . . Maggots upon the flesh of the poor! Corrupt filth!"

He raised his glass to those about him.

The stranger rose from his seat to ask, with seeming indifference, "You saw him die, you say?"

"Yes, and dealt him the violence he deserved, sparing him nothing!" He spat contemptuously upon the floor, then rubbed the spittle from his lips. "Yes. Thanks be to God, I saw him die, and that puking wife and brat beside him . . . None was spared! What is more. I followed that tumbril bearing the Chevalier de Riberac almost into the city of Chartres itself, running beside it, with taunts and blows, glorying in the death of the old regime . . . a true citizen of the people's army."

There was pride and venom in Raoul's voice, but sickness in his throat which all but choked him. Yet he spoke with such arrogant scorn that none challenged him . . . His hatred was real. They did not doubt it . . . There burned within him, feverish and all-consuming, a fury akin to madness. When the friend he awaited had come to sit beside him, he saw in Raoul only an old man, weary and spent of passion, and grieved that he was so changed. Raoul had done what was needed, and felt no shame at his betrayal. His promise to Armande de Valandré absolved him, and if God were just and all-forgiving, He would grant His absolution too.

With his plans for Hélène's and Jean-Luc's safe passage argued and confirmed, and the dues exchanged, Raoul walked the familiar path through woods and fields to Riberac. The stench of carnage and smoking timbers remained, and only the walls still stood, gaunt as ruined teeth, blackened and useless. A flock of predatory birds rose as he approached. A black cloud; scavenging, pecking at the charred remnants of animal flesh, as hostile as the violence about them . . . All was scorched, empty, devoid of life save they . . . devoured in the holocaust of hatred and revenge. Raoul could not weep nor cry aloud, for the rage in him and the pity ran too deep . . . He would have run screaming to ward off the returning carrion, flailing at them, damning their obscenity, but could not . . . the obscenity lay not in them, but those who had wrought the carnage upon others of their kind . . . The silence deepened about him, and as he turned to leave, he did not know if it were the beating of their wings or of his own heart he heard; their cries of protest or his own . . . Black as dead leaves, they clustered still; black as the trees and grass; black as the ruined walls of Riberac . . . Dear God! He was too old to bear this pain. Too tired. Let there be no more killing, he prayed. No more grief . . . He made his way, slowly and painfully, back to those who awaited him, knowing that the horror of it must remain his own. He could bear his own grief, as he must, but not the added anguish of theirs . . .

When Raoul had returned to the small lakeside copse where he had left them, Jean-Luc had run excitedly to greet him, taking the old man affectionately by the hand. Then he had confided hesitantly, as though half-ashamed,

"I will miss the old mule, Raoul . . . you will not sell him . . . allow him to be slaughtered? He is deserving of better . . ."

He had flung his thin arms about the mule's coarse maned neck, shielding and protecting him.

"No. You may be sure of it." Raoul's tone was purposefully

45

brisk. "I shall have need of both mule and cart to return to Valandré."

Jean-Luc's face was a tight mask of pain and disbelief, but he made no sound. It was Hélène who cried out,

"You would leave us, Raoul? But why? You cannot! What should we do without you? Where would we go?

Raoul said quietly,

"I cannot come with you. Do not ask it of me. It will grieve me to refuse, and serve no purpose . . . I have done what the Comte de Valandré charged me to do. I will see you set safely upon a boat for England . . . and there you will find many friends who have been similarly persecuted, emigrés like yourselves . . . Monsieur le Comte has made arrangements with his bankers in London so that you will have access to whatever monies you require . . . I shall deliver to you his letters of introduction and credit before you leave . . ."

"But you will not travel to England with us, Raoul?" Hélène de Valandré's voice was low, expressionless.

"No. That I cannot do . . . I must go back to Valandré . . . the chateau. There is work for me . . . I must do what I am able to preserve what I may, until you return . . . God willing . . ."

It would not do to confess that he feared that Armande de Valandré's body was already removed, mutilated perhaps, flaunted by those very barbarians who had hacked him down . . . They were savages, bloodthirsty, inhuman.

"Then you will put yourself in peril!" It was as if Hélène de Valandré had known his thoughts, "They will recognise you, Raoul, and mete out punishment."

"No. The murdering, Parisian rabble will have turned their violence elsewhere . . . they are scavengers, thieves, moving on constantly to wherever there is gain . . . The people of Valandré have no quarrel with me, no hatred . . . They will be regretting all that has . . ." he hesitated, "all that greed and weakness forced them to condone . . ."

Jean-Luc turned in a sudden fury, and pushing Raoul roughly aside ran blindly to the water's edge and, splashing and crying out noisily, waded deeper into the lake, submerging himself again and again.

"Jean-Luc!" The comtesse, alarmed, would have run after

46

him to remonstrate, but Raoul said, laying a restraining hand upon her arm,

"We each have our own way of grieving . . . finding salvation . . . Are they not your own words, Hélène? We each have our own way of exorcising anger, hurt, our own devils . . . Jean-Luc is a child who has been forced to manhood too soon . . . Let him come to terms with my betrayal . . . for that is what he feels my leaving him to be . . . When he is ready, he will return and apologise with grace, keeping his own dignity . . . We must allow him that . . ."

Hélène de Valandré reached up impulsively and kissed Raoul's darkly shadowed cheek, then turned and ran swiftly to the water's edge.

The fisherman's hut stood solitary and bleak above the cliffs and headland of Cap Frehel. It was set about with heather and broom and a tangle of stunted, wind-burned scrub which all but barred access to it, save for the single pathway worn by the lone fisherman's coming and going . . . This was a wild and savage coast, the cliffs rising rocky and sheer from the Atlantic breakers which pounded restlessly at their feet . . . Its violence had gouged out deep hollows and gulleys in the grey rock, its surface jagged, its rough hewn ledges home for scavenging sea birds. They wheeled and screamed ceaselessly, as if to drown the echoes of the pounding surf; their droppings a crust of frosted white upon the cliff faces and upon the scarred finger of rock, pointing from its curled fist of stone, clenched beneath the surf . . . Raoul had manoeuvred the mule only with the greatest difficulty along the narrow track, its teeth bared, eyes showing white with fear as the low bushes and bramble tore at its legs, and had, eventually, secured it to a rusting iron ring which had been set firm into the stone beside the hut. Then, further restricted by a stout rope found in the hut, it demonstrated its perversity by cropping contentedly at the salt-washed turf, its former wilfulness forgotten . . . In the falling dusk, Hélène de Valandré could scarcely make out the distant waves, save as a flung whiteness against the greyness of sky and sea . . . a restlessness of seagulls. Yet she could smell the clean salted edge to the wind and the scent of creeping thyme beneath her sabots, and felt the balm of what was familiar and loved ease her.

47

Before dawn, she awoke to find Raoul shaking her shoulder and bidding her make ready, for it was time to leave. They must be at Erquy within the hour, he said, for the fishermen would be ready with the tide, and waiting to embark.

"It would be better to say our farewells here," he said, as Jean-Luc, alerted by the sounds of movement, rubbed the sleep from his eyes and came to stand beside them. "There will be little time upon the shore," Raoul continued, "and such things are safer said in privacy . . ."

They ate a near-silent meal, for none had appetite. Their parting hung heavily between them, and for Hélène and Jean-Luc, the loss of their own country and the promise of life in another seemed more penance than adventure . . . Raoul delivered to Hélène the letters of credit and introduction which Armand de Valandré had bidden him protect, and within that pouch which held her jewels, she now placed the few Louis d'or remaining. They would serve her well, the old servant promised, for gold knew no frontiers, or barriers of language or creed . . .

When all was completed, there was a silence between them, each of them filled with emotions too excoriating to reveal.

"Goodbye, Raoul . . ." Jean-Luc had rehearsed the words so confidently in his mind, determined to speak with all the dignity of a man. He would not forget that he was the Vicomte de Saint Hilaire, and must show courage and breeding. He would not admit, even to himself, that Armand de Valandré might yet be dead . . . "Goodbye, Raoul . . ." he repeated, clasping the old seneschal by the arm, as a comrade might. "You have been a kind and loyal friend . . ." Then Jean-Luc's face crumbled into that of a frightened child, despite his efforts to control it, and he wept loudly and with desperation, burying his face in Raoul's coat front as the old man patted the boy's head helplessly, too consumed with grief to utter a word of comfort. When the sobs had died away, and Jean-Luc was stilled again, drained of all emotion, Hélène de Valandré said gently,

"You are as dear to us as our own flesh and blood, Raoul, and whatever befalls, there will not be a day of my life when I shall not bless the memory of you, and thank God for your goodness . . ."

She embraced him most tenderly, and he, in turn, held her with sorrow and affection in his heart, thinking that she was all

48

that he had ever thought of, or prayed for, in a child of his own flesh . . . Once more he would be alone, and without them his wound would be deeper, and the remaining years powerless to heal the hurt . . .

At Erquy, their goodbyes were muted and subdued, for there were few words, and those stilted and cramped by the nearness of others . . . Raoul, standing beside the mule and cart, stood straight and tall, waving until he could see them no more for tears, and even then he was loath to turn away and admit the reality of their leaving. The sounds of the sea and the wild calls of the sea birds became confused in his own mind with the weeping of the two as they had left the shore, and he fancied that he could hear them still, calling out to him.

He wiped a tired hand across his eyes, then climbed upon the cart . . . He tried to tell the mule to move, but the words thickened and died in his throat. With a jerk upon the reins, he, and the mule, began the long journey to Valandré.

The wind from the south, although favourable to the small fishing boat, blew chill, and Hélène de Valandré was grateful for the thick cloak which Raoul had provided for her. Jean-Luc, after his first spasm of grief, grew intent upon watching the seamen at their work, while they, knowing the endless fascination of a vessel under sail, and Jean-Luc's need, strove to keep both his hands and his mind occupied. The fishing boat was a small and simple craft, but the men who sailed her knew every centimetre of the coast and the vagaries of its tides and currents. They were as keenly aware of the perils from submerged rocks, and those swiftly formed sandbanks, dredged by the force of restless wave and storm from the ocean floor . . .

Once out in the open sea, the wind grew stronger and more forceful, with the sails bellying full and the thrust of the boat purposeful and unhindered. Hélène de Valandré was grateful to sit alone, free from questioning and the need for response, although the cleaving of the prow through water and the swell of the sea increasingly disturbed her.

Soon she was gripped by a violent feeling of nausea; a cold sickness which seemed to seep into every pore and cell of her body, so that every movement became an agony almost impossible to survive. Her legs, when she struggled to her feet, seemed not to belong to her, they were so leaden and strange, and when, by a supreme effort of will which left her pale and sweating, she reached the edge of the boat, it was to collapse, retching painfully over its side . . .

For an hour and more she lay inert and almost unaware of her surroundings, vomiting miserably, and longing for the ease of oblivion in sleep, or even in death itself . . . Never had she felt so violent a despair or sickness . . . Nothing had prepared her for the all-consuming horror of it, or the unutterable weariness of body and spirit . . .

Hélène was unaware when the wind from the south unexpectedly changed direction, blowing fiercely now from the east, with the crewmen working despairingly to keep the vessel on course. Trapped in the peaks and troughs of the fierce Atlantic waves, and by the rising strength of the gale, the small craft was helpless, the fishermen impotent to control her . . . Hour after hour, lashed by storm and flurries of rain and icy hail, the boat drifted, pitched and fell, useless as an abandoned toy. The towering Atlantic waves crashed and thundered upon the deck, splintering boards, shredding the canvas of the sails; all hopes of reaching the English coast forsaken as those cowering aboard . . . As unpredictably as it had arisen, the storm died, the silence as eerie as the sea's calm . . . Without warning the wind had changed direction yet again, veering now, more kindly, from the south-west . . . Yet none on board was capable of guiding the boat as, battered by the ferocity of sea and weather, it was inexorably swirled and harried by the treacherous currents of the channel towards the coast of Wales . . . Even when finally driven ashore, and beached upon the flat rock and shingle of a natural creek, coldness and exhaustion defeated them, and they were unable to struggle ashore . . . Then, mercifully, willing hands made the craft secure and lifted them gently on to land . . . but Hélène de Valandré had strength neither to walk nor speak her gratitude, as Jean-Luc somehow rose and struggled to her side, chafing her cold hands with his own. Desperate to rouse her, he tried to cry out the single word, "Maman!" but the sound cracked and splintered in his throat. Harsh. Unintelligible, as strange sounding as the language of those around him . . .

CHAPTER 5

The two fishermen from France had been assisted to the cottage of a poor fishwife nearby, grateful for the support of their rescuers. Jean-Luc, exhausted, and barely able to stand, had been carried to safety upon the back of one of the men who had dragged the boat ashore. He had protested helplessly, fearful to leave his mother's side, but Hélène de Valandré was as unaware of his solicitude as of the strangers surrounding her. Fatigue and sorrow had so overburdened her mind that, unable to bear the hurt of it, she had escaped into a deep and cleansing sleep.

When she had finally awakened, it was to find herself in the house of an unknown clergyman and his young family. She had been washed and tended by gentle hands, her wounds and bruises eased. Moreover, she was dressed in a clean cambric nightgown, trimmed with lace, and the bed-covers were of well laundered linen, fresh with the scent of lavender and rosemary from the bushes upon which they had been hung. She had opened her eyes wide in sudden fear, not recognising the room nor the woman seated beside her . . . She was a small, shy-eyed woman of Hélène's own age, and wearing a gown of softest pearl grey, a ribbon-trimmed house-bonnet part covering her pale, ringletted hair.

Terror and memory made her cry aloud.

"Jean-Luc?"

The stranger laid aside her embroidery and came at once to stand beside her, taking Hélène's hands calmly and reassuringly into her own, and saying compassionately,

"He is safe, Madame . . ." She moved quietly to the door and murmured in an undertone to someone without. In moments, Jean-Luc was in the room, dressed in the style of an English gentleman, his face naked with joyous relief as he hurled himself

51

at her bedside. Then, cheeks aflame, he had struggled awkwardly free of her tearful embrace.

"Well, my peasant . . .?" Hélène's words, innocently spoken, were a knife thrust within her; Jean-Luc's intent face, so like Armand de Valandré's, a raw twist of the blade within the wound. Lacerating. Drawing blood . . . She closed her eyes, and fought to staunch the hurt of it, saying swiftly, "Now you are a fine young gentleman again . . ."

He smiled mischievously, saying with a hint of his old spirit, "I hope, Maman, that my fine clothes do not deceive you."

"No, Jean-Luc . . . I am proud of you, for what you are . . . for what you have done, as Papa would be . . ." her voice faltered and broke, then she steadied herself, to add with honesty, "Some lessons are hard-learned, my son, but they are the ones we do not forget . . . They make us what we are . . ."

He nodded.

"I have a new friend, Maman!" he blurted, face flushed with excited pleasure. "He is nine years old, like me, and he is named David . . . He speaks French so well . . . He is going to become a British soldier when he is a man, as I will become one of the Royal Guard when we return to France . . . Is that not splendid?" he demanded.

"Splendid, my dear . . ." her voice was tired, fading. "When we return . . ." She felt gladness and regret that, childlike, for Jean-Luc the present already deadened the past. The woman at the door silently motioned him to leave, and he dutifully obeyed, first touching Hélène de Valandré's cheek with gentleness.

"Au revoir, Maman. A bientôt . . . Soon." The English word sounded strange to her ears.

"Au 'voir, my son."

As Hélène's eyelids, grown heavy, began to close, despite all her efforts to force them apart, the woman in grey took out a pouch from the recesses of her gown and, crossing to the bedside, placed it in the invalid's hands, closing Hélène's fingers softly about it.

"Your jewels are safe, Madame la Comtesse . . ."

"Jewels?" Hélène de Valandré murmured, confused.

"It is good to retain some memory of past happiness . . . in possessions loved . . . They will bring you comfort . . ."

Comfort? thought Hélène de Valandré. What a strange word to use . . . Stones are cold, lifeless things, without flesh or meaning . . . Had they been spilled into the sea, and lost, it would have brought me no grief! No. Comfort is in people, and when they are dead, like Armand . . . and the others . . . there is nothing in heaven or all the earth to ease the loss . . .

"David? Jean-Luc's friend?" she begged, her words scarcely audible.

"My son, Madame."

Hélène de Valandré nodded.

"They are . . ." she hesitated, searching for a word, "our jewels. Our true wealth . . . You have other children, Madame?"

"I am Charlotte . . . Charlotte Tudor . . . and, yes, I have a daughter, a babe but three months old . . . Her name is Sarah . . ."

"Then you are rich indeed" The blue-veined eyelids opened briefly, and Hélène de Valandré's eyes were dark with unbearable hurt. "I beg, Madame . . . Charlotte, that you will open this pouch, for my hands are awkward . . . clumsy with weakness, and take out the little bracelet of gold marguerites, with the crest upon it . . . It was my own christening gift from my parents as a child, and now I shall have no daughter of my own . . ."

Charlotte Tudor did as she was bid, and took out the delicately beautiful little bracelet.

"It would please me if you would let her wear it . . . for her joy in it will exorcise all the sadness of the past . . . It belongs to a time of my childish happiness . . . an innocence I can never recapture . . . It should be worn only by one who is happy and loved, and hold nothing but good memories . . ."

Charlotte Tudor tried to thank her, but Hélène de Valandré's eyes were already closed in sleep.

"A blessed shutting out of a world too different and lonely to yet face . . ." Charlotte Tudor thought, compassionately.

Whether in sleep or wakefulness, Hélène de Valandré might have told her, the sorrow was always the same.

Three weeks had passed since the violence of the storm had driven the small fishing boat from Erquy into Newton Creek, on the southern shores of Wales. Hélène de Valandré's terrified

53

cry for Jean-Luc had been the first sign of her return to reason
. . . Until then she had lain in a fever of delirium, recognising
no-one, unwilling, or unable, to be recalled to living . . .
Charlotte Tudor and her elderly serving maid had nursed her
devotedly, although the physician had declared it certain that
she could not long survive the horrors she had been forced to
witness and endure . . . Oppressed by nightmare memories,
sleeping or waking, she knew no ease . . . Yet, frail and
pitiful as she seemed, there was a core of strength within
her, and fear for Jean-Luc gave her purpose . . . For her
own part, she would have given up the struggle to return to
an existence which held no hope for her, no joy. She must do
what Armand de Valandré had planned for his son; see that
his hopes were made flesh . . . The clergyman, Josiah Tudor,
was a kindly man and honest, she was convinced, and she
willingly entrusted Armand's letters of credit and documents
to his safekeeping. He would take no payment for the kindness
shown to them in offering them shelter and board, declaring
it both duty and privilege to help those in need . . . When
Charlotte Tudor thought she divined in Hélène de Valandré a
return of strength, Josiah Tudor saw more clearly . . . He saw
only that her stubborn pride of spirit sustained her, as it had
sustained her on that long road from Valandré. It was not her
spirit, but her flesh, weakened by grief and ill-use, which freed
her at the last; loosing her tenuous hold on life as inevitably as
a leaf freed by the wind. A submission as natural, and robbed
of hurt.

It was Jean-Luc who bore the hurt, crying out in a bewilderment of rage and disbelief, believing himself wholly forsaken
. . . She had been buried in the small churchyard, beside the
church, in an alien soil amid an alien people. Yet they had
proved more merciful than her own. Jean-Luc had hated that
brittle earth which claimed her, but had hated even more those
who had tortured and murdered her as surely as those pathetic
victims, her parents, upon their funeral cart . . . God willing,
he would take her home to Valandré, he vowed. It was his
duty, more, a sacred trust. He would work and fight to that
end; die, if need be. He would take revenge upon all those who
had wrought this vileness, deal them blow for blow, blood for
blood. He had stood at Hélène de Valandré's graveside, rigid,

dry-eyed, for all his tears were shed, and Josiah Tudor, who preached forgiveness, saw none of it in the child. He saw, with pity, a hatred which he feared could only fester and root deep, then finally destroy. It was an obsession which would cripple Jean-Luc's future life.

Charlotte Tudor would gladly have kept the boy for her own, and begged, in vain, to be allowed to do so. He was already dear to her, and her own son, David, added his pleas to hers. Jean-Luc, he protested, was more than a friend and companion, he was as close as a brother born . . . Josiah Tudor knew as inexorably as Jean-Luc himself that the boy's future lay elsewhere, and although it grieved him to do so, he knew how he must act. Hélène de Valandré had trusted him, more, charged him, to obey her husband's wishes . . . So it was that, braving tears and accusations, and with heaviness of spirit, he took a company stage coach to London, with Jean-Luc silent and dispirited beside him. Each knew where his duty lay, but it brought no comfort, merely solution. The journey had been long, and the inns unwelcoming, and they could not know whether welcome or rejection awaited them at their journey's end.

Distressed by Jean-Luc's apathy, the good clergyman had blurted gruffly, against his better judgement, "If it should prove . . . unendurable, my boy, you had best send word to me. I shall come at once. You may make a home with Mrs Tudor and me . . ."

Jean-Luc had felt an upsurge of hope, a yearning to return to that ready haven of kindness, yet knew he must not.

"I thank you, sir, for your kindness to . . ." he hesitated . . . "to us both. I shall not forget it . . . but it is my father's wish that I go . . ." Jean-Luc's manner was stiff, his voice deliberately cold to mask his disappointment. Josiah Tudor was not deceived.

"I do not doubt your father's love for you, nor yours for him . . ." he said kindly. "His thought was all for your safety, your future inheritance . . . as is right and proper. He could not deliver you into my charge, for he did not know me . . ."

"No, sir . . ."

"But," declared the clergyman more firmly, "you came to me by God's will. He saw fit to entrust you to my care . . . I will not betray Him, nor you . . . I will leave you with your

55

guardian only if I believe him to be an honest man, who will do what is best for you, you understand?" Jean-Luc had nodded wordlessly.

When the coach had stopped before a large, imposing house in an elegant square overlooking well tended gardens, Jean-Luc had slipped his hand tentatively into Josiah Tudor's, and found it comfortingly covered and held firm. The boy's face was pallid, his fingers trembling, and Josiah Tudor gripped them more firmly. There was a rawness in the clergyman's chest, and a weight of grief and pity, and it was hard to know whether he or the child was comforter.

The owner of the house which Jean-Luc and the Reverend Josiah Tudor now approached with a mingling of caution and curiosity was a military man, General Sir Frederick Loosely. His courage was legendary; his grasp of battle strategy and command unrivalled. He was authoritarian, demanding, and as rigid in his bearing as in his code of conduct and in his expectations of others. Those men who served under him in war, as those in his own household, feared and loved him, and were jealously loyal. He was a man of action; swift to decision. Yet, as he awaited the coming of the innocuous little clergyman from Wales and 'the boy', as he termed him, he was barely less apprehensive than they . . .

The letter from Armand de Valandré, brought to him by company stage coach and messenger at Josiah Tudor's bidding, had disconcerted him. How could an irascible soldier, a bachelor, and of advanced years, play guardian to an unknown child? It was ludicrous; impossible! Loosely had never suffered fools gladly, and boys, particularly foreigners, not at all. He would set him in the care of one of the emigré community in London, he decided. Yes, that was the solution. There were many escaped aristocrats, fleeing Madame la Guillotine, penniless and in want. He would pay such a family handsomely to care for the boy. He would be among his own kind. They would speak his own language, keep alive the traditions and mores expected of him, understand his past, and plan his future . . . And yet . . . Loosely's thin, aquiline features were marred by a frown, and he grunted audibly. And yet, the boy had been pledged into his care. A debt owed, a debt to be repaid. A matter of honour . . . His mind bridged the years between, and he was amidst the stench and carnage of war, possessed by excitement and terror, driven by the primeval urge to survive . . . It was only the places which changed; the names of the battles; the faces of the men . . . The violence of cannon and musket, the smell of cordite, the noise and fury, the confusion of horses screaming, and men, were as inevitable as the wounded and dead . . .

General Wolfe and the capture of Montreal by the British . . . Storming the Heights of Abraham, that rocky cliff face, sheer, scarred, seemingly impenetrable; held by the French, rank upon rank of men, and horse-drawn cannon; foot-soldiers, cavalry, rained upon by rock and cannon from above, fighting for precarious hold, the living inexorably replaced by the dead. The warm, thick smell of blood and torn flesh, the butchered, the fear-crazed, the anonymous dead . . .

Yet, stormed it they had, and taken Montreal. A victory to celebrate and laud forever . . . Yet, upon the Heights, it was a different battle. The enemy was real, and the fighting with bayonet, rifle and musket . . . One saw one's enemy, face to face; the bewilderment; the terror and revulsion; the fury of the soldiers to kill or be killed. The pathos. The courage. The kinship. The waste . . .

Loosely had been bayonetted in the thigh, and felt neither pain, nor terror of death. Nothing, save surprise. He had fallen, as though in a dream, awaiting the final thrust of raw steel that would kill him . . . His gaze had been unwavering. He had neither flinched nor cried aloud as the bayonet was raised to strike . . . Then his adversary had stared at him for a long moment, as if in sudden recognition, then inexplicably turned away . . .

Loosely had been herded with the other captives of the French, those wounded and those sightless, able to drag themselves upright, or be supported by others of their kind . . . A straggling column of humanity, dispirited and uselessly flawed . . . When the French retreated, near to defeat, the cry had been to murder the prisoners, and flee . . . It was that French officer whose bayonet had entered Loosely's flesh who damned the act and those who demanded it, his anger and contempt a scourge . . . They had been spared only upon the orders of Michel, Comte de Valandré . . .

They were enemies sworn. Yet there had been instant recognition between them; some bonding of blood. A silent acknowledgement, perhaps, of kinship of courage and worth . . .

Their paths had crossed in war and uneasy peace, and a strange friendship had grown, intermittent and undemanding, until now . . . Michel de Valandré's son, Armand, asked only repayment of a debt. A life spared by his father for the promise of life for his young son . . . There was no confusion in General Loosely's mind now; no hesitation as to what he must do. Only the certainty of what was owed. Money was not enough. He must give of himself; lend time and protection to the boy to secure his future . . . He hoped the boy was tractable and without foreign affectations and ways. God knows, Jean-Luc de Valandré had suffered more than many a grown man. But he, Loosely, would stand no nonsense; no whining self-pity or heathenish ways . . . Hearing the discreet knock upon the outer door, the general assumed his fiercest, most bellicose expression, and stood, waiting to do battle . . . When the Reverend Josiah Tudor and his charge had been ushered into the library, General Loosely strove to hide his immediate discomfiture. He had drawn himself martially erect, stern, autocratic, and seemingly totally in command of the situation. His tone had been brusque, but his eyes kindly, as he made welcome the ill-matched pair. He had thanked the clergyman stiltedly for the care of his ward, to that good cleric's palpable embarrassment. Then he had turned his scrutiny upon Jean-Luc, demanding curtly, "Well, boy? And what am I to make of you?"

The abrupt harshness with which the question was delivered made Josiah Tudor glance apprehensively towards the child, but Jean-Luc was not intimidated.

"Whatever you think fitting, Monsieur . . . Sir," he corrected himself, adding courteously, "I am in your hands."

The general's gruff laughter was spontaneous and warm, and Josiah Tudor relaxed with an audible sigh, although he still held the old gentleman in uncomfortable awe . . . Jean-Luc saw reflected in the English general not the military exactness of Michel de Valandré, whom he hardly recalled, but the human kindness of the Chevalier de Riberac; an innate honesty, to himself and others. The general saw a boy far younger than

58

he had been led to expect, pale, and with recent suffering and loss bruising his eyes. Yet the eyes themselves were alert and intelligent, surveying him now candidly, and so like his old friend's, Michel de Valandré's, that he felt the burn of tears behind his own, and said roughly, to hide his weakness of loss,

"What is it that you wish to do? What become?"

"I wish to return to Valandré, sir, and be the Comte de Valandré. To kill those who killed my . . . father, and Maman . . ."

There was such conviction in his childish voice, such implacable hatred that Josiah Tudor, alarmed, had moved forward to reason with him, but General Loosely's glance of harsh warning silenced him.

"Then you must learn those things which will serve you best . . ." the old gentleman said quietly. "It is not enough to fight blindly, and to hate . . . You must learn to walk with reason and control, to study, plan, and find real purpose in life . . . to become the man your father would have you be . . ."

The clergyman's eyes met the general's above the boy's bowed head, and there was compassion and understanding in their glances, and gratitude in Josiah Tudor's nod of acknowledgement.

"When, sir, may I begin?" The question if abrupt, was courteously spoken.

"Tomorrow you shall leave for my house in Cornwall, and I shall follow you to the coast as soon as I am able . . . I shall engage a tutor from among the French emigrés to instruct you, and a competent Englishman to help you perfect the language . . ."

At Jean-Luc's startled disclaimer, he declared firmly, "It is necessary that you become, outwardly, an English gentleman, if you are to enter an English boarding school . . . Is that not so, Mr Tudor?" he demanded.

"Yes, that is so . . ."

"It will not all be unremitting study," General Loosely assured him, more kindly. "You may sail, and ride, and hunt, and have the freedom of the woods and estate, as before . . ."

The naked hurt upon the child's face made the old man falter, and he damned his clumsiness, and strove to make amends.

"You will not lose sight of Mr Tudor," he said quickly, "and he has written to me of your friendship with his son, who will be companion to you, and visit, I am sure, when his studies allow . . ."

Seeing the uncertainty upon the clergyman's face, and knowing it was born of reluctance to speak of the poverty of his calling, General Loosely had said with sincerity,

"I am grateful, sir, that you do me the courtesy of remaining as a guest under my roof. I am too much alone, and feel the lack of congenial company, such as yours."

Josiah Tudor had made gentle acknowledgement, but his host had brushed his thanks aside, protesting,

"It is I, sir, who owe you a debt of gratitude for your care of my ward and others less . . ." He had faltered awkwardly, face crimson, only to repeat, "Yes, it is I who owe you a debt . . ." Then, with a return of his old briskness, he had insisted, "You must make use of my small travelling coach, sir, upon your return . . . indeed, whenever you have need. The company stages are ill-kept and unreliable; a foretaste of purgatory! Designed, certainly, to mortify the flesh!" He had chuckled delightedly, and the clergyman had, good-naturedly, laughed with him, aware of the tact and generosity with which the offer had been made.

"I hope, Mr Tudor, that you and your son will not become as strangers, but will visit us here, as in Cornwall, whenever you are able, sir . . ." His eyes had been unashamedly pleading as he added with honesty, "We have need of true friends . . ."

His glance at Jean-Luc had been concerned and compassionate.

Upon the morrow, before Jean-Luc had been set into the carriage for his journey to Cornwall, his leave-taking of the general had been disciplined and firm, and he had shown no apprehension at what lay before him . . . Yet, for a few moments, he had clung despairingly to Josiah Tudor, dry-eyed with sorrow, yet so reluctant to let him go that the clergyman had, finally, to prise the child's fingers from their grip upon the cloth of his coat.

"I promised that I would only let you remain if I believed your guardian to be a good and honest man," he murmured so quietly that none but Jean-Luc could hear. "He is a fine man, and will treat you always with kindness and affection. He will direct your future, but never forget what is owed to your past . . ."

"Yes, sir." Jean-Luc's acceptance was subdued, and he did not look up, but made his way, unseeing, to the coach. Josiah Tudor, who had grown to love the boy for his courage and for himself, felt a weight of loss which grieved him as much as any he had known, and heard only the clopping of hooves, the rattling of the coach wheels and the familiar sounds of movement. He could see nothing, for his eyes were useless with tears. Yet he knew that the words of comfort he had spoken to Jean-Luc were true. In the night, when Jean-Luc had screamed aloud, awakened by the nightmare of the past, it was his guardian, the general, who had hurried immediately to the boy. He had thrust all offers of help aside, speaking to Jean-Luc with quiet solicitude, calming, reassuring, settling him to comforting sleep . . . Josiah Tudor, lying wakeful, had heard the old man's returning footsteps an hour or more later, and knew that he had sat beside the boy, unseen, patient, reliable, as he would always prove. The clergyman had few fears for Jean-Luc's present, or his future. He prayed to God, most earnestly, that they should not be embittered and destroyed by the hatreds of the past.

Why, then, did the words echo and re-echo in his head, as fiercely as if spoken aloud?

"They have sown the wind, and they shall reap the whirlwind."

Part Two

YORKSHIRE 1807

CHAPTER 6

The November wind swept cold and thin across the moor. It came with a sigh as bleak as the carrier's own as he sought, in vain, to shield himself behind the shelter of his halted cart. As mean and inescapable as the moor itself, he thought, anxious now to be rid of this God-forsaken place, and once more upon his journeying. His stout boots and leggings and warm, home-spun clothes, beneath the rough canvas smock, were proof only against the dry crispness of ice and snow, not this dampness which swirled from marsh and sodden earth. It penetrated fibres and flesh, seeming to settle in the bones, as if the barren vastness of the land defeated it, and it, too, sought escape. He stamped his booted feet upon the stony track aside the cottage gate as he awaited his passenger, slapping his numbed hands hard against his shoulders for warmth. The shock of pain as blood stirred the nerve ends of his fingertips forced tears to his eyes and an involuntary cry to his lips. The horse, harnessed to the poor, ill-fashioned cart, echoing its master's impatience, restlessly pawed the ground. Its soft upper lip curled high over yellowed teeth as it tossed its head and snickered fretfully, breath clouding the air.

Within the cottage, upon hearing the carrier's cart, Sarah Tudor felt a stirring of fear; a sadness. She could not regret leaving this forsaken place. It had been neither home to her nor comfort. It had been shelter, no more . . . She could not weep for that poor, bewildered husk of a creature, her father, buried these four days. Josiah Tudor had been dead in all save flesh these many months. That final emptiness of mind and feeling, laid deep in the Yorkshire earth was a stranger. He was no-one she knew.

She might have wept for the loss of what he had once been; father, comforter, protector and friend . . . Sarah did not weep.

The past was a closed book. Finished. Ended as surely as he . . . To reopen its pages would be a weakness. A painful betrayal.

Yet, still, the memories came crowding in . . . fierce, insistent. Her mother's death of a fever some five years ago. Her own struggle, as a twelve year old girl, to take upon herself the running of their home, and her father's grief. She relived her rage and sorrow; powerless to halt her father's retreat into that apathy which gave him refuge from reality and hurt. A slow disintegration . . . She had fought bitterly and long, trying to hide from others that which could not be hid . . . There had been little money, and none willing to comfort her, for David, her brother, was long gone; soldier to a half-mad king of an empire he could not recall.

For four years she had struggled to repair their life, holding it together jealously, until it broke as grievously as Josiah Tudor himself.

The Poor Law guardians, her father's kindness and self-denial forgotten, had declared that he must return to his place of birth, lest he become a charge upon the parish. It was the law; but she, able-bodied, and born in the hamlet, might enter the workhouse, if she so chose . . .

She did not choose. Nor did she beg aid from those he had so freely helped . . . She might have sought work as a seamstress, or a governess, had she been so minded . . . Yet, how could she leave him alone, by day or night? Or deliver him into the hands of another? By bartering the few pieces of saleable furniture remaining, and those small remembrances of her mother most precious to her, she had raised enough money to journey to Yorkshire. They had travelled by carrier's cart, and upon the cheaper of the company stages, sleeping in barns and byres, for they could not afford even the meanest of the inns . . . They had come, at last, to this poor cottage, which was all that remained of his holdings . . . and he had shown neither recognition, nor awareness of her uselessly falling tears.

Sarah Tudor had sold the cottage for the pittance it would bring, to pay for Josiah Tudor's simple funeral trappings. She had done so without regret, save that she feared that her brother might search, and never find her again, should his regiment unexpectedly return . . . She might have sent word of her plight to General Sir Frederick Loosely, who had secured her brother's

66

commission. Yet she was too proud and independent of spirit to seek his aid . . . He was a good man, and kind, she knew, for he had sent word at her mother's funeral, begging that they forgive his absence, since sickness and infirmity laid him low. He had pleaded most urgently that they inform him of their needs and difficulties, should any arise . . . He regretted only his helplessness, and that his ward, Jean-Luc de Valandré, was absent with his old regiment of the line in India. The boy, as Josiah well knew, held Mrs Tudor in deep affection, and would have wished to pay his honest respects . . . It would grieve him sorely when he learnt of her death.

The carrier's harsh knocking upon the cottage door recalled Sarah from the past, as he returned disconsolately to his cart. The door to the cottage opened, and a small, delicately-boned figure emerged hesitantly from within, clad in a lavender dress and cloak and a matching bonnet. She paused for a moment, as if determining between the austere, stone greyness of what was familiar and known, or the comfortless greyness beyond. Then, the decision made, the young woman turned and closed the door, her gloved hand resting briefly upon the knob, and stooped to retrieve the objects she had placed upon the step, secured within a soft-hued Kashmiri shawl. Her face was shadowed by the brim of her bonnet, and the carrier knew only by her slenderness and the soft fluidity of her movement beneath the folds of her cloak, and the pretty inadequacy of her slippers, that she was young. Yet, when she moved forward to take her burden and place it with those piled high upon the cart, he was surprised, not merely by the delicate perfection of her oval face and the wide-spaced hazel eyes 'neath the fine brows, but her serenity and composure. In truth, she was scarcely more than a child. Yet there was a gravity in her bearing which spoke of grief survived.

"If you please, sir . . .," her voice was quiet, but firm, "I will take my bundle upon my knees . . ."

He nodded and, offering his arm, assisted her on to the narrow perch beside his own, then followed her upon the cart, taking the reins and flicking the pony into life.

She did not look back, but sat unnaturally straight, her bundle clutched tight within her hands. He would have spoken some word, but saw the trembling of her lips, quickly stilled, and the gleam of tears behind her lashes, and said nothing. The carrier was not a harsh man, and had sired four daughters of his own, with as many dead in infancy, and knew that what could not be changed in life was ill served by sympathy. 'T were best accepted first as last. He had made many such journeys with those bereaved or dispossessed. It was not a task he relished, for many were old and bewildered, and all were sick at heart. But work was hard to find, and a man had to live as best he could, or starve. There were others ready and all too willing to take his place, should he refuse, so what would compassion avail him or the poor, benighted devils he transported? Nothing. Save to set him beside them in the misery of pauperdom . . . He smiled wrily, "The road to the workhouse." It was easily said. A threat to young children to halt them at their mischief, or spur a feckless lad to effort . . . He had used the words himself, and often, with a lightness that brought him shame . . .

"It is far off, sir? This . . . place whither we are bound?" "What's that . . .?" The gentle voice had startled him. "No," he said, recovering himself, "'tis but five miles or so at most. We shall be there ere long, have no fear . . ." He cursed himself for an insensitive fool. His florid face, made raw by wind and weather, grew redder yet as he jerked hard upon the reins and noisily cleared his throat. Then, afraid of silence, he blurted, "I am sorry. It was ill-spoken . . ." A small gloved hand reached out to rest lightly upon his, and was as lightly withdrawn. So swift it was, and unexpected, that he might have thought it imagined, had she not said, "I beg, sir, that you will not distress yourself on my account. I see that you are an honest man, sensitive to the misfortunes of others . . . That words have less power to wound than the actions of others is a lesson I have early learned . . . I have met with little enough kindness of late, and am grateful for yours . . . I would not have it soured by regret."

"Then I will say no more," he promised gruffly, "save to add that you are a brave little maid."

His large raw-boned hands fidgetted upon the reins. "Aye," he thought, "and she would need every ounce of that courage, else her spirit would be crushed all too soon."

Around them the bleak moor stretched endlessly, the track set about by rushy marshland, its colour faded with the dying year to

68

the browns and ochre of fallen leaves, lifeless and decaying. Mist rose from the wetness of bog and turf; a purple-grey shroud, thinning as it rose to reveal sudden outcrops and boulders of stone, hurled randomly, it seemed, as though some rage within the earth itself erupted into violence . . .

Here and there, occasional sheep grazed, distance making them blurred and inanimate, scarcely distinguishable from the stones. The few near at hand showed no fear and little curiosity as the cart creaked and trundled by, for the moor was theirs, and passing strangers of little relevance . . . Save for a lone bird, wheeling and circling overhead, its ragged wings outstretched, there seemed no other living creatures in this sad wilderness, save for the silent occupants of the cart and the horse which drew it, its rhythmic hoofbeats upon the stony way, and the jangling of its harness, loud on the misted air, and the grumbling creak of the cartwheels.

Mile followed mile, with no change in the landscape and no word spoken, for carrier and girl were engrossed in their own thoughts.

"This damnable war with the French has much to answer for!" the carrier thought. "Like the wings of that predatory bird above them, it brought darkness and fear, and none could shelter, or escape the bloodiness of beak and talons . . . The girl beside him was gently bred, of that he was sure, for her speech was elegant, and her clothes those of a gentlewoman, although worn and oft mended. Too young to admit of a husband killed in battle? Her father, then, fallen at war? There were many young women so afflicted, and there would be many more. At least the poor, such as he, were used to deprivation and the daily grind of poverty . . ."

"We will soon be approaching the village, . . ." he warned, "if you will make ready."

"I am ready, sir," she said quietly, "for whatever lies before me. The poorhouse will offer me shelter and safety. A new life . . . I must not dwell upon what is past and ended, for regret is a bitter companion . . ."

"Indeed," he said gravely, "and I could have wished you a better one upon this journey, but I am a man awkward with words . . . you understand?" She nodded, saying with dignity, "I thank you, sir, for your concern for me . . . a stranger . . ."

Her voice was low, and he wondered what memory had the power to force such raw colour to her cheeks, with that defiant firming of mouth and chin, as she raised her head high. He felt a stirring of regret, a sadness he could not explain. He studied his coarse hands upon the reins, fingers thickened and chafed by weather, then his worn leggings and boots, as if they might give him the answer to what ailed him. The gulf between them was too wide to bridge by words . . . He sighed . . . She was a pretty lass, and proud, with rare spirit . . . It would not be easy for her. There were many who would seek to humble and break her, for such was the way of the world. He turned towards her and clumsily touched her arm, weathered face anxious.

"In but a few minutes we will be at the poorhouse. It lies beyond that spur of rock, hidden from view. I will help you from the cart, and open the iron gates for you."

"I thank you, sir. I shall be grateful if you will close them behind me."

The horse, with the force of long habit, slowed as they approached the rocky outcrop with the fall of white water dropping as a thin cataract into the worn gully beneath. She heard the splash of the animal's hooves through water, and the blurred sound of the wheels of the cart, then, before them, stood the gaunt, unlovely grey stone of the workhouse, starkly uncompromising. The carrier halted the cart and scrambled stiffly from his perch and strode to where she sat, and lifted her down clumsily to the damp turf, exclaiming vexedly, "Your pretty slippers are all but ruined, lass, and your bonnet and cloak soaked through with mist and weather . . ." adding remorsefully, "I should have offered you the dry sacking from my cart. 'Twas remiss of me . . ."

"The clothes I wear are all I now own, sir," she said, smiling, "and will be exchanged too soon for others of a more serviceable kind. I arrive as I am to lend me courage . . . It is not vanity alone, nor the need to impress others, that prompts me to dress thus, but the need to impress upon myself that this is what I am, and shall remain, whatever humiliation awaits me . . ."

The carrier did not know what impulse prompted him, for he was a reserved man, and oft-times abrasive, yet the words sprang honestly to his lips and he could not reject them, "I am a poor man, and my life is hard, and the work I do brings little

70

reward . . . I am richer, my maid, for having met you. I pass this way each week at this time. Should there be any letter or message you have need to send, or journey to make . . ." he hesitated, seeking the right words, "or simply to speak to one who counts himself a friend, then you have but to seek me out . . ."

The young woman's face was aglow with real pleasure, her eyes bright, as, aware of the embarrassment which caused him to shuffle and clasp his arms about him and look away, she replied earnestly, "It will give comfort to me, sir, to know I have such a friend . . ." She placed her bundle upon the step of the cart and untied the loose knots that secured the Indian shawl, searching anxiously, then taking something within her gloved hand. "I pray, sir, that you will accept this token of my regard and gratitude . . . I beg you will not offend me by rejecting it, for it would grieve me sadly . . ."

She laid a small gold stock pin upon his calloused palm, made in the likeness of a fox's head. Seeing the stubborn refusal upon his face, and hearing the objections springing to his lips, she cried urgently, "I will not pretend, sir, that the gift is of no account, or that I will not feel its loss . . . It belonged to my father, lately buried, and there is none other to care for me, for my brother was . . . is missing these many months in the wars with the French. I have no money, but had I some, I would not insult your honesty by offering you payment. I give you what is of value to me, believing you worthy of it . . ."

The carrier felt a thickness in his throat and an ache within him as he said, in a voice he scarce recognised as his own, "I shall not part with it, my dear . . . but treasure it as you have done . . ." He turned and struggled with the massive iron gates, scarce able to lift the ring and swing them open on their hinges for her to enter within.

"Your name, lass?" he said helplessly, "I do not know your name, should your brother or any other come seeking you . . ."

She said gravely, "There is no-one else, sir . . . but I am called Sarah . . . Sarah Tudor . . ."

"Then may God protect you, Sarah Tudor . . ."

His muttered words were lost in the clanging of the great gates as they closed behind her. He turned back to the cart and clambered heavily aboard. Before he took up the reins, he removed the fox-head stock pin from his rough smock and, wrapping it in a piece of torn linen which he kept for binding, should he meet with some accident upon the road, he placed it carefully in the pigskin pouch which held his few coins, and secured it about his neck for safekeeping. Then he settled a plug of tobacco in his cheek, and lifted the reins. He had never possessed so valuable a thing as the fox-head pin, nor thought to . . . Yet there was no joy in its ownership. Like his rare indulgence in tobacco, it brought only the dry taste of ashes. "Walk on!" he commanded the pony, jerking hard at the reins. In his thoughts was the picture of that slight young figure walking along that seemingly endless path to what was unknown.

Even with God's protection, he thought, the way would prove hard, and the journey crueller than his own.

CHAPTER 7

Jean-Luc de Valandré, prisoner-of-war aboard the rotting hulk of a British man o' war upon the mudflats of Portsmouth harbour, would have preferred a prison cell. He had known many such cells, but none which had been able to secure him. It was true that he had given his parole as an officer of the Hussars, that he would not attempt to escape. Yet, who but the British would consider such word to be binding? Had not Napoleon himself declared it a sacred duty to break free, and return to fight beside him for the glory of France and the Republic . . .

It was less a vessel than a tomb, Jean-Luc thought disgustedly. It stank of the sea, of human sweat and flesh, and the slimy dankness of timbers waterlogged . . . It was a damnably soulless place, for captors and imprisoned alike; men denied even the comfort and distractions of women and strong drink; those universal panaceas for men deprived. No street women would consent to being smuggled aboard, not even the lowest doxies and trollops of the port. The French were their enemy, heathen beasts, coarse and brutalised, and a harlot's life, however ill-used she be, was all she had. It was kinder than the unknown face of death, with its promised retribution . . .

Jean-Luc was not sure that death could be more destructive of human flesh than this wretched travesty of a ship which now imprisoned him. It was an ugly, desecrated skeleton of a craft, deprived of masts and rigging, without cannon or arms, denied even the power of movement, save that monotonous rising and falling with the tide . . . He hated the stench of its waterlogged timbers, assailed by barnacle and worm and countless unseen scavengers, eroding as fiercely from within as the storms without . . . Dear God! There was always noise . . . the chatter of men and guards, the rhythmic thudding of the pumps that cleared

73

the seeping water from the bilges, the shouts and clamour as provisions were hauled aboard, or the guard relieved . . . It was always cold. The winds came icily off the sea, finding bleak entry, with mist and fog, where the guns had once made shelter . . . There was always drenching spray and, when a storm arose, such violence of movement that sickness and terror overcame captives and captors alike . . . Then, the rolling of the hulk with the creaking of its timbers, and the pitch and toss of the waves seemed likely to send them all hurtling to the ocean floor . . . Oftimes, Jean-Luc would have welcomed such oblivion, for the retching and vomiting seemed scarcely more tolerable than death itself . . .

Jean-Luc de Valandré, or Luc Nolais as he chose to be called, made ready to escape . . . He had left nothing to chance. His credentials as the man he now was, or purported to be, had been established with meticulous care. Were it not so, his own life would have undoubtedly been forfeit, as those of so many other emigrés, aristocrats surviving the massacres of the revolution . . . Even with the uncrowned king incarcerated, and stripped of lands and possessions and his right to rule, supporters remained fiercely loyal to his cause . . . as they had to Louis XVI. That their king had suffered ill-use, and finally public execution, as many of their own families, served only to strengthen their allegiance. Theirs was a bonding of blood and sacrifice . . . each one pledged, upon oath, to return to France, and claim what was morally his own. Those who had been brutally murdered in the people's revolution, or survived, only to die in exile, would be avenged by those living . . . Jean-Luc, Comte de Valandré, had much to avenge.

Lieutenant Nolais was a man liked by few, even of his own kind, although grudgingly respected. He was solitary, and his abrasiveness discouraged all attempts at friendship. Yet, none could doubt his courage . . . Had he not proved it by twice escaping from fortified prisoner-of-war camps, held by the British to be impregnable? With no word of English, he had fled from that bastion upon Dartmoor, surviving its wildness, and evading capture for almost a month. Upon finally being forced to the hulks, manacled and chained, he was still contemptuously shouting curses at his captors. Neither solitary confinement nor the most brutal of beatings by the more vindictive of his guards had quenched his defiance, nor his spirit . . .

To the guards, Luc Nolais was the archetypal Frenchman, arrogant, cocksure, boastful . . . like his damned French Emperor, he strutted and paraded, a raucous, posturing bantam; all noise and fury . . . Punishment was invariably received coldly, but with scorn, and seemed only to stiffen the prisoner's conviction and resolve.

One of the guards, a pocked and foul-mouthed fellow, and swift to violence, had contemptuously christened him, 'The French Fox . . .' And there was indeed some deep, atavistic ruthlessness in him; some blood lust, cold and insatiable as the animal's own. Nolais was not, the guard once declared bitterly, the kind of prisoner to turn one's back on . . . He would seize opportunity; strike without warning . . .

To fulfil his prophecy, he had been struck down savagely by his own rifle butt, as Luc Nolais, crashing it against the guard's skull, leapt, after the barest hesitation, into the icy greyness of sea and enveloping fog. The impact when he had hurled himself from the deck and struck water had all but knocked the breath from his lungs, and when he had surfaced, gasping, he thought that he must die from the viciousness of the cold and the rawness in his breast, but the shouts and cries of discovery from the hulk, and the hail of shot upon the surface of the sea alerted him despite himself . . . For a while he trod water, grateful for the fog which muffled sound and hid him from view . . . Neither those on board nor the guards circling the hulk by boat could do more than guess at his whereabouts as, with quiet determination, he swam for the shore. The clothes he wore hampered his movements, becoming heavy and waterlogged, dragging him relentlessly, and slowing his pace . . . In the urgency of escape, there had been no time to discard the more cumbersome garments, and now there was no opportunity . . . His limbs grew heavy and stiff, and his breathing laboured as he swam, sometimes below the surface, sometimes gulping painfully for air. It seemed to him that, try as he might to muffle sound, the fierce splashing of water must draw the guards to him . . . In his own ears, it sounded hideously loud, and the harsh thudding of his heart in his rib cage seemed to deafen his mind and his senses to all else, so that, confused and barely conscious, he believed that they must be as aware of it as he. He swam, now, mechanically, almost without volition, deprived of sight and direction by the cold greyness of fog. The few sounds which penetrated its thickness were muffled, unrecognisable for what they were. All was strangely featureless and distorted, adding to his growing feeling of unreality, so that he seemed to be struggling to break free, not from the water, but some cold, oppressive dream which dragged him remorselessly below its surface, again and again, until exhaustion and terror robbed him of all will to survive . . . The sea was in his eyes and ears, filling his mouth and lungs, and he had no more strength to fight it. He felt it closing over him, cold, and salt-tasting as blood . . . He felt neither sorrow nor fear, only a blessed calm; a certain knowledge that the pain of it was over . . . The soreness had left his breast, and that scalding hurt as he gulped raw breath into his lungs. He closed his eyes and willed himself to struggle no more, as the sea claimed him . . . He had tried, and failed . . . There was nothing but rest from weariness, then darkness, oblivion . . . He was too tired now to mutter even that childhood prayer which came unbidden to his mind, with all the restless, crowding ghosts and echoes of things past . . . There were a child's tears upon his face; a child's helplessness, and no warm arms to make him safe . . . He felt nothing as the current swirled and sucked, coldly unyielding, bearing him determinedly in its grasp.

General Sir Frederick Loosely sat, severely erect, in the high-backed chair regarding his visitor impassively. The old gentleman's gaunt face was as attenuated as his frame, but his fine eyes, faded with age, were shrewdly assessing. Only a barely perceptible tremor of his hands upon the desk betrayed his nervous anxiety as he demanded, voice steady, "You have news of an escaped prisoner-of-war, you say?"

"I have, sir . . . to be delivered to you, and no other . . . Those were my orders."

"This . . . prisoner?" His tone was curtly indifferent.

"The man they call 'The Fox', sir . . . One, Luc Nolais. It seems he struck down a guard upon the hulks, and escaped into the sea . . ."

"Escaped, you say? How? When there are armed guards

upon the hulks, and sharpshooters upon the shore . . .?" he demanded irritably. "Was there some collusion . . .? Some laxity . . .?"

"No, sir. It would appear not . . . although there will be a deeper and more stringent enquiry," he paused, before claiming awkwardly, "It is thought he will be apprehended soon, and returned in shackles . . ."

"Thought, you say? Thought! Action is needed, not thought . . . It is a public disgrace and scandal that he was allowed to escape . . . Was he not wounded by the rifle fire?"

"It is not thought . . ." Alerted by the white anger about the General's mouth, he amended carefully, "It is not known, sir.Nor if he survived to the shore . . . The sea was icy, and the fog was . . ."

"Hell and damnation, sir!" expostulated the general. "Are you all cretins and nincompoops? Blind, sir? Such incompetence is unbelievable! No man under my command would have dared to make such excuse . . . The army has been lax, sir, and it grieves me . . ."

The messenger's spine was as rigid as the general's, his jaw as tense, until the irascible command released him.

"You may go, sir!"

The messenger contrived not to betray, even by the flicker of an eyelid, his relief, but saluted, and turned abruptly upon his heel, only to be halted by the icy command,

"You will bring me immediate news of this . . . this creature. The Fox, you say?" He spoke the name disparagingly.

"Yes, sir. The French Fox . . . for his cunning . . ."

"Then we must be as cunning as he; as ruthless and swift to kill. That is our answer . . ."

His eyes were closed, his eyelids so blue-veined as to seem bruised in the waxen face. The visitor made no reply, for there was none to be made.

General Loosely sat for a while, aware of the painful thudding of his heart and the rawness of his breastbone. This strange weakness and lethargy had bedevilled him of late, and he wiped irritably at the sweat which beaded his mouth and hairline . . . Thought of the messenger, and his deliberate harshness to him, brought a wry smile to his lips. Was it the Roman emperors, or the Greeks, who killed the bearers of bad tidings? He could not now recall . . . for age and confusion of mind were inseparable . . .

His memory of Jean-Luc was clear, and his fear for him a physical hurt, so acute that he almost cried aloud with the vileness of it . . . Strange that he had never felt fear for his own safety, only the boy . . . his ward. Had he been right, he wondered again, to do what Jean-Luc asked; to prepare him for such a revenge? He could not believe it to be so . . . Yet, perhaps, from that very first day, he had known it to be inevitable, pre-ordained. The boy's whole life had been wrought and fashioned to this end. At least he had been trained to the limit of his endurance, sometimes even beyond that limit, and none could fault him for courage . . . Strangely, the knowledge brought the general no comfort. Courage, without caution, or the fear of death, too-often led to recklessness . . .

Well, the plans had been well laid, and the guard, well briefed to allow the prisoner's escape, had played his part well . . . He would be rewarded . . . Yet, had he escaped? The hail of bullets was real. The dangers of drowning, or recapture, should he survive, an ever-present threat, for none could be trusted; so vital was Jean-Luc's mission, and the prize.

"You know that you must stand alone in this, Jean-Luc," he had warned him. "That none will openly aid you, or protect you, should you fail . . .?"

"Yes, I understand. It is my choice I stand alone."

"If you are discovered . . ."

"If I am discovered, they will kill me with as little mercy as they showed my father, and kin . . . With as little mercy as I shall show to them, should need arise . . ."

The admission was calm, chilling in its certainty. He would become Luc Nolais. He would willingly face prison, then the wretchedness of life upon the prisoner-of-war hulks . . . He would become the Frenchman he played, blindly following the secret route which escaping French prisoners took, betraying to the English those who aided their escape to France, to serve in the little Corsican's army . . . He would not call him Emperor. He had not earned that right.

General Loosely felt old, and cruelly beset by weakness, as he rose from the desk . . . There was a coldness within him which the leaping flames of the fire in the grate could not ease.

He had prayed, this long time, that the hatred which Jean-Luc felt would die; that he would be purged of that cold rage which impelled him . . . Yet he could not think it. Jean-Luc, Comte de Valandré, or Luc Nolais, it was all the same. Both were one; that small boy upon that rough-hewn cart, who watched his grandparents humiliated and driven to their deaths, and his mother die . . . The flames of Valandré burned fierce within him, white-hot and devouring. The general could only pray that they would cleanse, even as they destroyed.

Jean-Luc struggled to uneasy consciousness in some unknown place, trying to still those terrors crowding in upon him . . . The mist seemed to seep into flesh and bone, clouding his very brain, so that he was incapable of thought or movement . . . When memory, and feeling, returned, it was with a pain so sharp that he actually cried aloud. It was as though every muscle and nerve pulsed raw, washed clean by the salt sting of the tide. His clenching fists trapped grains of wet sand, and he was aware that his legs still lay within the lap of foam of the sea's edge as he dragged himself with slow effort higher up the shore . . .

He lay there helplessly for a while, hearing only the slap and suck of the tide and his own harsh breathing . . . All about him in the fog, he knew, were expert sharpshooters, marksmen, who would not hesitate to wound or kill. His life was of no account. He was, once again, the active enemy, and would be hunted down as such . . .

But his life *was* of account, he thought despairingly, and that one task which his new life and the old had tempered and honed him to do . . . he must summon the will to rise; force strength into himself. Yet, try as he might, he could not . . . Exhaustion and weakness bedevilled him and, to his shame, he felt the tears of rage at his own impotence running uselessly from his eyes.

Somehow he crawled from the sea, dragging himself inch by awkward inch through the slime of the mud-flats and sand . . . It seeped through the cloth of his breeches and coat, and oozed through his splayed fingers, and when he fell forward, exhausted by effort, it filled his mouth and nostrils, suffocating as the fog about him.

Crawling, rising and stumbling, he made his way inland, aware only of the need to be away from the coast, and its dangers . . . The fog gave place to the deeper darkness of night, yet he dare not pause nor slacken his pace . . . Salt water had filled him with a raging thirst, and his water-logged hessian boots chafed the skin to broken flesh . . . Hour by hour, mile by mile, he walked, and when he could walk no more, he fell to his knees against a bleak outcrop of stone, and, exhausted and unable to rise, slept . . .

Feverish and beset by chills, he cried out wildly in his sleep . . . anguished by memories . . . He was upon the cart from Valandré, his mother and Raoul beside him . . . he could feel its movement, and smell the stench of rotted fruit and straw . . . The heat was all about him, searing flesh, burning him to ashes . . . The flames were flickering light, red as blood, devouring the chateau of Valandré, and when he tried to cry out, his voice was a croak in the dryness of his throat . . . The faces of the wild boars, tusked and savage, drew in on him, and other faces . . . his father, grandmère and grandpère upon the hideous cart, his mother, waxen and dead . . .

The man driving the cart had turned, and he was no-one Jean-Luc knew; the woman beside him chafed his cold hands and wiped the dried mud from his eyelids, and he felt it stiffening his face, cracking apart while his lips formed the rictus of a smile . . .

"Who are you, you poor scarecrow?" she asked.

"Luc Nolais . . . Lieutenant, Hussars . . ." The words, long rehearsed, came instinctively, and he knew, even as he spoke them, that it would mean a return to the hulks . . . Yet he was too weakened to care. "Well, Luc Nolais," the voice of the man at the reins returned softly in French. "We have been awaiting you . . . It is as well we came searching . . ." Dream, or reality? Imagination, or death? Jean-Luc de Valandré closed his eyes. In God's good time, he would know.

CHAPTER 8

Within the poorhouse, Sarah Tudor's thoughts, too, were upon the past, for its sadness was more endurable than the reality of the present.

She had quickly been taught that, in surrendering herself to paupery, she had surrendered all rights, save that to exist. She must wear the coarse grey uniform; work as instructed, and renounce her few possessions. She must curtsey always to those in authority over her, and speak only when commanded to do so . . . She must eat the mean, pitifully inadequate food provided, even though the prayers of gratitude demanded caught in her throat as sourly . . . She must obey instantly. Never question. Punishment for laziness or insubordination would be severe . . . Could any punishment, she wondered, be harsher than what she now endured? The price of the charity, so grudgingly given, was too high; a slavery of flesh . . . Yet, they could not possess nor shackle her mind and spirit. When the time was right . . .

She had endured the humiliation of being stripped of her clothing, and seeing it burned, 'for fear it proves verminous'. She had been forced to bathe in a wooden tub of cold water, under the watchful gaze of the housekeeper; a coarse bully of a woman, blowsy and foul-tongued . . . The ball of lye and tallow had been rough, and the brush and flannel with which she had been commanded to scrub herself, excoriating, a penance to be endured . . . Her hair had been shorn by another pauper, and with it, Sarah felt, her last shred of dignity and pride . . . The pauper, a deaf mute, had been hesitant, and her hands as gently compassionate as her gaze, which held the words of comfort and apology she was powerless to speak . . . The tears of rage and self-pity which scalded Sarah's eyes did not fall. She had found a friend, one imprisoned more viciously and inescapably than she . . .

"Jane Grey! Go!"

The housekeeper's command was curtly dismissive, but the pauper, not hearing, remained, clasping her rough-skinned hands firmly about Sarah's in comfort. The housekeeper, incensed, had shaken the woman violently by the arm, and thrust her savagely without. "The woman is a fool!" she muttered. "Stupid! Witless . . ." she added spitefully. "No more than an animal, and of less use . . ." Sarah had said nothing, but stood quite still amid the cut and fallen locks of her hair, their lifelessness obscene . . . She felt that she had been violated, made unclean, less by the barbarism of the act than by the housekeeper's words. Her eyes were insolently accusing, her contempt plain, as she sank into the curtsey demanded, never shifting her gaze. She had learnt when not to speak. She would know, as inexorably, when to act.

If the enforced austerity of her new life, and the work-house uniform, had failed to quench Sarah's spirit, then the workmaster, Oliver Sidebottom, seemed admirably equipped to succeed. He sat imperiously behind his desk, deliberately not rising when she entered, in order to point out her subservience . . . Despite the ugly anonymity of her dress, there was about her some quality which disturbed him; an inherent superiority which could not be hid. He stared at her coldly, unspeaking.

Sarah, in turn, stared assessingly at him. There was a fop-pishness about him; some lack of manliness, not disguised by the careful elegance of his clothes. Beneath his immaculately powdered and ribboned bag-wig, his skull was narrow-boned, and his tapering nose and chin lent him a sly, vulpine quality, accentuated by the short upper lip and small, pointed teeth. He looked, she decided, like nothing so much as a pert fox, aspiring to be a dandy.

He surprised her smile of amusement, and flushed, declaring with acerbity, "I asked you, ma'am, which work you felt yourself best suited for . . . what qualities you felt you had to offer, although, it seems that politeness and concentration are not amongst them."

"Since I am able to read and write, sir, and have learnt from my father some knowledge of French, history, geography and literature, I had hoped that I might offer myself as a governess."

"A governess!" The exclamation was of genuine amusement and incredulity, "A governess, you say? There is small demand for pauper governesses! Who would employ such a person to teach their children, and mix with their family? The idea is inconceivable . . ."

"Then, perhaps, you will permit me to teach the pauper women and children in your care, sir . . .? Their lives are bitterly empty and restricted. To be able to read would broaden their horizons; give them pleasure . . ."

"Broaden their horizons? Give them pleasure?" he repeated, unable to repress his impatience. "You are naive, ma'am, and, I go so far as to say, impertinent! Their horizons are bounded by what they are. As for pleasure, they may find it in work, for this institution is what its name implies – a workhouse! If you have no more pertinent suggestion to make, then it must be my duty to instruct you . . ."

"Could I not nurse those who are sick within the institution, sir?" she persisted stubbornly. "I have knowledge of sickness, sir, for I tended my mother and my father, over many years. There must be those here who are equally frail and aged, unfitted to work, and in need of such care . . ." She broke off confusedly as he continued to stare at her, unspeaking, expression unreadable. "There will be infants who are ailing, perhaps, or nursing mothers, weakened by childbirth . . . I have oft times visited such women, in my father's parishes, and ministered to them . . ."

"With nourishing soups, no doubt, and charitable gifts?" His tone was scathingly dismissive. "I remind you that you are now one of those poor, ma'am. A pauper! Living upon the charity of others . . . Those who are no longer able-bodied and capable of earning their keep are sent elsewhere . . . Nursing mothers surrender their infants to others to wet-nurse, and must return to work. It is . . . unfortunate that so few of the newborn survive . . . barely two in every hundred, I believe . . ." Then, alert to Sarah's stricken expression, he added maliciously, "This is not due to any lack of care on our part . . . rather to the fecklessness of those women who bear them . . . If they are unwed, and their unfortunate infants bastardised, they cannot expect to be admitted into any hospital, even should some complication occur . . . None will accept them, rightly judging them to be

83

promiscuous and undeserving of such aid . . . To treat them
would be to offend all decency, and encourage such immorality
. . . These women are nothing but degenerates, ma'am!"

"You do not find them deserving of pity, sir?"

"Indeed, I do not!" Anger engorged his face and the veins of
his neck, and even reddened the whites of his eyes. "They bring
such suffering upon themselves by their own licentiousness . . .
They alone are culpable!"

"And the children, sir?"

"The sins of the fathers," he quoted sententiously. Then,
awkward and shamefaced at his blunder, he blustered peevishly, "I will not discuss it more! The matter is ended. I have
listened long enough to your absurd ramblings! You have tried
my patience, ma'am! You will be informed of your duties . . .
those I deem suited to your . . . experience and talents."

Sarah could not doubt that it gave him a perverse pleasure
to assign her only the most menial and degrading of tasks. She
grew adept at scrubbing hallways and floors, the emptying of
chamberslops, and the carrying of coal, the endless scouring of
pots and skillets with rottenstone and sand, the washing and
ironing of the paupers' clothing and bedding in the steam-laden
dampness of the laundry . . . Her hands grew chapped and raw.
Her resentment grew. Yet she performed her tasks obediently,
and with a diligence which none could fault.

Her only true solace and help was Jane Grey, and they often
laboured side by side, the most hateful task made bearable by
their companionship. It was, perhaps, an affinity of outcasts,
for both were separated by barriers of difference from others
of their kind. Jane Grey had been so trapped in her carapace
of silence that none had thought her other than idiot; slow,
and uncomprehending. Yet she was sensitive and intelligent;
the blows and contempt of those in authority an added torment. Sarah helped her break free . . . She evolved a simple
sign-language, and marvelled at Jane Grey's quick eagerness
in learning. What could not be easily explained by touch,
was explained in mime, and by the repeated slow mouthing
of words . . . Soon they were so adept at this 'language' that
others, drawn by amusement or curiosity, began to imitate,
then master it, too . . . Jane Grey, released from solitariness,
grew daily more confident. Those paupers who had previously

shunned her from embarrassment, or belief that she was an imbecile, made shamefaced amends. Such acceptance was a rebirth for Jane Grey. An awakening. Her plain, broad face lost its look of dull incomprehension, her eyes grew lively. Animation made her seem young, and almost pretty . . . and those who had dismissed her as elderly were chastened to learn from her that she was no more than nine and twenty years old . . . Her debt of gratitude to Sarah was never touched upon; yet her devotion spoke words enough. Jane Grey would willingly have died for her . . . Her constant fear was that they would be forced to part. Sarah would not long endure that servitude which had been Jane's from childhood . . . She would break the yoke, cleanly, and with finality. Jane did not know if even being freed from her own yoke of silence would be comfort enough for that.

Sarah, who had no former knowledge of workhouse life, found the petty restrictions as chafing as the harsh clothing which she now wore . . . The workmaster, and the house-keeper, despite the authority of the unseen Board of Guardians, appeared omnipotent. Their word was ineluctable law . . . The more venial offences, such as laziness, were punished by shaming and ridicule, the offender denied food, and forced to publicly parade her sins, and beg absolution . . . The aim was always to humiliate and degrade. Blows and ill-treatment were so commonplace as to go unrecorded, whippings were not unknown. Persistent lying, insubordination, or theft of food, brought penalty of solitary confinement in the cellars beneath; in darkness, and denied all comfort save water . . . Those who escaped and stole to survive were faced with the pillory or stocks, at the command of the justices . . . Few had the will to escape, for who would shelter them? Nor did they steal from one another. It is useless to steal from another as deprived as oneself . . . The cruellest punishment of all, Sarah thought, was in separating husband from wife; parent from child . . . Many such families were never to be reunited, the men forced to labour in fields, or upon the roads; the women at menial tasks within the workhouse, or in the sculleries of houses without . . . the children 'sold' into the slavery of chimneys, mines, brickyards, or upon farms.

It was her abhorrence of this rule which brought Sarah to disaster.

Within the vast dining hall, the paupers were assembled like a flock of sombre grey birds; the workmaster, the housekeeper, and their subordinates, raised high on a platform above.

The workmaster walked with slow deliberation to the lectern. The shuffling of the paupers grew subdued, their faces downcast.

The workmaster remained standing until every sound was stilled, every movement halted, then began to read tonelessly from the Beatitudes . . .

"Blessed are the meek . . . Blessed are the poor in spirit . . . Blessed are the merciful . . ."

There was a startled cry from somewhere behind Sarah's table, and what sounded like a long, drawn-out sigh, lost in the clatter and confusion of a bench being overturned . . . The workmaster went on reading, determinedly unperturbed by the clamour, incurious as to its source . . . Incredibly, no-one upon the platform moved, or showed change of expression, their faces, with those of the paupers, blank in their deaf concentration . . . Sarah turned and looked behind her, and glimpsed a pauper woman, head lying against the overturned bench, her clothing smeared with the soup from the broken bowl which lay in fragments about her, its contents spilled upon her, perhaps as she sought to steady herself.

Sarah ran towards her, scarcely aware of the rows of pallid faces about her, desperate only to give aid . . . The woman was breathing, but in some deep swoon, and blood from the raw wound made by a piercing shard, oozed from her forehead. Her hand, when Sarah took it into her own, was clammy with sweat, yet terrifyingly cold. She could not doubt, from the woman's swollen breasts and rounded belly, that she was with child, and that weakness and, perhaps, hunger, had caused her to fall.

"Leave her!" The workmaster's voice was cold with anger. "Return to your place!"

Sarah was staunching the blood as best she could with a rag, wrenched awkwardly from the hem of her petticoat, but it was useless, for the blood-flow had soaked it through. She ripped more violently at her clothing . . .

"Return!"

The single word held such fury that Sarah briefly hesitated. The woman's hand tightened upon hers as her mouth tried clumsily to form the words which Sarah had to bend low to hear.

"Please . . . I beg you, do as he says, or it will be the worse for us both . . ."

Sarah arose unsteadily, leaving the blood-soaked rags pressed to the wound. The woman's eyes, when they had gazed into Sarah's, had been frightened, pleading, and her agitation so intense that she could only obey . . . Yet it grieved her, and filled her with despair. The pauper's sickly pallor boded ill for the child she carried, Sarah was convinced, and for the woman herself. The only colour had been in the crimson flow of blood, and in the dark shadows bruising her eyes, and the blueness of lips . . . Sarah walked to her place beside Jane Grey, conscious that the eyes of those seated upon the platform were regarding her with cold censure . . . Indeed, in the housekeeper's narrowed eyes, there was naked hostility. Nonetheless, she turned defiantly to reassure herself as to the sick woman's safety. Sarah saw, with gratitude, that she had recovered sufficiently to have dragged herself to her feet. She was now supporting herself awkwardly upon the table-edge with one hand, the other holding the bloodied rag to her forehead. That blood which escaped continued dripping remorselessly from mouth and chin, to darken the bodice of her gown. Bare minutes had elapsed from the harsh sounds of her falling to Sarah's involuntary movement to her side, but time seemed endlessly frozen . . . It might have been a lifetime that had passed, so remote was it all, and unreal . . . Oliver Sidebottom closed the bible. His voice, when he spoke, was cold, and his enunciation precise. "You will have noticed that there is one among us who has much to learn. It seems that she is impetuous, and has scant regard for authority, rules, or, indeed, God Himself. She places herself above the sanctity of our simple prayers . . . We must ensure, then, that she is elevated to . . . a fitting position, the position of those irreverent and profane . . . Those who seek to usurp proper authority . . . Those who think themselves to be above the humble, God-fearing mass . . ."

"I think myself a human being, sir . . ." She could not regret the rebuke, only the terrified confusion upon Jane Grey's face, as the workmaster descended, tight-lipped, and ordered her removal to the cellars beneath.

Sarah, alone, remained unaware of the workmaster's return to the dais, and his angry command that they repeat his words,

"She is arrogant and unworthy of charity . . ."

There was an embarrassed muttering of the words from those upon the platform, dying away foolishly. The pauper women remained silent. Colour flamed into the workmaster's face as he blustered,

"Repeat after me . . . She is arrogant and unworthy . . ."

Again there was a shamed, barely audible, muttering from beside him, but the paupers made no sound.

He saw that the faces of those assembled beside the benches and tables below were not bewildered, as he had supposed, but obdurate, firm in their refusal to obey. Their unappetising meal lay untouched before them, the soup slowly congealing, its surface yellowed with pale globules of fat . . . the bread untasted. Despite their fatigue and hunger, all remained standing, even the pregnant woman Sarah had aided, her face sallow as parchment, the blood crusting upon her forehead.

The workmaster was almost beside himself with rage at such wilful public contempt for his authority, yet he was powerless to name any one of them as a ringleader in the mutiny. None had incited, threatened or coerced. Indeed, none had uttered a word. He could not even hope to separate and make example of those displaying insolence, for their faces were uniformly blank. Sidebottom studied them helplessly, turning to those upon the platform behind him, seeking inspiration, but finding none . . . There was, he realised, no rule to deal with total, silent rebellion. White with anger, he dismissed them to their beds.

When Sarah was first left alone in the alien darkness, she had to steel herself not to scream aloud and beg release . . . She grew as afraid of silence as of sound. All was intensified and made menacing by the impenetrable blackness. She fancied that she heard the scrabbling of rats in the straw which served as a bed, and always she lay in terror of sleep, lest they run over her, unseen, or gnaw at her flesh . . . Even the harmless dripping of water from the stone walls became a torture, so loud and monotonous that she feared her own heartbeats thudded in her head . . . Should *they* die, then she must die too . . . She tried to occupy her mind . . . She prayed. Wept. Sang aloud . . . She lost all sense of time . . . believed herself abandoned to madness or death.

When the housekeeper came, with a lantern, to release her, the candleflame seemed so bright that it hurt her eyes . . . The housekeeper's face had been made grotesque in the halo of light, and she had grasped Sarah's arm roughly, thrusting her ahead, watching her stumble awkwardly up the stone steps to the hall above.

"I hope that you have learned a lesson, Miss, and that it will serve you well . . ." she declared spitefully. "Do not forget it!"

"No, ma'am." Sarah's voice was as expressionless as her eyes. "You may be sure that I will not forget it."

She had been imprisoned, she learnt, but two days. Yet the remembrance of it would not lessen in a lifetime.

CHAPTER 9

The carrier had halted at the farm. There, with the willing help of the farmer and his cowman, he had manhandled the sacks of potatoes onto his cart. They were brawny men both, and the carrier as powerfully muscular, but the awkwardness of handling his cargo, and the weight of it, had made him sweat-stained and heated, despite the wind's coldness . . . There would be help aplenty at the workhouse, he felt sure, and some of the women as robust and hardened by toil as any farm labourer . . . His thoughts had turned to the pauper woman he had carried there a few short weeks ago . . . She was a gentle, frail-boned young maid, he reflected, and soft-spoken. How would she fare in the coarse roughness of toil and workhouse living? He would not ask the housekeeper, for she was a lumpen creature, harsh and unfeeling, but he would dearly like to know if Sarah Tudor fared well . . . He had kept the little fox-head pin well hidden, even from his good wife, for she would have urged him to sell it, declaring it too fine a thing for a rough carrier upon the road . . . Yet it had become to him a pledge; a kindness freely offered for a kindness freely shown . . . A talisman. He would not part with it . . . He had learnt from the scullery maid of Sarah's punishment, and the reason for it, and regret, and pity for her, lay more heavily upon him than the physical burdens he bore . . . She was but one among many, and he was powerless to help.

When, a week later, he took as passenger upon his cart, the local midwife from the village, he learnt that she would have him drive her to the poorhouse to aid a pauper woman in awkward labour. Upon an impulse, he bade her deliver a message to Sarah Tudor, or to any in sympathy with her, if she would. The midwife's glance had been keenly assessing.

"What would you have me say?"

90

"That I shall be passing the gates of the workhouse each Thursday morning at eight o' the clock."
The midwife, who knew the carrier for a loyal husband, and good provider for his brood, asked no question of him, nor did she hesitate.

"She shall be told . . . never fear."

He had nodded, satisfied, and said no more. Complicity, if proved, could cost the midwife dear. He would not dwell upon what his rashness might cost him, and others . . . 'twere better they remained in ignorance.

The workmaster had not forgotten Sarah Tudor's open defiance of him, and the silent scorn of the paupers . . . It had demeaned and humiliated him before all. Oliver Sidebottom was not a man to forgive easily the slights of others . . . She was arrogant. A conceited nonentity; scarcely worthy of his attention . . . Her punishment had been well deserved, and he could not doubt that it had proved salutary . . . The evidence was in her pallor, and the shadowed darkness about her eyes, as she stood tiredly before him . . . 'A bruised reed.' He did not know why the words sprang to his mind, 'a bruised reed which bows in the wind, but does not break . . .' Well, he would see that she was broken. It was his God-given duty.

"Well, ma'am, it is to be hoped that you have profited from your punishment . . . that you have had time for reflection . . ."

"Yes, sir." Her voice was low, strained, as though it cost her effort.

"I do not think you will repeat your mistake."

"No, sir."

"You will be expected to make public apology, you understand? To accept full responsibility for your pride and arrogance . . ."

"Yes, sir." Her voice was firmer now. "I accept full responsibility for what I did . . . and I will not deny it."

Did he detect a flicker of insolence, amusement even, in Sarah Tudor's eyes? . . . No, he must be mistaken. They were regarding him steadily now, expression clear and ingenuous. Why, then, did he feel set at a disadvantage? Irritation made him brusque.

"It seems that you have aspirations beyond your present employment, ma'am." It was said mockingly.

91

When Sarah remained silent, he continued coldly, "I have found you the employment you deserve, without the workhouse." As, bewildered, she sought to murmur her gratitude, he cut in tersely, "No, do not thank me, ma'am. You are a disruptive influence upon those within these walls; obstinate and prideful . . ."

"I am to be a governess, sir?"

"Indeed not!" He permitted himself a condescending smile. "It seems that you still harbour ideas absurdly above your station! You will be a scullery maid, at the house of the chairman of the Board of Guardians, Sir John Hambrook . . . That is the work for which you have shown aptitude."

She had scarcely heard his last contemptuous words, so appalled was she at the prospect.

"I believe, ma'am, you are fortunate to have made Sir John's acquaintance, in your . . . former life."

Fortunate! She almost cried the word aloud in her anger. Yes, she had made his acquaintance, and bitterly lived to regret it. It was he who had bought their cottage and furnishings for a pittance . . . knowing her powerless to turn elsewhere. He had harried her unmercifully during her father's sickness; treating that good man, Josiah Tudor, with open disdain, dismissing him as a provincial cleric, sickly, and confused of mind . . . Sarah, to whom his unsolicited visits were a trial, had grown to fear and dislike him . . . Denied her father's protection, Hambrook's manner had grown proprietary and over-familiar . . . She, in turn, grew punctilious at keeping him at a distance, physically, and in speech, always beyond his reach . . . On the few occasions when he had brushed past her, by accident, or Sarah had been forced to take his hand, in leaving, his touch had repelled her . . . He was a prurient, slimy creature, and she despised him. Memory of his florid, supercilious face and his obese fleshiness filled her with disgust. He was gross in every way.

"I believe that Sir John was kind enough to arrange for your admittance to this institution . . . knowing you to be destitute . . . A pauper . . ."

Sidebottom's eyes were slyly knowledgeable in the narrow fox-face. "Well, I hope, ma'am, that you will show due gratitude that he takes so . . . personal an interest in you. You are privileged indeed."

"If I am to leave the workhouse, sir," surprisingly her voice was calm to her own ears, "I should wish to have returned to me my father's bible, my christening bracelet, and those few remembrances of my past which I still possess . . ."

"You possess nothing, ma'am!" His tone was as incisive as a whip lash. "You *are* nothing. Even those clothes you wear are the property of this institution! The food you eat, shelter . . . all are provided from the charity of others!"

"They do not possess *me*, sir." The quietly spoken words were a rebuke.

"Do they not? As a pauper, you have no rights. Your future is for others to command. Your body is of more worth dead than living . . . since a corpse may be legally sold . . . Should you die a pauper, then you will be buried, uncoffined, in an unmarked grave . . . That is the law . . . You should be grateful that . . ." he paused, momentarily at a loss.

"That you have reminded me of my worth?" The question was innocently spoken. "Yes, sir, I am grateful for that . . ." Her face was innocent of guile, her words sincere. Why, then, did he feel the sting of her contempt, the assurance that it was she who was in command? With a peremptory wave of his hand, he dismissed her.

Jane Grey was aware that Sarah must escape the workhouse, rather than be delivered into Sir John Hambrook's house . . . Fact, not rumour, of his physical ill-treatment of the pauper women, supposedly in his "care", gave proof enough of his decadence. His sexual abuses were well known enough, yet a pauper's sworn word against him valueless . . . Jane Grey was grieved by Sarah's distress at being refused her few treasures, yet she knew that the workmaster would not be swayed. Such command over the lives and property of others gave him his only power . . . Sarah, it was agreed, would leave upon the morrow, taking her chance to board the carrier's cart . . . The leave taking of the two women that night had been muted, their tears held back lest others suspect . . . Yet each felt a keenness of loss, lacerating, laying raw; as cruel as a bereavement.

In the first half light, Jane Grey had shaken Sarah awake as, confused with sleep, she had cried out in alarm . . . Jane had closed Sarah's hand over the gold christening bracelet. It was the only solace she could offer, and Sarah wept then, for she knew that in returning it, Jane Grey had risked all . . . Discovery would have brought an accusation of theft; a court trial before the justices . . . It would have meant imprisonment at a house of correction, with punishment upon the treadmill or worse . . . Men and women had been publicly flogged, then sentenced to hanging, for being found guilty of stealing a loaf of bread . . .

The escape proved easier than Sarah dared to hope. Yet why should it have been otherwise? Few willingly ventured within the poorhouse walls, save those dispossessed and driven by hunger and need. Fewer ventured without. The moor was bleak and denied all shelter. The choice was stark; slavery and grudging life within, or starvation and death without. To those flayed by circumstance and robbed of spirit, pauperdom was no more than another grief to bear.

But Sarah had refused to be broken in mind or spirit. Her constant goad was to escape; to live rather than survive. The carrier's cart would take her to freedom, provide deliverance. Even if it did not, the unknown moor was less to be feared than the certainty of what otherwise lay ahead.

She set her plans carefully to make escape, for if they failed she would not have the carrier harmed. The workmaster would see that he paid heavily for such involvement . . . Sarah did not delude herself that Sidebottom cared whether she lived or died. He was as sensitive to her survival as to the fate of all other paupers in his care. His sole interest lay in procuring her services for Sir John Hambrook; to sell her as cheaply as those few treasures of her former life. To ingratiate himself, and humble her.

She would neither be humbled nor sold! When those who worked beside her in the scullery of the poorhouse were fully occupied, she made excuse and walked boldly without. She would not follow the main pathway to the gates lest she be glimpsed from the windows, or her escape bring reprisal upon the innocent pauper at the gatehouse.

With her heart beating violently and a coldness within her, she walked with outward confidence towards the kitchen garden of the men's quarters beyond. She had thought to find it deserted, but a lone pauper was engaged upon wresting some parsnips from the frozen earth. His hands clung raw-fleshed to the blade of his knife, fingers mottled as brawn. He glanced up and nodded, his smile a pained grimace from the cold, then stoically returned to his labours. Beyond, in the far distance, Sarah saw with dismay a crowd of pauper men, hacking at and crushing stones, their rough grey clothing blending with stone and sky. They were as drably intent as scavenging birds, and seemingly as incurious.

There was no gateway within the garden, no option save to pass among them or to scale the high stone wall. That, or return to the poorhouse, defeated.

With an anguished surge of resolve Sarah ran to the wall, fingers scrabbling desperately at the thick stems of ivy, nails tearing and scraping as she hauled herself painfully upwards. She hung perilously before slowly inching her way, awkward boots finding few footholds in the rough stone . . . She ached in every muscle and nerve, and could scarcely breathe for terror, expecting, every moment, to hear the harsh cries of the men alerting those within.

When by some miracle she gained the top of the wall, Sarah crouched like some hunted animal, bracing herself to leap to freedom. She glanced towards where the pauper men stood. They uttered no cry, shouted no warning, frozen in feature and movement, then returning to their toil.

Sarah had hurled herself from the wall, falling hard onto the dead bracken and tussocks beneath. The violence of her fall knocked the breath from her body, then she found herself gasping and hauling herself awkwardly to her feet, stumbling, running, aching in every bruised limb as she made her way to the open moor and the shelter of a rocky outcrop.

She waited there, trembling with cold and fear. There had been no hue and cry, no dogs' baying, nothing save the coming of the awaited cart. She had clambered numbly aboard, the carrier had flicked urgently at the reins, and the pony had moved on with no shouted command to stop, none suspecting.

He had not spoken, but the grasp of his work-roughened hands had been firm as he hauled her beside him on the board. In truth, he found it hard to speak, for so changed was she, so pallid and thin, her long hair savagely cropped. Only her fine hazel eyes stayed vitally alive, unchanged by suffering . . . The carrier was not a vindictive man, but he cursed Oliver Sidebottom silently, and fluently, for the anguish he had wrought.

"You had best change your clothing when we reach that little copse yonder," he said gruffly. "I have brought a boy's clothing; a smock and and beaver cap, such as the drovers' lads wear . . ."

He cut her gratitude short, insisting,

"A lone woman would fare ill upon the roads . . ." He had thrust the bundle of old clothing into her arms, saying, "Your boots will serve well enough, for you will wear leggings of Bristol brown paper, as others do."

When she had returned, her hateful workhouse dress abandoned, he had said,

"We must soonest be on our way. I shall take you as far as I am able, then deliver you to the care of another. A friend who will see that you join the drovers' trail. It is all I can offer. Yet it cannot be worse than that which you have fled." He had grown flustered, saying quickly, "There is a loaf within this clean flour sack, and some ale, and cheese . . . and a purse with the few poor coppers I can spare."

Her impulsive embrace and warm kiss had all but tumbled him from his perch, as she asked,

"But how, sir, could you know that I would come today?"

"I have carried the clothing with me, and food, ma'am, . . . lest you should have the need . . ." he said simply "'tis plain you are a lady of quality, ill-fitted for workhouse life."

"As you, sir, are a gentleman of quality." Despite her resolution, tears burned in her eyes, then spilled.

"Now, now . . ." he said, face crimsoning as he clumsily patted her hand. "There is naught in all the world to weep about . . . and we are almost at the crossroads, where my friend awaits."

"I do not know your name, sir!"

"'Tis no great matter . . . but I am Jacob the carrier to all hereabouts . . ." he hesitated awkwardly. "I would not ask where you go . . . save that your brother might come searching . . . What shall I tell him?"

Sarah hesitated. "I do not know what the future holds . . . but tell him I shall be going home. He will understand."

The crossroads was in sight, and he cautioned the pony, then bade it halt.

The tears had dried upon her face, and she dismounted, clasping the sack fiercely, as though she clung to him, fearful to see him go.

"God bless you, sir!"

"And God bless you, Sarah Tudor . . . Yes, may God bless you!"

The grinding of the cartwheels and the creaking of the cart died away, and he had not looked back, keeping his gaze fixedly on the road ahead. He was seeing nothing. He had not told the girl that the midwife had told him that very morn that the babe within the workhouse had perished at birth, and the pauper woman who bore it had not long survived . . . "Worn out," the midwife said, "with toil and hunger. She had cried out her husband's name, begging he be brought to her, but none had heeded, although he was lodged in the poorhouse, but a stone's throw away!" The carrier was a kindhearted man, and had protested bitterly at the cruelty of it. "'Twas a blessing," the midwife gave opinion, "for what comfort awaited either one of them? They would have been kept apart by man, and now were joined forever in God."

She was an honest woman, and well meaning, but the carrier's bile rose and all but choked him. And what of the husband's loss, he wanted to cry out, but did not, for it would have been less than useless. "Paupers," she said kindly, "are different from folks such as we." The carrier sighed aloud. He was glad that Sarah Tudor had cared for that poor woman, as he was glad that he had aided Sarah in turn. He set the pony to trotting, to dispel the coldness, not knowing the coldness lay within.

Jean-Luc was painfully aware of the dangers which faced him, should his true identity and purpose be known. He could expect no aid from the British, and no mercy from the French. He was alone now, and lived or died by his own wits. Yet, fatigue and sickness so enervated him that the remorselessness of his questioners flayed his nerves raw. He had become Luc Nolais in all save blood, believed himself prepared, inviolate. Yet his interlocutors gave him no peace, by day or night, probing his mind and past, demanding, accusing, trying always to incriminate and trap . . . He grew afraid of sleep, and suspicious of all he ate or drank, lest it be drugged. He lived in terror of a relapse into unconsciousness, lest he betray himself. The three unidentified Frenchmen who took turn to question him were alike only in their thoroughness. Their violation of mind and flesh was no less brutal for lack of emotion. Jean-Luc, vengeful, and bruised in body, could have wished himself their detachment; isolation from all which plagued him. The woman, who had spoken kindly to him upon the cart, fed him and tended his practical needs . . . She addressed him with gentleness, seemingly compassionate. Yet he knew that in her kindness, and his instinctive response to it, lay greater danger. As the days of his detention increased, and with them the ferocity of his questioning and ill-treatment, so did his chances of acceptance. Jean-Luc was sure of nothing now, save his will to survive, and do what he had planned. He would close the route for escaping French prisoners. Those who created it should be brought to justice. He could not think of it as a betrayal. Napoleon was a tyrant; a crude butcher, with hands still reddened by the blood of the murdered.

His henchmen had found Jean-Luc. Now, all he had to do was to find *them* from the least to the greatest. He only hoped that the British, too, had discovered his whereabouts, and held him under surveillance, unable to strike. When the time was right, they would seek contact, he knew, but how, or when, was in their keeping . . . It would take his interrogators weeks, or months, before his new identity was checked in France . . . and, even then, it would be verified that such a man existed, whereabouts unknown. Who were these people who had rescued him? Spies of Napoleon, nurtured secretly? Escaped prisoners such as he? Emigrés, corrupted for money or favour? Blackmailed perhaps into turning traitor to the king, and their own kind? British politicians, seeking promises of power and opportunity? Jean-Luc heard his questioners returning, and, with them, a return of that nausea and fear he could never totally subdue. He stiffened, knowing it must begin again, and willed himself to face it.

The final surrender had been unexpected, for they had shown no signs of accepting him, nor of slackening their unremitting hold. Yet, suddenly, he was one of their own. Had their enquiries aboard the hulk and in the prisoner-of-war camps convinced them? Had they received confirmation from France that Luc Nolais did, indeed, exist? Or was it his own stubborn resistance which had triumphed? He knew only that their hostility towards him was ended, as were their beatings and cold interrogation. He was their equal; a friend of The Republic; a soldier of proven courage. Yet he did not relax his guard. He listened intently, and forgot nothing, neither names nor associates, nor meeting places, carelessly mentioned. He was aware that this proved no more than a single cell in the meticulously constructed honeycomb of conspiracy . . . isolated from all, save those few identical cells surrounding them. Yet, it was a beginning. He would recognise his gaolers, and give firm evidence against them when need arose, but his real aim must be to identify those who ruled them; those in power within the hierarchy. He was unprepared when opportunity came. Blindfolded, and without warning, he had been hurried, at night, to a waiting coach. He had tried desperately upon the long journey to keep his dulled senses alert, memorising each twist and turn upon the way, assessing each obstacle, trying vainly to identify the change from cobbles to highway, from country to town . . . So it had been re-enacted on the second stage of his enforced journey, and upon the third. His stays had been brief, the questioning resumed, yet none had successfully challenged him, nor broken his assumed cover . . . None that is, save one.

Jean-Luc had been aware of a growing tension and increased activity in the safe house. The daily inquisition he was forced to endure had grown perfunctory, an over-familiar ritual, without zest or meaning. Yet his questioners, indeed, the whole atmosphere, was charged with ill-suppressed excitement. They seemed to be awaiting some event or person of importance. He did not doubt that his future was to be decided, and his final destination made known. Through careful listening, and the negligence of his keepers, who occasionally conversed in English, believing him ignorant of the language, he pieced together a profile of the expected visitor. His name was never mentioned. Yet his position in the upper echelons was plain.

He was a man of undisputed authority; the personal emissary of the man who provided the escape committee's funds. He was, it seemed, the final arbiter upon how an escaping prisoner should be dealt with, and where he might be sent. Upon his word lay acceptance or rejection. He held the power of life or death.

When Jean-Luc had been summoned before the committee, he had prepared himself thoroughly to answer those questions about his motives, and his background, he expected . . . What he had not expected was to recognise his questioner. Sir Ewen Charlesworth, Member of Parliament, landowner and philanthropist, stared at Jean-Luc. Try as he might, Jean-Luc could not completely subdue the nervous trembling of his hands and the fear which clawed at his ribs, threatening to betray him. He had met Charlesworth at his guardian's house. Jean-Luc had been not more than fifteen years of age, and immersed in his studies at his tutor's instruction, but Charlesworth's manner had been plainly bored, his acknowledgement tepid.

The gaze he now turned upon Jean-Luc was incisive and critical, missing nothing. He seemed momentarily disturbed, frowning in concentration, before declaring curtly,

"It appears, Lieutenant Nolais, that your ordeal has taken harsh toll . . . You had best be seated."

There had been no sign of recognition upon Charlesworth's face; no overt accusation in his tone. Yet Jean-Luc felt oppressed by uncertainty. Had his interlocutor forgotten their earlier meeting? It would seem so; as it would seem that he had accepted Jean-Luc's pallor and nervousness as natural reactions to his escape and the enforced interrogation and hardship he had endured.

The interrogation which he now faced was more determinedly invasive than any before. Charlesworth showed as little expression as an automaton; his control as rigid as his purpose, and as unalterable . . . Jean-Luc, mind sharpened by anxiety, had answered tersely, and without error, and to Charlesworth's apparent satisfaction.

"It seems, Lieutenant Nolais, that the appellation, 'The French Fox', is well deserved. You have much of that animal's cunning evasiveness." Jean-Luc, scarcely daring to breathe, waited, as he concluded, ". . . and all of its wildness and fierce courage, if our reports are to be believed."

Once again the words were almost too carefully neutral. Then Charlesworth gave a wry smile, and stood up, holding out a hand in acceptance. Jean-Luc's smile was faultless, his handshake firm. Yet he was beset with unresolved fears . . . Had Charlesworth recognised him? If so, then why had he not been openly accused as a traitor? Was it a skilfully contrived and sadistic game which his adversary chose to play? A way to lead him to others who owed fidelity to the Crown of France? It was true that at their first meeting, Jean-Luc had been no more than a boy; an object of little importance, and less interest . . . and yet . . .? Ewen Charlesworth's gaunt ascetic face stayed in his mind, the deep-set eyes, coldly expressionless or excoriatingly alive . . . The face of a fanatic; one who would sacrifice all, even himself, for a cause. A man, perhaps, too like Jean-Luc, Comte de Valandré.

When Jean-Luc had been informed that in one week he was to leave for London, and would thereafter travel to Ireland, then embark for France, he felt less sanguine than he had hoped . . . Charlesworth, General Loosely had informed him, had shown open sympathy with the revolution in France, and had tried to stir up rebellion and mayhem in England, to further his ambitions. No doubt, he would be well rewarded by the republic, should he succeed. Jean-Luc would sooner see him damned.

CHAPTER 10

At the crossroads, Sarah Tudor had waited with increasing impatience for the arrival of Jacob the carrier's friend. The onset of winter had brought no lessening of damp and cold, and bleak as the rawness of the day was the rawness of grief at leaving Jane Grey . . . That, and the carrier's unexpected kindness, had forced treacherous tears to her eyes. Even as they fell upon her cheeks, the keenness of the wind had scourged them dry, so that she could snuffle and gulp, believing that it was the cruelty of the weather which wrought such hurt . . . With the creaking of a distant cart upon the byway, terror so bedevilled her that she all but turned and fled into the wild sanctuary of the moor. They had come to order her back to that cold tomb of a workhouse, or to deliver her to Sir John Hambrook's house . . . She would not return! No, not even at risk of living wild on the moor, perishing even . . . They would add to the crime of her escape, the theft of the bracelet . . . Gaol or the gallows would await her then . . .

The carrier upon the wool-cart saw no gentlewoman waiting, only a thin, shorn waif of a lad, so terrified that the wide hazel eyes seemed to dominate the small oval face . . .

"Sarah Tudor?" He had not been able to hide his uncertainty, although Jacob had warned him that she would be properly disguised.

"Yes, sir . . . That is my name."

"Then you had better climb aboard," he said gruffly, to hide his concern. "You will get used to the smell of the skinned fleeces within the sacks. 'Tis the oil, no more . . . They will make a comfortable enough bed, although you will stink as high as they by our journey's end . . ."

"It will be more comfort than I have known in the past, sir," there was no self-pity in her tone, "and I thank you."

Embarrassed, he thrust her thanks aside.

"You will need to work," he reminded quickly, "and as hard as any apprentice lad . . . I carry no passengers."

"I have learnt to work, sir, and will not shirk. I am strong . . ."

He nodded, thinking compassionately that for all her frailness of body, there was a strength within her which would serve her well.

"'Tis plain you must change your name, or you will be in trouble else. I had best call you Tudor, then, although 'tis a fancy enough name for a carrier's jacklad . . ." His plump, good-natured face had dissolved into a smile so broad that his eyes all but disappeared into his rubicund flesh. "Tudor . . ." he repeated. "Aye, 'tis a name fit for a king!"

"And what must I call you, sir?"

"Mr Fowles. That is how a hired lad would address me . . ." He hesitated, before awkwardly blurting, "'tis not pride which demands it, but your safety, you understand?"

"Yes, Mr Fowles. I am grateful."

He sniffed deprecatingly, then cleared his throat and flicked at the reins.

"A . . . young woman, even a lad, alone, and in London, runs grave risk . . ." His polished cheeks grew ruddier still as he struggled for words of explanation. "There are those who prey upon others . . . the weak and the helpless . . . 'tis not only for the slavery of work, you understand . . .? Jacob has told me that you are gently bred . . . a daughter of the manse . . ." His words were stilted, his discomfiture acute.

"Yes, Mr Fowles, it is true that my father was a clergyman . . . and a good man . . ." she said quietly, "but I have not been untouched by the harshness of life, nor remained innocent of life's evils, or its cruelty . . . I am sensitive, sir, of your concern . . ."

"Then you will have refuge there? Friends?" he persisted.

"Yes, sir. An old gentleman whom my father greatly respected for his integrity and kindness of heart . . . I will beg that he finds me brief employment as a governess, that I may pay for my return to my old home, in Wales . . . for I do not ask for charity."

She was a frail enough thing, delicate almost, but firm of purpose and spirit, Joe Fowles thought. Aloud, he said, "Aye, charity grudgingly given can leave a sour taste, my dear . . . my lad," he corrected himself, "but do not let it sour you, else you will be no better than those who seek to humiliate and bring you down."

Sarah's thin hands rested briefly upon Joe Fowles' calloused, toil-grimed fist upon the reins, and he nodded, unspeaking. Then he turned away, shouting useless directions to the horse, lest she see how it had grieved him, that her hand was no less work-scarred than his own.

The journey upon the cart had been long and tedious, with many a halt upon the way to deliver the fleeces aboard. They had slept in the shelter of hedges and ditches, taking food and rest where they might. London had appalled her, with its clamour and bustle and the crowded hovels, so closely leaning that the sordid alleys between scarce caught the sunlight. Sarah had helped Fowles unload the cart, to many a muttered oath and undeserved clout for her slowness from those she strove to aid . . . She ached in every bone from the rattling of the cart ride, and her flesh was as bruised by the journey as by the sly blows she received . . . These were the lowest, most insalubrious, parts of London, she was aware, and yet, even here, she was not out of place . . . She was aware that she stank as rancidly as the skins upon the cart, and was as grimed and dishevelled as those around her, for she had but the one suit of clothes, and those, like her ugly cropped hair, grease-stained and unbecoming . . .

She had memorised Sir Frederick Loosely's address, and had almost decided not to appeal for his aid, so degraded and, she feared, verminous was she . . . It was Fowles' sternness, alone, which decided her, for he would brook no weakness nor argument, but delivered her to the door, not without misgivings as fierce as her own . . . Her hesitant request to see Sir Frederick Loosely had met with outraged refusal and disdain from the scullery maid, who was pleased to send her packing. Her timid insistence merely provoked further wrath, and a warning to be off before the dogs were set upon her, to teach her the manners she lacked.

"Sir Frederick would not see the likes of you, even were

he here! As for me, I would be blind, or a madwoman, to admit you!"

In a last fury of despair, Sarah had jammed her booted foot hard in the door, to halt its closure, and Joe Fowles had leapt bellicosely from the cart to add his might and invective to hers. Before he could reach her, the scullery maid had kicked Sarah's foot viciously aside, and made to slam shut the door, screaming, "Take telling! He is gone to Cornwall! Not here! You understand?"

"Please!" Sarah was close to tears, and all but sick with rage and disappointment, "Please! I beg that you will tell the general that his friend, Josiah Tudor, is dead . . ."

The door slammed noisily shut, and she did not know if the servant heard, for she did not return, although Sarah beat with her fists upon the wood until pain numbed them. But it did not numb her despair, and Fowles lifted her easily, and with tenderness, into his arms, feeling the wetness of her tears upon his shirtfront, and set her upon the perch of the cart, saying helplessly, "Do not cry, my maid . . . 'tis not the end of the world . . . to make you take on so . . . You shall reach your home, in the safe company of my friends, the drovers, as Jacob planned . . . 'tis best not to be beholden to others . . . to make your own way, honestly, and by your own efforts . . ."

He spoke with such conviction that Sarah rewarded him with a watery smile through her tears . . . In truth, he was as plagued by doubts as she.

Fowles had taken Sarah upon the cart to the cheap lodging house where the drovers gathered while their business in London was transacted . . . Those who drove their herds and flocks the many hundreds of miles, to be sold at Smithfield, were mainly God-fearing men, he declared, honest and to be admired. They were entrusted with commissions to the banks and trading houses, and would deliver important documents to attorneys or private citizens upon the way . . . Licensed drovers, he explained, were men of property, over the age of thirty, and known to be of honest reputation . . . Moreover, they were industrious, literate, and of proven good character, as they had need to be . . . He did not add that those in their employ were not always as reliable as their masters. They were

taken on another's word, at the yearly hirings or cattle marts
. . . The master drovers were rare judges of human character,
as they were of beasts, but a labourer's brute strength and glib
tongue could sometimes deceive, and give him preference.

"Aye, the drovers are splendid men!" Fowles insisted, to calm
her fears, and his own, "hard-working, reliable and frugal . . ."
Frugal they most assuredly were, Sarah thought wryly, for the
lodging house was no better than a hovel, as squalid without as
within. Its owner had emerged through the open doorway at the
sound of the cart's halting. Sarah saw a blowsy, coarse-featured
woman, all shapeless flesh beneath food-stained garments . . .
Yet, a smiling slattern, whose good nature redeemed her
slovenly ways . . . She had gone, at once, in search of the
drover whom Fowles wished to see, grumbling as she walked
upon swollen, ungainly feet . . . When she returned, it was
with a brawny, dark-jowled man at her heels, his face sullen
and unwelcoming. She had thrust a morsel of strong cheese
and a crust into Sarah's hands, exclaiming,

"God's truth, my lad, you are a skinny enough creature!
You look more in need of victuals than your master's poor
nag!" She had dug Fowles in the ribs playfully, demanding, strident-voiced, "Do you starve him, Carrier? He has
less flesh than a skinned rabbit. I'll warrant you feed well
enough yourself!" Her raucous laughter was stilled by the
impatience of the drover beside her, who thrust her aside,
to say, testily, "Jed Parker is not here . . . He has business,
and will not return ere nightfall. You may bargain with me in
his stead!"

Sarah, who had been eating the crust with voracious enjoyment, felt it stick in her throat, appetite lost. Surely Mr Fowles
would not deliver her into this taciturn creature's care? She
looked to him in mute appeal, but his eyes were upon the
drover, anxious, and indecisive . . . Then, making up his mind,
he declared, "My jacklad would return to Wales, upon the
drovers' roads . . ." Fowles hesitated . . . "I would deliver him
to Jed's care."

"It will cost you dear! He will be neither use nor ornament
upon the way!" the drover exclaimed disparagingly. "We have
lads enough to feed." He glanced towards Sarah, demanding
ill-temperedly, "Well, boy, have you coins enough to pay your
way?" Sarah had shaken her head, made dumb by his hostility.

"Nonsense, Tudor, lad!" Fowles' grip upon Sarah's arm was meant to be reassuring, his plump face wreathed in triumphant smiles. "You have laboured well, and rightly earned your passage home! 'Tis only just and fair that you be recompensed . . ."

Sarah's throat was too constricted with nervousness for her to make argument or appeal. She saw that the unknown drover's face was alive, now, with cunning and cupidity. So, to her dismay, the bargaining began, good-humoured at first, then increasingly bitter and acrimonious. The owner of the lodging house had given Sarah a smile of wry commiseration, then shrugged her broad shoulders and returned wordlessly within. The bargain was struck, then sealed with a handshake, and Fowles delivered the coins to the drover. The man's fingers closed hard over them, and he made no attempt to hide a smirk of satisfaction before commanding sharply,

"You there, lad! Climb down from that cart!" Then, with increasing impatience, "Are you deaf? Shape your stumps, boy, and get yourself within! I will not wait all day!"

"No!" Fowles' rebuttal was harsh. "I will deliver him to the care of Jed Perkins, no other . . . else he stops with me!" The drover, red-faced, was all blustering irritation and threats, but the carrier remained unmoved.

"'Tis no odds to me . . ." the drover declared peevishly, at length, "I have other business, with men of importance . . . not jacklads and carriers! Men of influence and wealth!" Then, as if already regretting his indiscretion, he turned sourly upon his heel. The young man who scornfully brushed him aside as he scowlingly re-entered the lodging house, was, despite his coarse-spun drover's clothing, an arresting figure. He stood well over six feet in height, broad of shoulder, his bearing arrogantly erect. His skin was burnished by wind and weather, his hair bleached by the sun to the ripe paleness of corn. He returned Fowles' respectfully murmured greeting courteously, but his gaze was keenly penetrating, missing nothing, even the wretchedly snivelling jacklad, woe begone and filthy, upon the stinking cart. The stranger's vivid blue eyes stared, then his mouth tugged, irresistibly, into a smile.

"The world beyond is a colder place than a carrier's cart, as I have reason to know . . ." he said unexpectedly, adding with awkward kindness, "Whatever it is that grieves you so . . . it will pass . . . believe it . . . Here!" He delved into the pocket of his breeches, and tossed a sixpence in Sarah's direction, and she trapped it in her fist, forgetting to thank him in her eagerness.

Jean-Luc, Comte de Valandré, went smiling upon his way, but Sarah Tudor only wept the harder, because she was leaving Fowles, who had been so generous-hearted in all his dealings, and had only her true welfare at heart . . . She wept for Jane Grey, and her father, and herself, and a world beyond that would assuredly be 'colder than a carrier's cart . . .' But most of all, she wept because she was ugly, and stank of rancid sheep fat and hides, and her pretty hair was shorn, and she looked like a carrier's jacklad, and because a handsome young man had shown her pity.

Not all Mr Fowles' exclamations at her good fortune, or clumsy solicitude, could stem her tears.

General Sir Frederick Loosely had returned from Cornwall to London, not in the best of humours at his decrepitude and weakness of limb . . . Each time he travelled, it seemed, the journey grew longer and his stamina less . . . Damn it! he thought irascibly, what ails me? I am not a cripple. Useless. In my dotage! He cursed that onset of old age and decay which so restricted and plagued him . . . He missed the boy, Jean-Luc, too; his company. No. No longer a boy, but a man, he reminded himself. Alive or dead? Those who might have told him, he had begged to hold their silence, lest it set his ward, and his mission, at risk. He must wait, with patience . . . but patience, like energy and blood, grew thinner in the old.

He had been grieved to hear news of his old companion's, Josiah Tudor's, death, for he had been an honest man, and a loyal friend . . . Besides, it brought closer the reality of his own nearness to the grave's edge . . . He had questioned the servants, most stringently, about the message, and by whom it had been delivered. Yet, none save the scullery maid had been able to give answer . . . She was, he thought without rancour, a dull-witted creature, slow to express herself, and her memory poor.

"'Twas a dirty ragamuffin, who stank to high heaven,

108

sir . . ." was all she could recall. "Upon a cart it was, a cart with a brown horse . . ."

Sir Frederick had written to Josiah Tudor's daughter, offering aid, and would have travelled to Yorkshire himself, had not he been afflicted with some congestion of the lungs which hindered his breathing . . . A result of the cold journey from the house in Cornwall, his physician warned, and sternly forbade further travel . . . When his letter of condolence remained unanswered, the general had given a close friend use of his travelling coach to travel to Yorkshire. He was instructed to return with Josiah's daughter . . . for it was not fitting that she remain alone. Her brother was absent with his regiment, and the young gentlewoman herself no more than sixteen or seventeen years of age . . .

The friend had returned, disconsolate, to admit that his careful enquiries had come to naught . . . She had, he was led to believe, been admitted, briefly, to the poorhouse as a pauper . . . Yet the workmaster, one Oliver Sidebottom, had denied all knowledge of her, or her whereabouts. He gave, as his opinion, that Sidebottom was pretentious and self-opinionated; an ignorant, self-seeking fellow, with only his own interests at heart . . . Yet it had been impossible to move him from his denial, and in it he had been supported by the new owner of Josiah Tudor's cottage . . . a poor, isolated place, near to rack and ruin . . . Sir John Hambrook had declared the matter to be firmly closed. It would be profitless to pursue it . . . Yet he had not reckoned upon Sir Frederick Loosely's tenacity . . . He would, he declared, never stop seeking the child, Sarah Tudor . . . It was the only thing he could now do for Josiah Tudor. Enquiries must be made at all the places she once knew, and beyond. He would not rest easy in his mind until Sarah Tudor was safely found.

Sir Frederick had been disturbed, indeed, aggravated, by an unsolicited call upon him by Sir Ewen Charlesworth, a man he detested . . . Yet, curiosity as to the reason for the visit, and apprehension lest Jean-Luc be in some way involved, forced him to be civil and to welcome him courteously. "I trust, sir, that you will forgive this . . . impulsive visit, and trust that it is not an inappropriate time to call upon you."

"Indeed, no . . ." General Loosely had murmured polite

denial, "I had heard, sir, of your unfortunate ill-health, and as I had business in the vicinity, I felt it incumbent upon me to call and enquire as to your progress . . ."

"I thank you for your concern, Sir Ewen . . ." Try as he might, the general could infuse no warmth into his tone. "It was a most trifling indisposition, I do assure you . . . scarce worth the mention . . . More a matter of age than infirmity . . ."

Charlesworth had made flattering homage to the general's evident vigour and mental agility, and so the innocuous conversation had continued, fortified by glasses of the best Canary wine . . . The conventional trivialities exhausted, Charlesworth came to the real purpose of his visit.

"And your ward, sir? The young Frenchman? . . . An erudite young fellow, if I correctly recall, intelligent, and eager to learn . . . He studied the wine in his glass, saying inconsequentially, "His name, sir, for the moment escapes me . . ."

"The Comte de Valandré, sir . . ." The general spoke curtly.

"And where is he now, sir? I should like to renew our . . . slight acquaintanceship."

"He is, sir, where every red-blooded gentleman of honour should be . . . fighting to preserve the country which gave him adoption after that . . . French débâcle. He is abroad, sir, with my regiment of the line . . ."

General Loosely had spoken calmly, but with such pride of conviction, that his affection for his ward was clear.

Sir Ewen had murmured approval, then deftly turned the conversation, before reluctantly taking his leave. As he stepped into his waiting carriage, he thought, ill-temperedly, I was wrong, then, to suspect . . . The prisoner, Luc Nolais, *was* what he seemed. It had been no more than a foolish aberration on his part; monstrous stupidity! Thank God he had not brought his suspicions to his superior's notice, else it would have laid him open to ridicule and contempt . . . General Loosely, despite his advanced age, was a man of influence, and much respected; a dangerous adversary . . . well, at least the matter was settled beyond all reasonable doubt, and it had been achieved skilfully, and without the old general even suspecting.

CHAPTER 11

Upon the morrow, Fowles had taken Sarah to an inn upon the outskirts of the city, to meet with the assembled drovers. To Sarah's relief, Jed Perkins, the head drover, had turned out to be as kindly as the carrier had claimed. He was a massive fellow, in size and strength, but, as if to belie it, his manner was mild and his speech, as his movements, cheerfully unhurried. He exuded confidence, and there was no hiding his generosity of nature. Sarah, despite her regret at losing the carrier's companionship, felt no qualms at surrendering herself to the drover's protection. There had been an ugly confrontation when Jed had discovered that his underling, Jim Parslowe, had demanded payment from his good friend . . . The words exchanged between the two drovers had been abrasive, their anger harsh. But there was no denying who was master. Parslowe, shamefaced, had been forced to return to Fowles the money extracted for Sarah's safe passage . . . Fowles, in turn, had delivered it to Sarah, declaring it payment honestly earned, and she had been grateful for his selflessness. Yet, it had been too public a whipping. Jim Parslowe, humiliated, and resentful that his authority had been eroded before all, had turned his wrath upon Sarah. He had flayed her with foul-tongued curses and invective, and would have dealt her a physical blow, had not Jed Perkins stepped between them. Parslowe was much the smaller man, although wiry and hard-muscled from toil, and fury had made him reckless. It seemed that the argument must end in violence, and the watchers were as tensely fearful as those involved.

"There is free ale for all who would drink!"

The landlord's voice, lusty and far-carrying, penetrated to every corner of the yard . . . There was an incredulous silence, followed by a murmur of disbelief, before the full intelligence of his words was understood. Then, jovial and florid-faced, he barely had time to remove himself safely within, before the inn was crowded with the exuberant, jostling throng . . . The would-be antagonists were stilled, undecided . . . then Perkins had put an arm to Parslowe's shoulder, and guided him within. Parslowe had gone, stiff-backed and grudging, first turning his malevolent gaze upon Sarah . . . Fowles, disturbed by the drover's malice, was fearful of what revenge he might be prompted to take. Yet he was powerless now to aid her. He must rely on Jed Perkins' protection.

"Best follow them inside, Tudor, lad," he ordered gruffly, "or they will suspect you else . . ." He hesitated, before saying clumsily. "We will make our parting careless, as men would do . . . There must be no foolishness . . . no tears, you understand?"

Sarah had nodded dumbly.

Within, they were quickly swallowed up in the excited clamour of men, and girls, victualling themselves, and discussing who their likely benefactor might be . . . but the landlord, tight-lipped, would not be drawn, for all their persuasion.

The handsome young drover, who had given Sarah a sixpence, stood head and shoulders above the surging crowd, drinking his ale with satisfaction, laughing, joking, the centre of an amused throng . . . Seeing Fowles taking Sarah's hand in awkward parting, he had thrust his way determinedly to where they stood, saying, "If you would leave, carrier, you may trust your lad to my care . . ."

Fowles had studied him for a long moment, unspeaking, then, satisfied, had nodded, and abruptly walked away. Without glancing back, he had climbed upon the cart and urged the horse into life . . . He had seen the young drover covertly watching Sarah within the tavern, his face alert with puzzlement. Fowles had no doubts as to whom the drovers' anonymous benefactor would prove to be, nor could he fail to trust him. He suspected, too, that the stranger knew of Sarah's disguise . . . She was a brave-spirited creature, the carrier thought, and he would miss her company sorely upon the long haul back to Yorkshire.

Within the inn, Sarah was trying to master her ale, but its rough, unpalatable taste only sickened and defeated her. The stranger beside her took it from her, vastly amused, and drained the tankard at a draught, remarking,

"It is not to your taste . . . We may hope my company will suit
you better. You shall bed beside me, lad, 'neath some hedge
or dry wall, wherever we may find shelter . . . We shall cling
together for warmth and comfort. What do you say?"

Sarah said nothing; indeed, she was incapable of uttering so
much as a word, but a slow flush seeped from her neck to stain
her face. In an anguish of confusion, she had nodded assent.

Her protector's eyes were a most arresting shade of blue,
and quite startlingly knowledgeable. They were regarding her
benignly now, but with the surest gleam of amusement. She
felt certain that the offer was kindly meant, but could be
certain of nothing else . . . save that mixture of new and
violently unexpected emotions which assailed her. Excitement.
Apprehension, and above all, a shamefully disturbing desire to
which she could not yet put name.

The band of drovers, guards, graziers and their lads, with
the accompanying women, had set out agreeably refreshed
upon the first leg of their journey to Wales. There were
twenty and more in all, and Tudor, the carrier's jacklad,
had been relegated to the rear of the small procession, in
the company of his peers. Luc, at Jed's beckoning, had gone
to walk beside him at the head of the exodus. Their pace
was keen, their strides well matched, and soon they were in
earnest conversation, their laughter and that of their fellows
drifting cheerfully back. The drovers' lads, surrounding Sarah,
jostled and pushed for advantage, briskly argumentative, each
striding out in a furious bid to outdistance the others . . . Yet
there was no real malice in them. Their boisterous exuberance
was as natural as that of young puppies, as was their urge to
compete and prove themselves . . . Although they chivvied
and harangued the carrier's jacklad when he lagged behind,
deriding him as puny, and asking if they might hire a funeral
cart to carry him, their childish mockery was more to bolster
their own achievements, rather than to belittle his.

Inevitably, Sarah found herself in the company of the slower
paced women, who were strolling more sedately, but always
within sight and sound of the men. The boldest of them, an
amiable body of some thirty years of age, seeing the pinched
exhaustion upon the new lad's face, and his frailness, had
gathered him firmly under her maternal wing . . . She was

113

a jaunty companion, and handsomely built, with a mane of dark, copper-coloured hair, intelligent eyes, and a humorous mouth. She would have been uncommonly beautiful, Sarah thought, had it not been for the disastrous showering of freckles disfiguring her pale skin. They lent her a strangely animal look, distinctive, and not wholly unattractive, like some ginger and white furred cat; a brindled dog, or a spirited piebald . . .

Becky Hendry, for so the red-headed woman was named, had a natural gift for mimicry. As they walked, she kept them amused with her scurrilous imitations of employers at whose hands she had suffered; the pompous, the wheedling, the lecherous, the mean . . . The characters took form and substance before their eyes, her observation wickedly accurate, as vividly alive and fleshed as she. Her audience's hilarity grew so noisily unrestrained that Jed Perkins and Luc glanced back, openly amused at the women's innocent high spirits. Yet, she had served to diminish their fears with her own; to cleanse and make bearable. Their seasonal work as weeders, fruit pickers, hop gatherers and scullions laid them open to the abuse and harassment of such men . . . Their work, and their poverty. Sarah, miserably recalling to mind Sir John Hambrook and the odious workmaster, stumbled, and all but fell . . . Becky Hendry's arm was instantly firm 'neath her elbow, to steady her, but Sarah's startled cry, and her shape and flesh as she leaned hard against her, had confirmed Becky's suspicion. The carrier's lad was undoubtedly a woman; small-breasted, and delicately formed. She might have been forgiven then for giving full rein to her acting talents in unmasking the charade . . . It would have won her that all-devouring attention which she so fervently craved. Yet Becky did not speak. She saw in the jacklad's vulnerability the pattern of all their lives, their inner fears, rejection and hurts . . . She did not know from whom, or what, the jacklad fled. It was none of her affair . . . Aloud, she exclaimed brashly, and with exquisite feeling,

"By heaven, jacklad, you stink! Worse than a midden! I'll swear Jed Perkins could hire you to keep the foxes away! You shall bathe at the first stream or duck-pond we come to."

Swift colour had flowed into Sarah's cheeks as Becky, prancing fastidiously, had held her at a distance, nose wrinkling, to add slyly, "Aye . . . you shall bathe with the drovers' lads, and we shall sit back and enjoy the frolics!"

The laughter and lewd jesting of the other women had made Sarah cringe, and her high colour had receded, stranding raw burns of crimson upon her cheeks . . . Becky, who was not an unkind girl, aware of her victim's distress, and the reason for it, felt a stirring of shame. Under cover of the women's continuing ribaldry, she had murmured, "I know, jacklad, that you are no more a lad than I . . ."

Resisting Sarah's terrified denial and her attempts to pull away, she had gripped her arm more firmly, saying urgently, "None shall learn of it from me, I swear!"

Her gaze had been honest, and her expression kind, and Sarah's painful relief had forced the sting of tears to her eyes, and she was powerless to halt them.

"See!" exclaimed Becky, vexedly, to the others, "we have made this poor jacklad cry with our foolish prattling!"

Immediately they were all remorse and concern, awkwardly comforting, begging the lad to pay no heed to their nonsense, for they had meant him no harm.

Luc, in glancing back, had seen the tears smeared childishly upon the lad's flushed face, and his clumsy efforts to wipe them away, and had felt a rush of protectiveness quite alien to him . . . Confused, he had missed his step, and Jed Perkins, following his gaze, realised what had so distressed him . . .

Jed's thoughts, as Becky Hendry's, were tinged with pity and concern . . . Of Sarah's history, he knew all, of Luc's, nothing. Yet experience had taught him that the man who walked beside him as eagerly sought escape, and that he, too, travelled in disguise. Luc was a gentleman born, despite his drover's clothing, and whatever drove him so remorselessly might well end in death; another's or his own . . . As for Sarah Tudor, it was plain that Luc recognised her for the woman she was, or, worse, foolishly believed her no more than a half-grown child . . . She saw him as a man; strong, protective . . . Such innocent emotion could all too quickly ignite into passion in a girl as lonely and gently nurtured as she . . . That would bring danger to them both. But the greatest danger lay in Jim Parslowe ever discovering that Sarah Tudor was a woman . . . He was a vindictive creature, vain and unpredictable, with a streak of deliberate cruelty . . . The blows and curses he dealt her as a jacklad might be easier to bear than his uses for her then.

They seemed, to Sarah, to have been walking for days rather than hours. The noonday sun was high and bright, but lacking in warmth. Sarah would have sworn that its heat had seeped into her own flesh and lay trapped beneath those layers of restrictive clothing which chafed and irritated her so. She felt it escape in slow runnels between her breasts, and gather in the creases of her body. It beaded her hairline and upper lip, clinging, persistent as raindrops upon her crudely shorn hair. Sarah had never thought that she could yearn for the stinking verminous discomfort of the carrier's cart, but she thought of it longingly now, as salvation and refuge. She had forced herself to walk beside the women, lest, in falling back, she be forgotten and deserted. She would not complain, nor beg for rest, for none, save she, showed discomfort . . . Her limbs ached, and her skin blistered then rubbed to raw flesh under the rasping of her boots, but still she trudged stubbornly onwards . . . After a time came the ease of numbness; that deadening of pain and feeling which grows from exhaustion . . . She moved, now, like an automaton, movements stilted and jerky, as though prescribed, and not of her own volition . . . Jed Perkins, glancing back and seeing Sarah's set face and painful efforts to stay upon her feet, called a halt upon the outskirts of a small village, where they might rest in a meadow and sheltering copse . . . Sarah had barely summoned strength enough to eat the oatbread and strong cheese which one of the women had distributed among them from her pack, but the ale, poured into a salt-glaze pitcher and passed among them, no longer seemed repugnant, and she drank of it eagerly to quench her raging thirst.

The drovers' lads, pleasantly sated, and with their aggression blunted by the rough and tumble of horseplay, sought other diversions. They set themselves to dam the small stream which flowed through the lower pastures, and make a pool in which to bathe. Their high-pitched voices, raucous and excited, had drifted back from behind the thorn hedge which hid them from view, until, work completed, they stripped off their clothing, and splashed and floundered into the ice-cold water. Their screams of shocked outrage had made the women and drovers

116

laugh aloud, and Jed Perkins, Parslowe and Luc had risen from the grass to watch their antics . . . It was all mild, harmless amusement, give or take a little over-enthusiastic ducking, until Parslowe had muttered an instruction to their leader . . . The boy, a cumbersome, slow-witted lout, had not hesitated, but had lumbered out of the stream, barely pausing to cover his nakedness, before blundering to where the women sat . . . He had grasped Sarah's arm viciously, dragging her to her feet, too startled and terrified to make proper resistance.

"What do you want of me?" Her voice was nervously pitched.

"Mr Parslowe would have you bathe, jacklad . . . Your stench offends him!"

He had dragged her roughly to the water's edge, ignoring her frantic cries and the angry protests of the women . . . Indeed, they seemed to add to his febrile excitement as, bullying and thrusting, he had forced her mercilessly ahead . . . Becky Hendry had scrambled to her feet and tried to drag the aggressor away, but he would not be halted, shaking her off so roughly that she stumbled to her knees.

"Now, jacklad! Clean off your filth! Join the fun and games!" He had held her poised at the water's edge, spurred by the cries of the other lads and her violent trembling. He had pulled at her shirt, so violently that it had ripped away, as, sobbing and beating at him with her fists, she had wrenched herself from his grasp and hurled herself bodily into the shallow stream, trying, in vain, to hide the nakedness of her breasts.

The laughter of the lads had died into shamed incredulous silence as Sarah had looked despairingly about her, trying, in anguish, to hold together the ravaged cloth, and her pride. Tears of pain and humiliation all but blinded her as Luc stepped into the stream to cover her with his coat and lead her gently to the bank . . . Jed Perkins had ordered the lads from the water, bidding them, harshly, to prepare themselves to be upon their way. His voice had been stiff with ill-suppressed rage, and his contempt a whiplash, but his excoriating anger was not for them, but Jim Parslowe . . . Chastened, and awkward in their discomfort, the boys had straggled ashore and dressed . . . No word was spoken, no resentment shown, for the game no longer mattered . . . It was ended.

Jim Parslowe, appalled at the unexpected savagery of the head-drover's anger, had tried to set blame upon his drover's lad, sullenly denying his own part in it . . . It had been no more than a youthful prank, he claimed; high-spirited nonsense. He had looked around him for support, but the women's faces held only hostility, the men's, disgust, and he had shuffled uneasily in his boots before moving away, inwardly seething, but with a spurious show of arrogance.

Jed Perkins, grim-faced, had motioned Becky Hendry aside, making stilted explanation before telling her to remain behind with Sarah Tudor. "There is a post-house no more than half a mile along the byway . . . we will await you there," he promised, adding, "Try to calm her, Becky. She is in need of kindness, and you are the kindest woman I know . . . for all your heedless laughter and mocking ways . . ."

He had flushed scarlet, expecting her usual sharp-tongued or jocular reply, but she merely nodded, eyes unnaturally bright. "You will need to calm her . . . give her courage to rejoin us upon the road, as she must . . . She has been shamed and humiliated before all. It will not be easy, Becky, but I look to you!" Then he had added with gruff self-consciousness. "That common sense is your greatest asset, no man could deny!"

To his confusion, Becky had taken his great gnarled fist gently within her hands. Her vivid blue eyes looked mischievously into his own dark eyes through a fringe of red-gold lashes as she dissolved into sudden laughter.

"And if I lend her my courage, Jed, then where will I find enough to speak those words to you which one day must be said?"

Puzzled, he had smiled, then clumsily withdrawn his hand from hers, and, shrugging good-naturedly, had ambled upon his way. Becky was a strange creature, he thought, bewildered; volatile and unpredictable, as fiery as her own red hair . . . yet with a core of unexpected tenderness . . . She was too exotic and rare a creature for a life of wandering the roads . . . Yet, Spring and Autumn, she came, unfailingly as the seasons, to walk beside them, and seek whatever work she might find . . . lively, generous, admired and courted by many a hopeful drover and, doubtless, men of means beyond. He sighed. He had been a widower these seven long years, and had naught to offer a woman, save the remnants of caring, and a life of hardship and toil upon the roads . . . Becky Hendry's vital, laughing face, with its glowing flame of red hair, burned in his mind . . . He did not doubt that she would be kind to Sarah Tudor . . .

Becky had given to Sarah a precious washball of lye and tallow, to bathe herself in the pool which the drover lads had dammed . . . The women, despite their poverty, had searched among their few, meagre possessions to find garments to clothe her. Without prompting, they gave of their best, those things jealously purchased against the day of their return to the village or hamlet from whence they had sprung. Young or old, firm-fleshed as Becky, or dry-boned and spare, they had made their offerings.

Sarah, skin scrubbed clean and dried upon rough flannel, her damp hair agonisingly brushed by Becky into a shining halo about her delicate oval face, stood garbed in her new-found finery. So slender was she that one of the women had been cleverly inspired to tie a colourful scarf as a sash at the waistline of her borrowed blue skirt, and to clumsily tack up its hem . . . They had set out irrepressibly when all was completed, chattering and jostling like a flock of noisy starlings upon their way.

Jed Perkins, hearing the cheerful clamour from within the post inn, had hurried to the door, and stood there, with Luc beside him, and Parslowe scowling, wry-faced.

It was Luc whose face had shown the most comical, open-mouthed astonishment at the transformation wrought. Then he had impulsively hurried forward to offer Sarah his arm and escort her showily within.

"A privilege, ma'am." His eyes were frankly admiring, then creased around with delighted laughter as she readily responded in kind. Placing her work-roughened hand upon his, and touching her skirts with graceful elegance, she had swept into a faultless curtsey, murmuring, "You do me too much honour, sir . . ."

"Indeed, ma'am, it would be impossible to honour you enough . . ." Their exchanged glances, mocking at first, had stilled in sudden recognition; each grown gravely aware of the intimacy which bound them, and aware of no others . . . Amidst the eager, explosive babble of excitement and amusement which surrounded them, Jem Parslowe, alone, remained silent and grim.

Within the post-house, Sarah, who had lodged for safekeeping with Jed Perkins that money which she had earned upon the wool cart, bade him spend some now. There should be gin for the women, if they chose, and rough ale for the drovers' lads, and victuals for all upon their way.

The rawness of her feet and her exhaustion were forgotten as they set out, refreshed, once more, upon the long way . . . Luc had walked a while beside her, telling himself that it was pity for her which stirred him so . . . That, and admiration for her courage and that fierce will to survive the blows, poverty and humiliation thrust upon her. Sarah was only grateful that he was at her side, and asked no more. Yet memory of his demanding that she sleep comfortingly beside him intruded . . . filling her with secret pleasure and pain; a depth of longing new to her . . .

Yet he had not come to seek her, but had slept that night within the warmth of a tavern and posting house, sharing a drover's room with Jed Perkins. Sarah, as was the way of things, slept in the cold, bare shelter of stone wall, with Becky beside her . . . She had slept ill, her mind a maelstrom of swirling thoughts and emotions she dare not give name to, nor even confess.

Jean-Luc de Valandré, in the comfort of his goose-feather bed, told himself that he was an imbecile, a cretin. The girl was a mere child. He had known, and taken, many women, giving always of his flesh, without heart . . . He had grown adept at extricating himself, emotions unscathed, from the courtship of gentlewomen, and the earthier pursuit of more lusty flesh. Always such affairs had been a harmless diversion. Nothing, and no-one, must deflect him from his obsession to return, in triumph, to Valandré.

Why, then, did Sarah's delicate-boned face with its slanting, hazel eyes fill him with such restless thoughts? Why did it come between him and sleep? She was an innocent, and what he felt for her was no more than – honest concern. The protection of a brother. Hell and damnation! It was ludicrous! Beyond all enduring! To even contemplate such an affair would be to drive her into danger as violent as his own . . . He would dwell no more upon her, but banish her from his mind . . . He slept . . . but could not banish her from his dreams.

CHAPTER 12

When the little band of drovers and their followers set out upon the morrow, Sarah's spirits were optimistic, her step light, despite the rawness of her feet . . . The change in her, Becky Hendry thought, amused, was as radical as that change from jacklad to gentlewoman, and as impossible to ignore. The reason for her new-found happiness was plain. She was besotted by the handsome new drover, Luc, and had neither the wit nor experience to hide it . . . Sarah's eyes strayed to him too often, her tenderness laid bare. Such naked devotion, Becky feared, would serve only to alarm rather than intrigue . . . For a man as virile and experienced as Luc, the thrill of pursuit, the chase, would prove as stimulating as the capture . . . The final surrender must be his, as well as hers . . . Of one thing Becky was certain; this man, Luc, was as much a stranger to the drovers' drifts as to the drover's life . . . There was some restlessness within him; some violence of need, damped down, yet ready, upon an instant, to ignite . . . That he was dangerous, she was convinced, as she was convinced that the passionate need which scourged him was of the mind, rather than the flesh . . . Who and what Luc was did not concern her. It was none of her affair. Each one of them upon the drovers' roads had some secret to hide, some sin, or fear, to expurgate. The past was another country, explored, long gone.

The country through which they moved, now, was fertile, the last leaves of Autumn a dying splendour upon the trees, the pleached hedges still bright with the purple-red leaves of bramble and elder, and crimsoned berries. Above them, with the fading of dawn, the sky was no more than a pale reflection, holding firm promise of a fine, clear day.

Yet Luc had not walked beside them, nor eaten with them, nor made any but the meanest acknowledgement of Sarah's existence. She was, he had made plain, of no more interest to him than any other. Flushed and shamed, she had hidden her bewilderment, laughing and chattering to all with feverish animation never glancing at him. Yet she ached with hurt.

"Tomorrow," Becky had promised, to ease Sarah's melancholy, "Jed will walk us to Farnham Fair! 'Tis the merriest of places, and the greatest gathering of the year. Oh, but you will love it, Sarah, for its bustle and gaiety . . . There will be pedlars and freaks beyond imagining, and sweetmeats, and the liveliest music and dance . . .! All the world will be there, for none could resist such joyousness!" Sarah had feigned excitement, but for the rest of the women the glorious anticipation was real. Farnham Fair promised adventure far removed from their harsh, workaday lives. A holy day to treasure in memory, and with pence enough to spare.

"Will everyone take part? Jed and . . . the others?"

Sarah's question had been carelessly posed, but Becky was undeceived. "Yes! Every last one, you may depend. 'tis a fine chance to do business, make contact with others of their kind. When all is safely done, they will find cheer in celebration . . . eating, drinking, play; whatever they choose . . . 'tis a rare old opportunity for courtship and display . . ." Sarah had nodded, but her thoughts were not turned solely to Luc, but upon Jane Grey, and her own shameful ingratitude. How dearly Jane would have relished such freedom and merriment, although she was deaf to both music and laughter. Well, she would take herself humbly to Farnham Fair, Sarah decided. She would rise upon the morrow, as gay and carefree as any meadow lark, and as filled with delight. She would dance with any and all who asked her. She would not spare a moment's thoughts, nor waste grief, on any undeserving. She would not name him 'Luc', even in her own mind, for even to dwell upon him, secretly, brought too painful a hurt.

That night the women slept in the shelter of a hayloft above the byre and stables of an inn. Jed Perkins, Parslowe and Luc slept within the inn itself, for they alone could afford to squander the four pence demanded. When the great drive along the drift roads to London, or the Essex salt marshes to fatten their herds and beasts was under way, the drovers, guards and women slept beside their animals in the fields, always alert to protect them. Now, relieved of such duties, they settled wherever they might find comfort . . . That evening, the tavern had echoed to carefree gaiety, the skilled music of Jed's concertina, and the singing and dancing bringing lively entertainment. The villages and hamlets upon the drovers' ways were isolated; poor rural communities, eager to provide cheap grazing . . . The drovers' coming was an event and adventure keenly awaited and welcomed by all . . . Becky Hendry's wicked mimicry and outrageous rhyming had so amused and captivated the landlord that he had given her use of the hayloft . . . Yet the ostler, a dour, ill-mannered man, face heavily scarred with cowpox, had not fallen such easy prey to her charms . . . He had demanded payment of a halfpenny from each of the women, and not all their wheedling, grumbling, or final abuse could move him. Nevertheless, it was, they admitted in his absence, a halfpenny well spent . . . It was a cold, crisp night, with the promise of frost to come in the early hours. Through the cracks in the loose wood of the loft, Sarah could see the hung moon, perfectly rounded, the stars beside it glittering as sharp crystals of ice. Beside her, the other six women slept, their sighs and movements an echo of those of the fidgetting horses in the stable beneath. From their stalls rose the warm animal smells of the cows; their sweat and fresh ordure, the sweetness of their breath clotting the air.

Sarah, glancing once more towards the pierced sky, saw a dark figure emerging from the inn, shadowy in the light of the moon. A silhouette, no more, but instantly recognisable as Luc. He had hesitated only briefly upon the cobbled yard, glancing so intently towards the stable-loft that Sarah would have sworn that he observed her with that same clarity with which she viewed him. Under the thin light of the moon, his corn-coloured hair was leached to silver, his face a paleness. She actually drew back into the shadowed darkness to avoid his gaze, before dismissing herself as a dreamer, and fool. It was not her company he sought, for he swiftly left the stable-yard for the pathway beyond, which led to the hamlet through which they had earlier trudged. Was he as restless as she; as beset by doubts and confusion? Was it privacy he sought? The solace of his own company, or the company of another? The thought of Luc's planned assignation with a woman unknown filled Sarah with such a rage of pain that she all but cried aloud.

Even as she watched the deserted yard, hesitant as to whether to follow him, another figure left the doorway of the inn. A man, she felt certain, but smaller and more wiry than Luc. His face was hidden 'neath the broad-brimmed hat, but he wore the drover's clothing of rough Cambrian frieze, the coarse breeches with leggings. Not Jed. She would have known him for his height and bulk. Jim Parslowe, then? A coldness of certainty chilled her, and she found herself trembling as violently as if she, too, walked abroad. She could not believe that they conspired together in some dishonesty! Parslowe must mean to do Luc physical harm . . . angered, perhaps, by Luc's defence of her. She had lain awake, strangely fearful, yet unwilling to confide her anxiety, even to Becky.

She had seen Jim Parslowe's swift return, and, long afterwards, the return of Luc himself. Yet it brought her neither relief nor solution. She lay sleepless until cockcrow, hearing the scrabbling of mice and stable rats in the straw below, and the restless unease of the beasts in their stalls. When the other women's excited chatter and preparations for Farnham Fair began, she took herself into the deserted yard. She had washed herself stoically in the freezing well-water of the inn, first using the bucket upon its chain to break its crusting of ice. It brought her as little comfort as the night.

They had eaten a breakfast of ryebread, cold fat bacon and ale at the inn, not begrudging the landlord his extra pence upon so special a day. They had bought no victuals to eat upon the roads, for there would be treats aplenty at Farnham Fair, and it would not do to blunt their appetites. Jed declared the drovers' lads to be "as high-strung as harps, and drawn tight with over-excitement." But he had indulgently given them sixpence apiece from his own pocket, which had served to excite them the more. The drovers strode confidently out, behind them the lads, and the women in their sprigged cotton dresses, carefully hoarded. Some wore prettily trimmed bonnets, and those who could not afford them had threaded bright ribbons into their hair. Becky carried a pair of shoes in her sack, dark blue, and soft as glove leather, fitted to her feet by a cordwainer. Delicate as spun glass they were, and as tenderly cherished, although she might have worn them out through gazing at them and touching

125

them alone . . . Upon the road to Farnham Fair she wore rough boots, with the others, for her dainty shoes were too precious for everyday wear.

A crispness of hoar frost lingered upon the grass, for the sun was not yet high, but, despite the chill, not one of the women saw fit to cover her finery with a woollen shawl. When the frost dissolved in the warmth of the sun, their boot soles made silvered patterns upon the wayside grass to mark their passing.

There were many who hurried to doorway and gate to witness the drovers' stepping out, for they were a bonny sight, with their spirits high and their greetings courteous. They seemed so joyously young and, for this one memorable day, carefree, and work free, and none could grudge them their innocent pleasure.

Luc, alone of the little company, seemed subdued and pre-occupied. Jed, who had shared a room with him, had marked his absence in the night, but had not spoken of it. A man's love life, or his urge to be solitary, were no business of any other. It was occupation enough to settle one's own affairs! Besides, Luc was merely passenger, not drover, and vouched for by Jim Parslowe as an honest man . . . Jed, who was as shrewd a judge of human character as he was of sheep and cattle, would have trusted Luc with his life. Yet, if pressed, he would have admitted that he would have been loath to trust Jim Parslowe himself, even with his money . . . Still, he was the best working drover Jed had ever hired, knowledgeable and industrious, and worth any two men . . . His wages were well earned . . . Yet there was a streak of intolerance in him; a cruel impatience with the lads, and contempt for the women. He was too swift to belittle and decry . . .

Becky Hendry had come forward to walk beside Jed, proud in her pretty, blue dress, eyes mischievously teasing in the freckled face . . . Under the sun, her beribboned hair was a copper cloud, her eyes vivid as Bristol blue glass.

"And will you dance with me at Farnham Fair, master?"

Jed laughed, despite his embarrassment at being singled out before all, for she was a bold and warming sight.

"That I will not! For I am clumsier than an ox, and as much a stranger to dancing . . ."

126

"Then I will teach you!" she promised pertly, "Every last twist and turn, every hold, every embrace . . ." There was a challenge in her raised chin and the clear eyes, and all about them were swept with laughter at her nonsense . . . "Well, Jed Perkins?" Her eyes no longer teased, but had grown grave and intent, quietly pleading.

"Then I will dance with you, and gladly!" he said, handsomely, and the drovers' lads had whistled and cheered, unable to hide their exuberance at the prospect of such a singular diversion.

Becky had simply nodded, and returned to stand beside Sarah, her smile uncommonly wide.

Jed Perkins, painfully ill at ease, had wondered why, of all the company, Becky had chosen to ask him . . . To embarrass and confound me, he thought disconsolately; to make me look a fool. Yet he could not honestly believe it to be so. Becky was without malice, or meanness. Yet, what had he to offer? He was a clumsy, great clod of a fellow, more suited to tending a sick ewe, or driving a herd, than dancing . . . Yet the prospect of holding Becky's soft flesh in his arms was pleasantly disturbing, a promise he would not willingly forgo.

"I shall make a fool of myself," he confided shamefacedly to Luc, "a proper laughing stock! I am as suited to dancing as . . . as an ox to the spinet! I am ill at ease with women . . . cannot find words."

"Then let Becky do the talking," Luc had laughingly advised.

"But she will expect answer . . . How will I know what to say, or do?" Jed's broad, ingenuous face was creased in concern.

"You will know. Believe me, you will know!"

Luc's reply was amused, emphatic. Yet, as he fell into step beside Jed, his own thoughts were as confused. At the safe house, last night, he had been told only of his next destination . . . no more. How would he make contact with the British, tell them of the little he had so far gleaned, the arrangements made? He was certain that Jim Parslowe had followed him to the house. Precaution on the part of his masters, or spleen upon the drover's part? An opportunity, perhaps, to betray him? He wished he knew. Upon one course he was adamant. He would have no dealings with women at the fair. There would be no sporting, no dancing. Upon that he was firm . . . Unlike Jed, none would persuade him.

Two miles or so along the road from the inn, they had heard the harsh, unmistakable calls of the drovers, urging their beasts to the fair. Their loud cries of "Heiptrw Ho!" gave piercing warning that carts and waggons must halt, farmers secure their flocks and herds, and those who walked the roads seek shelter . . . It was no idle threat, for the cattle were driven in their hundreds, a seething, trampling mass, fickle and temperamental. A stampede into a market town could bring risk of injury or death to those unfortunates in its path, and cruel devastation . . . Sarah, who had never before encountered such a vast herd, was terrified, for the beasts ahead had halted, making the way impassable. The fury and noise of their cries was almost deafening, their flanks wedged tight, a crushing tide of hide and horn and rolling, anguished eyes . . .

With no word spoken, Jed and the drovers and lads had hurried to help to control the panicked herd and restore good order. Becky, and the other women too, unmindful of their fair-day clothes, had lent what aid they might. But Sarah, although shamed into action, had been so terrified of one monster, who had turned its wrath upon her, mouth hanging saliva, eyes wild, that she had cravenly turned and fled, her screams adding to the confusion . . . Luc seemed to be of as little use as she, although he had immediately joined the affray, working at Jim Parslowe's impatient command, aware, all the while, of the contempt in which he held his efforts.

When Sarah had tentatively crept back, Luc's glance had met hers with amusement and understanding.

"I hope, ma'am," he said, doffing his wide-brimmed hat, and making an exaggerated bow, "that your day at the fair brings you more . . . welcome partners . . ."

"And I, sir, return the hope that you are more adept at dancing than droving!" she replied, stung to acerbity. He had laughed unaffectedly then, adding to her pique and uncertainty, before helping Jed and the others to right the carriage which lay upturned in the ditch beside the road, and had been the evident cause of the disturbance. The owner of the curricle, an elegant dandy, was having high words with the chief drover of the herd, his lean face flushed and choleric. Moreover, he was threatening, with explicit gestures, to horsewhip the drover "within an inch of his useless life." The drover, in turn, was threatening him with murder, disembowellment, plague and pestilence, with a few harrowing curses thrown in for good measure . . . They were ready to exchange blows, when Jed, with his good common sense, had intervened to cool tempers and pacify.

At his command, the curricle had been righted and set back upon the road, with no damage to the horse, save shock, and none which could not be mended to the fine carriage. Its owner, also undamaged, save in pride, had been soothed by Jed, although still glowering and sullen-faced.

Sarah's eyes were upon Luc. He had taken the hand of the young woman passenger from the curricle, and helped her from the far bank of the ditch, where she had been cowering, apparently terrified. She was trembling uncontrollably, and his handling of her was gentle, but assured and compassionate . . . All that could be seen of her was the pretty muslin dress and pelisse of dark blue silk, with the matching bonnet, from which a pale gold-cluster of ringlets escaped . . . Her face had been hidden by her bonnet-brim, yet, when she looked up into Luc's face, it was not terror she showed, but lively amusement, her shoulders shaking with irrepressible humour . . . She was, without doubt, the most exquisitely beautiful creature that Sarah had ever seen, perfect in feature and colouring, elegant in figure, fashionably modish in dress . . . All of virtue that Sarah was not. Jed, Jim Parslowe, and each of the drovers' lads had stared at her in awed disbelief, silenced by amazement. The women, more grudgingly impressed, recognised for the first time the tawdriness of their own clothing, their dishevelled state, then the roughened coarseness of their hands, the clumsiness of their boots.

The young gentlewoman had smiled demurely into Luc's handsome face, thanking him prettily, before declaring,

"What a delightful adventure! I may hope our journey to Farnham Fair brings such . . . lingering pleasure . . ."

She had withdrawn her hand from Luc's with every show of reluctance, her blue eyes teasing, smile warm with intimacy shared . . . The owner of the curricle had nodded curtly at Luc as he had helped her gallantly into the carriage, then had driven away with arrogant disdain for the safety of the women alongside.

They, too, had continued upon their way, the men vocal now about the stranger's loveliness and brave spirit, the women subdued. They picked their awkward way around the steaming cow-muck and through the churned filth of the roadside, cleaning their boots upon the tussocks of coarse grass . . . The day seemed cooler, less full of bright promise, as if the sun lay shadowed behind a cloud . . . Becky, glancing at Sarah's set face, and aware of the reason for her misery, ventured consolingly, "We will have such a time of it at the fair . . . 'tis meant for common folk such as we, and not the 'quality'! We shall buy ribbons and lace for our petticoats from the pedlars, and the prettiest fairings, too . . . and have our fortunes told by a true Romany!" She had taken Sarah's arm impulsively, and stepped out jauntily upon the way.

Sarah had forced herself to smile and pretend enthusiasm . . . keeping her eyes determinedly from Luc all the while . . . She needed no gypsy to chart her future. It promised to be as barren, and joyless, as her past.

CHAPTER 13

It would have been impossible to have long remained despondent at Farnham Fair. It was a scene of such spontaneous gaiety that Sarah could not remain aloof. It was more than a mere fair. It was shop and market, business house and meeting place; the scene of joyous reunions, of bargaining, courting, and simply being seen. Sarah and Becky, swept up in the colourful vitality of the crowd which surged about them, were dazzled by the excitement, and determined to sample all. Jed had business to transact with stock-breeders and farmers, and letters and commissions to deliver from friends at home. His bland, good-natured face was crimsoned with pleasure and ale, as he set cheerfully about his duties. There were woollen stockings to provide for the stallholders, knitted by candlelight by the cottagers of Wales. They were reputed to be the best stockings in all the country, and dearly sought after, for Welsh sheep were known to be sweet-fleshed, and their wool thicker, and more vigorous, than any other. He carried carefully within his pack hand-crocheted collars of gossamer lace, made by the ancients at their firesides in the long winter months. He would not rest, Becky knew, until he had sold every last one, for the few poor coppers they would provide their makers would be a godsend, and was eagerly awaited upon his return.

Becky and Sarah, separated from the rest, sampled all the rich delights on offer. They ate sweetmeats, pancakes, oranges, and crisp Kentish cobs . . . They bought hair ribbons and petticoat lace, needles and thread . . . They watched jugglers and fire-eaters, a camel, and a dancing bear upon a chain . . . They viewed waxworks and automata, and a monkey band. There were slack rope walkers, tightrope walkers, and freaks; one woman amazingly covered in fur, a pig with two heads, and 'an elf', but eighteen inches tall, in a suit of green fustian and a cap with tin bells . . . They watched bare-knuckled pugilistic contests; saw Jim Parslowe humbled and defeated.

Despite all Becky's earnest persuasion, Sarah would not enter the gypsy's tent to have her fortune told, but waited indulgently without, while Becky squandered a sixpence. It was then that Sarah, glancing idly about her at the milling crowd, saw Luc, his face bent attentively over the woman from the overturned carriage. They were talking earnestly, and passed so close by without seeing her that she might have put out a hand and touched Luc's arm. But it was his beautiful companion who took his arm in eager possession, flawless face raised alluringly to his, mouth soft with shared pleasure. Luc's handsome features were alive with interest, and he stood head and shoulders above the crowd in every way. Sarah, her promise to wait for Becky forgotten, thrust her way fiercely through the swirling tide of bodies to keep them in sight, impelled by bewildered hurt, then a devouring rage of jealousy.

She had watched them walk towards the entrance of a coppice which bordered the fair, then disappear within, and she was aware only of a coldness deeper than pain as, rage spent, she turned away. She did not at first see Jed, nor feel his comforting hand upon her arm, for her eyes were blurred with stupid tears, her flesh numb.

"We had best find Becky," he said, "for my work here is done, and I have promised that we will dance together."

She had nodded, unable to speak.

Sarah had watched Becky and Jed Perkins dance, a fixed smile upon her face, and a surging misery within. She had found Jed's clumsiness endearing, and his awkward protection of Becky too painfully revealing to bear. Becky's radiant happiness was a flame, lighting her from within, as brightly glowing as her beribboned hair. Sarah could not grudge her such transparent pleasure, nor cloud it with misery. The lively music of the fiddlers, the concertina, flutes and drums, and the gaiety of the dancing had drawn a crowd, their enjoyment, as their intake of ale, ever wilder and more abandoned. Sarah had found herself, unwillingly at first, drawn into the feverish whirl of activity. She had stepped out obligingly with Jed and his drovers, and smilingly encouraged the drovers' lads in their clog-footed exuberance, even Huw Jenkins, that slow-witted, moon-faced creature who had dragged her to the stream to bathe. His shambling awkwardness, and shy pleasure in her company, had shamed away the last hard core of bitterness. He was no longer a threat, held no menace. He was, after all, no more than a child, unwillingly trapped in a man's flesh, but with a child's simplicity of mind, and as gentle and biddable. Soon warmed by Huw's innocent enjoyment, Sarah had grown as light-hearted and carefree as he.

Jim Parslowe was only too eager to dispel her mood. He was well aware that Becky Hendry and she had witnessed his thrashing at the boxing booth, and his pride smarted as painfully as his bruised flesh. There had been no attempt to hide their triumph at his defeat. Sarah had felt unable to refuse his request to dance with him without giving open offence, for she had partnered all others. Reluctantly, and with foreboding, she had accepted him.

His arms had tightened about her, forcing her close, imprisoning her . . . His face was a grotesquely swollen mask, ugly, disfigured; his warm flesh, pressed hard against her own, a hateful obscenity. She had tried to wrench herself free, but it seemed to excite him the more. There was a smile of lasciviousness upon his face as his body forced pruriently close. He was determined, she knew, to humiliate and insult her before all, to make her the butt of the crowd's lewdness, their jeering amusement. Sarah closed her eyes, sickened with shame.

Jed had moved forward, shaking off Becky's restraining hand, a cold fury within him. But it was Luc who stepped forward before he could act, wrenching Jim Parslowe away, felling him with a blow which all but dislocated his head from his spine. There had been a wild, triumphant cheering from the onlookers as Parslowe's neck had snapped backwards, and he had staggered, face foolish with surprise, then fallen to the ground. He was as insensible to the ignominy of being dragged clear of the dancers, by Huw Jenkins and the drovers' lads, as to their mocking, irreverent laughter.

Sarah's emotions had veered from joy at her unexpected deliverance to mortification, then cold rage. She would have flounced scornfully away had not Luc expertly swept her into his arms, and danced her away before she could make movement or protest.

"I fear, ma'am," he said, glancing negligently towards where Jim Parslowe lay, "that your partner proved no more to your liking than the drovers' herd."

"And I am sure, sir," she countered with malice, "that yours, and your . . . exploration in the woods were wholly to your liking!" She had missed a step in her agitation, but with practised ease he had steadied her unobtrusively, murmuring with dry amusement, "Indeed. And you, ma'am, must be greatly relieved."

"How so?

Her tone was cutting.

"You expressed the hope that my dancing was more skilful than my droving . . . I hope, ma'am, that I have reassured you upon that score. My mastery of the polite arts is absolute."

"As is your overweening conceit, sir!"

He was arrogant, deceitful, pompous, and totally obnoxious, Sarah thought vexedly, but he had drawn her close. His eyes were no longer amused and arrogant, but tenderly perceptive, and she did not attempt to pull away from him, although she felt the hardness of his breast-bone against her thin bodice, and the warmth of his flesh. It was nothing like being held by Jim Parslowe; indeed, it produced a sensation of such new and exquisite pleasure that she hoped it might never end. If this were all of his touch and nearness she would ever know, then she would remember, and grieve, it. For the moment she was content to lay her head in the curve of his shoulder, and forget.

The contact with Luc by the British had been made at the fair so skilfully that he doubted that even Jim Parslowe had been alerted to it. The woman, Mary Grantley, had been a friend from early childhood, and the widow of a lieutenant in his former regiment. She had played her part impeccably, signalling by firm pressure upon his arm, and the anguished warning in her eyes, that he must, on no account, acknowledge her. Her escort had been privy to the secret, but his rage at the overturning of the carriage had been real, and his anger against the drover raw . . . His vehemence had served to further strengthen Luc's position, and to divert suspicion from himself. As a gentlewoman, Mary's walk with him into the woods had publicly compromised her, Luc knew, but she had brushed his protests aside. She knew no-one living in the county, she declared tartly, and even had she done so, then she would have discounted the risks for the gain involved. Sheldon, her husband, would have wished it so. Luc had given her all the information he had gleaned, and the place of his last briefing by the French, and the address of the safe house to which he must next report. It was little enough to act upon, he feared, but the British might set a watch upon the houses, or use it to other advantage. He was bound, eventually, for Ireland, and thence to France.

She would assure Sir Frederick of his safety, she promised, for none could suspect a visit from her as being made other than from pure affection. She loved the general as dearly as a father, and he had been all of kindness to . . . Sheldon, (she had hesitated over his name), and to her, in that bleak aftermath of her widowhood. She had kissed Luc with sisterly affection, bidding him take care, and adding that she would pray, most earnestly, for his safe return. General Loosely was old, and less able to bear the hurts of death and loss than she. She spoke the words quietly, as a simple fact, demanding no sympathy, and without self-pity.

"You are as brave and splendid a woman as you are beautiful," Luc had said with sincerity.

"No." the denial had been swift. "Without Sheldon, Luc, I have little to lose, nothing to live for . . . In doing this work, I give meaning to his memory, and to mine . . ."

He had escorted her to the edge of the wood, seeing her return to the carriage and her fretfully impatient escort, who had driven away without a backward glance. There had been sly nudges and knowing winks exchanged between the bystanders at the scene as he had made his way purposefully towards the throbbing vitality of the music and dancing, bent solely upon watching others . . . Yet Sarah's vulnerability, and Jim Parslowe's open abuse of her, had forced him to action, and he could not wholly regret it. It was, he told himself, the impulse of a moment; a kindness offered, then ended. But was it ended . . .? Jim Parslowe was as unlikely to forgive past offenders as he.

The excitement of that day at Farnham Fair was relived over many a long mile on the journeying to Wales, as it would later be told and retold at many a cottage hearth. For simple folk, its

135

wonders were beyond the power of imagining, and those who had witnessed them were privileged, and earned the envy and respect of all.

Jim Parslowe's public humiliation by Luc had not noticeably improved his disposition. Indeed, he had, if possible, grown even more taciturn and difficult to appease, and the drovers' lads were careful not to offend him.

The company was bound for Faringdon, where Jed was to collect some leather saddle-bags for a farmer friend from a master saddler's shop. They had halted just beyond the fair, at a village green in the lee of a churchyard wall, to take their bearings, and to position their bulging packs more comfortably . . . Scarcely had they paused when the excitement began in earnest. The blacksmiths at the open smithy nearby were shoeing those few bullocks which had shed their shoes upon that long, rough trail along the drovers' roads from Wales . . . In Jed's eyes, at least, it was a sight to rival any at the fair, and a rare treat to witness . . . He had, he boasted proudly to Luc, many a time witnessed the throwing and shoeing of as many as two and three hundred cattle before the start of a trek, and seen many a skilled overthrower gored, or trampled, by an enraged beast.

The drovers and lads had crowded eagerly to the field beside the smithy, to shout encouragement to the 'fellers' whose duty it was to catch and fell the animals, and make them safe for the shoeing . . . It was a hazardous venture for the men, and no less fraught with danger for the beasts; a well-matched contest of strength, cunning and endurance . . .

Luc and Jed had watched with wary interest the capture of the first bullock. The 'feller' had thrown a rope to secure the beast's horns, while his partner bent its forelegs, and gave a quick wrench of the horns, which sprawled it to the grass . . . Its legs were swiftly bound, and tied to a forked iron, driven hard into the ground. The blacksmiths then hurried forward to the tethered bullock, and while one deftly trimmed its hooves, another nailed the shoes of light iron to the cloven hooves . . . two skilfully shaped shoes to each split hoof.

With the first ox shod, and led away to join the herd, the women had prudently retreated to a corner of the field, out of range of the anguished bellowing and tossing horns of the next. There was danger, not only in its flailing hooves, but from the sheer crushing weight of it, should it fall . . . Becky, alone, remained uneasily near, her care not for her own safety, but Jed's.

Jim Parslowe had irritated both overthrowers and smiths by his muttered contempt for their skills and ill-spoken advice. Finally, one of the blacksmiths, whose temper was as abrasive as Parslowe's own, had erupted in anger, declaring, "Since you are so damned clever, you had best take over! Show us your skills!"

A nod to the ox-feller and his helper had made them stand aside, cynical, and not a little amused to witness the drover's rough initiation.

Parslowe had swaggered confidently forward to accept the challenge, unexpectedly issuing one of his own.

"We had best make a proper contest of it," he had declared brashly.

"What do you say, Jed? Are you man enough, and willing? Or does your prowess begin and end with dancing with women at Farnham Fair?"

There was a derisive sneer in his voice, and Jed had been quick to confound it.

"Yes, we will make it a contest," he declared coldly, "and an honest wager. The man who fails, and withdraws, to pay the fellers the sixpence they are owed for overthrowing each beast . . . Agreed?"

"Agreed."

"Then you had best choose yourself a helper . . . I shall pick Luc."

Parslowe's swift scowl had betrayed his annoyance, but he had recovered to declare, evenly enough, "Then I shall take Huw Jenkins," adding with an insolence meant to provoke. "An untrained lad will serve me well enough . . . Otherwise, I should have too clear an advantage . . ."

Jed's lips had tightened, as colour had flowed to mottle face and neck, but he had made no reply, save to motion Luc to join him. Huw Jenkins, bewildered and proud, had shambled over to stand beside Jim Parslowe. There was a grin of foolish delight upon his face at being chosen, and no hint of the danger incurred. If Parslowe had named him for his massive strength and obstinacy, then Huw was blessedly unaware of it.

Parslowe had expertly roped the first black ox by its horns, and Huw Jenkins had subdued it with a force and stubbornness exceeding the beast's own. Yet his slowness of thought and movement had earned him victory at a harsh price . . . Sweating, aching, as bruised in spirit as in limb, he had finally achieved his aim, and stood ready to match his opponents, throw for throw.

Sarah, although terrified, had been unable to resist the drama of the man against beast struggle, and had crept, unwillingly, to stand beside Becky in her vigil.

Jed had roped the next ox with deceptive ease, and Luc, too, had acquitted himself well, using skill and agility, as well as brute strength, to secure the beast, that the blacksmith might safely shoe it.

With the second of his attempts, Jim Parslowe had braced himself for action, first glancing complacently at those around him, then curtly ordering Huw Jenkins to stand prepared . . . The lad had driven the iron fork into the earth with a few massive blows of the sledgehammer, ready to hold the ox when safely roped . . . Jed, whose gaze was fixed firmly upon Parslowe's face, had seen him glancing involuntarily towards Sarah, a smile of malicious satisfaction upon his thin face . . . Then, in a split second, the rope Parslowe threw about the ox's horns had slipped its hold, and the creature, wild with a fury of terror, had turned, snorting, and pawing the earth, then, lowering its head, had charged blindly. At Jed's cry of alarm, the watchers had scattered; all save Sarah, who stood directly in its path, rooted to the earth with shock. She heard the angry snorting of its breath, the thunderous pounding of its hooves upon the turf, and saw the rolling whiteness of its eyes . . . but was powerless to move or make sound. Huw Jenkins, with a scream of anguish, had moved ponderously towards her, to protect her bodily, but Luc was swifter, and had hurled him aside, to take full force of the impact. Even as the enraged ox caught him a blow with its broad head, hurling him to the ground, Jed, with one of the ox-fellers, had thrown ropes around the animal's horns and, with the aid of the drovers, had gradually subdued it . . . Luc, who had been trampled, then thrown clear, by its powerful hooves, lay motionless . . .

Sarah had run to him and fallen to the grass beside him, lifting his head, cradling him in a terror of guilt and despair, rocking to and fro in her anguish. It was Jed who had gently lifted her from him, and Becky, white-faced, who had led her compassionately away.

The blacksmith who owned the forge had sent two of his apprentice lads scurrying to the undertaker's for a stretcher of poles and hide. Then, they had carried Luc to the blacksmith's house adjoining the smithy, and set him upon the box-bed aside the fire . . . Luc had remained insensible throughout, and Jed had declared that none would proceed to Faringdon until the extent of his injuries was known . . . Sarah, who felt that she alone was to blame had elected to nurse him, and Becky had insisted upon keeping watch all night beside her at Luc's bed . . . There had been no mention of seeking the aid of a physician. Such indulgences were beyond the pockets of the poor . . . Even had they, somehow, been able to raise the shillings for his services, there was no physician in the surrounding villages, and the one at Farnham reluctant to venture so far afield, and to the humbler cottages. A passing drover would scarcely be thought worthy of a visit, or a fee.

Jed, who had seen many drovers injured, or crippled, at their trade, feared that Luc's unconsciousness was the result of some contusion to the brain. He bitterly regretted that he had risen to Parslowe's jibes and taunts, and had become an unwitting accomplice in the accident . . . if accident it proved to be. It grieved him most to see Sarah's wretchedness and self-reproach, and it was in a mood of seething anger that he finally rejoined the drovers and their lads at the local inn.

All were chastened by Luc's misfortune, but Huw Jenkins was past consoling, counting himself responsible for all that had occurred. He had failed . . . He was stupid and clumsy, and had disgraced himself beyond redemption . . . Jed Perkins would surely tell him to go . . . that he had no more use for him . . . He would be forced to find his way alone, and none would again employ him . . . He wept unashamedly, his moon face ugly in its hurt, eyes swollen and raw-rimmed. Jed, who had entered the tavern, would have gone to the lad to soothe his misery, and tell him he was not to blame, but Jim Parslowe was there before him. He had dealt the boy a vicious blow across the face, ordering,

"Stop that snivelling, else you will feel the full weight of my fist! Then you will have something to snivel about! You are a fool, Jenkins . . . a useless incompetent!"

Before he could strike him again, Jed had grasped his upturned arm, imprisoning it like a vice. His voice, when he spoke, was equally cold and inescapable.

"Damn your eyes, Parslowe! If you so much as raise a hand to him again, I swear that I shall deal you blow for blow! Do not revenge yourself on the lad for your own incompetence and carelessness . . . You are to blame, and no other!"

Parslowe had wrenched his arm free; the look he cast at Huw Jenkins so malevolent and filled with disgust that the lad had shuffled out, head bent, too abject to stay . . . There was a silence in the inn so intense that it was palpable, as the two adversaries faced each other, wordlessly battling for supremacy. None had ever seen Jed so icily venomous, and it was Jim Parslowe who first dropped his gaze, mumbling resentfully,

"An accident . . . no more . . ."

"If any man here could prove it otherwise . . ." Jed's voice was so low that Parslowe alone could hear it, "then you would be lying in Luc's stead . . ."

Parslowe, face flushed, had walked abruptly away, delving into his breeches pocket, and insolently tossing a handful of small coins upon the bar where the young ox-feller stood. His voice was carelessly contemptuous.

"My repayment of that . . . small debt which is owed you . . . payment of your worth," The ox-feller had simply turned, forcing aside the blacksmith's restraining hand, and Jed was afeared that it was Parslowe who would be felled, with the brutal finality he deserved. With a dismissive sweep of his hand, the ox-feller had sent the coins hurtling to the sawdust of the floor, saying quietly,

"I am paid for felling oxen, sir, not harmless women . . . or honest men . . . You may keep your pence. I would sooner be handling beasts of the field than human carrion . . . Their filth can more easily be washed away . . ."

He had returned to his ale, and soon the tavern was filled again with murmured talk. Jed had walked outside then, and brought Huw Jenkins back with him, speaking to him with patience, and setting a tankard of ale in his awkward hands, and the lad had been innocently delighted to find a hoard of small, unclaimed coppers at his feet.

CHAPTER 14

In the stone-flagged kitchen of the blacksmith's cottage, Becky and Sarah had kept quiet vigil. Luc had stirred occasionally, as if trying to break that membrane which imprisoned him, sealing him from sight and sound. Once, when Sarah had bent over him, to apply a vinegar-soaked cloth to cool his brow, his eyes had opened wide. Yet they had held neither recognition, nor even puzzlement, blank as the eyes of the newborn, or the newly dead . . . Without, the early morning air grew chill, but the kindly blacksmith had built the fire high with logs and turf, and the thick stone walls held out the dankness of the rising mists . . . Despite her efforts to stay awake, the warmth of the fire had caused Becky to yawn, then doze, sitting upright in the oaken settle in the inglenook . . . Sarah could neither relax nor sleep, although they had promised to take turn and turn about at nursing Luc . . . There was a tenseness in her waiting; a desperation such as she had never known . . . Sarah would willingly have forced her own warm flesh and blood into his, to quicken his coldness of flesh, set breath to his lips, given life itself to restore his own . . . She could no longer deny, even to herself, how deeply she loved him . . . How cruel, then, that she should be the cause of his dying; how strangely ironic if he, who felt nothing for her, should have given his own life to save hers. If Luc should die, then her life would hold nothing . . . No! More terrifyingly still, it would hold remorse and grief of loss; a future made sterile by the past . . .

Sarah had bent to touch the curve of Luc's jaw, and, knowing herself unseen, caressing it with the tenderness of a lover. The flesh of his cheek was wet with her foolishly shed tears, and she shamefacedly soothed them away with her fingertips, then impulsively dried them with a kiss.

Luc had stirred restlessly, and she had instinctively drawn

back, fearful lest he be aware of how easily she had betrayed herself . . .

He seemed nearer, now, to the surface of consciousness; struggling to break through, his movements stronger and more violent. She would have called out to Becky, but Luc was trying desperately to speak, the words, at first, blurred and unintelligible. She knelt beside the box-bed and bent her head low, the better to hear him.

"No, Maman! No, Maman!" the voice was that of a child, shrill, and in terror. "C'est Grandmère et Grandpère! Ils sont morts . . ." There was such a depth of sorrow and pain in his remembrance that Sarah's hand had gone involuntarily to his, enclosing it. Yet her pain was greater, and with it came a revulsion of horror and disbelief . . . Luc was a Frenchman! A spy, even! No emigré would need to hide himself cravenly behind the identity of another, repudiating the past. Those who had fled the Revolution were looked upon with sympathy, and might declare themselves with pride . . . Bonaparte was the enemy . . . Dear God! What was she to do? Her every instinct was to betray him for what he was . . . Her own brother was missing on the battlefield, brutally slaughtered even, by the French . . . She would be betraying not only herself, but David, should Luc stay free . . . And how many others might she send, unknowingly, to their deaths? There was such a confusion of emotions within her that she could neither think nor withdraw her hand from his.

"Sarah?"

Becky had awakened with a cry, and Luc's eyes had opened too, to focus enquiringly upon Sarah. The doubts and bewilderment upon her face were reflected, at first, upon his own. Then came realisation; the certainty that he had betrayed himself, that Sarah knew . . . They had stared at each other for a long moment in an agony of indecision. Luc's eyes had been silently pleading, her own accusingly cold.

Then she had removed her fingers from Luc's, exclaiming with determinedly brittle lightness,

"See Becky! Luc is awake! We need have no more fears for his safety . . ."

Even as she spoke the words, her voice cracked, then treacherously died away . . . Becky, believing that it sprang from an anguish of relief, put a comforting arm about her shoulders. Sarah could not bear to look towards Luc. She had committed herself to his protection; openly declared herself. Yet it brought only a weight of grief at what had been sacrificed . . . Becky, sensitive to the heightened tension between the pair, was at a loss to know how best to heal the awkwardness.

"Sarah has not left your side," she ventured. "She has nursed you most devotedly," adding tartly, to hide her real concern, "You are a brave man, Luc . . . foolishly so."

Foolishly so . . . The words echoed in Luc's mind as accusingly as in Sarah's. He had saved her life, and now she held the absolute power to save his. It should have bound them more closely together; united them. The reality was that it forced them more cruelly apart, and neither could confess it to the other, or give reason why it should be.

It had taken two full days for Luc's strength to return enough for him to force himself from his bed, and into a fireside chair. He was bruised and battered in flesh and bone, and ached in every raw nerve . . . Becky and Sarah had protested most vehemently that he was foolish to exert himself so, but he was deaf to both anger and persuasion . . . His one fear was that he could not reach the safe house in Cirencester in time, for Jed still had business to transact in Farrington . . . Luc could not trust Jim Parslowe to go in his stead, since he did not know how deep the drover's involvement with the French lay . . . Political conviction, or money alone? There was no way of ascertaining without revealing too much of himself. He had briefly considered confiding in Jed, whose integrity and discretion he could trust, but would not commit him to the danger such knowledge must inevitably bring.

Jed, seeing Luc's agitation at holding them back, had tried to reassure him. The men and boys had found work piecemeal upon the farms, and the women, too, in local gardens and houses, he had patiently explained. There was no real urgency to return, for they were grateful for those few extra shillings they could earn, to help them through winter. Yet Luc was adamant. He would hinder them no longer. They must set off as soon as ever they were able, and he with them . . . Not all Becky's and Sarah's remonstrances, nor Jed's measured pleas, would dissuade him.

Jed Perkins was no fool, and knew that some fiercer need impelled Luc, although he doubted his strength to walk with them, even at the women's less taxing pace . . . Yet he gave his consent. They would leave upon the morrow, he promised, yet not at dawn, but in early afternoon . . . that the company might give notice to those who employed them, and collect the wages earned . . . Luc was aware that it was but a ploy to save him from humiliation upon his first day's march, but was grateful for Jed's kindness. "He is not yet fit enough . . ." Sarah had objected abrasively, for she did not wish to be deprived of Luc's nearness, and his dependence on her care. The closeness enforced upon them by his sickness had brought her pleasure and pain, but to relinquish such intimacy would be past enduring.

Jed said, with quiet authority,

"It is best that we leave. Luc's injuries are mending . . ." Then, seeing Sarah's dismay, he rebuked more sharply than he intended, "We may all thank God, most devoutly, that no bones were broken, and that he escaped goring by the ox . . . Such piercing wounds fester and grow corrupt, and are slow to heal . . ."

Becky was quick to murmur agreement, and Sarah's response was as fervently made.

"Such piercing wounds are slow to heal . . ."

Jed's kindly spoken words, Sarah felt, might as honestly have been said of her.

At midday upon the morrow, all were assembled without the smithy, and eager to depart. The blacksmith, as generous in kindness as in flesh, had staunchly refused all offers of payment, first from Jed, and then from Luc himself.

"I take payment only for labour at my craft," he protested firmly, "Not for helping those in distress . . . 'tis privilege and duty to be neighbourly, as the Good Book says . . . Let that be an end to it!"

Yet he had suggested a transaction which suited Jed well, and did not injure his own dignity. When the smith had bidden farewell and safe journey to Becky and Sarah, whom he had grown to admire and hold in affection, he accompanied them without the cottage.

144

Luc, walking behind them, and, to his shame, feeling weak and light-headed still, had, at first, protested volubly about the pony and ill-made farm cart awaiting him . . . Jed had been adamant. Luc might take his choice; either to climb within, or find his way alone. If they were to make up those days lost, he insisted gruffly, then they must travel without further hindrance . . . He would brook no more argument.

The blacksmith, seeing the set stubbornness of Luc's jaw, and Jed's equal determination to render him aid, whether he wanted it or not, intervened to prevent open conflict. "The terms have not yet been agreed for the hiring," he reminded curtly. "'Tis not charity, but business, we discuss, and the carrier's livelihood! You had best make up your minds, and now, for time and money is awasting!"

Luc had immediately insisted upon paying the carrier's fee to transport their goods and chattels to Faringdon, and his own passage beside them on the cart, should need arise or, indeed, for any made weary or footsore by the road . . . The bargain was sealed, and Jed made no objection. He had simply smiled, and shaken the blacksmith's hand, declaring warmly that it would please him to do business with him when next they passed that way.

Before Luc had time to consider, or demur, the blacksmith had raised him powerfully to the perch beside the carrier, wishing him,

"God speed upon the way, sir, and deliverance from further hurt." Luc had replied courteously, for it was not his nature to do otherwise.

"'Twas a kindness well done, sir, and without giving offence," the smith's apprentice said as the cart moved off.

"A man's dignity is as easily wounded as his flesh," the blacksmith said, entering the forge, "and harder to mend, lad, than iron at an anvil . . . I hope 'twill bring him some comfort, for 'tis certain that old cart will not!"

The ragged little procession of drovers, their women, and their lads, had made its leisurely way to Farrington, with Luc fretting and jolting uncomfortably upon the cart. The carrier was a dour, introverted fellow, with more care for the road ahead than for idle chatter. Luc had eventually given up all efforts to cultivate his company, for the strain of making laborious

145

conversation grew more painful than the ride. They had met with many small bands of drovers upon the way, urging sheep, cattle and hogs along the drifts, for there were markets aplenty for their stock from Michaelmas through until Christmastide . . . There was a warm companionship of the road between such drovers and others of their kind, and Luc was glad to clamber down to hear their news and cheerful banter, and to break bread with them in some nearby tavern, or sprawled upon the grass. Often, Jed and others bought pitchers of milk from the women accompanying the herds, for it was warm and fresh-tasting, and made the vendors a few precious coppers to squander upon a pedlar's hoard or at the next fair.

To Sarah's extreme chagrin, and Luc's amusement, it was she who was forced to ride passenger beside him upon the cart. The drovers sedulously avoided the coaching roads, unwilling to pay the high tolls demanded at the toll-houses, or suffer the delays and inconvenience to their beasts . . . The drovers' highways were poor, and awkwardly surfaced, made doubly hazardous by erosion from hooves and weather . . . Sarah's bootsoles had worn thin, and tiredness had caused her to stumble, twisting her ankle clumsily. At first, angry with herself, she had limped on, ignoring the distress it caused her, and refusing all Becky's pleas to rest awhile, or, at least, to support herself upon the tailgate of the cart. When, at last, they came to a brief halt beside a stream, Sarah had painfully eased off her boot, to cool her foot in the water . . . It had throbbed and ached, its flesh reddened and swollen grotesquely, and, despite her efforts, she could not squeeze it back into her boot, even when, in disgust, she tore out the leather lacing . . . Jed, quelling her argument, had lifted her bodily onto the cart, to Becky's secret delight and amusement.

"I hope, sir, that I do not incommode you . . ." she said stiffly to Luc.

"On the contrary, ma'am. I can scarce contain my pleasure at such . . . salubrious company."

His tone was gently mocking.

"I shall descend as soon as ever I am fit, sir. You may depend upon it."

"As I, ma'am."

They sat in silence for a time, then Luc ventured gently, "We are not enemies, Sarah . . ."

"Are we not? Then I admit I was under a misapprehension, sir . . ." Her eyes had filled with scalding tears, and she had blinked them back angrily, defying them to fall and further humiliate her.

"You are in pain, ma'am?" He asked in troubled concern.

"Yes, I am in pain . . ."

They knew it was not of physical hurt she spoke, but something deeper.

"I relied upon your kindness, not long since, Sarah . . ."

His words were hesitant, for he was unsure of what he could safely admit. "I trusted you then, and took your . . . care with gratitude. Will you not, now, surrender your care and your trust to me?"

His eyes were gravely questioning, his need raw, and Sarah could not bear to see him so painfully humbled.

"Yes, I shall trust you, Luc . . . whatever comes."

The promise was made, and she knew it to be binding. He had taken her hand, and drawn her closer to him, so that her head rested comfortingly upon his shoulder.

She thought that she felt the gentle pressure of his lips upon her hair, but could not be sure. She could be sure of nothing save that she loved him, and believed him as incapable of treachery as of deliberate hurt. She would seek no explanation, ask nothing of him that he could not give. For the moment, his nearness was enough.

Becky, glancing towards them with ill-concealed satisfaction, had said to Jed Perkins,

"It seems that Luc is a-courting Sarah, Jed . . ."

He had followed her gaze, observing sceptically, "There is more to courting than fussing a maid . . ."

"And how would you know?" she demanded pertly. "You are as much a stranger to polite courting as . . . an Anglesey ox!"

He had laughed delightedly, demanding slyly, "And what nonsense did that gypsy sell you for your silver, at Farnham Fair?"

"She said that I could never hope to be a great lady, nor rest secure by my own warm hearth . . .'tis my future to walk the drovers' roads, and seek no more of life . . ."

Jed's ingenuous face had grown pained as he blurted with awkward compassion,

147

"It is not always the way of things, Becky. Do not take on and fret . . . There is many a man able, aye, and willing, to prove her wrong, depend on it!"

"I do, Jed," she said innocently, "I do . . . And if that is my fate, as she foretold, then I will not take on, nor fret, but accept it bravely."

Despite their injuries, Sarah's and Luc's interlude as prisoners upon the carrier's cart had brought relaxation and pleasure to them both. Luc had assiduously set out to amuse her, and to offer her distraction, and in doing so had surprisingly found a palliative for his own ills. Their shared laughter had been easy and spontaneous, their companionship close. Each had delightedly found the other to be intelligent, articulate, and physically pleasing . . . and yet, there was always some hidden barrier of reserve. Their exploration of minds and emotions excluded the past. It was a dangerous country, and not to be shared.

They had stayed only briefly at Faringdon, that Jed might deliver the letters entrusted to his care, and to collect the goods from the saddlery . . . Sarah's and Luc's quitting of the farm cart, and taking to the road, had brought good-humoured jesting and bawdiness from the rest, and Becky had them all convulsed with mirth at her wicked parody of their limping and staggering gait . . . Huw Jenkins alone had seen no humour in her act, frowning, and settling himself beside Sarah as friend and guard. She had been touched by the tenderness with which he watched over her, eager, always, to smooth her way and offer protection. Huw was, she had learnt, all devoted child-like affection; his simplicity of mind trapped in a shambling awkwardness of body. It seemed that they lacked coordination, were somehow independent, one of the other, as if a child's brain had been thrust haphazardly into an adult's flesh, and remained bewildered . . .

Luc, too, had grown fond of the lad, and while not overtly protecting him from the taunts and petty cruelties of others, which would have spurred them to more, watched over him unobtrusively. He made sure that Huw earned his pence, not merely at the most menial and degrading tasks, and that his share of food and ale was fair and equitable.

Huw, in turn, accepted Luc with a dog-like devotion, obedient to his command, eager always to gain his approval. Luc, who knew that, sooner or later, he must leave the drovers, would confidently have left Sarah to the lad's care, certain that he would have defended her with his life, if need arose. Yet Luc knew, as certainly, that it was Sarah who would have ended in caring protectively for Huw, making decisions, planning the course the future must take.

It was only after calculating the risks involved, and much anguish of mind, that Luc decided to confide in Jed, and to place Sarah in his keeping. Jed had listened carefully, showing neither censure nor disbelief, then had promised that he would do as Luc asked. He would, he promised, matter-of-factly, see that Sarah was never in want of friendship or aid. He owned a small farm, little more than a holding, at Stormy Down, in Glamorgan . . . Upon Luc's return from France, he had best search for Sarah there, for Jed would offer her home and employment.

"Should I not return," Luc said, "I trust you, Jed, to deliver a letter to one who cares, and will take her as friend and companion . . . A widow, who will treat her with that kindness she deserves . . ."

"The gentlewoman you met at the fair?" Jed hazarded.

Luc nodded, venturing no explanation, save to say, "She works to the same end . . ."

"And Jim Parslowe? How is he involved?"

"I admit, Jed, that I do not know." Luc admitted.

"Then do not trust him. He is a vindictive man . . . ruled by love of self, and money . . . He would sell you, and any other, for gain . . . Be warned!"

"Yet you employ him, Jed?"

"This once, and no more . . . 'twas he who came seeking me out, at the Autumn hirings . . . I confess I can find no fault with his labour, for he is skilled and willing . . ." Jed shook his head regretfully, "but there is resentment and disharmony wherever he is found. There is a meanness in him, some evil strain, as in a rogue beast, you understand? Bad blood, which can never be bred out."

"You will see that Sarah comes to no harm from him, Jed?"

"I will." Jed hesitated. "And Sarah, Luc? Would you have me tell her the true reason for your flight . . . make promise, or explanation?"

"No. It is better not."

There was a silence between them, until Jed said quickly, "It will grieve her, Luc . . . of that I am sure. She is not one to give affection lightly."

"Nor I." Luc's voice was low, barely audible, "but I can offer her nothing, explain nothing. I cannot even give promise of my return. Would it not be cruel to ask her to wait? Has she not already known loss, and suffering, enough?"

"I do not know," Jed admitted with honesty. "I do not know, Luc, if it would grieve her more to feel herself abandoned as worthless, or to lose all with your death. She will need help and affection, you may be sure . . ."

"And you will give it to her?"

"Aye, readily, for what it is worth . . . but I know little of women and their needs . . ." he paused, "Becky, now, Becky Hendry is kind, for all her posturing and heedless ways. She has a loving heart . . . She will know how best to give comfort."

"I fancy," Luc said with conviction, "that Becky would willingly give such comfort to you . . . if you would allow her . . ."

"Nonsense!" Jed's denial was brisk, his cheeks suffused with warm colour. "'Tis only her foolish prattling way. Becky teases and flirts with all, without meaning or serious intent. I am not a fool, Luc! I do not deceive myself!"

Luc said quietly, "No, you are not a fool, Jed. You are a man of integrity. A good friend. A man to be trusted."

Jed had made no false protestations, but had answered with honesty, "I thank you for that, Luc, for I know it was not lightly spoken, but truly meant. 'Tis plain to me that you are a gentleman bred. I am a working drover, poor, and rough-spoken . . . Yet a man's wealth lies, not in what he owns, or wears, but in what he is. You are a true gentleman . . . one who treats *all* with natural courtesy . . . aye, even poor Huw Jenkins, and never diminish their sense of worth. I am pleased to call you 'friend'."

Raw with embarrassment at revealing his feelings so openly, Jed had grimaced, blinked rapidly, then held out his broad, work-calloused hand, and Luc had taken it gratefully in his own. It was the longest speech that Jed had ever been known to make, and Luc would remember and cherish it, every last word.

CHAPTER 15

Upon the outskirts of Cirencester, Luc had paid the carrier handsomely for his services, and then dismissed him. So unexpectedly extravagant was the tip that the poor fellow, who was by nature taciturn, was rendered incapable of any speech at all . . . A fervent handclasp and broad smile had served to convey his gratitude as, with a tug at his forelock and a nod and grunt to all about him, he had set the horse and farm cart back upon its way.

Luc's leave taking of Sarah had been scarcely more auspicious. He had offered no explanation, made no mention of when he might return. He had paid her no overt attention, but treated her with that same casual good humour which he showed to all . . . Sarah, in turn, had schooled herself to make her farewells equally light and unemotional. Jed, alone, sensed that undercurrent of repressed emotion which swirled beneath the surface calm; dangerous, unseen. Luc, who cared for her safety as much as his own, could not openly declare himself, nor beg her to wait for him. Sarah, beset by puzzlement and hurt, thought him coldly uncaring: Luc plainly could not trust her. She had been foolish, she scolded herself, for believing that she meant more to him than any other of the drovers' women. His life and interest lay elsewhere. Memory of the gentlewoman at the fair pricked her with jealous rage, adding shame to her sense of rejection . . . She would not further demean herself. She had humiliated herself enough. He was a conceited, overbearing and odious creature, vain and self-centred! How could she have been deceived by him? If he never returned, it would not distress her. It would be a reprieve, a deliverance even . . . Yet, as she watched Luc walk away, all her brave efforts to convince herself died. She was bereft . . . as torn and purposeless as a drifted leaf, life as brittly ended.

Jed, seeing Sarah standing proudly dry-eyed and erect, did not go to her, for he was aware of Jim Parslowe's slyly triumphant gaze . . . Jed would have motioned to Becky to move to comfort Sarah, unobtrusively, but there was no need. In an instant, she was beside her of her own volition, all brisk cheerfulness and affectionate warmth. Oh, but she was a kind and loving creature, and loyal, Jed thought gratefully, as they continued upon their way. As if he had spoken the words aloud, Becky turned, and smiled at him. The morning sun had burnished her hair to a red-gold cloud, and seemed to have entered her flesh itself, glowing from within, brilliant and translucent as a flame . . . Her beauty caught at Jed's throat with an actual physical pain, and the smile he gave her in return was wryly twisted before it died away . . . But the yearning persisted stubbornly; unquenchable, promising hurt . . . Jed knew that he loved her. Luc's words about Becky's real feelings towards him returned to his mind, insistent, inevitable with every step upon the track . . . True, or false? Mocking, or kindly spoken? Jed would not deceive himself by believing that Becky could care for him, or the harshness of a life spent forever trudging the drovers' roads. She was deserving of better . . .

Luc's thoughts had been scarcely more sanguine as he edged his way along the crowded pavements of Cirencester and across the cobbled streets, dodging the skittering hooves of the horses and the remorselessly clattering carriage wheels. It was a thriving, bustling market town, with all busily intent upon transacting their business, and not averse to thrusting and jostling aside any who hindered it . . . Waggons and farm carts, piled high with vegetables and farm produce, were a constant hazard, and the flocks of noisily bewildered sheep, and the harsh shouts of the drovers, added to the chaotic disorder . . . The stench of the animals' warm droppings and oily fleeces rose pungent upon the cold air, and Luc consoled himself with the thought that in this bucolic company, at least, he would, mercifully, pass unnoticed.

Everywhere there were drovers and farm labourers and the occasional florid faced farmer, appetite and wits sharpened by shrewd bargaining. Many a demurely bonnetted countrywoman anxiously strove to sell her eggs to the highest bidder . . .

The men would take their ease later at the taverns and inns, boasting of their triumphs over their ale, and the apple-cheeked countrywomen would sup reflectively upon their gin, their hands straying occasionally to the coins jingling comfortingly in their pockets. This would be their own, undisputed 'nest egg' reward for those cold risings at dawn, and the darkness fierce with foxes.

Luc's thoughts turned to Sarah and the cold savagery of the life she endured, and his sudden longing for her, and to release her from it was a rawness at his breastbone. He damned the violence of it as he damned the chance which had brought them together. He could not allow himself to love her. He had no emotion to spare for anything save the revenge he had planned for so long. To disseminate it would be an unforgivable weakness – a betrayal. He tried, vainly, to summon to mind the ravaged faces of his grandmother and grandfather, the Chevalier de Riberac, as they gazed helplessly at him from their funeral cart . . . But all Luc saw, as he raised the knocker upon the door of the house he had sought, was Sarah's face, delicately oval, fine-boned, her hazel eyes filled with rejection and hurt. The shattering of the silence as metal struck forcefully upon metal seemed to echo that conflict within himself . . . Then, all was forgotten as the door was abruptly opened, and he was drawn firmly within the house.

The dwelling was as unprepossessing within as without; the cottage, Luc supposed, of some artisan or lowly craftsman. It was carefully chosen for its anonymity, and indistinguishable from all others in the row . . . In such a setting, the arrival of a drover such as he would arouse no interest, stir no memory.

The six men seated at the scrubbed table before the kitchen fire were attired no more elegantly than he, their working clothing grimed and serviceable. They were untidy, and poorly shod, their jowls darkly unshaven, faces sullenly unsmiling. Once Luc might have been deceived and taken them for common labourers upon the farms or roads. Yet, now, he was aware that they acted a charade as determinedly as he . . . Their hands were soft-skinned under their layering of dirt, their faces unburned by winds and weather, their voices, although disguised, cultured. They were gentlemen playing a part as deviously, and with as much at stake as he.

Their catechism had been severe, their questions swift, and well rehearsed, and phrased to trap him. He bore them no ill-will for their efforts, only for their allegiance to 'The Corsican'. He matched their cunning with his own, and believed that, in the end, he had outwitted and convinced them.

Yet he was aware, too, that they had absolute knowledge of him upon every mile of the long, harsh journey from the hulks; his contacts, his injury from felling the black ox, his companions, his forays by day and by night . . . Jim Parslowe, then, was in their hire; a paid spy and traitor . . . It was no more than Luc had expected, and, from the evidence, he believed that he had covered his tracks well, outwitted his enemy. He had no fears for himself, but only for Sarah, Jed, and the others. Parslowe was an ill-natured little reptile, slimy, and swift to strike. His chosen victims were those like Huw Jenkins, defenceless and unsuspecting, their very innocence feeding his savagery. Luc had warned Jed of his suspicions and could do no more. He must rely on his friend's vigilance and discretion to give protection . . . Yet, fear of Parslowe's sly malevolence and revenge intruded, as real a danger to him as he faced his inquisitors as to those he loved. With practised ruthlessness, Luc cast his concern aside, and concentrated upon his present enemy.

Sarah had fallen behind Jed and Becky upon the drift road into Cirencester, grateful to be alone with her own thoughts. Jed had answered, in reply to her insistent questioning, that he did not know when Luc was expected to return, or if he meant to return at all. Concern for her had made Jed unusually surly and abrasive, and he had added curtly,

"'Tis his own life! I am not his keeper! He must do as he thinks fit . . . Let that be an end to it!"

Becky, startled at his vehemence, had glared at him in rebuke, and he had coloured shamefacedly, finding refuge in blustering that he had trouble enough in shepherding those remaining, let alone any straying!

"You women are more trouble than a flock of five hundred Welsh runts!" he had grumbled half-heartedly, "and as foolish and woolly-minded!"

"Then you had best lead, rather than drive us!" Becky had

154

advised pertly. "'Tis the drover's skill and patience which serve best, not temper!"

A smile had touched Jed's mouth, but he had answered firmly,

"A drover does not look to a sheep for instruction, nor intelligence, only obedience . . ."

Becky had erupted into mock wrath, and answered in kind, and Sarah, taking advantage of their bickering, had slowed her pace, to fall behind.

She had little time for self-pity, since Huw Jenkins, sensing, but not understanding, her distress, had ambled forward to walk beside her. So concerned and lugubrious was his plump moon-face, and so awkward his attempts to cheer her, that Sarah could not long remain aloof, and soon they were talking companionably. Their good spirits were further restored by the sight of a flock of geese being driven from a by-way and on to the road before them. The reluctant creatures grew hissing and venomous, their combined cackling and the aggressive flexing of their wings a greater deterrent than the snarls of the dogs which guarded them . . . They were a handsome sight, all proud arrogance and defiance, and the cautious darting and retreating of the dogs which gathered them, and their sly wariness, provided welcome amusement . . . But of greater fascination to Sarah were the strange shoes the geese wore; bizarre stilts to protect their feet upon the roads . . . They were little more than spikes, an inch or more in length, with carefully fastened uppers. Their normal waddling was strange enough, but with the grotesque handicap of sandals, they moved with that comical, rolling gait of sailors, unsteady upon their shore-legs . . . Huw Jenkins, shouting his delight at the spectacle, laughed until the tears ran down his cheeks, clutching his broad belly, choking so fiercely with mirth that Sarah had to thump him hard upon the back to settle his breathing. Indeed, so contagious was his laughter that even the geese's owner joined in the hilarity, as convulsed with mirth as the rest.

It was then that Sarah, who, for safekeeping, wore her precious christening bracelet concealed at her neck, felt its cord snap . . . Her hand went involuntarily to her throat in an effort to save it. Too late. The pretty trinket fell to

155

the roadside, striking upon the cobbles, its delicate tracery of marguerites gleaming gold.

There had been a startled pause, laughter stilled, before Huw Jenkins had bent low, fumbling clumsily to retrieve it . . . It was Jim Parslowe who had snatched it greedily from the lad's hand, his fist closing triumphantly over it. Sarah's eyes were anguished, Parslowe's coldly accusing as he muttered, raising it high that she might not reclaim it,

"Well, what a pretty thing we have here . . . Too pretty, and too valuable, I swear, for a drover's maid to come by honestly . . .!"

Jed, lips tight with anger, had moved towards him, with Becky, taut and white-faced, at his side, but neither had spoken. With the rest of the subdued company, they gazed imploringly at Sarah, willing her to make denial and explanation. Shock and bewilderment showed in her face as, with voice barely audible, she murmured,

"It was come by honestly. It is my own . . . a gift . . ."

"And who would have made a pauper woman such a gift?" his tone was scathing. "Some fine gentleman, perhaps, for favours given? And what did you sell for it, ma'am? Yourself? I'll swear, you made the better bargain!"

Two spots of colour burned high on Sarah's cheeks, and her eyes were bright with anger and unshed tears, as she delivered a blow of sheer hatred to his grinning face. In a moment, he had grasped her wrist, twisting it so fiercely that she cried aloud, tears of pain and humiliation choking her . . . She tried to tear herself free, but she could not. Parslowe's grip stayed vice-like, his eyes insolently mocking, as he taunted,

"We would not stoop to thieving!"

"Nor she!" Becky's denial was fierce. "Let her explain . . .!" Becky's eyes were pleading, her voice uncertain. "Sarah . . .?"

"She will explain to the justices!" Parslowe exclaimed, "and plead before them . . . like any other accused . . ." His face pressed sickeningly close to Sarah's, his warm breath foetid upon her cheek, as he spat out the words vindictively, "You may plead that you are a whore, Miss . . . a slut, and a common thief . . ."

"That is enough!"

Jed had stepped menacingly towards him, fist raised to strike, but Huw Jenkins was before him, delivering him such a blow that Parslowe rocked upon his feet, before dropping to his knees, mouth gaping blood.

He had been rendered near senseless by the force and ferocity of the blow, but none moved to aid him.

It was Luc's voice which unexpectedly broke the silence, as he stepped forward from the edge of the group where he had been hidden from view, and had taken the bracelet from Parslowe's unresisting hand. He had studied its delicate tracery, face unreadable, then looked at Sarah searchingly for a long, anguished moment. His tone, when at last he spoke, was coolly authoritative.

"It is a pretty enough trinket . . . but not of gold . . . some base metal . . . Useless. Valueless. I do not doubt it was bought for pence from some pedlar's tray, or a fairing stall . . ."

The listening company, anxiety released, found escape in laughter, wave upon wave of it. Parslowe, still dazed, a bruised swelling already darkening his cheekbone, felt it surge around him, choking, suffocating, drowning him with humiliation . . . It echoed in the bones of his skull, and filled his ears; scornful, raw with derision. To his chagrin, it was the idiot, Huw Jenkins, who laughed longest and loudest of all.

Parslowe had somehow summoned strength enough to rise to his feet, staggering, and wiping his bloodied mouth with the heel of his hand. The scowling glance he cast at Huw Jenkins was malevolent and filled with hatred. Jed, intercepting it, knew that it boded ill for the lad, and determined to watch over him, unobserved, for he did not doubt that Parslowe would take early revenge. He would bully and harass the boy unmercifully, and make him look dull-witted and useless before all. The violence to Huw's confidence would be crueller than the blows he would be forced to bear, and longer lasting . . . Jed damned the ill chance which had brought Jim Parslowe to the Welsh hirings . . . or was it chance? With hindsight, he would have sworn that it was Parslowe who had carefully hand-picked him, each step of the way carefully planned to suit his own purpose . . . He was a mealy-mouthed fellow, vicious and arrogant, a disruptive influence upon all. Normally, Jed would not have hesitated in dismissing him. Yet, now, knowledge of Luc's mission, and suspicion of Parslowe's involvement, stayed his hand . . . Jed sighed loudly, and Becky put a comforting hand to his elbow, eyes questioning.

"We had best be upon the road," he declared, "Time is awasting, and money with it! There will be work and pleasure at Cirencester fair."

He had glanced at the drovers, the women and the lads, and they had closed ranks obediently behind him, shuffling and finding place, their minds already upon the promise of the town ahead . . . Jed's eyes had settled briefly upon Huw Jenkins, huge, childlike, a foolish grin of satisfaction upon his face. Jim Parslowe had taken his allotted place at the head of the company, beside Jed and the drovers, all spurious cockiness and assertion despite his bruised face . . . Jed's gaze lingered longest upon Luc, and upon Sarah, who walked beside him. There was no joyousness in their reunion. What was it, he wondered, that ailed Luc? Some awkwardness at the safe house, perhaps? Some fear of discovery, or of what he knew lay ahead? Certainly his face was a mask of cold anger and suspicion, hiding some intolerable hurt . . . Sarah, in turn, was plainly bewildered, made prickly by resentment and wounded pride. They walked rigidly apart, purposely isolated, anxious lest they accidentally touch . . .

"Dear Lord!" exclaimed Jed in exasperation, "'Tis more like a funeral wake we march to than a fair! I have seen brighter faces on black Anglesey cattle! All this for a piece of . . . useless trumpery! It is beyond all sense and reason! Has the world gone mad, Becky, or have I?"

"No, Jed." her hand crept into his. "You are the sanest man I know!"

"Would you create so over some silly gew-gaw? Some . . . bauble, Becky? Some foolish bracelet or ring?"

"I would value the giver, Jed." Her voice was low.

He looked at her in puzzlement, then, "I'll be damned if you don't show more sense than the plaguey lot of them, Becky!" he approved, and wondered why she laughed with real delight.

Luc and Sarah had walked silently together for a mile or more, each wanting to comfort, or confront, the other, yet not daring to force their emotions into words . . . Sarah held

158

stiffly aloof, shamed lest he think her a thief, and grieved that he did not openly support her. Luc could find no easy way of showing that he trusted her. His mind was in a turmoil; memory excoriating, laying bare . . . He could not question her about the bracelet without either revealing his past, or convincing her that he had no faith in her honesty. Yet, he yearned to know how it had come into her possession. Sarah would not offer explanation, since she believed that he should trust her implicitly. If he could not, then it were better ended.

It was Becky who had moved to heal the wounds they nursed, throwing herself on to the grass beside Sarah as she struggled to eat her rye bread and cheese upon the wayside verge. Luc sat moodily beside her, gazing, unseeingly, ahead in self-imposed isolation from the rest. Sarah had all but choked upon the bread she stubbornly ate, tasting it dry and flavourless as ashes, her throat constricted with angry tears . . . Becky had stretched out a hand admiringly to the pretty golden bracelet which Sarah had retied about her neck, no longer hidden, but worn defiantly now over the bodice of her dress.

"Oh, but it is a pretty thing, Sarah!" she exclaimed impulsively, demanding so ingenuously that Sarah could not take hurt, "How did you come by it?"

Luc, who had seemed abstracted, looked up, face intent, as Sarah blurted defiantly,

"It was a christening gift . . . My own. Given to me by someone who loved me . . . A lady of France, an emigrée . . . for kindness shown."

The tears which threatened now thickened her voice, and Becky would have moved to reassure her, had she not glimpsed Luc's pained disbelief. So still and ashen-faced was he that Becky grew afraid, eyes anxiously searching the crowd for Jed. She did not know what plagued Luc so . . . unless it was fear that Sarah might speak as recklessly to others of her links with the French . . . their sworn enemy. Becky had struggled awkwardly to her feet, looking about her wildly, until, seeing Jed in earnest conversation with one of the drovers' lads, she had made to hurry towards him.

"This . . . lady of whom you speak . . ." Luc's voice was tense, scarcely audible, "What was her name? Tell me her name!"

He had gripped Sarah's arm with such ferocity that she had

cried out in pain, then stood, numbed to silence by his intensity, helpless, even, to wrench herself free. "For the love of God, Sarah! Her name!"

"The Comtesse de Valandré . . . Hélène de Riberac."

Luc had uttered no word, standing so still and bloodless that it seemed he no longer breathed. His eyes were tightly closed, but Becky, poised uncertainly for flight, saw the tears squeezed painfully between his lashes, before she fled, and could, herself, have wept. When she reached Jed's side, and drew him away to make garbled explanation, she turned, and was amazed to see Sarah and Luc in warm embrace, Luc's lips lovingly exploring her cheeks, her hair, her throat, then finding the soft eagerness of her lips.

"By all heaven and the angels, Jed!" Becky exclaimed, "I swear I do not understand."

"Nor will you try! Nor speak of what you heard to any living soul, if you value your safety, and theirs!"

There was such rough urgency in his warning as he glanced involuntarily towards Jim Parslowe and the others that Becky had kept her silence. Jim Parslowe had come swiftly, unheard, to stand beside them, saying slyly to Becky,

"It seems your . . . pauper friend has hidden charms . . . or can it be that . . . useless ornament at her neck which intrigues him so? It might bear closer inspection, for I fancy it has a history as curious as her own."

Becky, despite his goading, refused to be drawn, but,

"Hell and damnation, man!" Jed exploded, fist held menacingly close to Parslowe's bruised face.

"Will you not take telling, man? 'tis ended, and none of your affair!" Parslowe had stared hard into Jed's enraged eyes before saying languidly, "You are right, Jed . . . It is none of my affair."

Surprised into silence, Jed's belligerent gaze had faltered, fists dropping impotently to his sides, as Parslowe had goaded, with sly innocence,

"No more is it yours! I only wonder it stirs such a rage in you."

Jed had shifted awkwardly, fighting to keep control of himself and his tongue, finally blurting, in an effort to divert him, "My rage is because so . . . trivial a thing has led to rancour and blows between my friends . . . drovers upon the roads," adding

160

with wry humour, "You are more pulped and swollen than a windfall plum, and scarcely more handsome. Admit it, Jim. 'tis not worth the aggravation for some useless frippery . . . a tuppenny fairing!"

Parslowe had regarded him stolidly, face expressionless, then turned, and demanded abruptly of Becky,

"And what is your opinion? A useless thing? Valueless? Tawdry, perhaps, and not of gold . . .?"

Becky had hesitated, biting her lip, glancing towards Jed.

"Come, Becky!" Parslowe's tone was purposely bland, "you have inspected it closely . . . held it in your hand, discussed it even . . . What do you say? Did you not notice that it bore some crest? An inscription, within, in some foreign tongue . . .?"

"Why, Jim, 'tis one and the same to me . . ." she said without hesitation, "whether 'tis in English, Welsh, or even Chinese. I can neither read nor write, as Jed well knows." She smiled at Jed radiantly. "It is no shame, nor grief, to me, for I was never learnt by others." She looked at Parslowe challengingly, saying pertly, "I'll wager you could no more read it than I."

Parslowe had coloured dully, but made no reply, his glance straying venomously towards Luc, who stood with his arms encircling Sarah's shoulders. Her face was upturned radiantly towards his, their joyous discovery of each other made plain. Becky had darted a wickedly triumphant look at Jed, pleading with mock humility,

"I beg, Jed, that you will not think the less of me for my ignorance . . . 'tis well known that you are a clever man, who can figure, read and write, as all licensed drovers must, and that you put a value on book learning."

"I put a greater value on honesty, Becky," he responded straightfaced, "for that, like wisdom, is a skill which cannot be taught."

He had stretched out his arm with courteous formality, that she might lay her hand upon his. He made smiling appeal to Parslowe, demanding indulgently,

"Is she not a force to be reckoned with? Becky is as quick-witted as she is handsome, and as kind hearted to all."

Parslowe, scowling, had muttered non-committally, then moved away gracelessly to join the drovers' lads. Huw Jenkins had hitherto felt as little relish for his master's enforced company

161

as the rest, but his stock was high with his fellows because he had struck him in fair contest, and without reprisal. In his naivete, Huw greeted Parslowe with a cockiness verging on condescension, his moon-face as childishly innocent and welcoming as he.

CHAPTER 16

Luc's and Sarah's providential discovery of each other and their shared past seemed to illumine Sarah from within. She was possessed, now, of a glowing beauty, the special radiance of one who loves absolutely, and is loved in return. She exuded happiness. There was no trace of that poor, shorn waif, skinny and ill-used, who had joined the drovers as a carrier's lad. Her flesh had grown rounded and firm upon her womanly body; her skin was burnished and her cheeks warmly coloured by outdoor living. Her cropped hair had grown longer and more luxuriant, framing the oval delicacy of her face. Perhaps the greatest transformation was not the physical, but the inner change wrought in her. Sarah's clear, intelligent eyes held humour now, and an unashamed passion for the flesh of another. She was a woman, confident in love, and for the first time in her young life, she felt protected, aroused, and wholly content.

There had been grief, too, in learning of Luc's past, yet relief from those suspicions which had tormented her from the time of his sickness, when she had learned that he was French . . . His sorrow over her brother's death upon the battlefield was deep, for he had shared a companionship of childhood and growing with him, more binding, even, than her own. To Sarah, ten years removed from him in age, David had been a hero and protector, to Luc he had been a friend. More, a link with the one period of remembered joy in his life, that blessed period of renewal and calm after the terrifying holocaust of Luc's past . . . It had been a friendship of equals, instinctive and undemanding, which had grown and deepened in strength as inevitably as they.

"David and Jonathan," the Reverend Josiah Tudor had affectionately called them, "brothers in life, and only by the violence of death divided . . ."

163

Memories of that good, gentle man, Sarah's father, and her mother's warm generosity, had filled them both with gratitude and regret, and drawn them closer with pity for the courage and suffering of Hélène and Armand de Valandré, whom Sarah would never know . . . Yet it was as though she had always known them, and they, her. The silken strands of the loving dead, spun from their caring, held them. A web. A protection. As if the future had been planned and patterned by them, drawn from their flesh, as Luc and Sarah had been formed from their bone and blood.

It seemed to Sarah that she could never tire of Luc's nearness. She wanted, always, to reach out and touch him to convey her tenderness and joy in him through her fingertips, the joining of flesh. It seemed as if all her former life and teachings had been forgotten. She felt no reserve, no barrier, between them. Had Luc demanded it, she would have given herself to him, wholly, and with gladness. She would have felt neither awkwardness nor shame, only the passionate fulfilment of being possessed in body, as in mind and spirit . . . But Luc, although he loved her fiercely, was obsessed with protecting her from harm. Had he loved her less, he would have taken her, as he had taken other women, with the natural impetuosity and heedlessness of the young. He was passionate and virile, and Sarah aroused in him a need and yearning which his body cried out to fulfil . . . Yet he would not . . . She was deserving of better; a settled home and a future which the dangerous life he had chosen could not provide. He could promise her nothing; offer her nothing, not even the certainty of his return . . . Worse, he could not even confide in her the truth of his mission, for if he did, her danger would be as great as his own . . . He was bedevilled by doubts and uncertainties as never before. For the first time in his life the promise of revenge against those who had killed those he loved failed to stimulate and excite him . . . Excitement lay in Sarah's warmth and soft flesh, and their kisses, and the sweetness and pain of their embraces . . . Once more, he thought with irony, living happiness eluded him, shadowed always by the debt he owed to the dead, and the past.

Jed, seeing Luc's torment, was afraid. A momentary indiscretion, a careless word, could end in tragedy, he knew. Despite his earlier judgement, he had spoken to Luc when they were alone and unlikely to be overheard, counselling him to tell Sarah all. It would be wiser, he said, were Luc to confide in Becky too, for she was a loyal and trustworthy friend, and Sarah might well have need of her generous comforting.

"And will you have need of Becky's comforting, too?" Luc asked shrewdly.

"I shall wed her, if she is awilling," Jed had declared, "for I will find none better to care for me . . ."

"And to love you," Luc had said.

"It is enough that I love her. I would expect no more. She will be a kind and loyal partner, and will know the perils and loneliness of the road . . ." He had broken off, embarrassed at having revealed so much of himself, before adding with painful honesty, "My wife was a good woman, Luc, frugal and methodical in her ways . . . Yet there was no laughter in her, no joy in living, you understand?"

Luc had answered quietly, "But Becky is all gaiety and tenderness, and will love you until the day she dies . . ."

Jed had shaken his head stubbornly.

"I am as stolid and obstinate as those poor beasts I tend . . ." he said simply, "and my life as monotonous as theirs . . . Becky . . . Well, she is all fire and wildness, as colourfully glowing as her hair . . . I would not want to dull her joyousness, Luc, nor bring her regret . . . I am a simple man, awkward and plain with words."

"Then speak to her simply, and plainly," Luc answered, "and as truthfully as you have spoken to me . . . I swear that Becky will not regret it, no more will you . . ."

Jed had nodded, unconvinced.

"I wish I had your certainty," he said, smiling.

"I am certain only of this moment and of what is past," Luc said ruefully, "I dare not think too deeply of what might lie ahead."

Jed's face grew sober with contrition, "The future is new country to us all," he said, "and none can tell with certainty what lies ahead . . ."

"But it will be the kinder for your friendship," Luc declared.

"I pray to God that it may prove so . . ." Jed said. "Yes, I pray that, most earnestly."

General Sir Frederick Loosely, from his vantage point at the library window, had watched with admiration the progress of the elegant carriage across the square. It was, he thought, a sight to delight even the most rheumy and jaundiced eye; so delicate, and finely balanced was the equipage. The finely-bred horses, two perfectly matched chestnut mares, stepped proudly, heads tossing, arrogant nostrils flared, as befitted their superior status. The coachman and the liveried postillion, who descended post-haste to pull down the steps, were, Sir Frederick thought with a wry smile, more aristocratic in appearance than any duke. The general was not, by nature, an abnormally inquisitive man, but a faint hope was stirring that the occupant of the carriage, his unexpected guest, might prove as diverting. He was not disappointed. It was with a cry of genuine pleasure that he left the library, brushing aside the footman who had already reached the door, and welcoming Mary Grantley delightedly. She had not responded to his formal bow and greeting with a modest curtsey, but had flung her arms impulsively about him, setting a kiss upon his withered cheek, eyes bright with affection.

"Oh, my dear child," he had declared without dissembling. "What a rare joy it is to see you! You grow more pretty and more elegant by the hour . . ."

"And more welcome, sir?"

"As welcome as you have always been, and will always be, my dear!" There was no mistaking his sincerity. "You have brought a warmth of sunshine to an old man's winter discontent . . ."

He had relieved Mary of her bonnet and pelisse, and handed them to the footman, then, with an arm encircling her shoulder, had drawn her into the familiar solace of his library. A fire of applewood burned steadily in the hearth, crackling, and giving off darting, aromatic flame . . . Its scent was the familiar essence of childhood distilled; of her growing years with Luc . . . There was a welcome as warm as Sir Frederick's own in the shabbiness of old, loved things. The faded colours of the worn Aubusson carpeting, the smell of old leather and musty vellum pages, the mingled aromas of ink, sand, wax and mellowed wood . . . Here, in this room, her past and childhood lingered still. Nothing had changed . . . Nothing, she thought with a pain of regret, save the two people within, and those so cruelly

166

lost without; Sheldon, David Tudor, and soon, perhaps, Luc himself. She recalled herself with an effort to hear Sir Frederick saying, kindly, "We shall take tea here, Mary, my dear, if you will allow it. It is warm and familiar to me, and eases my old bones. Besides, the drawing room is too austere and solemn a place . . . suited only to dull and formal acquaintanceships . . . You and Luc are all I own of family . . ."

"I would choose no other place . . ." Mary said gently, "and no other companion . . ." save those who cannot be here . . . The words, unspoken, lay heavily between them. Mary added quietly, to salve their hurt, "I have news of Luc."

"You have seen him? He is safe, then?" His dignified, fine-drawn face was suddenly vivid with hope as he exclaimed, "You must tell me all! Every last detail! Was he well? Did he speak . . . kindly of me? How did you meet . . .?" Then, rebuking himself for such unsoldierly lack of reticence, he said shamefacedly, "You will forgive an old man his foolishness, Mary . . . Old age and solitariness are poor companions, and I forget those natural courtesies due to a more welcome guest."

Mary had smiled disarmingly, and leant over and kissed his cheek, saying, "I would be grieved if your concern for Luc were any less, or his for you . . . There are messages and good wishes aplenty, which he taxed me, most fervently, to deliver, sir . . . I shall begin at the beginning, and omit not one single word . . ."

When all was related, retold, and discussed at considerable length, Sir Frederick summoned that tea be brought. Mary presided, and Sir Frederick, seeing her so beautiful and assured, and so graceful in all her ways, saw, as clearly, the child he had known and loved. In the firelight, her hair still gleamed pale gold, but the face, then, had been innocent of hurt, the small hands lifting, with effort, the heavy silver tea-kettle, pride of achievement in every bright glance. She was exquisite now, in her maturity, but how bitter had been the price, how grievous her loss . . . He had sighed involuntarily, and Mary, handing him the delicate cup and saucer, and seeing them tremble in his hands, had felt a compassionate tenderness. How suddenly he had grown old, she thought. Age had crept upon him unnoticed. He seemed smaller; shrunken in flesh, less resolute in spirit, diminished in every way.

"Luc is a man to trust . . ." she said quietly. "A man like you, for you have given him your own values, inspired him with your own courage . . . He will survive, as you have survived . . ."

"I thank you for that, Mary, my dear . . ." His voice had been unsteady. "I do not fear for his courage, only his need for revenge . . . It has crippled him in life . . . I am too old to bear the loss of any life, save my own."

Her face had been stricken with concern, eyes raw with pity, yet she had made no denial, save to murmur, "Yes, the death of another, whether one is young or old, is a grief . . . a burden, almost too heavy to be borne . . . but we bear it, for there is no other course . . ."

He had set down his cup upon the small table beside him, and leaned towards her, to say, with remorse, "You must forgive an old man's insensitivity, my dear, and his thoughtless ramblings . . . I fear the second childhood makes me as heedlessly selfish as the first . . ." He had reached out to take her hand affectionately in his own, and she was grieved by its cold fleshlessness and the frailty of bone. He had looked at her intently, before confessing, "Josiah Tudor's death has been more sorrow than I would allow . . . There are too few friends remaining. The loss of the kindest and most loyal of them . . ." he faltered, "well, it leaves a gap which cannot be measured, or filled."

"It was a shock, sir? . . . Unexpected?"

"No . . . not unexpected." He smiled wryly. "At such an age, every moment is a gift from God . . . one lives on borrowed time." He stated it as a fact, and without self-pity. "Oh, but it is David's young life I grieve; all that bright promise gone to waste . . ."

"He was a good friend to Luc . . . and generous hearted." Mary's voice was low. "As a child, I believed him god-like, invincible . . ." she hesitated before asking, voice troubled, "Was there not a sister, sir; a much younger child?"

"Indeed . . . I have searched for her sedulously, but to no avail . . . Yet, I will not give up, for Josiah's sake, and her own. She is scarcely more than a child, but seventeen years of age, and, by all reports, without money or friendship . . . I believe that she was forced into a pauper's life, and somehow escaped, although none will swear to the truth of it."

"But if she escaped, sir, does not that give you greater hope . . .?"

He shook his head regretfully.

"Escaped where, and to what . . .? She is a young gentlewoman, Mary, as gently nurtured as you. Innocent, and with no means of making her living or countering the harshness of the world . . . No, I have little hope that she will remain untouched by the cruelties of life, and the rapacity of others . . ."

"But you will not cease searching for her?"

"No, I will not cease searching for her . . ." he promised, "but I am old, and time is not infinite . . . no more am I . . ." There was an appeal in his voice, although no further word was spoken.

"You would have me take over your task . . . should you fail?"

"Yes, I would value that above all else, my dear."

"Then you have my promise."

Mary's keen blue eyes looked steadily into Sir Frederick's tired, opaque ones, and he nodded, satisfied as, filled with grateful love for her, as his eyes with tears.

Huw Jenkins was happier than at any time in the whole of his life, for he had been a foundling, farmed out from his earliest days. He had worked for a pittance as a child labourer upon the poorer farms and holdings, and often for no more than a crust of bread, and a place in the hay, beside the animals, where he might lay his head . . . He had suffered blows and curses from those whom he had served for his so-called idleness, for, although his body had grown, he remained slow in wits and comprehension . . . Jed, finding him in one such place, half-starved, and unmercifully beaten, had persuaded his master to part with him for no more cost than a firkin of ale . . . Huw had been bought from slavery into such freedom as he had never known, freedom from hunger and thirst, freedom from rootlessness, and freedom from the gratuitous violence and persecution he had suffered almost from the day of his abandonment upon the steps of the paupers' home . . . Jed had watched over him carefully, and been rewarded by the outcast's loyalty and honest devotion . . . Huw had proved a tireless worker, unresentful, and eager to please. Jim Parslowe, alone, had treated the lad with open contempt, bullying and belittling him before others, making him clumsy and confused . . . Finally, anger had flared high between the two drovers, and Jed had warned Parslowe of the consequences, should he persist. For a time the threat had brought Huw protection from Parslowe's worst excesses, but the lad's spirited defence of Sarah, and the punishment he had so publicly and humiliatingly heaped upon the master drover had been more than Parslowe was prepared to bear . . .

After a hard day's work, Huw had been whiling away a few hours at a tavern beyond Cirencester with the rest of the drovers' lads. He had supped cheerfully at his ale, played a few games of shuffleboard, reluctant to leave the warmth of the inn and the undemanding company, even when the rest had tried to persuade him to depart. It would be a long day's march upon the morrow, they reminded him, and they must rise before dawn to be upon their way. He had remained stubbornly obdurate, insisting that he would follow them later, declaring,

"I am not a child to be tucked abed when it grows dark, nor am I afeared of ghosts and suchlike . . . I am a grown man, and shall come when I am ready."

There had been a spatter of applause and encouragement from Huw's newfound cronies, for he was generous in treating them to ale. Eventually, growing weary of pleading with him, his disgruntled companions had left, with a promise that he would follow them to the barn where they had found comfortable overnight shelter.

He had not arrived. By sunrise, the drovers' lads had grown apprehensive for his safety, and fearful to tell Jed, lest he accuse them of selfishness and deliberate neglect. Huw Jenkins was childlike in mind, and in need of their protection . . . When, finally, shamefaced, they had confessed his absence, Jed, terrified that he had been set upon by footpads, and robbed for his few pence, ordered that a search be made, and all thought of moving on without him be dismissed from mind.

The drovers and their lads, and the womenfolk with them, had hunted for him with growing desperation. They had explored meadows and small copses, barns and outhouses, lofts, and even abandoned pigstys. They had peered behind hedges and into hollows and ditches, searching wherever a man might have fallen, or a body been hid . . .

Sarah and Becky, and others among the women, had been weeping openly, fearful for his life, and Jed and others who were no more optimistic of his chances of survival were unable to pacify them or calm their fears.

At length, it was the landlord of the tavern who had discovered the truth of it from a farm boy, partial to his ale, who had witnessed all . . .

Huw Jenkins had been press-ganged into being a sailor against Napoleon, weeping, and screaming aloud, fighting as he had never fought before . . . Bludgeoned, and barely conscious, he had been dragged violently away, and there was not a man, lad, or woman, among the listening company who did not feel his terror and revulsion, as if it were their own . . . There was no more to be done, and little to be said, save by the farm boy, who had insisted, most vehemently, that Huw Jenkins had known his betrayer, the man who had seen him manhandled so viciously away.

"Did you catch a glimpse of his face, lad?" Jed had demanded with cold anger.

"No, sir, that I did not! I was afeared for myself, and the night was dark, save for the light of a sailor's lantern . . ."

"You saw nothing, then?"

"I saw him spit in the face of the man who had betrayed him, although he was so beaten, and weakened that he could scarce find strength, sir, to raise his head . . ."

"Damn him for his treachery!" Jed exclaimed, "whoever he is, and wherever he be! May God bring him the misery he brought to that poor forsaken creature . . . May he never rest easy, for as long as he shall live!"

Becky had taken Jed's arm, and led him gently away, her own tears still wet upon her cheeks. She had kissed him openly, and held his hand tight, although her own grief was a hard knot within her, and she feared it would never dissolve. She knew, in her own mind, that it was Jim Parslowe who had sold Huw Jenkins back into slavery. Without proof, she could do nothing but watch, wait, and hope to take revenge.

The spirits of the whole company had grown low with the

boy's abduction, and Sarah, although loving Luc, and grateful for his nearness, could not shake off her overwhelming unease and misery. The drovers' progress towards Gloucester had been laggardly, and none had sought work nor found real diversion at the taverns . . . At first, they had tried to follow the roads which Huw's assailants might have taken, but all their enquiries and searching had come to naught, and they had finally been forced to return to the familiar drovers' way, admitting defeat.

The weather, which had been damp and uncertain, with early mists and fog at dusk, turned suddenly cold. The skies grew as leaden as their spirits, and a chill north-easterly wind cut them through. Luc had bought Sarah a cloak of homespun wool from an old cottager at her loom, and Sarah was grateful for its enveloping warmth, as for the affection which had prompted its purchase . . . They no longer slept in the open, for the nights were bitter with frost, and the dew which settled upon their clothing froze as icily as the ponds and streams. The muddy surfaces of the roads became as slippery as glass, slowing their progress, and the vegetables which they bought cheaply for nourishment were locked into rock-hard earth. Even the blackened branches of the trees, stark against the pewter sky, were sheathed in ice, and the few brittle flowers in the cottagers' gardens mildewed and coffined by winter . . .

Even Jed grew fractious and unreasonable, concern for them and pity for Huw Jenkins making him churlishly demanding . . . The women, ill-equipped for the weather in their lighter clothing, shivered, and lagged carelessly behind, fingers and toes so pained and unresponsive that they sometimes wept . . . The few shillings they had so frugally saved were squandered now on mulled ale, or occasional bowls of thick soup at the taverns; as much to thaw their frozen flesh as to fill their empty bellies . . . Their hands, clutching the steaming bowls and tankards, throbbed with exquisite pain. Their nostrils ran; their eyes watered as freely as their mouths. Chilblains blossomed upon their fingertips, swollen and red, ripe as holly berries . . . Always, they were loath to leave the comforting warmth of the hostelries, and each day, the way grew harder, their progress slower . . .

Luc knew where his French masters had commanded him to leave the drovers, at Coleford in the densely wooded Forest of Dean, beyond Gloucester . . . He confided in no-one, not even Jed, for it would have served only to depress them further. Besides, Sarah's increasing nervousness, and despair at his leaving, added to his own, would have served to alert Jim Parslowe to their complicity. Jed and his small band of followers faced hazards enough in surviving hardship and weather. Luc would not add the dangers of revenge, and possible death, to their burdens.

Upon the flat river plain of the Severn, as they neared Gloucester city, the biting chill of the north-east wind suddenly lifted. The sky, which had earlier been heavy with lowering clouds, grew dark. Snow began to fall, soft and misted at first, melting upon their upturned faces, dissolving upon their lips and lashes. Then, inevitably, it began to thicken, falling insistently now, the flakes larger, and soft as curled feathers, as light, and without sound . . . Before them the cathedral rose, grey and leaden as the sky, its soaring, pinnacled tower and its spread of dark stone veiled and softened by snow . . . Its misted beauty was strangely moving and awe inspiring, as if some great primeval beast, cumbrous and seemingly dead, had suddenly stirred from its slumbers . . . Sarah's grip had tightened upon Luc's hand, and she said, glimpsing the teeming streets and sordid alleyways surrounding it,

"How beautiful a thing to be cursed by so much poverty . . ."

"Not cursed, but blessed . . ." Luc answered quietly. "Poverty has built it . . . stone by stone, penny by penny . . . You see in it the face of God, and man's sacrifice and labour. A labour of love . . ."

"But so much beauty and squalor, Luc, side by side . . ."

"As in life, and living . . ." Luc reminded. "They have created a thing of of beauty, Sarah, and one which will endure, to inspire others . . . It is a tribute to God's love, and their own . . . an affirmation . . ."

She looked at him, intent but unspeaking, as he continued quietly, "It is that same affirmation I now make to you. There will be no other, I swear. I shall love you until I die, and beyond the grave itself, if God so wills it . . ."

"As I shall love you . . ." her vow was whispered, softly and gently as the falling snow. It settled in melting flakes upon her hair and eyelashes, and in the folds of her dark cloak, and on

173

the worn, misshapen boots. Ugly. Restricting. Luc saw only the pure beauty of her face, and the love she bore him. He took her in his arms, and kissed her with passion and gratitude, uncaring of those about them. Indeed, for Luc, they had ceased to exist . . . Sarah's lips were cold, and tasted of sweetness and snow, warmth and salt, and he knew that it was her tears he tasted, and the sorrow of a parting which must surely come.

CHAPTER 17

It had taken them a little over a week to reach Gloucester, held up as they were by their unsuccessful search for Huw Jenkins and the inclemency of the weather.

Becky had told Jed of her fears, angrily insisting that Jim Parslowe was responsible for alerting the press gang, and demanding that he be dismissed. Jed, whose suspicions were equally aroused, had vainly tried to calm and reason with her, declaring that there was no proof of Parslowe's active involvement in, or, indeed, knowledge of the affair.

"You cannot openly accuse him, Becky!" Jed had remonstrated.

"And why not, may I ask?"

"Because right is on his side . . ."

"Right! What right is there in abducting a man? In dealing him violence, and wrecking his life, as that poor, simple wretch, Huw Jenkins's life has been . . .?" Her eyes had been brimming with unshed tears, her mouth trembling, and Jed would dearly have loved to take her in his arms and comfort her, but he steeled himself to say, sharply, "He would simply call you a mischief-maker, and a liar, Becky. He would deny all knowledge of the affair . . ."

"'Tis not 'an affair'," she cried vexedly, "'tis a crime, let us be straight upon it! Are you afraid of him?" she taunted, "afeared that he might deal you a blow?"

"Damn it, Becky!" Jed had exclaimed indignantly, "I am afeared of no man, nor of the truth, as well you know! If I *am* afeared, 'tis because I would not see you humbled, and made a laughing stock! Parslowe is a vindictive man, never doubt it . . . It would please him to make you grovel!"

"Grovel! Grovel did you say? It seems to me, Jed, that it is you who are simple-minded, not that poor benighted drover's lad! 'Tis a pity they did not pressgang *you* into being a sailor! I could wish there was an ocean between us, for I do not think highly of those who so cravenly forsake their true friends."

Jed had stared at her, shocked and outraged by the unfairness of her charge, unable to trust himself to make reply.

"See!" she persisted triumphantly. "You do not deny it! Cannot! Well, Jed Perkins, *I* shall not forsake him, nor rest until he is found."

With a defiant toss of her bright hair and a shrug of her shoulders, she was away into the snow, and escaping he knew not where . . . Becky had no clear plan in mind, but during their altercation, she had glimpsed Jim Parslowe lingering slyly, then slipping surreptitiously away, believing himself unseen . . . She would follow him, and find proof of his treachery, whatever dangers it involved.

Jed, seeing her disappearing so impulsively into the swirling snow, felt a cold fear. She was a damnably volatile and infuriating creature, he knew, but the truth was that he loved her, and could not let her go alone . . . Becky was courageous and totally unpredictable, and anger would rob her of what little caution she possessed . . . Determinedly, he made to follow her.

Becky, barely able to see Jim Parslowe's shrouded figure for the violently thickening flakes, was already feeling afraid. She regretted the rashness which had made her speak so cruelly to Jed, and regretted even more the foolishness which had driven her to pursuit . . . Jed had been sensible and restrained, despite her stridency and the accusations she had made against him, too shameful to recall . . . She could scarce see her hand before her face, much less be sure that the blurred shape ahead was Jim Parslowe . . . She was lost . . . irrevocably, lost, and would never be able to return to the safety and protection of Jed and the drovers . . . She was a hot-headed fool! An imbecile! God, alone, knew what dangers lay ahead of her from footpads and strangers. A woman alone was fair game for rogues or ruthless pimps, who would sell her into whoredom . . . and if they did, it was no more than she deserved! She was a fool, and an ingrate! Jed was well rid of her . . . She began to cry, quietly at first, then with great gulping sobs . . . the only sound in the deadened, snow-filled air . . . Should she turn

176

back? Struggle on? Her flesh and brain were cold-numbed. She could no longer feel, nor reason . . . They would find her body frozen, lifeless, in the drifted snow, and bury her in a pauper's grave, uncoffined, and without a winding sheet, with none to mourn, or even remember . . . Yet, would that be crueller to bear than never setting eyes upon Jed again, or meeting the wrath of Jim Parslowe when he discovered that she shadowed him . . .?

Suddenly, without warning, her footfalls deadened by the snow, she chanced upon him, standing irresolutely before an unwieldy spread of buildings, with massive, iron-hung gates. Becky had pressed herself against the rough bark of a sycamore tree, scarcely daring to breathe, or even to peer, terrified, around it . . .

What manner of place was it? she wondered. Some institution, certainly; perhaps a poorhouse or foundling home, a prison, even . . . Jim Parslowe, with a swift, furtive glance about him, and thinking himself unobserved, entered the courtyard, and halted briefly at some small wooden messuage, or shed . . . Becky, intrigued enough to lose all sense of danger, had crept from her hiding place, and pressed her hands to the iron-spiked railings, the better to peer within . . . The flakes of snow were falling more heavily now, large, and soft as curled goose-feathers. The forms she saw were blurred, greyly indistinguishable, scarce recognisable as living. Even as she stared, and tried to make sense of what she saw, an arm clasped itself around her waist in an iron grip, the hand upon her mouth so hard-pressing that she felt the warm saltiness of blood as her teeth pressed into her lip . . . More than anything, she felt a terror more weakening than any she had known . . . Becky was unable to cry aloud, unable, even, to move, for her limbs were paralysed . . .

"Becky!" the name was whispered urgently. "It is I, Jed! No! Do not cry out, nor turn suddenly . . . just come with me, quietly . . . without argument!"

His fear had communicated itself to her, and she did as he begged, feet stumbling and slithering in the drifted snow as he dragged her with him. When they were finally safe, Jed had abruptly halted, and released her hand, chafing it in his own to ease its frozen rawness.

"What was that place, Jed?" she asked. "Where was Jim Parslowe going? What doing? I do not understand . . ."

"This is a garrison town, Becky. The soldiery and militia are there . . . 'tis their barracks he seeks . . ."

"But why, Jed? What business would take him there?"

"Treachery, Becky. He means to inform upon Luc . . . to name him an escaped French prisoner. They will hunt him down, and kill him if needs be . . . We must return and warn him, see him safely away . . ."

"But the snow, Jed! How will Luc escape? He will not dare seek shelter . . . He cannot go!"

"He must . . ." said Jed with cold certainty. He had taken her arm and forced her onwards . . . Becky's feet were wet from the drifted snow which surged into her boots, and the sodden hem of her dress had chafed her legs to bare flesh . . . The cold easterly wind had stretched her face into a mask, her tears frozen to ice upon her cheeks . . . The pain of hurrying was almost too intense to bear, and Becky ached in every muscle and nerve, yet she made no murmur . . . Half blinded by snow, and with all sound deadened, she suffered Jed to lead her into the terrifying, alien landscape, trusting to him, as Luc must learn to trust . . .

Luc, Sarah, and the rest of the company had remained in shelter in a disused coach house at one of the drovers' taverns while awaiting Jed's return. It was thick-walled and dry, and the landlord, from whom they had purchased their ale and their victuals, had offered them use of his tinder box, and spared them some hog's fat candles to provide them light. None questioned why Jed had hurried away, although his strident argument with Becky had been smilingly remarked. It was the common opinion that he had gone to make his peace with her, and to pay whatever recompense was demanded. It was plain that poor Jed was besotted with her. Becky Hendry, as everyone knew full well, was as tempestuously unpredictable as the weather, and as impossible to control . . . It was not the blizzard which would prove hazardous to Jed, but Becky. As a master drover, he was a man of sound common sense, and experienced beyond the ordinary. He had knowledge of beasts, and was skilled in subduing them . . . Of women, he knew less than nothing . . . It was Becky who would lead him docilely back, and the ring through Jed's nose would be but a prelude to the one upon her finger . . .

Within the coach house, the drovers had been allowed to build a fire of kindling from the winter fuel heaped there . . . Its glow was warmly comforting, and in the vast stone spaciousness, even the rancid smell of the spluttering hog's fat candles seemed as remote as the blizzard without . . . The tavern keeper was a jovial, plump-cheeked fellow, as generous of heart as in girth, and had bidden them take freely from the mountain of sacks in his store. They might sing and dance and make merry as they chose, he added expansively, for the walls were thick and the coach house set apart, and they would disturb no-one with their frolicking. They had taken him at his word. With a firkin of strong ale in their tankards, sizzling invitingly from an iron poker thrust into the fire, and their hands and bellies warmed with potatoes crisped in woodash, they had eaten and supped their fill. Afterwards, the older of their company had dozed, replete, but the women and younger lads felt a renewal of vigour, and demanded some livelier diversion . . . Jed's cherished concertina had been borrowed from his pack; one of the drovers had obligingly tuned and tightened his fiddlestrings, and yet another had proudly produced a tambourine from his private hoard. The rest, as delightedly determined to please, had made use of whatever came to hand, horn combs in the thick Bristol brown paper they saved to make their workaday leggings, pot-lid cymbals, spoons beaten against metal platters, and spoons skilfully rattled between their fingers, to set the melody and rhythm tapping as restlessly as their feet.

There was laughter and excitement as spontaneous as the music, as Luc had swept Sarah into his arms with an exaggerated flourish, and danced her expertly across the stone-flagged floor. She had rested her head against the hardness of his breast, and he had held her closer, lowering his lips to her hair, and as she glanced up, eyes lovingly bright, kissing her with a tenderness of passion upon her softly parted lips. It was into this haven of relaxed cheerfulness that Jed and Becky had stumbled unawares. One of the heavy wooden doors to the coach house had been wrenched gratingly open upon its hinges, then sent crashing perilously against the stone by the fury of the wind. The

179

music within had faltered and died away as Jed had thrust Becky into the light. His mouth had been trying vainly to form words, but he was unable to speak for the icy numbness of his lips and throat . . . There had been a moment of shocked disbelief, the company frozen into silence, before they surged forward to aid them. Becky had stumbled, then fallen to her knees upon the flagstoned floor, too exhausted to rise . . . Jed stood foolishly watching, able to summon neither wits nor will. His garments were white with drifted snow, and he, wraithlike, more ghost than living blood and flesh.

Willing hands had lifted Becky to the fireside, and warmed ale was forced down her throat in an effort to bring back life and feeling to her useless limbs. Jed, too, had been half thrust, half carried, to the warmth of the fire . . . They had drowned all Jed's feeble protestations, refusing to listen to him until he was rested and restored. Yet, with every passing second, he grew more restive and anxious, until, finally, he would not be restrained, crying out vexedly,

"Have you all taken leave of your senses? Let me speak, I say! It is not I who am in danger, but Luc!"

"Luc? But how?" Sarah's voice was ragged with alarm.

"Hell and damnation!" Jed sent a proffered tankard of ale hurtling to the floor. "Will you not take telling? Must I read you the riot act before you will listen?"

There was a shuffling of feet, then shamefaced silence.

"Jim Parslowe has alerted the militia!" Jed declared. "Made claim that Luc is a spy for the French!"

"But why?" one of the women cried, "What madness drove him?"

"That same madness and envy which drove him to sell Huw Jenkins for gold." Jed's voice was unsteady, fatigue and emotion thickening it. "He would claim reward for his treachery, lying and cheating for his own ends . . ."

There was a murmur of anger and dismay from the drovers, with the women, equally enraged, and vociferous in their condemnation. Sarah, who was supporting Becky with her arm, and setting a tankard to her friend's lips, paused, face more pained and frozen than Becky's own.

"What is to be done, Jed?" she demanded helplessly, "should the militia come, Luc will be taken away . . . imprisoned."

"'Tis true!" one of the lads exclaimed impassionedly. "They will shackle and manhandle him, with no thought for his innocence! Shoot him as a French spy and traitor, as like as not!"

"Dear life!" Becky had regained some of her old strength and fierceness. "Have you no sense? No spirit? While you stand wailing, and wring your hands, Luc's accusers will be upon him! The snow will not long hinder them! Let him be upon his way . . ."

Without a word, Luc had taken up his pack, his swift pressure upon Sarah's fingers as he bent low to kiss her so fierce that it all but crushed her bones . . . He turned to Jed and made to thank him, but Jed grasped Luc's elbow, saying urgently,

"You must cross the river and meet us near Coleford, Forest of Dean . . . There is a small hut within the woods . . . A charcoal burner's poor dwelling. He is a drover like us, and was once upon the roads, until some accident to his leg near crippled him."

"His name?"

"Vaughan. George Vaughan . . . You need have no fear that he will betray you. He is an honest man, and will offer you food and shelter, until we come . . ."

Luc had briefly grasped Jed's hand, and they had stared at each other, their fears unspoken. Then Jed had nodded dismissal as two of the drovers had dragged open the coach house doors, straining to hold them fast against the fury of the storm.

Luc had immediately been swallowed into the devouring whiteness, and the drovers, the great doors all but torn from their grasp by the wind, had gratefully slammed them shut. There was silence from those in the room as the two men made their way to the fire, snow clinging to their frieze-cloth jackets, faces wetly reddened and glistening. The silence had been broken by the stamping of their boots upon the flagstones to scatter the melting snow . . . It was Becky who was comforter now, forgetting her own pain in Sarah's greater need . . . Jed, watching her compassionately, damned Jim Parslowe for the grief he had deliberately brought to them all.

"What of Parslowe?" one of the drovers at the fireside demanded aggressively. "Will he dare to return? Will he have the damnable gall?"

181

"He will return!" Jed replied with conviction.

"Then he will get more than he bargained for! He will feel the weight of my fist, and others . . . He will pay for his lying treachery, as dearly as Huw Jenkins and Luc . . ."

There was angry support from his companions, and insistent cries for revenge.

"No!" Jed's vehement denial shocked and sobered them. "No . . ." he repeated more quietly, "that is not the way . . . If you honestly aim to aid Luc, then you must pretend innocence . . . disclaim all knowledge of him, deny his existence . . . More, you will treat Jim Parslowe as if his deceit is unknown . . ."

"But how will that serve?" demanded a drover at the fireside.

"You must trust me," Jed declared stubbornly, "In this, as in all else . . . for I am unable to explain . . . I have never yet lied to you, nor led you to disaster . . ."

"No, you are a just man . . . fair in your dealings, and a good master. I could wish for no better . . . "The drover's tribute sprang honestly, and was echoed as sincerely all about him.

Jed had nodded, pleasure at their approval further reddening his broad face. Then,

"We had best return to our music and dancing," he advised, taking up the concertina which had earlier been hastily discarded upon his pack. As the familiar music grew in volume and richness, the others took up their makeshift instruments, and the younger drovers and women returned, self-consciously, to their dancing upon the stone-flagged floor . . . Sarah and Becky remained seated upon the dry sacking beside the flames, immured in their own thoughts, and not of a mind to celebrate . . .

"It will be all right . . ." Becky had comforted Sarah helplessly. "You will see it will all come aright in the end . . ."

Her eyes had met Jed's above the colourful swirling of the concertina's rhythmic ebb and flow . . . The smile he gave her had curled his lips, but his eyes were darkly unreadable. Becky felt a coldness of dread settle upon her, more insistent than the iciness within. She had sought reassurance, but found none. In Jed's face, she had seen only the grief of one who mourns the loss of another. For him, Luc was already trapped, and dead.

CHAPTER 18

Luc, moving blindly through a snow-scarred landscape, felt as isolated and abandoned as the unknown countryside he trod. He thanked God, most devoutly, for the stout drovers' clothing he wore, its rough Welsh frieze-cloth warmly protective. Yet, even its thickness, and the sturdy leggings and leather boots he wore, could not altogether keep out the wetness and chill. His feet sank uselessly into the soft drifts, and wind and flung snow whipped his exposed face and hands to redness with the raw pain of a burn . . . His broad-brimmed drovers' hat, long since fallen victim to the wind, which had snatched it greedily, then flung it beyond his reach. Luc had possessed neither strength enough, nor will, to retrieve it, and had floundered on, guided only by instinct. There would be a hue and cry, he knew . . . The militia, and the soldiery too, would already be searching, his name and description displayed in every tavern, and nailed upon every suitable fence-post and tree . . . His mouth twisted wryly. 'The French Fox'. An animal of known slyness and cunning, aggressively determined upon escape. Luc felt no aggression, and his cunning, with his strength of purpose, had deserted him. He had barely the will to survive . . . The pain which had wracked him troubled him no longer. He felt nothing, save a strange lethargy which bore him down as relentlessly as his limbs were dragged down into the thickening snow . . . His eyes ached from the glare of whiteness, and he was numbed in every muscle and nerve, even the blood within him seemed sluggishly frozen; a river slowed to ice, all life suspended . . . Luc did not know how many miles he had travelled. He had somehow forced himself onwards, unseeing, unthinking, thrusting instinctively through hostile climate and treacherous land . . .

When he could walk no more, he sank down in the lee of a dry-stone wall, and wept with hopelessness. If he fell asleep now, he would never awaken. The falling snow would be killer and tomb . . . He felt neither fear nor rage at his ending, only an overwhelming yearning for sleep. The drifted snow covered his face, and lay in the creases of his clothing. He felt nothing; saw nothing. Then, for a split second, his eyes had opened . . . This whiteness, then, was the bright emptiness of death.

The Gloucester militia, and then the garrison soldiery, had come searching for Luc Nolais, the escaped prisoner-of-war, as Jed had warned that they might. The snow had died away during the night, and they came to the tavern, battering upon the door, calling impatiently aloud until the landlord had appeared at the window . . . Shaken so abruptly from his sleep, his face was as pallid as the nightcap he wore, his fingers awkwardly mutinous as he strove to pull on his clothing. He had led them apprehensively to the coach house, which Jim Parslowe had named as Luc's hiding place. The officer in command of the militia had been surly and officious, the landlord trembling as much from terror as from cold as he feverishly sought to disclaim all knowledge of those within . . . Jed, who had lain sleepless, heard first the crunching of boots upon the compacted snow, then the violent throwing open of the coach house doors. Alarmed, he had struggled to his feet, glimpsing the cold glitter of the snow without, the haloed, yellow light of the pole-held lanterns, and, beyond, the pin-points of starlight piercing the darkened sky . . . Then the doors had been slammed shut.

The militia had treated the drovers and lads with the contemptuous arrogance of those new to power, and determined to prove their mastery. In their ignorant prejudice, they classed the drovers as useless vagrants, rootless, homeless, and of no account . . . They were crude and rough-tongued in their orders to the men, and their salacious jibes and insulting handling of the drovers' womenfolk had all but provoked a riot . . . Had Jed not intervened with determined calmness and authority to restore order, they might all have been taken into custody.

"We are not vagrants, but decent God-fearing folk . . . hard working, and beholden to no man . . . I am a master drover, licensed by the quarter sessions," 'he declared. "I am no vagrant, to be arrested, whipped, and pilloried . . ."

Jed had angrily withdrawn his drover's licence from the

pocket of his breeches, thrusting it at the officer of the militia, and demanding stiffly, "If it is this that you seek . . .?"

The officer, splendid in his frock coat and regimental cap, had brushed it peremptorily aside, saying curtly,

"It is a French spy that we seek. One Luc Nolais, a lieutenant in Napoleon's army, lately escaped the hulks."

"There is none of that name here!"

"Information has been laid against you. You are accused of knowingly sheltering him, and aiding his escape."

"Dear God!" Jed's cry was torn from him, "Who made such accusation? Do you take heed of every foul-mouthed lunatic who lays such filthy charge . . .? Every envious fool and parasite?"

Indignation had made him red-faced with choler and, for a moment, all but speechless . . . Then, recovering himself, he continued with deliberation and clarity, "I am an honest man. A loyal supporter of the king. A true patriot . . . let none dispute it! I would sooner be hanged . . . garrotted even, than aid that . . . whelp, Napoleon! I am no traitor . . . The real traitor is the man who made such lying accusation!"

So fierce and convincing was his indignation that the officer hesitated briefly, clearly undecided . . . Then he ordered that every drover, woman and lad be taken singly into the inn, and fully interrogated. Should any evidence of complicity be discovered, or any suspicions remain, then Jed and all others involved would be transported to the barracks, then made to stand trial in a court of law . . .

None had claimed personal knowledge of Luc. Indeed, they had denied his very existence. They would not be bullied, bribed, or frightened into admission, their refusal as stolid, their manner as phlegmatic as the stubborn oxen they drove . . . Becky, alone, of the company, volunteered to give information freely. It was her opinion, she averred, that the man they sought was an arrogant, overbearing little toad, who went by the name of Jim Parslowe . . . A slimy, venomous little reptile of a creature, who might well be the very traitor they sought . . . Had she not, with her own ears, heard him lay claim to speaking some foreign tongue? Besides, he had the look of a turncoat about him; some slyness in manner, a furtiveness even . . . Yes, it was to him they had best look, not among decent, law-abiding folk, hard working as the drovers.

The officer's supercilious and haughty expression had remained scrupulously unaltered, but the red-coated soldier who had escorted her within the inn had betrayed himself by the merest flicker of a smile, rigidly suppressed . . . Becky Hendry was a fine figure of a woman, he thought admiringly, with that wild mane of red hair, and a spirit and a temper to match, he did not doubt! As he marched her back to the coach house, he thrust his uniformed chest out proudly, so that, in the lantern light, the brass of his buttons gleamed bright. His head he held proudly erect, that the impressively spiked black helmet he wore might be shown to greater advantage. She could not dispute, he thought with satisfaction, that he cut a noble figure, neat and military. In the darkness of the yard, beyond the splintered lantern-light, he laid a caressing hand to her backside, only to be dealt so unexpected and violent a blow to his jaw that lantern and he went sprawling inelegantly into the snow . . . One of his companions had come swiftly running, alerted by the commotion, as the soldier hauled himself, shamefaced, to his feet, still awkwardly dazed. Becky had retrieved the lantern, and was holding it aloft. In its light, her face was innocently concerned.

"'Tis treacherous weather . . ." she ventured, "and scarce fitting for honest souls to be abroad . . . for fear of some mishap or sudden accident . . ." She had turned solicitously to her assailant, demanding, "Do you not agree, sir?"

He had muttered inaudibly beneath his breath, and his companion, relishing the situation, had offered slyly,

"Perhaps you would feel . . . safer in my company, ma'am?"

"'Tis not I who was in danger, sir," Becky responded pertly, "'tis always best to keep a balance . . . to keep one's hands and feet in their proper place . . . 'tis a lesson hard learned!"

With a toss of her bright head, she had delivered the lantern into his hand, them re-entered the coach house.

It had been a moment of welcome levity, but the only one amidst the sombre ruthlessness of the inquisition . . . Accusations and rebuttals had been made with equal forcefulness; none had yielded nor shifted ground. Grudgingly, the militia officer had acknowledged an impasse, if not defeat, and had tersely regrouped his men and marched them away. They had been

watched in resentful silence by the drovers' band, who had stood
in the snow-crusted yard until they were well clear of the tavern,
and their muffled footsteps dying . . . Then, spontaneously,
wave upon wave of cheers had broken, with laughter and
hugging by the women, and ribaldry by the cockier drovers' lads.
A measure of their relief . . . The landlord, authority and good
humour restored, had treated them all to a tankard of mulled
ale, stubbornly refusing all payment . . . Then, warmed by good
hops, and cheered by their victory, they had settled comfortably
to sleep, but not for long. The soldiers, when they arrived but
an hour later, were altogether more thorough and disciplined in
their interrogation, their manner brutal. The drovers, women
and lads, nervous and exhausted through confusion and lack of
sleep, seemed doltish, and aroused hostility. Their inquisitors
grew openly irritable, and could not hide their contempt . . .
Their scorn, instead of whipping the drovers into submission,
stirred them to angry rebellion . . . They became obdurate . . .
Their faces grew stubborn, their voices taciturn. Jed, who knew
them better than any other, knew that the soldiery and militia
had failed.

Neither goad nor persuasion would move them. If Luc were
captured, then it would not be through betrayal by his friends.
For the moment, his enemy, Jim Parslowe had failed. Luc's
future lay in God's hands. Jed could only pray that He would
prove merciful.

At Gloucester barracks, Jim Parslowe's interrogation had
been as savage, and unyielding, as if he were the renegade . . .
He had been harangued for his incompetence, and for wasting
the time and energies of troops and militia upon 'some fool's
errand . . . some jealous whim.' Worse, he had been actually
threatened with public trial for his venality; and warned that
the punishment, should he be found guilty, would prove cruelly
severe . . . Parslowe had grown, at first, aggressive, then abject,
and had pleaded to be allowed to return to the drovers, and he
would find proof of his accusation, he swore, and would be in
no danger, for none was aware that it was he who had informed
. . . The commanding officer had dismissed him arbitrarily,
scarcely bothering to hide his contempt . . . Jim Parslowe,
nursing his humiliation, had made his escape. As he left the

garrison, his head was held arrogantly high, his step upon the crispness of dry snow resolute . . . Yet, inwardly, he seethed with fury against those who had sneered, and slighted him, and against Jed Perkins and Luc. He would return, and take his revenge. He could conjure up convincing enough excuse for his absence. None would question it. As for Luc Nolais, he would surely return when he believed all danger ended . . . He would not long keep absent from that . . . slut, Sarah Tudor. When Nolais returned, he would find vengeance waiting, retribution . . . Jim Parslowe smiled wryly. He would not dwell upon what retribution the French might visit upon him, were they to discover that he had betrayed Luc Nolais, and them.

As suddenly, and quixotically as the blizzard had come, the weather turned around. The biting north-easterly wind died, and the air grew soft with the promise of rain. It fell, hesitantly at first, no more than a misted greyness, then with increasing steadiness . . . Luc, awakened from his exhausted slumbers, felt its warm moisture upon his face. His skin was icily stretched, his eyes raw-rimmed, and his neck and limbs cramped and barely capable of movement . . . The pain of flexing them brought such agony that he actually cried out, but he willed himself to drag himself upright by clinging to the wall of loose stones which had served to shelter him . . . At least he had survived the night . . . Yet the snow was already thinning, earth showing bare where the slanting rain drove, piercing as nails . . . His pursuers would gain advantage with daylight. With the snow gone, they would hunt unhindered, the fox, their prey, visible, and denied shelter . . . He had best be gone, and keep to the wilder, more remote, tracks, trusting to instinct and Providence for survival . . . Yet, when he moved, it was painfully, and with the burdensome difficulty of an old man, beset by tiredness and infirmity. Despite the thickness of his clothing, and his stout gaiters and boots beneath, he was chilled, excoriated by weather, as if the skin had been painfully torn away. He thought of Sarah and Jed, and the rest, and the warm shelter of the coach house, and felt a violence of rage and hatred against Jim Parslowe for his treachery . . . There was open warfare between them now. Luc's regret was that it had served to ensnare not Parslowe's legitimate prey, but those who were innocent, making them accomplices, setting them at risk . . . If Jed and his fellow drovers, women and lads were thought to be implicated in Luc's escape, and made to stand trial, then they might well lose not only their freedom, but their livelihood, and be forced into paupery . . . Luc's head throbbed abominably; he felt confused as to what to do . . . He knew that he must first cross the river Severn and find his way to Coleford . . . But once there, should he make for the safe house, as ordered, or join Jed and the drovers at the charcoal burner's hut? Would Parslowe's betrayal be already known to his French masters, he wondered? Would his own masters, the British, be sent word by the militia and soldiery? Would all his carefully laid schemes come to naught, his true identity be made known? Dear God! How he wished that he felt physically strong, and confident in mind, instead of beset by doubts . . . He shivered violently, as though with some ague, as he forced himself remorselessly upon his way . . . There was a dryness in his throat, and a tightness at his ribs, and he could not be sure if it were illness or despair which so weakened him . . . He would keep to the hedges and fields, the woods and poor cart-tracks, and steal food, and take shelter wherever he might . . . It was to have been his great adventure, the culmination of all that he had hoped for and so long planned. Why, then, did he feel so little joy?

The militia and troops had moved as swiftly as Luc had feared, searching tirelessly, and entering every small tavern and hostelry, farm and cottage upon the drovers' way . . . The melting snow had given Luc Nolais aid, they feared, for his tracks would now be obliterated, and he could more easily steal vegetables for sustenance from the sodden fields . . . Their pursuit of him was unceasing, their spirits high. When they tired, there were others to take their place, as eager and well trained as they . . . The French Fox would ultimately be cornered, and his animal cunning would be no match for muskets and rifles . . . They had orders to disarm and take him unscathed, that he might be questioned, then returned to the hulks . . . Yet none expected that he would willingly surrender. He would be savage and snarling to the end; an animal, like his namesake, vicious, and with an insatiable blood-lust . . . A creature to whom the killing was of as little account as death itself . . . If someone set a stray bullet into his brain, then none would enquire too closely, or long condemn . . . It was a code that Luc, himself, had learned to accept and live with. Trust only a dead enemy. There should be no other kind.

Jim Parslowe's return to the tavern coach house might well have proved rancorous, and the drovers' disgust with him made plain, had not Jed warned them to act peaceably. If they had expected Parslowe to come stealthily, they were soon disabused. He had entered brazenly, displaying all his old arrogant assurance, and boasting of the lucrative business he had transacted in Gloucester town. Sarah, appalled by his deceitfulness and glib lying, could scarcely bring herself to greet him with the courtesies owed to a returning traveller. Her voice was sharp, her words stilted and unconvincing . . . The rest of the company, following Jed's instruction, had seemingly accepted him as phlegmatically as they accepted all else. Parslowe, who had expected neither curiosity nor effusiveness from them, saw nothing unnatural in their indifference.

It was Becky, that accomplished actress, who had artlessly blurted out the story of their own adventures. In Parslowe's absence, she confided exultantly, they had known some rare excitement! The army and militia, both, had descended upon them, dragging them away and interrogating them most brutally . . . each and every one!

Parslowe had convincingly feigned shock and bewilderment, demanding angrily,

"But why, in God's Name? Of what are we accused . . .?"

"Harbouring a fugitive . . . an escaped Frenchman; a prisoner-of-war . . ."

"Then they are useless clods and imbeciles! Ignorant scum, no better than those traitors they seek!" His venom had been real, his resentment palpable. He had glanced about him challengingly, demanding, "And where is Luc? What involvement has he in all this?"

"None!" Jed's denial was curt, his voice incisive.

"But he is absent . . ."

"As you were absent . . . upon business of your own."

"Can you be sure that it was not he who informed against you . . .?" Parslowe jibed maliciously.

"As sure as I am of you . . ."

190

There was a tense silence before Parslowe demanded abrasively,

"What do you know of him? Nothing . . ."

"Nothing!" agreed Jed evenly, "save that he came upon your insistence, vouchsafed by you . . . If you have some knowledge which you have kept hidden . . .?"

"No . . . None." The denial was forced from him. "I know of nothing . . ."

"Then we had best be upon our way, while we are able, lest the snow return," Jed ordered curtly. "We have wasted time enough!"

Parslowe had nodded, and lifted his pack, then hesitated, sucking at his lip.

"He will join us at Coleford, then? Luc, I mean . . .? He will surely return if he has nothing to fear, nothing to hide . . ."

"He will return in his own good time, as you did, if he so wills it . . ." Jed said dismissively. "The place, and the reason, are his affair, and his, alone . . ."

Becky, who had taken her place beside him, had turned impulsively to Parslowe. Despite all Jed's warnings and remonstrances, her dislike for the man was plain.

"Whoever informed upon Jed was a fool and a scoundrel!" she declared abrasively, "Some envious half-wit, seeking to drag him down . . . as like as not to his own foul level . . . Who else would lie so maliciously? There is not one man, woman or lad among us who would willingly aid the French upstart! And none traitor and coward enough to serve him . . ."

There had been a murmurous swell of agreement from those within hearing, but Becky's gaze was firmly upon Parslowe.

"Do you not agree, Jim?" Her tone was pleasant, her expression innocent of guile.

"The . . . renegade they search for is all that you say, and more!" he exclaimed vindictively.

"The informer . . ." Becky corrected, "for we all know full well that there is no renegade among us, none who, for filthy gain, would sell his country and the lives of those who defend it . . ."

She had barely taken pause, when,

"That is enough!" Jed's command came, sharply incisive. "Becky, you have made your point. Do not labour it! We are all agreed. It serves no useful purpose to bicker and snarl at each other, like jealous dogs. Let us be on our way peaceably!"

Becky had flushed, chastened by the harshness of Jed's reprimand, and had fallen into step beside him as they quitted the tavern yard for the road. Parslowe, smiling maliciously at her discomfiture, had walked back to join the lads . . .

"I am sorry, Jed . . . my wayward tongue will be the death of me . . ."

Her cold hand had slipped apologetically into Jed's roughened palm.

"Then you had best curb it, Becky," he said with quiet conviction, "else it will be the death of others, too . . ."

CHAPTER 19

They had crossed the river at the stone-built bridge, and made tracks towards Coleford along the well worn drovers' roads. They had met many others of their calling, some known, and as many more strangers to them. Yet, always, Jed and his companions greeted them with a warm friendship, offering them aid with their beasts, and victuals or kindling from their hard-earned store . . . There was a feeling of cameraderie upon the drovers' roads, Jed declared proudly, "like no other upon God's good earth." It was a meeting of honest men, drawn close by hardship and toil, poverty and shared danger . . . Friendship was born between them, for they understood each other's lives with no word needed, or spoken. The drovers were a special breed; a race set apart . . .

From the itinerant drovers who gave them news, Jed learnt where the soldiers' makeshift camps were to be found, and where the militia gathered . . . By the time Jed's company had drawn near to Coleford, Forest of Dean, they had no need of vicarious information; their eyes gave evidence enough . . . The roads, and the forest itself, were teeming with soldiery and militia, intent upon some secret task. The drovers, with memories of their harsh interrogation clear, did not need to ask what duty so obsessed them . . . They hunted Luc Nolais . . . The French Fox. There was no other reason which could force them to arms, and to search with such fierce commitment.

Sarah, consumed with fear and pity for Luc, could not believe that he could escape. Becky, who was of like mind, had done her best to lift her friend's spirits, but to no avail. Indeed, save, perhaps, for Jim Parslowe, there was not a man, woman or lad among them who did not feel heavy of heart at the prospect of Luc's capture, and the punishment he would be forced to endure . . . He was innocent, they felt sure . . . Yet, what would innocence avail him? He would be imprisoned, tried, and, as like as not, shot, or hanged upon a gibbet, his skeleton picked clean of flesh by rat and scavenging bird . . . then left, a deterrent to others.

Jed and the rest had left the road, and made tracks into the thickness of the forest. The trees above them rose stark, the decayed leaves mildewing underfoot, and clinging, leechlike, to their boots. They would make their way along a little known path, used mainly by woodcutters and charcoal burners, one of whose number, George Vaughan, they now sought.

There had been a violence of crashing and stamping in the trees beyond, and cries, as of some great creature in pain. The sound held an anguish of terror; a torment which made the blood congeal in sudden fear . . . They had all halted, stricken, and even Jed, gripped by alarm, had felt sickness rise into his throat, its sourness choking him. The women had paused, terrified, and some of the lads had bolted, fleeing instinctively from whatever evil it was which threatened. The rest had waited, apprehensive, hardly daring to breathe as the blundering and cries grew louder, the fury greater with the enraged creature's approach . . . A wild boar, caught in a thicket, or wounded by a hunter's arrow or shot, Jed thought. Yet the cries were not wholly animal nor human . . . Jed had hurriedly crossed himself, then stood his ground.

That they recognised the creature which stood before them did not lessen their horror, rather compounded it. It was Huw Jenkins who faced them, a rifle clutched in his hands, some wildness in his manner and in his eyes, which spoke of madness . . . The broad, vacant face was bruised and bloodied, the skin torn by thorn and briar. The hands which clutched the rifle butt were trembling with agitation, scratched, and filthy and bleeding, the nails broken.

"Huw . . ." It was Sarah who had made move towards him, crying out his name with compassion, tears blinding her eyes. He paused for a moment, all suspicion, fingers tightening upon the trigger. Jed had pulled Sarah roughly aside, thrusting himself before her in protection.

"Huw, lad . . ." Jed's voice was rough with pity, "for God's sake, give me the rifle . . . We are your friends. None shall take you. None harm you . . ."

For a brief moment the boy's bloodied face creased in bewilderment as some inkling of recognition had come, some memory of times past. Jed had opened his arms wide, as though to a sorrowing child, offering haven and comfort, but Huw Jenkins made no move. He stood irresolute, confused as a whipped dog, unsure of whether to snarl defiance, or cower in defeat. The tears were coursing soundlessly down his cheeks, and wetness falling from his nostrils and the corners of his mouth. There was scarcely one among them who did not feel his grief as fiercely as if it were his own . . .

He had gazed around him at the sea of faces, pained, pitying, but strangers to him, all . . . He tried to make sense of what he saw, but terror and exhaustion were all he knew. They would take him away, again. Beat him. Starve him. Make him a butt for their cruel laughter . . . a figure of scorn. With the rifle in his hand, *he* was the master. The fear would stare back from their eyes. They would neither goad nor mock him. They would cringe and whimper, and hold off their blows.

Huw's confusion clouded his brain and eyes, but amongst those strangers who watched him, one face, alone, was clear . . . The face of an enemy. One of those arrogant, hostile faces which so haunted him, in sleep as in waking. The face of one who held him in contempt, cursing his slowness.

He had raised the rifle to take aim, as Jim Parslowe moved forward to disarm him. Parslowe's command had been coldly authoritarian, his mouth twisted in a sneer . . . Huw's finger had pressed hard upon the trigger. The sudden violence of the retort had sent him reeling, the rifle butt cracking his ribs with a bone-crushing hurt.

There had been fleeting surprise upon Jim Parslowe's face, then stark fury, before blood surged at his breastbone, monstrous, obscenely flowing . . . He stood, transfixed, then fell . . .

Huw Jenkins, appalled, and not understanding the viciousness he had wrought, had cried aloud, then stumbled away into the woods. His face had been a mask of horror, his eyes bleak, but he held the rifle to him jealously. Those watching had stood, frozen with disbelief, unable, even, to move to aid Parslowe, or to pursue his attacker . . . Memory of Huw Jenkins' ravaged face, haunted by madness, had stilled them all.

Jed had somehow found strength to move first, blundering to

where Parslowe lay. Yet, he knew, even before his hand had touched his coldness of flesh, that the drover was already dead.

"After him! After Huw Jenkins!" One of the older drovers had shouted urgently, "Quick! Else he will make his escape . . .!"

"No!" Jed's voice was raised, harsh, brooking no argument. "For the love of God, leave the lad be . . .!"

The man had hesitated, and the lads who had crept back glanced nervously shamefaced from one to the other, unwilling to act. The sounds of Huw's blundering flight through the trees, the rustling of dead leaves, and the snapping of twigs and branches had become blurred, softened by distance. Then, shattering the silence as cruelly as bone and flesh, the sound of a rifle shot and its dying echo . . .

Jed had started forward fiercely, and others would eagerly have followed him, but he bade them stay. He would go alone, he declared, for that was his duty as master, and his alone. It were better that they take the women to safety, as planned, else the militia and soldiery would soon enough be alerted.

"But what of Jim Parslowe?" Becky had asked despairingly.

"He must be left! None can aid him now . . . Our care must be for ourselves, and Luc . . ."

He had gone without further word to search for Huw Jenkins.

He had come across him lying in a small clearing in the forest, beside a pile of logs. The rifle shot had torn a wound in his side, already darkening and stiff with congealed blood . . . Huw's eyes were open, but dulled, opaque with the membrane of dying. Jed had fallen to the leafy earth beside him, lifting the poor, bloodied head, cradling him to him. The boy had spoken no word, but his grip had tightened upon Jed's fingers, and his eyes had grown wide. Then he had smiled, the blood from the corners of his mouth mingling with mucous and tears upon his bruised flesh. When Jed was certain that Huw was dead, he set him upon a bed of fallen leaves, and closed the eyelids over the sightless eyes, then he fell to his knees beside him, in prayer. The words that he spoke aloud should have brought Jed healing, assuaged his grief. Yet, when he rose, he was filled with a rage of anger so destructive that it seemed to rip him with physical pain. He cursed Jim Parslowe and all who brought violence upon those like Huw Jenkins, already broken in mind or spirit. He damned them for the answering violence they stirred in the helpless victims they chose. He damned the uselessness of life, and the cruelty of death. He damned the coarse and the uncaring. He damned himself, and his failure, most wretchedly of all . . .

He did not look back, but left the clearing to its dead. His feet were leaden, and his eyes plagued with unshed tears. It had been a bitter journey for Huw Jenkins and the drovers, dark and cold, and a colder journey lay ahead. Jed hoped that Huw would find, at its ending, that peace denied him in life, and the affection he sought . . . It was all meaningless else, and not worth a corpse's candle.

It seemed to Luc that he had been travelling across country for weeks rather than days, nerves taut, and with coldness and hunger his constant companions . . . He had kept well clear of the carriage roads and drovers' drifts, reasoning that the soldiers and militia would march more readily upon the highways, and his presence upon the familiar drovers' ways would be expected, and traps scrupulously laid . . . He had brought no pack with him. He wanted no hindrance upon the way, but he would have welcomed dry clothing, and a change of stockings and boots . . . The atmosphere was damp-laden, and his woollen garments weighed heavy with rain. It soaked into the fibres, as it soaked into his bones, chilling, and laying raw . . . He lived more roughly than the meanest vagrant, for he could afford to beg neither shelter nor work. The little money he carried was of no use to him. To buy, or barter, would have set him at risk . . . He stole swede and turnips from the frosted fields, to ease both thirst and hunger, and ate those few nuts and berries still remaining upon hedgegrows and thorn . . . He would, he had decided, make for the safe house at Coleford, rather than join the drovers at the charcoalburner's hut . . . The roads and villages would be teeming with soldiers and militia, he felt sure. They would not easily be deflected from their task, but would hunt him down relentlessly . . . The freeholders of the forest, believing him to be an escaped French prisoner of war, would betray him without remorse . . . He had many enemies and few friends, save Jed and the drovers. He would not willingly lead them into a greater danger than they already faced for harbouring him. If his emotions had ruled him, rather than

his mind and training, he would have risked all to see Sarah
– all, that is, save her life. His own life had been at risk from
the first, knowingly, and of his own volition . . . To lose Sarah
now would be as great a tragedy as any he had known. She was
as much a part of him as those of his own blood; those whom he
sought to atone . . . Was he obstinately sacrificing their future,
and their present, for a childhood promise to the dead past?
He could be sure of nothing, save that he loved Sarah, and
that the past was not dead, but living within him, as surely as
the blood of the de Valandreś and the de Riberacs . . . It was
a blood he would share with Sarah, and his sons, if God so
willed, as he would share the chateau and his inheritance . . .
Did the chateau de Valandré survive, or was it like those who
once dwelt within, dead ashes; spent, never to be rekindled to
life . . .? Even if it lay in ruins, Luc knew that he must, one
day, return, to exorcise the ghosts of the past; to lay their
troubled spirits to rest, and to bring peace to his own . . .

He had grown weary of walking, and hunger gnawed at him,
a pain beneath his ribs . . . It had been awkward to cross the
river unseen, and he had waded across at a shallow place,
remote, and little frequented, save by the wild creatures of
the forest, who came to drink . . . A hind had looked up,
startled, at his approach, and had fled, wide-eyed, upon its
delicate legs, its skin soft, and with the mottled paleness of
a mushroom . . . He had heard the grunting and rooting of
a wild boar, and the sounds of birds and small scampering
creatures, disturbed by his passing. For the moment, he was
as grateful to seek the sanctuary of the woods again as they
. . . He would find a warm, solitary place for shelter, and try to
sleep . . . His mind, he knew, would remain as active and alert
as his pained limbs, defying his exhaustion . . . He had forced
himself beyond the need for sleep . . . He could have wept with
tiredness, as he could have wept for all else . . . for the boy he
had been, and the man he was; for what was ended, and not
yet begun . . . Luc closed his eyes, but the picture remained
behind his eyelids, as real, and as elusive, as sleep. Luc had
dozed intermittently. At first every unrecognised sound had
raked him to consciousness, sweating, trembling, primed for
escape. Those noises familiar to forest dwellers were strange to

his ears . . . By night, his hearing grew more acute, sharpened by darkness and loss of sight. He learned to accept the gentle rustling of leaves upon the forest floor, the stirring of wind in the branches, the steady monotony of rain. Yet, the harsh call of a night-jar, or the strangely human cry of a screech owl remained alien and terrifying. The small nocturnal creatures, intent upon foraging, passed close by. Once, when the moon was high, Luc had watched the fussy, old man's shuffling of a badger as it had snuffled for grubs among the decaying leaves. Beyond, through the trees, he had glimpsed a vixen out hunting, sleekly alert, the painted triangles of face and ears raised in listening, her eyes aglow with amber light, and he had felt at one with her loneliness . . .

Now, by day, too, Luc had fallen into the habit of dozing, deep in the seclusion of the forest, snatching rest jealously whenever he might . . . He had been shallowly below the surface of sleep when the noise shattered him into watchfulness. A crack of exploding sound; unmistakably, a rifle shot . . . He had scrambled to his feet, senses alert, his every instinct to flee the sound . . . Some careless soldier or militia man must have accidentally fired, foolishly giving warning . . . Luc had fled away from the direction of the sound, through the bare-leaved trees, and towards the highway. A few minutes later, another shot cracked out as clear . . . Luc had paused momentarily, anxious and confused. Was it a trap, then? A clever ploy to send him running to where he could best be seen, best captured? Damnation! What was he to do . . .? His plans were already uselessly awry. He was twenty-four hours and more late for his meeting at the safe house . . . How long would they wait, knowing that he had been betrayed . . .? And what of his contact with the British? Mary Grantley had agreed to send someone to keep track of his movements upon the way. They would not have reckoned upon his leaving the drovers, and travelling secretly, and alone . . . Dear God! He was finished, and his work with him . . . He would be returned to the hulks, with no chance to again escape, and his punishment would be severe, even if those who sought him did not deliberately aim to cripple or kill . . .

There had been no more shooting, no further sight nor sound of his pursuers. Luc had, at first, kept himself prudently concealed within the trees which edged the highway, then finally ventured out . . . So intent was he upon watching the road ahead that the small coach had rounded the curve of the highway behind him, almost before he became aware of it . . . He had hesitated only briefly, then flung himself down the steep bank into the drainage ditch at the forest's edge . . . lying still, praying that he had been unseen . . . Stagnant water clogged his nostrils and mouth, and the dank slime of leaves covered him, chokingly.

"Luc! Luc!" The name, imperiously called, was in the unmistakable voice of Mary Grantley. Shamed, and disbelieving, he had dragged himself to his knees in the stinking ditchwater, then painfully scrambled out, mud and green scum covering him from head to heels . . . "Well, sir . . ." Mary's tone was gently mocking, and filled with affectionate laughter, "I congratulate you upon your disguise as a blackamoor. A masterpiece, Luc! I'll wager neither friend nor enemy would recognise you . . ."

"And which, ma'am, are you?"

Exhaustion and discomfort made him brusque, yet, despite himself, his lips twitched with reluctant amusement, and soon they were laughing companionably, as of old.

"I may never hope to meet a truer friend, Mary, nor . . . others a more beautiful enemy . . ." he apologised handsomely. She looked at him for a moment in silence, before recollecting the danger they were in, and urging hastily, "Quick, Luc! Climb within the coach! We have wasted time enough!" As he hesitated, she insisted, "Go! Without argument!"

Once safely within, stinking and squelching in his waterlogged boots, Luc had held himself stiffly from the fine leather seat, demanding, "And how will you explain so . . . elegant a passenger, should we be stopped by the militia?"

"We will not be! You may be assured of it. I have taken a house nearby, and am well known to the regiment and the militia as Sheldon's widow . . . They would harbour no suspicion against me . . ."

He had nodded, asking quietly, "And you have heard that I was betrayed to them?"

"Yes . . . but it might yet serve to your advantage with the French. Add to your credibility even . . ."

He had grimaced wryly, asking, "You did not think to bring me victuals, or a change of clothing . . .?"

"Indeed not!" She could not resist a smile. "How would you explain it to your French masters? You have lived rough, and existed as best you were able . . . You are a foul-smelling, disgusting skeleton of a creature, Luc, and precisely what they are expecting. It would scarcely serve if you arrived in full fig, and looking like Beau Brummel! You must trust to them to feed and clothe you . . ."

"You are a hard taskmaster, Mary!"

"Indeed, and if I were not, then your life, and others, might well be forfeit . . ." Her tone had been light, but neither could disclaim the truth of it.

"And shall we meet again, Mary, when my visit to the safe house is ended?" He hesitated, confessing, "I had planned to return to the Forest of Dean, to meet the drovers who have sheltered me . . ."

"Unwise, Luc! You will put them, and yourself, at risk! It is wiser that you remain only briefly at Coleford . . . Here, in Gloucestershire, the army and militia have full powers of arrest . . . Once beyond its borders, and into Monmouthshire, the fury of the search will lessen . . . Can you not meet the drovers at Monmouth town?"

"Yes . . ." The admission was made reluctantly, for he knew that Jed and Sarah would fear him to be captured or dead . . . Yet he saw the sense in it, and was forced to agree.

"And where shall I next see you?" he demanded at length.

"Coleford market place . . . There is a stall there . . . an old country-woman, selling the last of the season's apples, and hens' eggs, and faggots of sweet-scented herbs . . ." Her mouth curved into delighted laughter. "I'll swear, Luc, that were I to buy every nosegay upon the stall, this coach would still smell like a farmyard dunghill! No self-respecting fox would allow himself to reek so . . . not even a French fox!"

Even as she spoke, the coachman had drawn the horses to a halt in an isolated by-way, and he made ready to alight . . . Despite the grimed filthiness of his skin and clothing, she had reached over to touch his sleeve with her gloved hand, and to settle a light kiss upon his grimed cheek, saying with gentleness, "Your guardian sends you his most affectionate regards, and begs, as I, that you take good heed . . . There are those who have loved you from childhood and await your safe return . . ." Mary hesitated, meaning to speak to him of David Tudor, and Sir Frederick's grief at their young friend's loss, but did not. She could not willingly add to his burden of care. Luc, sensing her conflict and regret, said quietly,

"There is much in my past to be grateful for, Mary, as well as much to mourn . . . Without you and Sir Frederick, my childhood would have been barren indeed . . ."

Mary, startled by his intensity, would have delayed him, but at the old coachman's urgent command, Luc had already flung open the door, and made to alight.

"The coast is clear, sir . . . but you had best not linger!"

The coachman had raised his tricorne formally above the spare grey locks, sitting elegant and proud upon the box in his impressive livery. The disreputable vagrant he addressed had honoured him with a civil bow, smiling widely at the pretty gentlewoman at the window of the coach, and at the ludicrousness of the whole charade. Then, with the swiftness of a running fox, he was away again, into the woods and making towards Coleford . . . He had meant to tell Mary of Sarah, he thought regretfully, and to beg her to treat her with the affection of a sister, should he not return . . . Well, he would see her at Coleford market, and all could be explained and discussed. Even should disaster befall him, then Jed would honour his promise. Luc's footfalls, blurred by the rustling leaves, were as rhythmic as his own heartbeats, their sound lingering with his frosted breath upon the air. Now he felt neither hunger nor cold, only the exhilaration of a runner reaching his destination, a man determined upon finishing what was begun.

CHAPTER 20

By stealth and cunning, Luc had found his way at length to
the safe house at Coleford. Upon the fringes of the town,
he had bought from an astonished pedlar the entire contents
of his tray and pack, adding a further shilling to the guinea
offered for the purchase of the old campaigner's blackthorn
stick and shapeless hat . . . Like many another, wounded in
battle against the French, the ex-soldier had been eking out a
precarious living upon the roads, too proud to accept the slur
of paupery and the grudging charity it offered . . . He had
been voluble in calling down blessings upon Luc, showering
them as liberally as his reminiscences. He had served under
Sir Frederick Loosely, he had told Luc with pride; the finest
commander in the British army, and a true gentleman, for all
he was a martinet . . . There was not a soldier, living or dead,
who, having once fought under the general, had not respected
him for his truthfulness and his honest concern for the lower
ranks . . . The tribute was generously given, and as generously
received, and cherished . . . The old man's eyes had been bright
with memory and incipient tears as he had wiped a gnarled hand
across his lips, nodded, then marched erectly away, summoning
strength and past training . . . Luc had watched him go, feeling a
kinship with him; a shared warmth and affection for that sternly
autocratic old gentleman, who had formed and guided them in
their separate ways . . . The pedlar's tribute, Luc knew, would
have pleased the general as honestly as it pleased him . . .

His greeting by those at the safe house had been more
muted, but was, nonetheless, civil enough. The initial surprise
and recoil at the state and stench of him had been translated
into immediate command to the servants that a hip-bath and
hot water, towels and a wash-ball be brought, together with
suitable clean clothing . . . Luc had wallowed unashamedly in

the sybaritic pleasures of cleanliness, a luxury too long denied
him. It was, after all, he thought, but one small step from
godliness.

He had dressed himself in the garments set out for him, the
necessary accoutrements of the gentleman of quality. Their
delicate fabrics seemed alien to him now, their modish cut and
impeccable styling restrictive after the coarseness of his drovers'
clothes. The reflection which stared back from the looking
glass atop the toilet stand might have been some stranger;
his looks too weathered, his flesh too hard-muscled, despite
his new-found leanness, to be a well bred gentleman . . . The
irony of it did not escape him as he made his way, elegantly
clean-shaven, to the library where he was awaited. Jean Luc,
Comte de Valandré and Luc the drover were effectively dead.
He stood, now, in the guise of Luc Nolais, Officier de l'armée.
A man of many parts; acting but one. He hoped he would
convince them.

Afterwards, Luc had been amazed at the ease with which he
had duped them. His inquisitors already had firm knowledge
of his betrayal by Jim Parslowe, and Luc's own filthy and
dishevelled appearance had further convinced them of the
truth of his claim to have fled, and to have been living in
peril of his life.

"You have news of Jim Parslowe? Have questioned him?"
he demanded.

"He is dead . . ." The reply had been curt, emotionless.

"Dead? How?" Realisation came even as he uttered the
words. They must have killed Parslowe for his treachery! Shock
showed plain upon Luc's face.

"No," his informant disclaimed, as if the question had been
posed aloud, "He was killed by another . . . some useless dolt of
a fellow, a drover as witless as he . . ." He paused, watching Luc
intently. "It would seem," he continued superciliously, "that
Parslowe had sold him to recruiters, no less!"

Dear God! Luc thought, sickened. Poor childlike Huw Jenkins
had taken his revenge . . . Luc did not speak, lest pity for the lad
be betrayed in his voice.

"It seems that the militia and the military are quite satisfied
that no other was involved . . . They believe that Parslowe was

204

shot by the boy, a named deserter, who had bludgeoned his way from detention in the garrison, where he was held; the rifle he had stolen from the injured guard . . ."

"And the boy?" Luc's face was coldly expressionless.

"Dead . . . for the little it is worth. It will save the expense of a court martial or a hanging . . ." The tone was bored and dismissive. "or to better account, it will save us the . . . inconvenience of dealing with Parslowe's deceit, and might well save your skin . . ."

Luc had nodded, his manner as curtly indifferent as his informant's own, although he felt ripped through with pity for Huw Jenkins and his needless suffering and death.

There had been sounds of brisk argument in the passageway bordering the room, and an urgent knocking upon the library door. The man who had been questioning him had risen with irritation, and impatiently strode without, the door slamming shut behind him . . . Luc's hesitation had been brief. Swiftly and purposefully, he had moved around the desk to where the report as to his future destination lay. He read avidly and quickly, taking accurate mental note. . . . Past training had served to burn the information into his brain, as it had taught him speed and caution . . . Even before he heard the sounds of the argument diminishing, and his companion's returning footsteps, Luc was back in the place where he had previously stood, unflurried, and seemingly indifferent.

It was to Swansea, then, that he was to be next sent, and thence to Ireland . . . If that information proved correct, then what he had additionally gleaned could be given credence . . . Excitement rose within him so fierce that when his destination was confirmed, he feared that his exultation would betray him.

Yet none had challenged him, nor hindered him from leaving. He need no longer wear that filthy clothing which he had arrived in, he was informed benevolently. It was fitted only for burning . . . He would be safe now in the clothing of a gentleman. "I should like to join the drovers somewhere upon the way . . . at Monmouth town perhaps . . ." The assertion had been firmly made. "What purpose will it serve? It scarcely seems necessary . . ."

"There are possessions of mine which I would claim . . ."

the lie came easily, "besides, were I to disappear without farewell, or explanation, then the drovers might suspect that the soldiers and militia hunted me, as Jim Parslowe, no doubt, implied . . . I would not have them spread their suspicions along the way . . . and to others. There is danger enough . . ."

"Then you had best keep the clothes you wear well hid, and purchase drovers' clothing at Coleford market . . ." Luc had been handed a pouch of gold coins from a hidden drawer within the desk. "You will travel by coach, and like a true gentleman . . ."

"A gentleman of France." Luc's smile was wide and ingenuous.

"Yes, Lieutenant Nolais. A gentleman of France . . ."

Luc, refusing the offer of a carriage to convey him, had stepped out with confidence to the market at Coleford. He was well aware that he cut a trim, indeed, dandyish figure, well groomed, and sartorially splendid in his borrowed plumage. His grey doeskin inexpressibles were close fitting and wrinkle free, his darker roll-collar jacket, with its quilted velvet collar, a masterpiece of the tailor's art. His weskit in subtly toning brocade was every whit as elegant as his befrilled shirt and silken cravat. The high silk hat, cane, and slender hessian boots proclaimed him to be every modish inch a true gentleman of fashion. He did not doubt that Mary would approve the transformation wrought in him; his return to a more familiar guise. Of Sarah's reaction, he was less sure. She had known him only as a drover, as he, in turn, had seen her disguised, first as a simple carrier's lad, then in the coarse-spun drabbery of a working girl . . . It was as well, he thought with a smile, that he had pence enough to exchange his toggery for more mundane dress, or his reception by the drovers, their lads and womenfolk, would be somewhat less than ecstatic . . .

The old countrywoman and stallholder of whom Mary had spoken had evidently not been expecting so finely clad a gentleman. The deep-set eyes in her smiling crab-apple of a face had grown suspicious, her manner furtive . . . It had taken all Luc's tact and persuasive skills to convince her that he was indeed the simple drover she had been told to expect . . .

206

Finally, capitulating to his charm, she had led him reluctantly to the bleak one-up, one-down dwelling behind her crowded vegetable stall, and had left him, without explanation, in a cold, sparsely furnished room.

He had been a fool to venture here, and so distinctively attired, Luc thought ruefully. He was as out of place as . . . a bird of paradise among a flock of farmyard fowl. Mary would think him half-witted! And where was she? She had promised to await him, and she was a woman of her word. Nothing, save the gravest, most pressing calamity would keep her away . . .

Luc's feeling of unease increased, and the oppressive silence within the small dwelling seemed to close in on him. Was it a trap that he had unthinkingly entered? The military had set, then primed it, perhaps, with Mary as innocent bait . . .? Or had his acceptance by those at the Coleford house been a ploy to disarm him? Had they deliberately caused diversion that he might read and memorise the plans upon the desk? Had there been some unseen watcher; witness to his act of betrayal against his hosts . . .?

Luc was summoning resolve to creep, unnoticed, from the place, and to lose himself in the market-day crowds, when he heard the sound of hurried footsteps without . . . He moved, soft-footed, to the door, silver knobbed cane raised threateningly high, to halt the intruder.

The comical astonishment upon the old coachman's face was a sight which had Luc laughing aloud in mingled relief and amusement, so fierce an anticlimax was it . . . The old man had been, at first, alarmed, then apologetic, clutching his tricorne hat to his liveried breast, and declaring, face creased in puzzlement,

"I vow, sir, some mistake had been made . . . I had not been led to expect a gentleman . . . but a drover . . ."

"Then there is no mistake. You see both before you . . ."

The coachman had peered at Luc uncertainly, opaque eyes narrowing under the straggly locks of beribboned hair. Then, upon recognising him, "God bless my soul, sir! I can scarce credit the change!" he exclaimed, suddenly recollecting himself to add contritely, "I beg you will forgive my impertinence, sir . . . I meant no offence . . . my old eyes grow dim, you understand . . .?"

Luc had waved aside the rest of his stammered apology,

asking tersely, "Your mistress, Mrs Grantley? She does not accompany you . . .?"

"No, sir . . . She sends written regrets and explanation, which she charged me most vehemently to deliver to you, and no other."

He placed the heavily sealed note into Luc's hand.

Luc had read it at first impassively, then with growing concern, forehead creased in a perplexed frown . . .

"Mrs Grantley has already left for London then?"

"Indeed, sir. She spared no hesitation, but left as soon as the messenger arrived. She left upon the very same coach which had brought him, as soon as the horses were changed, and the coachman refreshed."

Luc had nodded absently, biting his lip in deep concentration. Then, mind made up, had asked that ink and quill be brought, with a parchment for writing.

"They are here, sir, within the drawer of the small table . . . I took the precaution of bringing them here, not an hour since. There would be none in a household such as this, where none can read nor write."

Luc had praised him for his prudence, then had begun to write sedulously, quill scratching harshly upon the thick parchment. When all was finished, he looked up, to say quietly,

"Mrs Grantley, your mistress, had told me that you are a man of integrity, one to be trusted implicitly . . . more friend than servant." The old man's face had flushed with pride, but his faded eyes had met Luc's gaze steadily.

"Your letter is safe in my hands, sir . . . I would protect it as I would my mistress herself, with my own life, if need be." There was no reproval in his tone, no arrogance, only truth. Luc said, "Then I am as privileged as Mary to call you friend." The old man had smiled his appreciation before confiding awkwardly, "There is a bundle of old clothing within the coach, sir . . . which my mistress bade me purchase at a market stall, and deliver into your keeping." He grimaced wryly as he studied Luc's finery, "'Tis not a gentleman's clothing, I fear . . . but, although well worn, it is clean enough, and not verminous . . ." he had hastened to reassure. "I am to make a bundle of whatever garments you now wear, and to place them in a clean sack, lest you have future need of them." He had hesitated before blurting in painful embarrassment, "Perhaps, sir, it would be . . . prudent to retain the small clothes you wear beneath, for rougher, less sensitive, folk make do." His seamed face had reddened dully as he confessed, "I admit, sir, it was as I feared, and I was neither able to find nor purchase any. You will understand it was altogether too delicate a matter to confide to a gentlewoman, like Mrs Grantley, sir. If you will follow me to the coach?" Luc had nodded with commendable gravity, and followed the coachman obediently without.

How strange the mores of a society, he thought, in which a woman, like Mary, must face the death of those she loves in the naked bloodiness of war and espionage . . . yet be shielded from all mention of the trappings of living flesh. It was a bizarre, oddly prudish, world, as unpredictable as the people within it . . . perhaps that was what made it bearable . . . His mind returned to Mary's letter, and the reason she gave for her visit to London. She had been summoned by Sir Frederick, she wrote, "on a matter of some urgency, and of the greatest personal concern." Luc hoped that it was not a visit to his guardian's sickbed it foreshadowed. If the old gentleman were failing in health, then it would certainly be Mary's company and comfort he would seek. She was as dear to him as a daughter, and as tenderly devoted as if she were his own warm flesh and blood. If Sir Frederick were to die in Luc's absence . . .? The thought bedevilled him, and would not be cast out, despite all Luc's efforts to be rational and objective. Again he wondered if he had been fair to the living in sacrificing them, and himself, in a crusade for the dead.

Mary had been as confused and apprehensive as Luc at Sir Frederick's plea that she return immediately to London. The general had made no further explanation, but Mary had known that only a matter of the greatest import would have made him write to her so impetuously. It was true that he had not connected her visit to Gloucestershire with her secret work for the government, or with Luc, believing that she merely rented a house in Gloucestershire to be near her remaining family and friends. It was a part of the countryside which she loved, and her visits had been frequent and often impulsively made since Sheldon's death.

When, tired from travel, she had alighted at Sir Frederick's house, it was early afternoon, and the sky wintry and leadenly overcast. The square was tranquil and deserted, its leafless trees dark-boled. There was a greyness in the light, as in the air itself, the gardens as frozen and faded in colour. It was Sir Frederick who had greeted her at the door, a little more gaunt, a little slower in his movements and speech, his manner subdued despite his pleasure at seeing her.

"There is something amiss, sir?" Her concern was real. "You are not sick? Distressed in some way? I have come as soon as ever I was able." He had watched as her fingers impatiently untied the ribbons of the pretty blue velvet bonnet which so perfectly matched her intelligent eyes, and waited as she unbuttoned her cape.

"No . . . my dear," his voice was gentle. "It is not for myself I summoned your aid . . . but for another. I remain well, thank God, but he . . ." Sir Frederick had taken her arm and drawn her towards the library, and, upon opening the door, had ushered her within.

A bright log fire blazed in the dog-grate below the marble chimneypiece, its dancing flames flickering light over all. It was at the cavernous winged chair of leather that Mary looked, a familiar dark head barely visible in its depths.

"David . . .? David Tudor . . .?" She did not know whether she had imagined the words spoken, or had actually breathed them aloud, for they brought no response, no movement. She had turned to Sir Frederick, face pale and perplexed, and he had thrust her gently forward. "You will excuse me, ma'am, if I am clumsy in movement, and slow to greet you as I ought." The occupant of the chair had risen with heavy awkwardness. "I confess that I did not expect so . . . rare and welcome a visitor."

"Nor I the blessing of your safe return, sir. Sir Frederick gave me no inkling."

Mary had inclined her face towards the general, partly to hide her conflict of emotions. He was not deceived. Her spontaneous joy at seeing David Tudor was tempered by sorrow at the change which war had wrought in him, physical and more deeply wounding. Then, as if bitterly ashamed of her withdrawal, and fearful lest David be made aware, Mary ran to him, as of old, flinging her arms about his neck, kissing him impetuously and with honest affection. He had rested his dark head gratefully against her soft cheek, feeling the yielding warmth of her flesh against his own. Her sweet-scented womanliness surrounded and enfolded him, gently and lovingly as her arms. A homecoming. A peace. Mary felt no such calm. Indeed, she was ripped by such an intensity of feeling that she all but cried out with its pain. Pity, compassion, regret . . . they were all part of it, but within its depths and her own was a fiercer, more consuming emotion; a physical stirring of that love which she had believed ended with Sheldon's death . . . So savage and unexpected was it that tears of angry rejection sprang to her eyes. Yet the tears which fell were silent and healing, for the misery of David Tudor's past and her own. They clung together; made one by childhood and sorrows shared, from need and knowledge. Sir Frederick had turned aside, glancing intently through the window and into the barren greyness of the deserted square. The winter shadows were lengthening, and the day was chill, yet, within, he felt a comforting warmth, as if the flames of the fire glowed, and sent heat through flesh and bone. He had been right to send for Mary. There were wounds which were quicker healed by a woman's touch, and in binding them, might not she find a healing salve for her own? When he had returned from the window, Mary was kneeling beside David Tudor's chair, pale hair translucent in the firelight, her gaze intent upon the young lieutenant's face.

"Was it sickness which brought you home? The wound to your leg?" Her voice was low, compassionate.

"No. I was exchanged for another prisoner of war." His mouth twisted wryly. "Soldier for soldier. Flesh for flesh. French or British, it makes no matter. When battle is ended, we are one and the same."

"You will not return to your regiment, then?" Her voice was anxiously pleading. "You will remain in England . . .?"

"No. I will return to fight, as soon as ever I am able. It is all the life I know . . . all I have ever wanted to do."

"But did you not give your parole to the French? Make promise to fight no more?"

"Only in that one skirmish in Spain, where I was captured. It is not binding on any other place, any other battle."

"But your wounds?"

211

"My leg is all but healed. I have already applied to rejoin my regiment. I await only my orders to leave."

"Then you will not long be here." Despite her fierce determination to make no unfair emotional claim upon him, Mary's voice was bleak. Sir Frederick, seeing the answering bleakness in the young man's eyes, said brusquely, "You will remain here, Mary, I am sure, and offer David the young companionship denied him by Luc's absence." It was less an invitation than a command. "You will doubtless find much to discuss . . . and I am poor enough company, for age makes me querulous and forgetful."

"Then I shall gratefully accept your hospitality, sir . . . notwithstanding your infirmity." Mary's demure acceptance was belied by the mischievous twitching of her lips. David Tudor's swift smile was equally as delighted as he courteously thanked his host. Mary, covertly watching the young lieutenant, was aware that the change wrought in him ran deep. He was handsome, certainly, but the youthful blandness of his features had been sharpened and refined, the lines of experience harsh scored. David's newfound maturity, Mary feared, had been painfully won. She dearly wanted to take him in her arms, with that innocent impulsiveness of their childhood days; to soothe away the hurts, dispel the shadowed wariness of his eyes . . . No, Mary thought compassionately, and with clear insight, I want to make him forget, but not as a child might, but a woman. To hold him, love him, become a part of his thoughts, and his flesh. I want him with tenderness and pity, but with passion, too. Sir Frederick, seeing the dark head and the pretty fair one held close together, as Mary knelt beside the boy, and hearing the gentle intimacy of their shared remembrances and laughter, smiled. He felt no sense of exclusion, no envious regret. If such singular affection had been denied him, then he had been the means, at least, of bringing it to others. He was a catalyst. Yet, unlike a catalyst, he had not remained unchanged by the nearness of others. He had found joy in Luc's guardianship; affection, too, from Mary and David and dear friends like Josiah Tudor. Had he but found Josiah's missing child, and seen Luc safe, then he would ask for nothing more of life. He prayed that the poor forsaken child, wherever she might be, would one day be found and brought safely home . . . David Tudor

212

had come to him broken in body, and emotionally spent with despair, all his efforts to trace his sister in Yorkshire and Wales come disappointingly to grief. Sir Frederick sighed. He would never stop searching for Josiah's girl, not while there was even the remotest chance that she lived, and while there was breath in his body. He suddenly felt tired, and apprehensive, and despairingly old.

CHAPTER 21

Jed's diminished little company had made its way to the charcoal burner's hut, deep within the Forest of Dean, as planned. The rain had ceased, and the weather grown bitterly cold, the ground icy and treacherous underfoot. They travelled dispiritedly now, even Becky's natural exuberance stilled. Even the knowledge of their nearness to Wales, and home, offered neither spur nor inducement . . . Too much had happened. Despite their anger against Jim Parslowe, and their dislike of his bullying arrogance, the flesh and blood reality of his death had served to chasten them. He had not been deserving of so bloody and demeaning an end . . . As for Huw Jenkins, that poor crazed soul, his life was better ended, for God, alone, could bring him forgiveness and comfort . . . He had been touched by tragedy from cradle to grave . . . They had wept for him, and pitied him, and believed him one of their own . . . Yet, none had understood him . . . He had been set apart by the destructive madness of others, and his own . . . They would not easily forget him.

Jed, grieved by the waste of Huw Jenkins' death, had made his way uneasily to join the others . . . He was possessed by a great weariness which he was unable to shake off . . . the black dog of despair. Memory of the grip of the lad's fingers upon his own, and the emptiness of death, excoriated him, ripping raw . . . He had stumbled, like a defeated old man, from the dead boy's side, scarce able to think for his grieving, nor see for tears . . . Had it been a deliberate taking of his own life, or tragic accident? It was all the same now . . . and none would ever know the truth of it.

Jed had been warmly received by his friend, George Vaughan, the charcoal burner, and made welcome at his fire. He had not spoken to him, nor to any other, of the horror of Huw's death . . . such things were best kept hidden . . . They had waited within the forest clearing for a full two days, the men restless, and the lads equally eager to be upon their way . . . Sarah, alone, had remained alert, anxiously watching, awaiting Luc's return . . . As the daylight hours had faded into darkness, she had remained seated beside the fire, stretching her cramped limbs, trying to peer into the surrounding darkness, alert to every movement and sound . . . When, at last, she had been forced to accept the truth that Luc was not coming, she had gathered her bundle with the rest and set it upon her shoulder . . . She had made no plea to Jed that they remain a while longer, nor had she wept. Quietly, she had made her thanks to the charcoal burner, then, dry-eyed, had walked beside Jed and Becky, shoulders firm, head held defiantly erect . . . So white-faced and forbidding was she that none had spoken Luc's name, nor tried to calm her grief.

Mile after mile, towards Monmouth town, she had walked preoccupied and unspeaking, keeping in step with the others, pausing when they paused, but neither eating nor drinking upon the way . . . Luc is dead . . . The words beat relentlessly into her brain, their sureness increasing with every forced step, every measured mile . . . She walked like an automaton, expression fixed, eyes blankly unseeing, her movements were as stilted, her emotions dead . . . She was nothing without him . . . It was his touch, alone, which had forced her to life . . . Becky had put a hand to Jed's arm, eyes raised to his in helpless appeal, then had made to speak sharply to Sarah. "Leave her be, Becky . . ." His eyes had held warning as firm as his answering pressure upon her arm . . . A time to grieve, Jed thought, wearily. We each have need of a time to grieve . : .

The market town of Monmouth had been alive with the bustling activities of drovers and their flocks, farmers, traders, and those intent upon bargaining . . . There were stalls heaped high with vegetable produce, freshly baked loaves, honeys and preserves, pickles and chutneys . . . with clothing and trinkets enough to brighten the most jaundiced and lack-lustre eye . . . Jed and the drovers had been greeted jocularly by others of their kind, and news and opinions were avidly exchanged, letters of credit presented, commissions executed, and private errands run.

They had crossed the humpbacked bridge crouched over the river Monnow, and walked through the splendidly arched gatehouse of the little town, and on past the tollhouse . . . They had made camp at Wyesham above the meandering river, and below the rolling greenness of the Kymin Hill. It was a lush and fertile countryside, well-leaved in spring and summer and even with the wooded hollows and hillsides winter-bare, it had an undeniable richness and splendour; the natural abundance of a river valley with its fecund alluvial soil.

It was here that Luc came, quietly, and unannounced, to join them. He had simply walked to the fire side and settled himself beside Jed, setting his pack to rest. The vociferous excitement of his welcome by the drovers and lads had brought the womenfolk hurrying from their makeshift beds, agog with curiosity at the disturbance.

Becky, roused from sleep by the clamour, had roughly shaken Sarah into wakefulness, bidding her come and join in the fun . . . Sarah had dutifully obeyed, but with neither speed nor enthusiasm, so that, finally, Becky felt honour bound to upbraid her for her sluggishness, declaring, sharp-tongued, "I do not know what ails you, Sarah!" although she knew full well. "You are long-faced as a sheep, and as spirited a companion . . ." When Sarah had sleepily appeared, with Becky beside her, the gibbous moon was high . . . Luc had risen from the fire side, and Sarah had stared at him foolishly, silenced by disbelief . . . Then, with an anguished cry, she had run straight into his arms, and he had lifted her bodily, hugging her close, then kissing her brazenly, and with such eloquent fervour, that drovers, lads, and even the women, had burst into spontaneous clapping and cheers, good humour restored . . . Neither Luc nor Sarah had heard, for they were oblivious to all save themselves and the passionate reunion of their flesh . . .

Long after most others were asleep, they had stayed awake beside the glowing wood-ash of the fire, talking of everything and nothing, as lovers do . . . wholly content with the moment and each other. They had known their reunion must be brief, but made no mention of their parting, nor of what griefs the future might hold.

Jed, lying wakeful, had glanced across at them, darkly silhouetted against the clouding moon. His throat ached with pity for Sarah's youthfulness, and the needless cruelty of the life she had suffered, and he prayed silently that, by God's good grace, she would be called upon to endure no more.

Luc and Sarah had fallen to sleep beside the spent ashes of the kindling, cheeks touching, arms entwined. Their present nearness and loving were more than either had dared to hope for, or believe . . . They made no demands for the morrow. 'Sufficient unto the day . . .'

David Tudor's orders to rejoin his regiment had arrived within the week, and for the first time in his army career he felt not only keen excitement and anticipation, but a sense of regret. The death of his father, Josiah Tudor, had been a cruel shock, and that it had occurred when David was a prisoner-of-war had given the tragedy an additional poignancy . . . The young lieutenant's grief was for the loss of his sister too, for all his efforts to trace her before his return to active service had been in vain . . . Was she alive, or dead? Starving? Forced, perhaps, into paupery, or near-slavery? She was, he thought despairingly, little more than a child; naive and gently nurtured, and he was haunted by uncertainty and fear as to what might have happened to her . . . Even his return to the coast of Wales, with its childhood haunts and friendships, had served only to exacerbate his distress . . . There were many parishioners and family friends who would willingly have counted her as one of their own, and given her shelter . . . Yet, Sarah had not returned to that one familiar place where she was known, and loved, and might have expected welcome . . .

With the dilemma of Sarah's absence unresolved, David Tudor had put his faith in Sir Frederick Loosely's determined will to succeed where he had failed . . . Mary Grantley, too, had been a generous ally, promising to continue the search unremittingly . . . Their childhood friendship had ripened into a deeper, all-embracing love; intense and consuming. There had been no reserve between them; no artifice. The time remaining to them was brief, and they had declared their love openly and with joy in their mutual discovery. There was a tenderness in their devotion which Sir Frederick, who held them both in affection, felt boded well for their future together . . . They had, both, attained maturity through early loss and personal

217

suffering. They would not easily be wrenched apart in spirit, nor defeated by physical absence . . . As their benefactor, he had good reason to feel sanguine . . . When, as Mary's unofficial guardian and long-time friend, the general had been approached by David Tudor, who tentatively declared his love for Mary, and his hopes that she would become his wife, the old gentleman had been well pleased . . . He had been generous in his delighted congratulations to them both . . . The need for his permission had, he knew, been no more than a courteous gesture on David's part; a civility. Yet, how grateful he was that they had so thoughtfully drawn him into their happiness . . . Their official engagement had been, of necessity, a hurried and private affair . . . for David would immediately be returning to his regiment, and Mary was a widow with no near kin of her own. Yet the absence of the usual lavish celebrations and strict social formalities had been no real sacrifice to either . . .

Their leave taking had been painful, for the future was uncertain, and they had shared so little time . . . Yet Mary, although plainly grieved, had neither wept nor clung to him in anguish, selfishly importuning him to stay . . . She had been first daughter, then widow, of a soldier . . . Her tears would only come later, bitterly, and when alone. She would not voice, even to herself, the fear that David would not return . . . Her work would continue secretly to aid the British, and, with God's blessing, to lessen the living hell and carnage that was war . . . David knew of Luc's part in the work, but not of her own, for she had begged Sir Frederick to tell him nothing. He would have need of all his courage and confidence for what lay ahead . . . It would serve no purpose to rob him of his peace of mind, and to bring grief to them both.

After Mary had made her farewell, in private, to David, she had stood, unobserved, at the window of the drawing room . . . Sir Frederick had taken the young lieutenant's hand to bid him Godspeed, then put a hand to his shoulder in friendship . . . The gesture had the solemn finality of a benediction; a blessing in parting, and David had stood motionless for a long moment, looking into Sir Frederick's eyes. The small scene held for Mary the frozen unreality of a dream. She seemed part of it, yet set apart . . . Tears blurred her eyes, and the two figures, the handsome young soldier and the aged general, seemed one and the same . . . a single entity, martial, proud, and defiantly erect . . . When Mary had impatiently shaken her head to ease away the tears, and looked up again, the carriage was already making its way along the cobblestones, the paired horses prancing elegantly, heads tossing, harness jangling, hooves ringing out like tocsins upon the winter air . . . Sir Frederick no longer looked martial and proud, but a tired and shrunken old man, weighed down by his years, and a weight of knowledge and regret . . .

When he had come within, deliberately straightening, then bracing himself to bring Mary comfort, she had run at once into his arms. He had felt the wetness of her tears upon his shirt front, and had soothed her as in childhood, murmuring, and stroking the pale gold hair . . . He had done so after Sheldon's death, and after the deaths of Mary's parents of a virulent fever which she alone had survived . . . The arms which held her were strong, the love undiminished, but she was aware of the frailness of his bones, the toll which age had demanded and cruelly taken of his flesh.

Mary's renewed tears were not for David alone, but for Sir Frederick, for Luc, and for herself. She wept for that security which they had unthinkingly shared, accepting, believing its innocence would never change . . . In the end, she could not have said which of them was the comforter, and which the comforted.

Luc had made no secret of the fact that his was but a fleeting visit to Monmouth to further his courtship of Sarah, and to renew his growing friendship with Jed, Becky and the drovers . . . He would not immediately be returning with them to the south Wales hinterland, but travelling across country through Abergavenny and the Vale of Neath, and thence to Swansea seaport, where he had urgent business to attend. None questioned the nature of it, for although they expressed regret at his leaving again so soon, they were, by character and occupation, stubbornly independent and well used to the comings and goings of others of their trade . . . Luc's courtship of Sarah, as Jed's of Becky, had been wholly approved. It was the most normal thing in all the world, they were agreed, for a man and maid, thrust so intimately together in the springtime of their lives, to respond as nature intended . . . There was naught amiss in loving . . . Yet, despite their familiarity with the cycles of animal life, and creation, their own moral code was strong and rigidly inflexible; perhaps as protection for themselves, and their way of life . . . As Luc had discovered, with the single exception of Jim Parslowe, the drovers were honest and God-fearing folk, hard working, loyal and compassionate . . . Many, as Jed was swift to boast, had become well known preachers and poets, the wayside their pulpit, and the changing countryside and seasons their inspiration . . . They were close to nature and mankind . . . but set their behaviour above that of the beasts, for were they not human beings, with immortal souls . . .? It was accepted that whereas lads and young maids might indulge in innocent flirtations, it was merely a prelude to congenial parting, or serious courtship . . . Courtship led to marriage; marriage to procreation . . . Jed and Luc were cognisant of the rules, and scrupulously obeyed them. Becky, for all her seeming wildness and exuberant ways, was known to be chaste, and loyal to Jed. Sarah was the daughter of a clergyman, a gentlewoman bred . . . There would be weddings, for sure, when lambing was over and done. Then the spring exodus would find them once more upon the well worn drovers' roads, and, as like as not, the newlyweds with them . . . It was a hard and taxing life, none would deny it, but it bred a comradeship like no other . . . In a year or so, give or take a season, Becky would doubtless turn broody, and settle herself securely into Jed's warm nest, her wandering done . . . She had the makings of a tidy wife and an affectionate and devoted mother . . . Life would never be dull for those about her, but if, sometimes, she yearned for that wider freedom of the drovers' drifts, and the open sky of a starlit night, then none, save she, would know of it . . . She would count Jed's love both miracle and blessing . . . the sweeter for coming to her late. She would walk beside him in all save flesh upon every familiar furlong of the roads, in storm and sunshine, good years and bad . . . When he could walk no more, she would tend him as patiently, and as lovingly, as he tended the flocks and herds within his care . . . That was the proper way of things for those who had made their vows before God . . . Once made, they must never be broken.

220

Luc had quietly arisen with the first glow of light and had hurried away, reluctant to face a tearful leave-taking from Sarah . . . She had been sleeping with the innocent soundness of a child, face flushed, lips gently parted, hair spread in soft disarray upon her pillow of dry leaves . . . She had stirred, and murmured involuntarily upon his leaving, one slim arm escaping the blanket of her cloak . . . Luc had paused, covertly, to watch her . . . There was a deeply protective tenderness within him, and regret, but they served only to stiffen his resolution. He must be away before Sarah and the rest awakened, for their sake and his own. He would travel on foot until the rest of the world stirred, and the real work of the day began . . . Before he reached the outskirts of Abergavenny, he would find a secluded copse or ill-frequented by-way, and change into his gentleman's clothing, and hire a chaise at the nearest livery stable or inn. The long journey to Swansea would be effected more quickly, and in comfort and safety. He had gold enough, and presence enough, to arouse no suspicion in others, and none would be seeking him in Monmouthshire or Wales. Memory of the information which he had been able to dispatch to Mary, and through her to the military, stayed vivid within his mind . . . It listed, from first to last, every known safe house in England and Wales, and even beyond the Irish Sea . . . More, it gave the names and credentials of those within; known adherents of and active fighters for Napoleon, and, more importantly, those whose allegiance had previously remained unknown . . . Turncoats from amongst the emigrés, eminent British statesmen, and others of power and influence, whose treachery had been well hid . . . Would his crusade now be ended at Swansea, or would he be expected to extend it into Ireland, and even beyond, to France? There would certainly be British soldiers already expertly observing him and those he had named . . . Men from some special unit, trained in counter-espionage and all that it entailed . . . Once in Swansea, his future would be made clear, its course set and immutable. Luc felt neither fear nor exhilaration, simply the calm certainty that he was nearing his journey's end. It seemed preordained, inevitable, yet, how much was owed to his childhood suffering and need for revenge, he would never be sure . . . He preferred to think of it as just retribution; God's will . . . If the price demanded should be his own life, then so be it. Luc's step upon the road was firm, his manner assured. He was, to all appearances, a working drover, rough-hewn, and striding purposefully, and alone . . . but he was not alone. Memory walked beside him, and the image of that delicate oval face, with eyes the shape and colour of hazel fruit, a ripeness of brown and silvery green . . . Sarah Tudor; vying insistently with the past.

CHAPTER 22

Luc had walked steadily for hours, relishing the crisp freshness of the early morning air and the stark beauty of the winter landscape . . . There were few others abroad, and those either lone drovers, herding small flocks of sheep, or geese, or farm labourers, whose day began with cock-crow and ended with dusk. They greeted Luc as one of their own kind, showing the companionship of those forced to isolation and toil, while others, more indolent, lie abed . . . When he was within first glimpse of the town, amidst its rolling hills, and with the brooding and unmistakable dark shape of the 'Sugar Loaf' beyond, Luc took sanctuary in a small beech coppice. There, safely screened from view by the closeness of its silver-barked trees, he emptied his pack of his gentleman's clothing, then exchanged them for the less salubrious garments he already wore. His discarded drover's clothing he neatly piled, and abandoned behind a tree . . . All he lacked now was a high silk hat and silver-topped cane . . . and they could be procured easily enough in any small town. He had gold enough, and to spare, and would visit the very first hatters of quality upon the way, then take himself to an inn or livery stables to hire a suitable gig.

So it was that Luc, attired as to the chateau born, returned to the highway. There was a smile lifting the corners of his mouth as he thought of the excitement of the first pauper or vagrant who stumbled unawares into the wood . . . His drovers' clothing would prove treasure indeed, and he did not grudge any man the use of it, for it had served him well.

His custom at the hatters and the livery stables delightedly courted and with his needs satisfied, Luc drove his horse and carriage expertly over the cobblestones, under the archway, and on to the main highway . . . The recommended inns and stables had served him well enough, and his journey had been surprisingly swift, despite the wretched inadequacy of the roads and the punitive tolls and delays at the turnpikes . . . When a man has been forced to tramp the drifts in every foulness of weather, Luc reflected, and with all his worldly goods in a sack upon his back, then a horse and carriage is a luxury beyond imagining . . . It is a lesson hard learned, and one not easy to forget.

The countryside through which he drove had been beautiful and swift-changing; a kaleidoscope of subdued colours and forms. Gently wooded meadows and plains with the blue of mountain ridges beyond had given way to the fertile Vale of Neath, aflame with dying ferns, a purpling of heather still misting its hills . . . There were cascading waterfalls, cataracts narrowly set into the cliffs and gorges, their waters falling sheer into foaming pools beneath. Then, surprisingly, the wide scything sweep of Swansea Bay with the rockiness of Gower beyond, and across the surging greyness of sea, the darker grey coasts of Somerset and Devon, and a lighter greyness of cloud and sky, so that the horizon, land and sea became blurred and indistinguishable, one from the other, like wet colour running and mingling haphazardly upon a page . . .

The prosperity of Swansea, Luc knew, was centred around its thriving seaport, and it was in the more prestigious avenues that the houses of the more affluent merchants and shipowners lay. Such dwellings were beyond sight of that squalor attendant upon a dockside, with its piled cargoes of minerals, its sweating humanity, and its bartered flesh . . . They were as distanced from the sordid stews and alleyways, and from the crowded, insanitary hovels of those who laboured to keep them in such opulent seclusion . . . Luc, passing by in his carriage, and glancing at the ornate facades of the merchants' houses, with their florid embellishments, was wryly amused . . . Their tombs, he thought, would, inevitably, be as flamboyant a memorial to their wealth. Success must demonstrably be seen and celebrated . . . A lavish memorial, in death, might serve to inspire others . . . A laudable aim; but to be taken on trust. To actively live in such a memorial and be alive to the envious respect upon the faces of others was triumph indeed . . .

He had returned the horse and carriage to the livery stables stipulated by its owner, and set out for the safe house. As always, the instructions given to him had been precise, and he had found his way through the splendidly named 'Salubrious Passage' towards the street he sought . . . The bustle and turmoil of life flowed on around him; the noise and detritus of human living . . . Children played upon the cobblestones, heedless of the filth and stench from the rotting vegetables and the human excrement which clogged the gutters. Lean curs snapped voraciously at every stinking morsel of gristle or trash thrown; whether from upper window or open doorway, whether edible or not . . . Poverty had become so familiar to him that Luc felt no revulsion, no disgust, only pity . . . His fine clothes were out of place here, but not he . . . If he aroused curiosity, it was open and without menace, and he felt no fear. Gradually the narrow cobbled alleyways had grown wider, the bleak hovels giving way to bigger, if no less crowded, dwellings, then finally to the stylish opulence of the houses of the rich.

The house Luc sought was secluded, and set amidst spacious, well-tended lawns. There was the satisfying crunch of small stones beneath Luc's hessian boots as he trod the curving carriageway to the porte-cochere. The house was splendidly Palladian in style. It was harmoniously proportioned, elegantly pillared and fenestrated, in fact, admirable in every way. Yet Luc was aware of some disharmony, an unease, springing not from the building, but within himself. It was a house lacking movement and sound, the windows blank, and with no evidence of life, even from the extensive stables and messuages beyond . . .

Luc had approached the door with reluctance, fearing that a trap was about to be sprung, and he the victim. His cautious tug upon the brass bell-pull had brought a liveried servant to the door, impeccably bewigged, and plainly expecting him, for he had been ushered immediately within . . . He had been shown into a small anteroom and courteously bidden to wait while the footman announced him . . . Luc had not seated himself, but remained rigidly standing as the minutes ticked by, then had begun to fidget, then prowl restlessly in the small confines of the room . . . He had, more than once, considered his gold half-hunter, growing ever more irritable at the enforced delay. He had been waiting a full twenty minutes, and would wait no more . . . Too angry, now, for caution, he had slipped out resolutely into the hall and, after a cursory glance about him, had surreptitiously tried the handles of the great double doors facing him . . . The handles had turned effortlessly and without jarring noise, and Luc had found himself in the oak-panelled library of the house, with its morocco-bound volumes of parchment and vellum . . . A log fire burned in the dog-grate, but Luc was as unaware of it as of the evocative smells of ink and leather, and of all else . . . All else, save the massive partner's desk and what lay awkwardly slumped over it. The man's face was hidden within his arms, his wig slipped clumsily awry, back hunched. From the awkwardness of his limbs, and his stillness, Luc knew that he was dead . . . His every instinct was to flee the place, but his limbs seemed as lifelessly frozen as those of the dead man at the desk, and he could gather neither will nor wits . . . The only sounds within the room were the crackling of the flames and his own violent heartbeats, and Luc did not know if they sounded aloud, or pulsed within his head . . . Luc's palms were damp with sweat, and he felt a prickling of fear at his nape, but he moved involuntarily towards the desk . . . There was a dryness in his throat, and a feeling of revulsion, as he forced himself to raise the corpse's stiffening head . . . There was no doubt that death had been from a gunshot wound. The mess of congealed blood and bone, torn flesh and hair, gave proof of what had been hidden, as did the gouts of dark blood upon the clothing, and the viscous pool of it upon the surface of the desk . . . The man was Sir Ewen Charlesworth. His skin was deeply cyanosed and icily cold, his jawbone already stiffening . . . The deep-set eyes were open. They held no cynicism now, no expression. They were clouded and unseeing. "Jean-Luc de Valandré?"

Startled and unnerved, Luc had swung around violently, fists instinctively raised. They had dropped uselessly to his sides as he stared into the face of his questioner, then at the twin barrels of the pistol in the man's hand. Neither face nor hand betrayed any flicker of nervous indecision.

"Jean-Luc de Valandré?" the question was repeated stonily. It was a trap, Luc knew. They were aware, then, of his betrayal,

226

his true identity. Luc's hesitation, although brief, seemed to him to last interminably. When he spoke, his voice was coolly controlled. "No. You mistake me for another . . . I am Luc Nolais, Lieutenant des Hussars . . ."

Fear lent him conviction and a certain arrogance. Yet the stranger's eyes remained as cold and steely as the pistol within his palm as he asked, with seeming indifference,

"Are they not one and the same, Monsieur le Comte de Valandré?" Luc had already tensed himself to spring and wrest the gun from his grasp when his adversary, forestalling the attack, stepped deftly aside . . . The gun remained steady and expertly trained upon Luc as he hurled himself impotently. In that split second, while he awaited the explosive force of the shot, and its crippling violence, he cursed himself for a fool. He had closed his eyes, awaiting the cracking of bone, the eruption of light and pain . . . There was nothing . . . In an agonised silence, he had waited, fearful of death, yet increasingly filled with rage. When, finally, he had dared to open his eyes, the man was regarding him quizically, saying with an ironic smile, "I fear it is sometimes hard to distinguish friend from enemy . . . Lieutenant Nolais. I concede that there is little to choose between our methods of interrogation . . ." Luc had remained impassive. "Cunning must be countered by cunning; brutality by brutality. Like by like, that is the rule of war . . . But I am preaching to the converted," he added drily, "I acknowledge you as a master of the art . . ." His pistol was still directed at Luc's chest, and primed to take aim. Luc and he regarded each other unyieldingly for a tense moment, neither willing to drop his gaze . . . Then, with bewildering suddenness, the pistol had been lowered.

"I see, Lieutenant Nolais, that you are still confused . . . Then let me explain . . ." His adversary's smile was wide now, and held genuine warmth. "I am friend, not enemy . . . Peter Hasquencort, former colonel in the Dragoons, but recently seconded to the Special Services regiment . . ."

His pistol had been carefully replaced beneath his coat, and his hand formally extended.

Luc had glanced from Hasquencort to the dead body at the desk, before coolly extending his own hand. Rage at the sheer effrontery at the trick practised upon him had given way to grudging admiration at its audacity. As Luc stretched out and grasped Hasquencort's hand, he felt amusement reluctantly bubbling within him, and soon he was laughing ruefully at the ludicrousness of the whole situation, his voice grown sharp with relief. His laughter had died away as he demanded shamefacedly of Hasquencort,

"Who killed Charlesworth? And why?"

"God alone knows!"

Hasquencort's mouth was wry. "It would have served us better had he lived . . ."

"Suicide?"

"There was a gun, certainly . . . beside the body . . ."

"But you are not convinced?"

"No . . . It was too neatly arranged . . . altogether too precise . . ." Hasquencort's voice was troubled. "The timing of it, the reason . . ." He broke off, perplexed, confessing, "I can make no sense of the whole damnable charade!"

"The servants? The man who admitted me . . .?"

"One of our own . . . The place was deserted . . . not a living soul . . ." He grimaced expressively towards Charlesworth's cadaver, adding drily, "He was already as silent as the grave, and his secrets as deep buried . . . We must look elsewhere for solution."

In answer to Luc's unspoken question, he admitted stiffly, and with some reluctance, "I concede that the fault was ours . . . We acted upon your information, de Valandré, but clumsily, and too late . . . We must look now to trap them in some other way . . ."

"You have searched him . . . Charlesworth, I mean, and the house?" "Minutely . . . We are not wholly amateurs, de Valandré; no more are they . . ." Luc's mouth twitched at the implied rebuke, but since he offered no apology, Hasquencort continued coldly, "The search will continue, of course, thoroughly and efficiently, until we are completely satisfied . . . but all evidence will, undoubtedly, have been removed or destroyed . . . This is real life, de Valandré!"

"Indeed. And Charlesworth would be the last to dispute it . . ." To his credit, Hasquencort had noticeably relaxed, and even summoned a smile before agreeing, "We can do little enough here, in all conscience . . . We had best be talking

228

elsewhere . . . and refreshing ourselves upon something more salubrious . . ."

"I confess that I shall be grateful for some stronger spirit than my own to fortify me . . ." Luc gave easy assent. "I like Charlesworth's company as little in death as in life . . ."

"But the prospect of searching him gives you little pleasure?"

"No." Luc admitted.

"Then it is best left to those more objective . . ." Hasquencort made to squire him without, adding, "Emotion and memory can be as real enemies as those we seek, and as treacherous!" He had hesitated, before continuing quietly, "It is from harsh experience I speak, de Valandré. I would have you believe it . . . They can betray you as easily . . ." Hasquencort's gaze was averted, and he seemed abstracted, as if mind and memory were also turned elsewhere. Yet Luc had no need to read his facial expression, or his eyes, to know with what painful honesty he spoke.

They had moved out of the library and into the hallway, but before Luc could make suitable reply, there had been an urgent knocking upon the door which had alerted and halted them both. An armed soldier who had been positioned close by had motioned the servant urgently aside, and then opened the door cautiously to investigate. The messenger who entered was sweat-stained and dishevelled, and as breathlessly winded as the lathered horse which Luc glimpsed upon the carriageway.

Hasquencort had read the message delivered in silence, brow furrowed in concentration . . . His face had, at first, been guardedly expressionless, but there was no concealing the excitement with which he thrust the letter into Luc's hand, or his fleeting smile of triumph.

"They have caught him, de Valandré!" Hasquecort could contain himself no longer . . . "Did you not see? The murderer . . . he already confessed!"

"He could scarcely deny it," ventured Luc, "since they found Charlesworth's engraved watch in his possession, as well as his gold, and other valuables . . . Strange that he would take such risk . . .?"

"Greed tempts the best of us, and makes us fools . . ." returned Hasquencort. "Besides, who knows what panic drove him? His instructions would have been clear . . . to kill, then to search for, and destroy, all evidence . . . His greed may well have cost him his life."

"And the lives of others, it is to be hoped," Luc agreed. "If his own life is at risk, he will have little to lose by incriminating others, and he might well gain more clemency than he deserves . . ." The messenger, who had lingered and still stood awkwardly by, said hesitantly, "There is another document, sir . . . I am instructed that it is to be delivered into the hands of a Lieutenant Luc Nolais, and no other . . . or returned with seal unbroken . . ."

Luc had stiffened, and glanced enquiringly at Hasquencort, who had shrugged his puzzlement, then curtly informed the messenger, "This is Lieutenant Nolais . . . You will deliver it to him, and await his reply."

Luc had scanned the letter rapidly, to say firmly, "There is no reply, save to give assurance that the orders were safely delivered, and will be obeyed."

He had glanced warningly at Hasquencort, who had curbed his curiosity until the messenger had been dismissed with orders to victual himself at the kitchens and see that his horse was watered, rested and fed . . . Then Luc had been steered towards a small but elegantly furnished drawing room, and the doors firmly shut. Hasquencort was evidently already familiar with the geography of the place, for he was able to pour two lavish glasses of cognac from a decanter upon the serving board, before demanding,

"Well? Am I to learn more of your future plans? I have been ordered only to assist your journey to Swansea docks, where a ship already awaits you, to take passage to Ireland . . . The carriage will arrive here in less than an hour, as directed."

He had broken off, staring expectantly at Luc.

"Then I suggest, sir, that you cancel it . . . or change its destination . . ." Luc said, straightfaced, "for I will be a passenger to London, with you . . . It seems that the safe houses have all been invaded, and those within them successfully captured . . ."

"And?"

"And I am instructed to report immediately to London, under your protection . . ." He smiled ruefully. "I am informed that those in Ireland will be dealt with by the army . . . There is one

230

clearing house only there, and its whereabouts already known . . . It seems, sir, that I am the only one able to identify those who interrogated, and gave . . . hospitality, to me and to others of my kind."

Hasquencort, appreciating the irony of it, broke into delighted laughter and extended his hand cordially, gripping Luc's hand in his own, then putting a welcoming hand to his shoulder. The urgent knocking upon the door of the room was as unexpected as it was startling, and both men had tensed apprehensively before Hasquencort's terse command of "Come!". The young officer who entered was supremely well disciplined, as military in his bearing as in his dress . . . The salute he gave was as impeccably tailored as his uniform. "Well?" Hasquencort demanded curtly.

"Papers, sir. Discovered in the search . . ."

Hasquencort had taken them and scanned them briefly, demanding irritably, "Why were they overlooked? Where were they found?"

"They were well concealed, sir . . . sewn into the dead man's coat, beneath the lining . . ."

Hasquencort had dismissed him with a grunted few words which might have been of approbation or censure, then turned to Luc.

"Letters of credit . . ." he declared brusquely.

"Concerning whom?"

"The bearer, Sir Ewen Charlesworth . . ."

"Foolish of him . . ." Luc exclaimed in puzzlement. "Unlike Charlesworth to be so indiscreet . . . It is not in character."

"Unless they served as insurance, protection of a sort . . .?"

"You think he suspected that he might be killed?"

"That . . . or he was unsuspecting, and murdered in panic, with his commission still to be fulfilled."

Hasquencort, who had been cursorily rifling through the papers to gather their gist, had stopped with a startled exclamation, face incredulous. He had thrust the letter into Luc's hand, saying harshly, "They were to be delivered by Charlesworth to a Swansea bank . . ." Then, irritated by Luc's slowness, he ordered sharply, "For God's sake, look to the signatory, man! You see who guarantees it?"

"Dear heaven!" Luc's outraged disbelief was as real as

Hasquencort's own. "Is it a hoax? A macabre joke on Charlesworth's part to confound us?"

Hasquencort said, with wry humour, "I hope to God that it proves so! I would not dare to openly accuse or interrogate him . . . It would need the army, and government, both, and the prime minister's consent . . ."

They had stared at each other in awed silence, until Hasquencort's lips had twitched involuntarily as he blurted,

"Upon my oath, de Valandré, I am sorely tempted to burn the damned things! If they prove a hoax, then my military career might as easily go up in flames and smoke . . . I will be guilty by association . . ." He gave a rueful smile. "Charlesworth might well have destroyed us both . . ."

"But if it is true . . ." Luc reminded, "then we shall have destroyed them all, from the least to the greatest, and Charlesworth will have been our unwitting ally."

"Poetic justice indeed!" murmured Hasquencort, without noticeable enthusiasm, and doggedly pouring twin glasses of cognac. He glanced up, to demand, "Well, de Valandré, what do you think? Was he their victim and dupe, or cunning enough to take full revenge . . .?" Luc shrugged, and raised the glass which Hasquencort had handed to him, saying, "Charlesworth is dead. That is the only certainty!"

CHAPTER 23

Jed and the drovers had made their way to the sea coast of Glamorgan upon the southernmost shores of Wales. Many of the women and lads had been returned to the hinterland and those smallholdings and simple stone cottages from whence they had come . . . Their coming had been long awaited, and their welcome by family and friends was rapturous, and as often warm with joyous laughter as tears . . . They were heroes all, for they had travelled far, and their small earnings would mean the difference between proud survival and paupery to those within . . . Small matter if they had served as the lowest of the low; weeders and scullions, humble graziers and unskilled lads . . . Here, they were deliverers all, and their worth unequalled . . . Jed had been feted and thanked most affectingly wherever he went, and treated with the respect owed to an honest and caring master . . . He had been the recipient of many small gifts of home-made cordials and receipts, but, flushed and happy as he was, it was Becky's pride in him which shone the brightest . . .

Sarah could not fail to be touched by the warmth and selfless generosity of those she met, or to cherish their caring, although her mind strayed often to Luc, and she could not be wholly at ease.

At the last, when all others had been delivered to their homes, Jed had proudly led Sarah and Becky to his own tiny farm upon the hills above the quiet hamlets of Nottage and Newton, where Sarah had once lived. It was a remote and windswept place, the stone dwelling ill-furnished and primitive, for all Jed's earnings were spent upon improving his small flock and herd. The animals had been tended in his absence by a wiry, wry-necked old man, a former drover, gnarled and twisted as a wind-bent tree . . . His wife, a spry old lady with hair like

233

thistledown, had greeted Jed with real affection, kissing him, then chiding him roundly for not having sent a lad ahead from the village to warn of her coming, that she might have had a nourishing meal prepared . . . Her faded eyes had grown keen with curiosity in her weathered face as they rested, first upon Becky, and then upon Sarah. Jed's explanations given, she had shyly taken Sarah's hand, quietly bidding her welcome. But, at Becky she had gazed long and hard; a scrutiny intense but without rancour. Then she had sucked in her lip consideringly and nodded approval at Jed, saying briskly,

"Aye, you have chosen handsomely, master, in spirit and flesh. 'Tis time you were settled, and with one knowing the needs and ways of a drover . . . and who will not fret at hardship and loneliness." She had carefully wiped her roughened hand upon the apron covering her red flannel skirt before drawing Becky to her in close embrace, declaring without self-consciousness, "My Daniel and I welcome you to Stormy Downs, my dear, for Jed's dear sake, and your own . . . He is an honest man, and there is no better friend and master in all the world . . . He will never treat you with other than fairness, you may be sure, for that is the way of it . . ."

Jed had shuffled awkwardly in his boots, too embarrassed even to attempt denial, but Becky's return embrace of the old woman was every whit as naturally loving as the glance she bestowed upon Jed.

Sarah, intercepting it, had felt a warmth of affection for them both, and a sense of indebtedness for the generosity with which they had taken her into their lives, and accepted her as one of their own. They were all remaining of family now, with her father and David gone, and Luc, perhaps, lost to her . . . Despite all her efforts to quell them, tears had risen to her eyes, and she felt the burn of them as they overflowed and fell.

"Oh, my poor dear, you are tired and cold . . ." the old woman exclaimed penitently. "What can I be thinking of to prattle and hinder you so? I will boil up a nice hot bowl of mutton cawl for you all, and Daniel shall build the fire high . . . and you shall take your rest . . . It has been a long harsh journey home!"

"Yes." Jed's compassionate gaze was upon Sarah as, with an

arm about her shoulders and Becky's, he had led them gently within his house. "Yes," he said, "It has been a long harsh journey home, and, for some, it is not yet ended . . . Pray God we may all find safety and peace."

Within the small, stone-built cottage across the field, Daniel Harris was watching his wife as she stirred the broth in the vast iron pot suspended from a chain over the open fire . . .

"Aye. 'Tis good to have him home again, Hetty," he agreed, echoing her words. "I have never felt Jed's absence more keenly than of late . . . nor the weight of my work heavier – 'tis age and infirmity that blight me, no doubt . . . My old flesh was ever less willing than the spirit . . ."

She had paused in her stirring to look at him in concern, willing herself to deny the changes in him, and yet, unable . . . Seeing her distress, he had said contritely,

"When summer comes, 'twill make things right again . . ." Then he had reached over impulsively to put an arm about her waist, declaring with affection, "There is none in all the world your equal at cooking, my love . . . You are the best of women, and the best of wives . . ." She had smiled her delight at his praise, turning to put a hand tenderly to his cheek.

"I'll wager that Jed will be saying as much to his own wife ere long . . ." she ventured with satisfaction.

"Not when he has a fill of your mutton cawl, Hetty," he insisted stoutly. "It is a treasure to set a body yearning . . ." he sniffed appreciatively.

"'Tis a filling of Jed's old cradle I most yearn for," she said. "That will be treasure enough . . ."

It was with strangely mixed feelings that David Tudor had hired a gig and driven himself straightway, to General Loosely's house in Salisbury Square . . . To his chagrin, he had been refused permission to rejoin his regiment. The medical officer had pronounced himself dissatisfied with the wound upon the young lieutenant's leg. It was painfully slow to heal, he declared, and in need of further treatment and rest. All David Tudor's protestations and pleas had availed him nothing. He was unfit for active service, the physician insisted, "and it would take at least a month before he would consent to re-examine

235

his patient, and give opinion . . ." From the window, he had surreptitiously watched the young man as he awkwardly descended the steps, and climbed into the carriage. He had been right in his prognosis, he decided. The wound remained livid and unhealed, but there were deeper wounds, and scars unseen . . . Captivity and privation had taken their toll. His decision had been made, not for David Tudor's sake alone. To command in battle, a man must lead with confidence and certainty; body and mind in harmony . . . There are no second chances . . .

David had arrived at the Square chastened and disconsolate, feeling his return to be a humiliating anticlimax . . . General Loosely, as was his custom, had taken himself to the library, to partake of his finest Canary wine, to idly turn pages, and to snooze beside the fire unseen. His leather armchair was vastly comfortable, and had become nicely moulded to the contours of his flesh. Moreover, its winged sides protected him from draughts and prying eyes . . . It was haven and solace both . . .

Mary, her farewells to David made, had remained in the drawing room, wretched, and too close to tears to attempt to read, or take up her sketching pad, or even her embroidery frame . . . She had wept so much that she was well aware of what a fright she had made of herself . . . Her nostrils were reddened and sore, her eyelids swollen, and her whole face felt shapeless and bruised . . . Yet she had neither the will nor wish to rouse herself.

The unexpected grating of carriage wheels upon the cobbles roused her from her apathy and sent her hurrying to the window . . . Dear Heaven!, she thought in pained disbelief as she watched David alighting, and handing the reins to a groom, why had he returned? What ails him? He looked so anxiously ill-at-ease that she almost wept anew. Then, her appearance and grief forgotten in her fury to comfort him, she ran from the room and through the hallway, brushing aside the startled footman in her effort to reach the door . . . When she had wrenched it open, she had flung herself down the steps and straight into David's arms, with no thought for reticence or propriety . . . He had kissed her with as little reserve, and General Loosely, grudgingly raked from sleep by the cacophony without, rose stiffly, and stumped, frowning, to the window to remonstrate . . . His scowling disapproval was replaced by a smile . . . a smile of quite absurd indulgence. It mattered not a jot to him that his guests made so public and indiscreet a display . . . It did not concern him that Mary was a respectable widow; a gentlewoman shamelessly defying convention . . . Nor that the young lieutenant was wilfully aiding and abetting her, indeed, encouraging her, in the scandalous act . . . He saw two young people, whom he loved, joyously reunited. Then, lest they think him an unwitting voyeur, he settled himself back in his armchair, and poured himself another glass of Canary wine, and contentedly awaited their coming. If David Tudor's wounds had caused him pain and grief, then, indirectly, they had brought him healing, too, with the promise of a future kinder than the past . . . Sir Frederick felt privileged to have played a part in it.

Luc and Peter Hasquencort had interviewed Joe Rees, the alleged murderer of Sir Ewen Charlesworth, at the barracks where he had been detained awaiting trial. The truculence and open contempt he had shown at his capture had vanished, now, with the realisation of what punishment might lie in store . . . He was a most abject and pathetic creature, overeager to unburden himself, and that others should be incriminated in his stead. He had confessed freely to being Charlesworth's killer, although he had shown no real regret save for his own capture . . . Nonetheless, they had gleaned useful information about those formerly manning the safe house with him at Swansea, and of their plans and present whereabouts . . . Rees's immediate superior, who had given him the order to kill Charlesworth, was already known to the British, and had been swiftly apprehended. Rees, himself, had been briefed to escape upon the fishing boat from Swansea docks, which was to have transported Luc to Ireland. Finally, it had been forced to sail without either, in order to catch the tide . . . It had been skilfully intercepted by a pilot cutter, its crew well armed, and those involved brought ashore to stand trial, together with two French prisoners-of-war, escaped from the hulks . . . Luc, who had interrogated both, had felt a certain grudging sympathy for them, despite the knowledge that they were avowed enemies,

237

and, to his own mind, traitors to France . . . How ironic, then, that they should have survived privation, and hostile interrogation by their own kind, only to be betrayed into his hands. Had they known his true identity, it would have proved the final humiliation. The French Fox was a living legend, an inspiration to all those compatriots who strove to escape prison camp or hulk . . . The true irony, Luc thought, lay in that each of them honestly believed his own to be the true cause, and himself to be the rightful defender of France . . .

Hasquencort, aware of the unresolved conflict within Luc, said quietly, when they were alone,

"I fear, de Valandré, that we too often forget that wars are fought, not by countries, but people, like ourselves . . ." When Luc made no reply, he continued, "The ultimate tragedy is that, in the end, there are no real winners, or losers, only survivors . . ."

"Then we must fight the harder to ensure that the just survive, and justice rules . . ." Luc admonished sharply.

"Indeed," Hasquencort agreed, "else there would be neither sense nor purpose in what we both, as soldiers, have chosen to do . . ." He smiled ruefully, confessing, "I sometimes wish that I could see as much of the battle as God, and as clearly, and be as impartial a judge . . ." He had looked at Luc shrewdly. "But we are human and fallible, de Valandré, and that is our weakness and strength in judging others . . . and best accepted, first as last."

Luc's first defiant encounter with Peter Hasquencort had given each of them a wary respect for the other. Respect had grown into liking, and an easy friendship had grown between the pair. Luc soon learned from their shared interrogation of the captured French prisoners-of-war, and others of Napoleon's sympathisers, that Hasquencort was shrewd, skilful, and highly successful at gleaning information. Luc saw in his disciplined bearing and manner much of General Loosely's innate authority. There was the same austerity of features and flesh, a rigidity of purpose which might have proved self-destructive had it not been tempered by patience and humour. The capture of the safe houses, and those within, had yielded useful information, but their most singular and disturbing find had been the note of credit upon Sir Ewen Charlesworth's dead body . . . Had he been suspected of being the informer who had betrayed the escape organisation to the British, and caused the invasion of the safe houses, and the destruction of the line? It would seem so . . . and if it proved to be the case, then he had as surely betrayed the man who had ordered his execution . . . Yet the difficulties in arresting Charlesworth's murderer, and bringing him to justice, would be acute. He was protected by his great wealth and power; his political influence, and the range of his philanthropy. The Duc de Saint Lo was no penniless French exile, deprived of his titles and patrimony. He was a friend, not only of kings and governments, but of the common people whose lives were the kinder for his charity . . . Neither Luc nor Hasquencort was certain that the Duc de Saint Lo could be successfully called to account . . . Indictment lay in the hands of the prime minister, Spencer Perceval, and his cabinet ministers. How much protection Saint Lo would receive from them would depend upon favours received, and the influence he still wielded . . . Luc and Hasquencort could only pray that it would not be enough to exempt him from interrogation and arrest, if need were proven . . . otherwise, all they had achieved would have been meaningless . . . He would be free to begin again.

On the windswept heights of Stormy Downs, Jed had returned to no easy rest. He had simply exchanged the labours and hardships of the road for more rigorous toil upon his bleak acres of pastureland with his own few beasts and scattered flock. The grazing was good, for the earth, despite the salt-laden winds from the sea, was richly productive . . . It grew root vegetables in the winter, and wheat and oats enough to be milled into flour . . . The herd provided milk, butter and cheese aplenty, with buttermilk for the calves. There were the occasional joints of tender mutton for cawl, or baking, and, the ultimate luxury, a yearly flitch of pearly pink bacon to be laboriously salted, and hung from the smoke-blackened rafters.

Jed was determined that, one day, he would purchase and breed a fine variety of cattle, superior to the ubiquitous Welsh runts favoured by others. It was to this end that he worked so sedulously as a master drover, living frugally upon the roads, and hoarding his small earnings . . . Already he possessed a pair of choicest Montgomery oxen, four black Castlemartin cattle with firm flesh and distinctive drooping horns . . . Jed boasted, too, a tiny flock of black-faced Jacob's sheep, renowned for their thick fleeces and superior wool, which would certainly earn him rich dividends . . . Yet these he would not drive to London, nor part with to the graziers who came persistently seeking them out . . . They were his pride and his treasure, and he would sooner have dismantled his farmhouse, stone by stone, then taken to the drovers roads for ever, rather than sacrifice his dream to another . . .

Now, with Becky beside him at the farm, Jed was visibly happier than at any time in his life . . . She worked alongside him tirelessly, from dawn until dusk, without carping or complaint, and taking upon herself every menial task, grateful to be in his company. Daniel and Hetty Harris, and those few outpaupers whom Jed could afford to occasionally employ, were totally enslaved by her, and Jed plainly besotted . . . For the first time in countless years, the farmhouse became again a place of gaiety and music, with a warmth as generous as Becky's own spirit . . . Sarah, too, despite her preoccupation with Luc's absence, seemed to grow more confidently at ease . . . She worked beside Hetty Harris as willing scullery maid and cook, cheerfully fetching and carrying water from the well, feeding the hens, and collecting the eggs, washing, scouring and sweeping. Becky, secure in Jed's love, and with her wedding set for three weeks hence, knew that it was fear for Luc's safety which drove her friend, and that in work and tiredness Sarah found salvation . . . Becky had tried, in vain, to persuade her to visit the village and church at Newton where she and Jed were to be wed, but Sarah would not . . . Josiah Tudor had been vicar of the parish, and memory and loss were now too raw to allow return . . . She had, at last, accepted that David, her brother, was dead, and that to speak of it to others would cruelly reopen old wounds that were best left scarred. She had tried to explain as much to Becky, but Becky had been dismissive, then obstinate, chiding her for her stubbornness . . . It was Jed who, seeing Sarah's distress, and sensitive to her hurt, had gently taken Becky aside, saying,

"Leave her be, Becky. The past is better dead and buried with those she has lost . . . Leave it until Luc's return."

"And if he does not return?"

"Then she must make her home here, with us . . . She is as near to us as kin. I would not see her homeless, and humbled further . . ."

Becky had clasped her arms about his broad neck, and kissed him soundly, declaring affectionately,

"You are the sweetest man God ever put breath into, Jed Perkins, and the kindest, and best . . . and I am the richest and most blessed of women . . ."

"You are satisfied with so little, Becky."

"No, my love . . . I am a woman of discernment and pride, and would have no other . . ."

His broad, ingenuous face had flushed and grown absurdly tender as he drew her to him, and bent his head to set a kiss to her soft lips . . . She had smiled at him afterwards, eyes ashine with affection, to explain hesitantly,

"I do not try to chivvy Sarah into returning to Newton from my own selfishness alone, Jed . . . I would have her share in my happiness, be bride maid to me, if she will . . ."

"I know, my love, but it must come of her own choosing . . . There are too many ghosts, too many sad memories, and the happiness of others might serve to make her feel her own loss the keener."

She had nodded, and squeezed Jed's hand, her eyes filling with compassionate tears for Sarah and all those denied her glistening happiness . . . Oh, but his Becky was a rare woman, he thought, and as tenderly loving as she was beautiful. He would never understand why she had chosen him, a rough, working drover, with naught to offer save a few bleak acres, and his love for her . . . She was a miracle, and one which he would never understand. But he would be thanking God for it, most humbly, for all the days of his life, and beyond.

CHAPTER 24

Luc had found no difficulty in identifying those assisting espionage within the safe houses. Their faces and voices were as vivid in his memory as the bruises he had suffered, and the scars he still bore . . . Their interrogation had proved harder. For the most part they were highly trained men, resourceful, and fanatically addicted to Napoleon's cause. The more advanced their position in the hierarchy, the more obstinate and contemptuous was their response . . . Their weakness lay in those like Joe Rees, tempted to murder for gain. He held no allegiance to the self-styled emperor, or to them, his only aim now, self-preservation. His blurted confession had been the knife-blade inserted to crack and force apart others, and gradually, and skilfully, Hasquencort had widened that rift . . . Luc could not help but admire his ruthless professionalism, for he was painfully aware that he lacked Hasquencort's objectivity. He could not divorce himself from remembrance of his treatment at their hands, and their arrogance infuriated him. Despite all Luc's efforts to remain detached and impartial, his antagonism too often surfaced with the need and opportunity to extract revenge.

It was while he was engaged upon interrogating such a prisoner that the special messenger arrived in haste . . . Luc had been immediately summoned by Hasquencort. The orders were urgent, and countermanded all others. They were to leave without delay for London. Upon the morrow, at three p.m., they would present themselves for interview at the War Office, in the presence of the Home Secretary, and Spencer Perceval. Hasquencort had grimaced at Luc, then shrugged his shoulders resignedly, but there was no mistaking his inner conflict. Despite all his efforts to appear calm, his face was as much a mixture of nervous excitement and doubts as Luc's own . . . This was the opportunity they sought. Properly exploited, it could mean an end to the web of espionage and deceit, as to the predator who had so skilfully spun it. It would no longer entrap . . . Yet, if they failed, they must sacrifice not only themselves, but the futures of countless others. There was no questioning, or dissent, for neither man could safely trust his voice to keep his emotions hidden . . . Their powers of speech and persuasion would be needed for the morrow. They must make ready to leave.

They had travelled to London in Hasquencort's small coach, arriving at such an ungodly hour that Luc had been grateful to accept his companion's offer of a bed for the night at the small bachelor apartment kept ready for him in his parents' house . . . Despite the incivility of the hour, a fire had been kept burning in the grate, and a servant had been aroused to prepare them a nourishing hot soup and a cold collation . . . Despite himself, Luc had eaten ravenously and with enjoyment, and his slumbers in the somewhat cramped bed had further restored him to humour. He could almost forget the weary catechism and ordeal which lay ahead.

He had arisen early, and aftei a light breakfast, and with Hasquencort's blessing, had arranged to be driven to Sir Frederick's house in Salisbury Square at a respectable hour. The old gentleman would be awake before dawn, Luc knew, for training and habit were well engrained, but age and temperament demanded a leisurely breakfast, if he were to remain equable. It was a fact of life which Luc had early learned and was scrupulous to observe.

His unexpected arrival had caused more excitement and furore than he could ever have foreseen, and Luc was equally as incredulous. When Sir Frederick had hurried from the library to welcome him, Luc had stared, mystified, at the gaunt stranger accompanying him, for a brief moment failing to recognise him as David Tudor. Then, before he had even greeted his guardian as he deserved, Luc and David were joyously clasping and tangling with each other as companionably as of old, amidst delighted cries and attempts at explanation.

When Mary had appeared, Luc's comical astonishment had been so complete that she had broken into spontaneous laughter, so helplessly amused that, for a while, she was quite unable to kiss him and welcome him teasingly, as a surrogate sister ought.

The news of their engagement had pleased him beyond measure, and, ensconced in Sir Frederick's sanctum, it had been celebrated fervently upon Canary wine, to the satisfaction of all.

It was then that Luc had nerved himself with courage enough to assure David Tudor that his sister lived, and that he was not only sure of her whereabouts and safety, but loved her as she loved him.

Luc had feared that he had blurted it too clumsily, and that David, still weakened from the aftermath of his imprisonment and wounds, might be too emotionally distraught to accept the truth of it . . . But it was Sir Frederick who had caused them concern, so pale and trembling with shock and agitation that Mary had been forced to minister to him with the silver vinaigrette from within the pocket of her gown . . .

It would have been impossible to recreate the intensity of the joy, anguish and relief within that room and deep within each one of them . . . They had wept and rejoiced and questioned and demanded. The shadows of the past had been dissolved by the merciful happiness of the present, the promise of the future, and none was too proud to openly thank God that it was so . . .

Luc's stay had been, of necessity, brief, and much still remained to be told and resolved, and as much, through circumstance, to be kept hidden . . . Mary had taken the first opportunity to secretly tell him of her elation that the safe houses had been raided, and the trail of espionage broken, although she had sensed his reserve, and asked for no explanation as to why he must leave.

"When all is ended . . ." he had promised, "I will explain, but there are reasons . . . strictures upon speaking freely, you understand?"

"Yes, my dear, when it is ended . . ." She had put a hand to his arm, and raised herself to set a kiss upon his cheek, then her intelligent eyes had looked searchingly into Luc's dark ones, and she had nodded. "I believe that for you, as for me, Luc, much is already ended . . . that pain which drove me, that violence which drove you so fiercely towards revenge . . . When all is ended, we will begin anew . . . There

244

will be no more need for secrets, no dissembling . . ." Luc had not spoken, but had lifted her hand and pressed its soft palm to his lips. She was wrong. It was not ended, and would never be, until Napoleon was vanquished, and he stood once more upon the soil of Valandré, its master and keeper . . .

Luc had returned to Peter Hasquencort's bachelor establishment so transfigured with excitement at finding David Tudor alive, and in good spirits, that he could scarcely speak coherently. It was only with the greatest forbearance and difficulty that Hasquencort was able to make sense of the garbled adventure he told. So bewildered was he by the complexities of the tale, and the relationship of one to another, that his repeated questions, and slowness, had driven Luc almost to the verge of distraction . . . Yet, with the gist of it absorbed, and news of David's betrothal to Mary, Jed's to Becky, and of Sarah's firm promise to Luc, his early confusion had given way to honest pleasure at his friend's newfound happiness, and his congratulations were sincere and unrestrained.

It had been hard to dispel Luc's euphoria, and return his mind to the immediate task ahead . . . their meeting with the Home Secretary and Spencer Perceval. Hasquencort did not doubt that it would prove bitter and acrimonious, and they would be regarded with mistrust. Saint Lo was a man of power and influence, and their combined word would count for little against his . . . Their only real proof of his treachery lay in the letter of credit, signed in his name, and given to Charlesworth . . . Would it suffice? Hasquencort was not sanguine . . . They were accusing a man of internationally accepted integrity of being, at best, a scoundrel, and at worst a traitor . . . Saint Lo's reputation was less likely to be in doubt than their own . . . They must present themselves well, and deliver their evidence and findings convincingly. It was with understandable misgivings that Hasquencort summoned the coach and a liveried coachman, with postillion, to drive them to the address they sought.

"If we are to present ourselves, then it had best be done stylishly . . ." Hasquencort declared philosophically, "although, I doubt we shall outdo Saint Lo's elegance . . ."

"It is his eloquence which worries me," Luc confessed, adding, "although I might hope that the gentlemen concerned would be perceptive enough to look beyond mere modishness."

245

"Indeed," Hasquencort agreed, straightfaced. "Perhaps you would have proved more convincing as a drover, Luc? It might have helped you separate the sheep from the goats . . ."

They had alighted with suitable gravity from the coach, and made their way within. From their impeccable sartorial elegance and air of quiet assurance, none in authority would have known of their turmoil.

The questioning had been as thoroughly abrasive as they had feared, and some among their interrogators had been openly critical and hostile . . . Yet Luc and Hasquencort had remained courteous and attentive, never vacillating from the truth nor showing offence . . . Eventually, their testimony given, and the letter of credit produced and fiercely debated, they had been asked to withdraw into an anteroom until final decision was made . . . They had waited in a fever of despair and impatience until the summons to re-enter came; too exhausted by emotion to discuss what the probable outcome might be.

It was not the Home Secretary nor any other member of the cabinet who rose to address them, but the prime minister, himself. Spencer Perceval had stared at them long and hard before announcing his decision, and the agonised suspense of those who waited had been palpable.

"The accusations you have made, sirs, are grave indeed . . ." he gave opinion. "The gentleman of whom we speak is a known financier and philanthropist; one whose credentials and integrity have never before been questioned . . ."

Luc's spirits had dropped, for the tenor of the speech was as cool as he had expected, and the rebuke plain.

"However . . ." Spencer Perceval had paused, to glance about him, and rub a hand uneasily across his lips. "However . . . None could doubt the efficiency of your methods, nor your dedication . . . nor, indeed, your own integrity. It has been brought to my attention that besides the written evidence of . . . some complicity in the affair by the Duc de Saint Lo, the coordinator of the escape route in Ireland is prepared to swear, upon oath, to Saint Lo's involvement . . . As you, sirs, I am prepared to put my duty to my country before all other considerations, personal and public. I therefore grant you full and unreserved permission to interview the Duc de Saint Lo . . . He is here, at my express command, and awaits your

246

questioning. It will, of course, be conducted in the presence of the Home Secretary, myself, and others I shall name. If you are prepared, gentlemen, then it is best undertaken without delay . . ."

General Loosely sat alone in his library, relishing its solitude, and his own. Its very familiarity was a reassurance to him, a beacon of safety, and permanence, in a sea of change. He was too old for change. That was the pity of it. It took too harsh a toll. He was better able to withstand the blows of circumstance than its favours. To the old, joy was a more destructive emotion than grief . . . He felt enervated, drained of all strength and will. His hands upon the book he held were loose-skinned, bone without flesh; parchment dry, and liver-spotted with age, a mummified corpse, he thought, desiccated, and made useless by age.

Then, remembrance of Luc's visit, David Tudor's triumphant return, and Mary's newfound love and happiness stirred and flowed through him, quickening as new blood. Dearest of all, he thought, and what he had prayed for most fervently, the certain knowledge that Josiah Tudor's daughter lived. He had so long despaired of finding her. It was final repayment of that debt owed to his friend for bringing Luc to him, and for offering the boy home and affection when he had been rejected, and in the cruellest need . . . Sir Frederick sighed. How strange it was that Luc should be the means to finding Sarah Tudor, and that he should love her as deeply and loyally as Josiah would have wished . . . what was the phrase he sought? It all but escaped him, for his memory grew poor, outworn with his flesh . . .

"There is a destiny which shapes our ends . . . rough hew them as we may." Yes, there was a certain irony in that, a justice . . . How much of life was preordained, or simply accident, and how much changed at our own volition? The book slipped from his fingers onto the wood-grained surface of the desk, waxed and worn smooth, the patina of age upon it, as upon himself, and all that surrounded him.

He must stir himself. This lethargy and self-analysis were indulgences he must not allow . . . David and Mary had travelled to the sea coast of Wales to bring Sarah home . . . They would be returning soon, and he must make ready to welcome them. He tried to rise, but his limbs were slow to respond, his bones stiff, and he was forced to ease himself upwards by leaning upon the desk for support . . . He damned his own weakness as he felt the prickling of tears behind his closed eyelids . . . None would see him here, and know that he wept, or why he wept. It was not for himself, but for Josiah Tudor. He wept silently, and with the dry painfulness of the old, for pity, and joy, and for those dead, and for those he would never see. Then he took the book and set it carefully in place upon the shelves.

Mary had tried to quell her fears that the journey from London to Wales would prove too taxing for David, but he was determined upon travelling to bring Sarah home. Physically he was still debilitated from his imprisonment and leg wound, and he was equally as vulnerable emotionally. Yet, with Sir Frederick, she believed that to forbid the journey would cause him more distress than the inevitable rigours of the road. She was firmly intent upon travelling with him, in Sir Frederick's larger travelling coach, with coachman and postillions, and guards well armed, lest they encounter a highwayman, or footpads when alighting at the inns. Mary had taken her lady's maid as chaperone, as much for her own comfort as to appease Sir Frederick's sensibilities. She was a good, reliable soul who had been Mary's nurse in childhood, and they held each other in affection. On a practical level, Mary was convinced that should David's wound become troublesome, or his sister prove in need of comforting, or aid, then Joan Pullen's experience and sound commonsense would serve them as well . . . It was certain that she would stand for no coarse impudence from servants, nor slothfulness from landlords upon the way . . . She would count it a duty to inspect both bedchambers and kitchen for cleanliness, and food for palatability, and give any defaulter the rough edge of her tongue.

Yet, despite Joan Pullen's virtuosity and the refinements of the coach, the journey had proved vastly uncomfortable. For Mary, even David's nearness, and the exquisite emotions it stirred within her, could not wholly compensate for the tedium of a long journey. Other distractions, even a reading of 'Patterson's Roads', with its erudite information about those landmarks and treasures to be observed upon the route, served only to tire her eyes and clog her brain, as the oleaginous food at the inns served to clog her appetite. She, who had always been so decisive and self-reliant, worried incessantly about David's health, and whether Sir Frederick might fret, or, perhaps, fall sick of an apoplexy, in their absence. She was equally troubled about Luc's new mission, and its secrecy. She fretted lest the jolting of the coach should aggravate David's leg wound, or lest their beds prove damp. Joan Pullen, who knew Mary better than any upon earth, knew that it was love which drove her, and fear that such happiness might, once again, be snatched too early from her grasp . . . Despite Mary's forebodings, and David's own, for he could not judge how the journey might end, they came, at length, to the village he knew. The familiar landmarks of his childhood, the church, the inns and village green, raked him with unbearable sadness, and his leg had stiffened into a throbbing pain . . . Mary, glimpsing his pallor and the beading of sweat upon his lips and brow, reached out and took his hand comfortingly into her own . . . Joan Pullen, seeing the tenderness of her gesture, recalled how many times she had rendered that same reassurance to Mary, the frightened child . . . David Tudor had smiled hesitantly before making apology and rising with awkwardness to open the window of the coach. The wind from the sea had whipped at his hair, and forced colour into his skin, and the smells of iodine, salt and sand, with its aroma of wild thyme, was all of his childhood as they took the road over the high hill, and to Stormy Downs.

The message delivered by word of mouth to Jed by a carrier who had met the stage coach at the inn was cryptic. Jed did not know whether it had simply become garbled upon the way or was a jest to provoke him, for it made little enough sense.

"Repeat it again, man . . . word for word!" he had ordered the impatient carrier.

"Hell and damnation, Jed!" he had cried vexedly. "Will you not take telling? That is all I know!" Yet he had repeated it obligingly, his face as bewildered as Jed's own.

"You are to expect a visit from London . . . from a gentleman

249

and lady of quality . . . There . . . let that be an end to it!
'Tis all I know! Would you have me lie, and invent it, to save
you confusion?"

"No . . ." Jed had answered sheepishly, and bade him
enter within, and sup and eat with them at table, if he
chose. The invitation had been accepted with indecent alac-
rity, for Hetty Harris's cooking was known to be an art.

The message had been repeated and discussed then, endlessly,
and afterwards, but none could find rhyme nor reason in it . . .

"A gentleman come to bargain for some Jacob's sheep, or to
purchase an ox?" Becky hazarded.

"More like 'tis someone seeking Jed, to drive a herd come
Spring . . ." Daniel countered.

"But a lady of quality . . ." Sarah reminded, in puzzlement.
"It is unlikely that she would travel for such a purpose . . ."

It was Jed's opinion that it was a message about Luc's return,
and that the carrier, and others before him, had got it somehow
twisted about . . . Yet, Jed would not speak of it to Sarah,
or even Becky, for he feared that were he wrong, their
disappointment would be great. "And what do you reckon
to it, Hetty?" Jed had asked as she dished up the steaming
piecrust of leeks and cheese.

"That 'tis better to fill one's belly with good victuals than
one's brain with idle guessing!" she had replied, and amidst
companionable laughter, they had taken her advice.

Jed had no way of knowing that the message had been sent
in good faith at Sir Frederick's command. The old gentleman
had deliberated upon it long and hard, wondering how best to
word it to cause the least emotional distress . . . Luc had told
him only that he was likely to be long absent upon a mission
of importance, and the decision was therefore Sir Frederick's
own. The drover Jed Perkins, whom Luc had spoken of most
kindly, would certainly need warning of David's and Mary's
coming, he reasoned, else he might be off upon his travels,
or buying stock elsewhere . . . The safest course was to give
warning of some unspecified visitor's arrival, that he might be
prepared . . . Yes, it would be kindest were Mary to break the
news of David's survival, and his search for Sarah, to the child
with gentleness, first.

Had he chosen the best way? Sir Frederick could not know, but had decided that it was the way that Josiah, himself, might have prepared it . . . Now, all that he could do was wait . . .

CHAPTER 25

Sarah had been feeding the hens in the cobbled yard, when she heard the distant rumble and creak of a coach along the wide cart-track of the lane . . . She had barely time to call out warning to Becky of the strangers' arrival, and to finish scattering the feed, before the carriage had halted, and the guard had dismounted to uncouple the farmyard gates and fling them wide.

The coach had travelled within, noisy upon its springs, the horses' hooves clattering, and throwing sparks from the cobblestones, and scattering the hens in a squawking blur of feathers . . .

Sarah's curiosity had kept her stiffly rooted to the place where she stood. The magnificence of the crested coach, with its liveried coachman and bewigged postillions, was a source of real delight to her, as were the four matched chestnut horses, fine-boned, and arrogantly proud of mien . . . This was no ordinary visit of a gentleman farmer, seeking stock, or Jed's services, she felt sure. This was the equipage of a nobleman, or one of distinction and power.

She had watched, intrigued, as a postillion had carefully lowered the steps of the coach, making ready for the passengers to alight . . . Sarah was as unaware of the rustic simplicity of her blue print dress and her wind-ruffled hair as of the appealing picture she made; all tawny hair and burnished skin, hazel eyes enquiringly bright.

As the door to the coach was opened, all she saw at first was a pair of dainty rose-pink slippers, emerging from beneath the hem of a delicately matching silk dress. The petticoats, too, were of silk, lace-edged, and expensively ruffled . . . When Mary had emerged into the daylight, clutching her reticule, and face alive with curiosity beneath her elegant bonnet, Sarah had given a cry of recognition, and despair . . . It *was* Luc returning, then! He had come, as promised, but bringing with him the woman from Farnham fair! A woman of his own kind, and one who loved him . . . How could he be so cruel? He had come to see Jed, Sarah thought bleakly, and bringing this beautiful gentlewoman as his bride . . .

Mary, seeing the conflict of emotions upon Sarah's face, and her suppressed rage and dismay, had faltered, and stood still. It was clear that David's sister disliked her. Her antagonism and resentment were plain . . . Yet they were strangers, one to the other. What was she to do? To say? Her usual presence of mind had deserted her, and fearful lest Sarah's anguish would make her turn and flee, Mary turned her face towards the carriage in mute appeal . . .

David, as bewildered by the abrasiveness of the meeting as the women involved, had thrown open the window, and descended in awkward haste. Sarah had at first stared, stupefied, then, with a cry wrenched from her throat, had hurled herself across the yard and into his arms, wetting his shirt front with her tears, unable even to speak his name for the joyous relief and gratitude within her . . . She had been conscious of how thin he was as he held her in his arms, and fleetingly aware of his clumsy and pained descent from the coach . . . But he was home, and safe, thank God! Whatever torments had etched themselves into the deep lines of his face, and ravaged him still, he was alive . . . David was alive!

Mary had stood numbly by, aching with weariness, but the tears she freely shed owed nothing to her journey. They were tears of loving compassion for David and this child unknown, who had found each other, when life and death and the harsh tragedy of war had torn them from all that was known. David, seeing Mary standing helplessly, her beautiful face uncertain with tears, had drawn Sarah towards her, arms encircling both, and making emotional explanation.

He could hazard no guess as to why Sarah had impulsively wrenched herself free of his grasp, and embraced Mary with such anguished fervour and remorse. The two women had remained locked in each other's arms, alternately weeping and laughing, their behaviour as incomprehensible as their murmured conversation. He had heard the name Luc amidst

a renewed outburst of cries, laughter, and muffled explanation
. . . The sheer emotionalism of women, and their love of drama,
was to blame, he decided. It was as involuntary and instinctive
to them as breathing, and he could never hope to understand
. . . He had been grateful when the sound of Jed's heavy boots,
clattering upon the yard as he crossed from the byre, took his
mind off speculation.

Jed's transparent delight and excitement at learning who the
visitors were was heartwarming. It was so extravagant and
unfeigned that none could remain aloof or unaffected . . .
His frank bucolic face was wreathed in smiles as he called
urgently to Becky to hurry from within to bid welcome.

"Oh, my love . . ." he exclaimed, "You will never guess who,
out of all the world, is come visiting . . . 'tis Sarah's brother, no
less! And this is his friend, and betrothed, Mrs Grantley . . ."

Becky, flustered from her usual self-possession, had mum-
bled acknowledgement and dropped a deferential curtsey to
the exquisitively dressed gentlewoman. But Mary was having
none of it, and eschewing all such formality, had kissed Becky
warmly upon the cheek, linking her arm through Becky's and
Sarah's both, and exclaiming warmly, "Oh, how right Luc was
in his descriptions of you! He claimed that Becky was as vividly
colourful as beech leaves in autumn, and that Sarah was the
sweetest and dearest girl to be found on earth . . . I cannot tell
you how dearly I have longed to meet you!"

Becky had glowed with happy pleasure at the compliment,
and Sarah had blushed prettily, saying with conviction,

"David is indeed fortunate, Mary, to have found you, for
your devotion to him is clear, as is his loving affection for
you . . ." Then, quietly, so that she might not be overheard,
she asked gravely, "Will he return to his regiment? I pray that
it may not be so . . . for the injury to his leg seems painful and
troublesome to him, and he would be set cruelly at risk . . ."

Mary's eyes were no less troubled than Sarah's own as she
confessed, voice low,

"Yes. He must soon return."

"But will you not grieve?" She would have recalled the words
had she been able, for they were blurted foolishly, and Sarah felt
shamed colour flame beneath her skin . . . Mary had answered,
with honesty,

"It would grieve me more were he to fear return . . . or feel himself to be a useless cripple . . . The army is his life, Sarah, and I would not have him choose, or demand it, to be otherwise . . ." Mary had hesitated, as if searching for words, before confessing quietly, "But you are right, I will grieve his leaving . . ."

Sarah had nodded, her fingers closing in understanding upon Mary's gloved hand, as she asked,

"And Luc? You have news of him? He has seen David? Knows of his escape . . .?"

"I can tell you only that he is safe . . ." Mary answered carefully, "and that his guardian, General Loosely, impatiently awaits your return with us to London."

Becky's involuntary cry of protest had been quickly smothered as Sarah had exclaimed, bewildered,

"But was not the general one of Papa's oldest friends, and David's mentor? Did he not pay for my brother's commission in his own regiment? I swear, Mary, that I am so confused and unsettled that I can scarce make sense of it all . . . Are you sure that Luc would not wish me to remain here with Jed and Becky . . .? What if he should return, and not find me . . .?"

"He will find you, wherever you may be." Mary said, gently. "I have known Luc and David from childhood." Her gaze had turned affectionately towards David, who was engrossed in earnest conversation with Jed, "Believe me, Sarah, they were as alike then as now . . . None will swerve them from their purpose, nor change their affection . . . Neither will admit defeat . . ."

Sarah said, wrily, "Then it will not make for an easy life."

"No . . . never easy, but always purposeful, and never dull . . ." Mary's smile was warm with some secret remembrance before she added, with quiet certainty, "Their loyalty will never be in doubt . . . That is why I believe Luc would have you return to London, to be with Sir Frederick."

"You are sure that General Loosely would welcome such intrusion . . . accept me? I would not have him forced to charity for Luc's sake alone . . ." Sarah was awkward with distress.

"Oh, my dear . . ." The hug which Mary had given her was fond and impetuous, "He has been searching most desperately

255

for you . . . He had no knowledge that Luc had ever met you, much less that you hoped to wed . . . No. It was from love of your father . . . a debt owed . . . It is that same love which he offers to you, and for your sake, and his own . . ." Her voice was unsteady. "He is an old man, and much alone, and it would be a kindness were you to be with him . . ."

"Then I will go."

The decision was made without reserve or hesitation, and Becky's face was as radiant with pleasure as Sarah's own as she led them proudly within . . .

If Becky had been briefly disconcerted at seeing so splendid an equipage and company within the yard, and wondered how on earth she was to feed them all, her natural optimism and good humour had soon reasserted itself. Nevertheless, she was pleased that Mary had shown the foresight to dispatch the coachman, the postillions and guard to 'The Ancient Briton Inn' at Newton, upon the coach, to victual themselves, with Daniel Harris as guide. Hetty and Joan Pullen had struck up an immediate friendship, for they were much alike in habit and inclination, and Mary's old nurse had been borne off in triumph, to dine most sumptuously upon Hetty's home-baked fare . . .

To Becky's relief, for Mary had put forward the reasons for it with the utmost tact and delicacy, a delectable hamper had been provided from the coach . . . It had been accepted with the handsome generosity with which it had been offered, and the unusual richness of fare had been enhanced, rather than diminished, by the simplicity of the surroundings in which it had been eaten.

Jed had provided the parsnip wine, a secret and highly potent receipt of Mrs Harris's, and toasts had been made with sincerity, and drunk to with enjoyment . . .

It was Mary who had innocently ventured, early in the meal, "Luc told us, Becky, that you are an actress born, a natural entertainer and mimic . . ."

"Indeed she is!" Jed's face had glowed with wine and vicarious pride. "There is none of her talent, I'll wager, not in London nor beyond . . . 'tis as natural to her as breathing . . . Is that not so, Sarah?" Sarah had smilingly agreed.

"Sir Frederick has powerful friends in the arts . . ." David

256

said impulsively, "men of influence and discretion . . . Owners of playhouses and the like . . . Would you have me speak to him, Becky?"

Jed had grown unnaturally still, his gaze upon Becky's face, his expression one of mingled pride and uncertainty.

"Would you have me speak to him?" David repeated, unaware of the tenseness surrounding him.

Becky's silence had stretched long, before she said, with quiet assurance,

"No. I thank you, sir . . . It was naught but a childish whim, a foolishness outgrown." She had turned her head towards Jed, her eyes warm with tenderness and candour. "My life, and my home, lie here with Jed. There is nothing beyond that could tempt me . . . nor bring me such joy, or fulfilment . . . 'tis Jed's love I have always sought, and not the applause of others . . ."

"Then you have found it . . ." Jed spoke the words with pride before all, although his throat was constricted with the joyous hurt of it. "You will not regret it, Becky, I swear it by all that I am, and own . . ."

"No. I will not regret it, Jed."

There had been such loving conviction in her tone that none could doubt it.

David Tudor had raised his glass, to say, with his glance resting upon each of them in turn, "I propose a solemn toast. To all those who have found true love. May it grow, and endure for ever . . ."

Each of them had raised a glass, and gratefully echoed his words, mind turned towards one present or absent . . . David's glass was lowered as he gazed with undisguised affection at Sarah . . . Then, he raised it again, eyes bright, to say, "To those who were lost, and are found again . . ."

It was only in Jed's mind that the words sprang, unbidden, as clearly as if he had spoken them aloud.

"To the return of the prodigal . . . my son."

And try as he might, he could not think why they so disturbed him, nor why it was Luc's ravaged face he saw.

The women's leavetaking had been tender, and tearfully made, and Jed's face had become uncomfortably reddened, his voice gruff, as he took David Tudor's proffered hand.

257

"I need not ask you to take good care of the little maid . . ." he said, "for I know that you are as joyous at finding her again as we are saddened at losing her."

"You will not lose me, Jed!" Sarah had hugged him fiercely, and set a loving kiss to his roughened cheek. "I shall return for your wedding . . . It is a given promise . . . None shall hinder, and nothing shall prevent it . . ."

He had nodded, pleased, then put an arm around Becky's shoulders, as if to will into her that strength and reassurance his own spirit lacked. Becky had not tried to stem her flow of tears, for it would have been useless. She was consumed with grief and regret, and as much with shame for her selfishness in grudging Sarah her new life . . . Yet they had been closer than kinsfolk, and shared so much of hardship and pleasure upon the drovers' roads . . . Such closeness would never come again.

David had gently taken his sister's arm and, with a word of reassurance, had helped her into the coach. Sarah's back had been stiff and her head held high, lest the tears which blurred her eyes spill over . . .

"Hush, now!" Jed commanded Becky sternly, for the sight of her sorrowful face, and the harsh painfulness of her tears, had all but set him to weeping too. "You have wept enough, Becky! 'Tis not fair to Sarah, for she will carry such memory upon her way, and be grieved the more . . ."

Becky had sniffed, and obediently dried her eyes upon her apron, although her nostrils remained pinched raw, and her eyelids pink-rimmed . . . Jed could not trust himself to speak with sympathy, though her misery grieved him sorely. Becky seemed to have leached away all colour and vitality with her tears; her skin drained and lifeless, and even the clouding glory of her hair dimmed and diminished as she . . .

"Hush, now," he cautioned again, as the carriage moved grindingly away, and Sarah's face showed pale at its window, a hand raised in farewell.

Daniel Harris and Hetty had stood watching the coach intently, until it was out of sight. Then, without speaking, Hetty had walked back, tiredly, into the house, and Daniel to the fields.

"They are gone, Jed . . ." Becky said dully.

"Aye . . . but Sarah will return. She made promise." He took her hand to lead her within, face earnest, as he declared, "'Tis not the ends of the earth she is gone to, Becky, but London . . . 'tis not many miles divide us . . ."

"She will be a gentlewoman, Jed." Her voice was bleak. "'Tis not only miles which will set us apart . . . but what she will be . . ."

"She will be what she has always been!" Jed's voice was firm. "Whether carrier's lad, drovers' woman, or gentlewoman . . . She will not change . . . Like you, she was ever a lady of quality."

Jed had meant only to cheer her, but Becky's tears began anew, and he cursed himself for his clumsy awkwardness with words. He was naught but a dolt and commonplace drover, he knew . . . He could not, for the life of him, recall what he had said to offend her.

Within the coach Sarah had tried to keep back her tears; her joy at finding David tinged with sadness for the loss of those whose caring had given her the will and means to survive. David, hearing her stifled sobs, and the painful gulping of her throat, would have spoken to comfort her, but Mary's swift shake of her head, and warning glance, stilled him . . . Mary made swift to talk to David quietly and earnestly on non-contentious topics, drawing his attention, and Joan Pullen's, to some prettily thatched house or unusual landmark upon the way, and soon Sarah's distress had abated, and she was able to compose herself, and join, tentatively, in the conversation.

Mary had made no mention of Sarah's parting from her friends, although she spoke with real warmth about Jed and Becky, Daniel and Hetty, and their patient industriousness, and the generosity of their welcome . . . Poor child, she thought, seeing, with pity, the bruised shadows darkening Sarah's eyes, and the emotion which exhausted her. The simple gown of sprigged blue cotton which Sarah was wearing was pathetically ill-made, and the poor cloak which covered it scarcely more flattering . . . Mary had brought with her a portmanteau of elegant gowns, pelisses, slippers and silk stockings, that Sarah might travel to London attired as a gentlewoman . . . Yet, when Sarah had confided proudly that her gown and boots had been a surprise gift from Jed and Becky, and the cloak bought for her by Luc, upon the drovers' road, Mary had let the matter lie . . .

259

It would have been cruelly offensive to have belittled the quality of the garments Sarah wore, and would have served to humiliate her friends . . . Mary, seated beside Joan Pullen, saw Sarah's eyes close briefly in respite, then open swiftly, as if she sought to keep aware of her new surroundings, and herself . . . Then, despite herself, her eyelids again closed, and her head drooped tiredly, and soon she was sleeping against David's shoulder, his arm tenderly supporting and encircling her.

"Poor lamb!" Joan Pullen said compassionately. "None will ever know the hardship of the life she was made to accept, nor the misery she was forced to endure . . . 'tis past dwelling upon!"

Mary answered quietly, "It has made her stronger in mind and spirit, of that I am sure. She will know more of the needs of the poor and disadvantaged than any, for she has shared in them . . ." She paused. "It must hold her in good stead when she returns, with Luc, to France, and Valandré . . ."

"The war is not yet ended!" David's interjection was abrupt, the rebuke clear.

"No . . ." Mary admitted penitently, "and its continuance will bring grief to us all . . . that is why I look ahead to kinder times, my dear . . ." she hesitated, adding, "and if I did not, the thought of parting, and what might lie in store, would prove unendurable . . ." Mary looked at him steadily, and with such naked affection, that he felt shame at his churlishness.

"I beg you will forgive me, my dear." The apology was painfully drawn from him. "The emotion of my meeting with Sarah, and the wretchedness of travel, rob me of good manners and sense . . . Yes. It will be a great day when the war is finally ended, and Sarah returns with Luc to France . . ."

His free hand reached out to touch Mary's fingertips as he confessed, "As great a day as my returning to you, for it is all that will comfort and sustain me . . ."

Sarah had stirred, and half-lifted her head from the curve of his shoulder, only to settle herself more firmly into sleep, David had smiled, and pursed his lips, declaring ruefully "Life will all be so strange to her, and new . . ."

"But never again so lonely and harsh, pray God!" Joan Pullen said fervently, "Never so harsh again . . ."

For Sarah, the journey to London had seemed never-ending,

and the halts at the inns only scarcely more tolerable. She had so long suffered privation that she could not attune herself to the orgy of gluttony and self-indulgence which so occupied her fellow travellers at the taverns, and upon the roads . . . At the first hostelry they had entered, Sarah's lowly clothing, which marked her as a servant, had caused her to be treated with condescension, and a bed made ready for her in the attic . . . Joan Pullen's wrath had intimidated the pompous innkeeper into making such abject and grovelling apology that Sarah's amusement had bubbled into laughter . . . Yet, it was a laughter so spontaneous and good-natured that the innkeeper had laughed too, relieved, and unable to take offence.

Mary, who had been inadvertent witness to the small drama, felt grateful that she had not been forced to intervene . . . Sarah's tact and humour would serve her well, she thought. It was a special gift, as rare as her ability to mix freely with both high and low . . . Was it born in her, Mary wondered, a relic of her vicarage life, or won, painfully, by her life upon the drovers' roads? Whatever its source, it would arm her for what lay ahead . . . Sarah had been neither humiliated nor resentful of the innkeeper's mistake. Yet, when she was alone in her room, she had peered into the yellow-stained looking glass as if it might somehow give answer to the questions in her mind . . . Who am I? Gentlewoman, or drovers' maid? Rich or poor? Where do I belong? I am of all worlds, and none . . . Her hand had closed hard upon the little christening bracelet worn beneath the bodice of her dress . . . She felt the coldness of metal cut into her hand; a reality. Memory and solace came flooding back. Her mother's gentle affection, Josiah Tudor's innate goodness and warmth of spirit. She saw his lined aesthete's face as clearly as if he stood beside her in flesh, and she knew the words he would use. They were the words he had spoken, with quiet affection, when, as a young child, she had asked him in perplexity, "But who am *I*, Papa? You are a clergyman, and Mama is a mother, and David is a soldier, now . . . But who am I? What am I . . .?"

"You are the dearest little girl who ever lived, Sarah, and my own sweet daughter . . ." he had raised her chin, to give her an indulgent smile and a kiss.

"But what else, Papa? What else?" she had persisted.

Josiah Tudor had lifted her on to his knee, and his face had grown as grave and intent as her own.

"You are Sarah Tudor, my love . . . a special girl, like no other upon earth . . . for we are, each of us, special to God and those who love us . . . Nothing which befalls you can alter that . . . You understand . . ." She had nodded, although she had not truly understood.

"You must remain special within, Sarah . . . believe in your own worth, whatever the estimate of the world, or others . . . Whatever attempts are made to turn or humiliate you, you must be true to yourself, for then no violence on earth can touch you, no bitterness destroy . . ."

They were words which had oftimes returned to comfort her in the days following his death, and in the aridness of the poorhouse, and upon the drifts . . .

I have tried, Papa, I have truly tried, she told him silently, but I lack your simple faith and charity . . . I am fearful for Luc, and David, of the future . . . I do not know if I have the courage to face losing them in war . . . I am bewildered and afraid, a child again . . . The face which stared back at her from the glass was her own, familiar and strange, eyes blurring her reflection with unshed tears. She held her eyelids wide to disperse the tears, and shook them roughly away. Then she opened the door of her room, and descended the stairs.

CHAPTER 26

When the coach had reached the outskirts of London, and then finally halted at Salisbury Square, Sarah's mind was filled with memories of her last visit to the elegant house, as a filthy, despairing carrier's lad. She had come, unheeded, to beg Sir Frederick's aid, for her own sake, and for the sake of the friendship he and her father had shared . . . Yet, she had been turned away by others, with a harsh word and a cruelty which had bitten deep, her shame and humiliation raw . . . Did the same rejection now await her, despite all Mary's firm assurances, and David's belief? It would grieve her were she to be tolerated merely for Luc's sake, or from the debt her father was owed . . . Yet, how could it be otherwise?

Sir Frederick had hurried to the door to greet them, his face gaunt and grave, looking with unease from one to the other, uncertain of how best to act . . . Sarah saw a tall, distinguished gentleman, forbiddingly austere. He saw a child in ugly, travelworn clothes, small oval face bleak with tiredness and apprehension . . . She seemed so pathetically lost and frail that his heart was wrenched with pity . . . It was the clumsy, workaday boots which most moved and unmanned him, for Luc had told him of the weary miles she had tramped in them, and the discomforts she had borne.

Sarah had lowered her head, fearing that his gaze, fixed rigidly upon her boots, spoke of disapprobation; his fastidious disgust at their awkwardness, and her own.

Yet, when she found courage to raise her head proudly, and look into his eyes, she saw such real compassion, and acceptance, that it might have been Josiah Tudor who stood in his stead . . . Without a word, she had run to him, and buried her face in the starched elegance of his shirtfront, and he had clasped her to him as gratefully, murmuring solace, smoothing her disarrayed hair . . . Then, with an effort, he had straightened, and with an arm about her thin shoulders, had led her within . . . Above Sarah's head, his fine eyes had been preternaturally bright, his mouth tender, as he had nodded his gratitude, first to Mary, then David. When he spoke, his voice was thickened, barely recognisable, "I thank God, most humbly, that you found her . . . that you brought her to me at last . . . I had all but despaired." His slender-boned fingers had clasped Sarah's small, roughened fist, as if fearful she might once more elude him. Sir Frederick had the strangest feeling that it was he, and not Sarah, who had come to the end of a long and arduous journey . . . He was the traveller returning; all that was past dissolved and forgotten in the joy of arrival . . . An exile safely home.

Luc had no knowledge that Sarah had been brought to Salisbury Square. He could spare little thought for anything beyond the urgency of the moment, the task of bringing the Duc de Saint Lo to confession, and the trial and justice he deserved.

Saint Lo had proved arrogant and contemptuously unyielding, but Hasquencort's interrogation and Luc's had been relentless, and their persistence as stubborn as his own . . . They had spared him nothing in their questioning, and so completely absorbed were they in their efforts to indict him that they had all but forgotten the silent presence of Spencer Perceval and the Home Secretary and his eagerly attentive acolytes . . . Saint Lo, who was known to them all, had watched their entry into the interrogation room sardonically, wrily amused at the embarrassed attempts at self- effacement . . . He was only too aware, Hasquencort knew, that his former friends and associates were as much on trial as he, and had almost as much to lose . . . The only difference lay in that if Saint Lo were proven guilty, then his death sentence would be immutable; *they* would certainly use all their powers of guile and persuasion to exonerate themselves . . . Yet, by the surreptitiousness of their entry, and the furtive way they took their seats, faces carefully averted or downcast, their dilemma was even more painful than Saint Lo's . . . He was aware of his own guilt, or innocence; they were not. Were his innocence formally established, then their denial of him would be hard to justify, and his patronage offered elsewhere . . .

Despite the rigours of the questioning, Saint Lo had, at first, remained detached, supercilious even, his saturnine face coldly expressionless. Gradually, as the swiftness and ferocity of his inquisition had increased, he had grown more assured, mocking even . . . as if he drew satisfaction from the quickening of wits and battle . . . He was undeniably an impressive figure, with a natural air of command and authority, and among those who listened to his measured replies to the accusations laid against him, some were plainly convinced . . . Saint Lo was plausible, certainly, Hasquencort thought drily, as so many rogues and liars are.

It was only when the letter of credit was unexpectedly produced, in evidence, that his self-assurance briefly deserted him . . . His proffered explanation, although glib, lacked credibility, and despite his denials, failed to convince . . . Luc and Hasquencort had given him no chance to recover his composure, probing, arguing, introducing new and damning evidence about the raiding of the safe houses, Charlesworth's death and the written affirmations of those arrested, and finally, the sworn testimony of the Irish commander as to his own, and Saint Lo's involvement and guilt.

If those present expected Saint Lo to bluster, and deny it, or to capitulate weakly, he did neither. Nor did he offer spurious excuse, nor make demands for clemency . . . He remained cynically aloof. His handsome, aquiline features retained their arrogance, his overbearing air of superiority remained unchanged. Even his admission of complicity was carelessly made, as if he gave passing rebuke to some ill-prepared servant . . . It was a matter, he somehow inferred, of no real consequence.

The prime minister, then his attendants, had risen, grim-faced, and without a glance or word to Saint Lo, but he had stared at them in silence, but with such fierce intensity that he might have been committing each man's features to memory for some future encounter . . .

It had, after all, been a sordid little tale, not of conviction and sacrifice for a cause, however misplaced, but of expediency . . . Saint Lo had been stripped of his lands and possessions, as so many other emigrés fleeing the revolution . . . Yet, at promise that his lands and titles would be restored with Napoleon's victory, he had accepted money from the traitor, and had become one, in turn . . . His wealth and position had been payment for a renunciation of all that he had formerly inherited and lost . . .

Saint Lo had spoken only to Luc after his confession of guilt. "You, de Valandré!" his voice had been imperious. "You, at least, must comprehend the reason . . . I did it to retrieve that which I had lost . . . my estates, and possessions . . . my status, and rank. Surely, sir, you, as a Frenchman, understand . . .?"

"No, sir." Luc's voice, although low, was lacerating in its contempt. "The price for my own inheritance had been paid in blood . . . I would not betray it, and those who died, by turning renegade . . . That much honesty is owed to France, the king, and those who died . . ."

"You are a fool, de Valandré!"

"Then I will find that easier to live with than betrayal." Luc's glance was scathing. "You have my pity, Saint Lo . . ."

"You are impertinent, de Valandré! I have need of no man's pity."

"You may reject it, as you have rejected all else . . ." Luc said quietly, and with a curt nod towards Hasquencort, turned abruptly on his heel. At the door, he paused briefly.

"I cannot doubt, Saint Lo, that you will find it easier to accept death than to live with what you are . . . Should you forget, there are too many murdered innocents to remind you . . ."

He had looked, Hasquencort thought, more austerely aristocratic than the Duc de Saint Lo himself . . . yet the nerve which twitched at Luc's cheek, and the trembling of his hands, had betrayed his anguish of mind . . . There would be other prisoners to identify and interrogate, but then Luc's involvement in espionage must cease. Without objectivity, he would be a risk to others, and to himself . . . He would recommend that de Valandré be returned to his regiment. Hasquencort's thoughts and gaze reluctantly returned to the prisoner, and he silently damned him and all those like him for their selfish cupidity . . . that meanness of soul which betrayed, not only themselves, but others . . . others like Luc de Valandré, to whom the past and the dead remained, not an old forgotten scar, but an open wound . . .

Sarah's transition into the life of the household in Salisbury Square had been immediate and painless. She had quickly learned to respect and trust Sir Frederick, and to discover in him those qualities of friendship which her father most prized . . . She felt no animosity towards those members of his household staff who had earlier held her in disdain, and was only grateful that they had failed to recognise her in her new guise as Sir Frederick's ward . . . Sarah needed no reminder of her days as a filthy, malnourished carrier's lad, with shorn head, who had but recently escaped from paupery . . . The misery of it remained branded upon her, and the scars would only slowly fade. Yet, it was her grief alone, and she would burden no other with memory of it. It had pleased her that David was close at hand, to tease, and protect her, as a brother . . . The affection between them, despite the disparity in their ages, was firm . . . the closer, perhaps, because of the tragedy of their loss, and separation . . . Mary had accepted Sarah with the greatest warmth, and for her own sake, as well as David's. Gradually, unobtrusively, she was helping Sarah to come to terms with her new life, taking pleasure in helping her to choose suitable clothes for her role as leisured gentlewoman reintroducing her to the polite arts and new, and sympathetic, friends . . . Sarah had, at first, been appalled at the wasteful extravagance of her purchases, and wracked with guilt at her self-indulgence. She had resented, too, the apparent aimlessness of the lives of gentlewomen in society; their endless visiting, the rigid mores and conventions, their overt dispensing of charity to those in need . . . Yet she slowly came to see that the deficiency was in herself, as much as they . . . It was a way of life to which they had been born and bred, as Becky and Hetty Harris had been born to theirs. There was no intrinsic virtue, or superiority, in either . . . They existed, and must learn to live amicably, side by side . . . Her greatest disappointment was that there had been no word from Luc, whose duties kept him occupied elsewhere, with no immediate prospect of release . . . Sarah delighted in the tenderness between David and Mary, their evident love and need . . . They seemed always to be reaching out, one for the other, in reminiscence as in flesh; as if contact in touch and words were, like time, too precious to be wasted . . . Sarah felt no jealousy, for she loved both Mary and her brother dearly, but their transparent happiness seemed to isolate her further, and to heighten her yearning for Luc . . . Sir Frederick, who watched over her affectionately, was troubled, for he knew how sudden and violent were the changes in her life . . . Yet he had pledged himself not to interfere in Sarah's life. He would neither counsel her nor guide, unless she invited him to do so. It was with some trepidation that she had gone to see him in his library, to ask his indulgence. His honest delight at Sarah's seeking him out had been evident, and he had begged her to be seated, grateful to see her grow calm and relaxed . . . He had, at first, made determinedly general conversation, and soon they were smiling, and discussing things equably. Then, he asked gently,

"Was there something in particular which brought you to me, Sarah?"

"Yes, sir . . . I should like your advice . . . and your help."

"Then I shall give them to you gladly . . . There is something which troubles your mind?"

"Rather someone, sir."

He had nodded, expecting some question about Luc, but, instead, Sarah had blurted, "There is a poor woman at the paupers' house in Yorkshire, sir . . ."

"A friend?"

"Indeed, sir . . . More to me than that . . . She gave me friendship and comfort when . . ." Sarah suddenly faltered, adding firmly, "when all seemed lost."

"What would you have me do, my dear?"

His response was immediate and concerned, for the whiteness of her face and her agitation greatly disturbed him. "Would you have me send for this poor woman . . . offer her home and employment?"

"No, sir . . . I would go to her myself, for I can make myself understood . . . a language of touch, sir, for Jane is both deaf and dumb, and knows no other." She paused, wondering how best to explain without giving offence and seeming to reject his generosity . . .

She said, at length, "I would not have her alarmed or bewildered, you understand? I owe her a return of that friendship which she gave to me . . ."

"Then I shall ask Mary and David to travel with you . . . for it is not fitting, or safe, that you travel alone . . ." He had checked himself, shaking his head ruefully, as he recalled that journey she had been forced to undertake unprotected. "It would please me, my dear," he said humbly, "were you to humour me, and travel as I wish . . ."

"Of course, sir! I would be a fool and an ingrate to spurn your care for me . . . You have already been more generous to me than I deserve . . ."

Sarah had risen and rushed to throw her arms impulsively about his neck, and to kiss his thin and desiccated cheek . . . He had flushed with pleasure at feeling her soft arms encircling him and hearing the depths of real affection in her words.

"Then it shall be done as you ask," he promised, "and your friend shall receive shelter and home here, for as long as she chooses . . ."

Oliver Sidebottom knew only that a gentleman's travelling coach had arrived at the poorhouse gate, and those within wished to gain admittance.

"Who is it? Did you not enquire?" he demanded irritably of the aged pauper who had come running to apprise him of it. The ancient had taken time to reply, for his ribs still ached, and his breath came painfully, from hurrying, and the rare excitement of it.

"No, sir . . ." he admitted, when he was able, "'twas not rightly my place, sir . . . for 'twas a fine coach, with servants wigged and liveried . . . and a painted crest upon its side . . . A rare sight . . . and gentlefolk of the quality within . . ."

"Fool!" Sidebottom had dismissed him with a muttered oath for his stupidity, and a clout to his head to mend his manners.

"Open the gates to them! Bid them come in . . . I shall attend them when I am suitably attired to greet such visitors . . ."

The pauper had lingered uncertainly for a moment.

"What ails you, man?" Sidebottom demanded petulantly. "Are you witless, as well as infirm? Go, I say . . . else they

269

will think it is Bedlam they have come to, and you one of its lunatics!"

Despite David's strictures, and Mary's pleas besides, Sarah stubbornly insisted that she must enter the poorhouse alone. It would not do, she said, to confuse and intimidate Jane Grey. She would explain her mission patiently to her friend, and in "the language of signs, and touch", which Jane trusted. It was only with gravest misgivings that they allowed Sarah to go. Her fear of the workmaster, and his ill-treatment of her and those unfortunate wretches in his care grieved them. For David's part, he would gladly have flayed Sidebottom, verbally, and in the flesh, for denying all knowledge of Sarah when he had come seeking news of his sister . . . The man was a conceited, pompous little nonentity; a humbug, and a fool! Should he distress Sarah in any way, or seek to intimidate her, David decided, then it would please him to teach the little jackanapes the lesson he deserved, his own injuries notwithstanding!

Sidebottom had not, at first, recognised Sarah, clad as she was in the stylishly elegant clothing of a gentlewoman of fashion . . . That she was one of the haute-monde was plain to him as he came forward, bewigged and foppish, to greet her . . . Despite the terror and rage which gripped her, Sarah's face, beneath her modish bonnet brim, was serene, her manner charmingly condescending . . .

"Mr Oliver Sidebottom, I believe . . .?"

He had faltered, some vestige of remembrance stirring within him . . . gnawing . . . strangely elusive.

"An honour to make your acquaintance, ma'am."

"Oh, but we are already well acquainted, Mr Sidebottom . . ."

The hand he had extended had dropped uneasily to his side, the short upper lip curled above the fox-like teeth.

"Indeed, ma'am?"

"Indeed, sir."

He had stared at her uncertainly, and without recognition . . . As the intensity of his scrutiny had increased, so had his discomfort. The oval face, high-cheeked, and delicately boned, seemed disturbingly familiar, as did the remarkable hazel eyes. He recalled them now, and their pride and arrogance, defiant above the grey homespun of her workhouse dress.

"Sarah Tudor . . .!" It was a cry of outrage.

"I see, sir, that your memory serves you as well as mine serves me . . ."

The sheer effrontery of it robbed him of words. The audacity! The brazen impertinence of the creature to return, and try to gain his respect . . . No doubt she was some rich man's whore. A harlot, taken from the streets for carnal amusement . . . When speech returned, and with it a cold anger, he declared frigidly, "State your business! I have little time to spare upon . . . paupers!"

"That, sir, is a fact well known to me . . ."

Sarah's quiet rejoinder, and her self-possession, raked him to fury, as he repeated testily, "State your business!"

"I believe, sir, that this will explain my errand . . ." She produced from her reticule a letter in General Loosely's hand, and with his seal. "My guardian, Sir Frederick Loosely, bids you attend me, and grant me your indulgence . . ."

Oliver Sidebottom had read in silence, his long nose and chin seeming to grow more pinched and pointed as his colour rose.

"I will send for Jane Grey . . ." he said disparagingly, "but it will avail you nothing . . . She is weak-minded, and a deaf mute . . . If you wish to take a pauper into service, it were better you chose one to do us credit . . ."

"The credit, sir, lies in what she is, and what she has overcome," Sarah was stung into replying. "Now, if you will send for her, it will oblige me!"

Seething with humiliation, but unable to refuse, he declared pompously, "As . . . master of this institution, and mindful of my responsibilities, I shall attend the interview . . ."

"No, sir!" Her denial was firm, "Sir Frederick, my guardian, specifically demanded that I see her alone, in private . . ." As he hesitated, Sarah insisted, "Alone, sir! Since you claim her to be simple-minded, and a deaf mute, your presence would be superfluous . . . a waste of your invaluable time."

With ill-grace, Sidebottom had sucked his lip between his teeth, turned upon his heel, and left. Sarah, although the victor, had found herself trembling at the exchange, as much as from his presence . . . He was an odious, prurient, little creature, sly and vindictive. She had thanked God that she would need to fear him no more.

The reunion between Sarah and Jane Grey had been filled with despairing tears, and a warmth of tenderness and laughter . . . It was as if the time between had never been, for the old companionship and loving intimacy seemed not diminished, but strengthened by absence.

The hideousness of the paupers' roughspun clothing seemed more cruel than ever against the contrast of Sarah's pretty elegance, in her gown and bonnet of rose-bud silk. Jane had touched the sleeve of Sarah's gown with reverence, delighting in its softness, and the clean purity of its line and colour . . . There had been no enviousness in her eyes, no bitterness, only the sheer pleasure of one grateful for the good fortune of another.

Jane's selflessness had chastened and humbled Sarah, and she had eagerly told her of Sir Frederick's wish that she, too, should make the house at Salisbury Square her home . . . At first, Sarah believed that Jane had misunderstood, for she had wept despairingly, unable to compose herself enough to make acceptance . . .

Yet, when she was able to make reply, it was not acceptance, but refusal, she made, generously, and with no wish to spurn the kindness so freely offered . . . Her fingers had been firm upon Sarah's palm as she tapped out the reasons, but her eyes bleak, and her mouth slack with hurt.

She must remain here, where she was of use to those who needed her, and of comfort. Sarah must remember how it had been . . . the woman who had died in childbirth, the aged, the infirm . . .? In the outside world, she would be nothing. A deaf mute, no more than that. Here, she was friend and comforter . . . Here, she would live and, one day, die.

Sarah had wept and pleaded, to no purpose, for at heart she knew that Jane was right . . . Sarah had been unable to persuade her to take clothing, food, or promise of financial help. She must live life by the rules of the workhouse, she insisted, or else bring anger upon herself, and others . . . There was nothing in all the world she needed, save assurance of Sarah's good fortune, and none could deny the reality of that.

In leaving, Sarah had spoken no word to Oliver Sidebottom, nor to the obese, florid faced gentleman dismounting from his carriage without the poorhouse door . . . He had doffed his hat

most eloquently, protuberant eyes alight with prurient curiosity
. . . Her nod of the head had been coldly formal in return, for
she was sure that Sir John Hambrook had failed to recognise
her . . . His full, sensuous lips had curled in a smile as he
had glanced back at the crested coach and liveried servants,
a postillion hurrying now to assist her to mount the step . . .

"A fine day, ma'am."

His overpowering presence was no threat to her now . . . His
avarice at robbing her of home and chattels, his lascivious plans
for her, no longer held power to hurt . . . He was a character
from another time, another life . . . A common lecher, elderly,
red-veined, and pitiable . . . "A fine day, sir." Her voice, gentle
and well-modulated, gave polite agreement . . . She was free
. . . The shackles of the past no longer bound and crippled her
. . . She was happy for herself, her release . . . but she wept
within for Jane Grey and all those who had no hope of release;
no hope at all . . . Then her eyes, too, were wet with tears as
she took David's proffered hand, as he drew her affectionately
within the coach.

David and Mary, upon hearing the outcome of her visit, would
have returned immediately to London, but Sarah was firm that
she had a debt to repay before she could leave with peace of
mind . . . They had humoured her, for they were aware of how
deeply Jane's refusal to leave the poorhouse had grieved and
disappointed her.

Jacob the Carrier had emerged, bewildered and apprehensive, from his rough stone dwelling when the coach had halted
upon the cobblestones without . . . His dealings were honest,
he knew, but never with 'the quality', and such a visit could
only mean that he had unwittingly angered some gentleman,
or his coachman, upon the road. Yet it was a gentlewoman
who descended the steps, and, to his horrified confusion, threw
her arms about him, as affectionately as if in greeting a friend,
one of her own class and station . . .

"No, ma'am . . ." He had protested, shock and fear making
him all but incoherent. "No, ma'am . . . 'tis some mistake . . .
I swear, I do not know you . . ."

"Do you not, Jacob?"

Some inflection in the voice had alerted him, but he gazed

273

at her without recognition still . . . She was as elegantly as fine a lady as he ever had seen . . . handsome, gracious, and her hazel eyes warm with laughter. It was then that he saw, in memory, the terrified girl from the poorhouse, head shorn, face grey as the rough homespun she wore . . . Only her eyes were the same, and the delicate oval of her face.

"The carrier's lad!" he made delighted exclamation. "By heaven and all the angels, 'tis the lad I delivered to Joe Fowles the carrier! Oh! 'Tis a rare blessing to see you, ma'am, and so well set up and elegant . . . 'twas plain to me you were gentry, even in your paupers' grey . . . Oh, 'tis a rare blessing, . . . a rare blessing . . ."

His gaze had turned, fascinated, upon the crested travelling coach, with its fine horses and liveried coachman and postillions. "You have business hereabouts, ma'am?" his smile was wide with pleasure. "I dare hazard that 'twas not the workmaster you sought?"

"It was you I sought, Jacob . . . to repay a longstanding debt."

Despite his fierce protestations, she had insisted upon payment of three gold coins, and as many more to deliver to Joe Fowles, with her warmest remembrance and gratitude.

"'Tis a fortune, ma'am . . ." he had declared, abashed, "and I have done nothing to earn it, save to offer what small comfort and aid I could . . . No, 'tis too generous, and 'twould shame me to take it . . ."

"And it would shame and grieve me if you did not . . ." Sarah's eyes were gravely entreating under her bonnet brim. "I beg that you will accept it, Jacob, if not as payment, then as an exchange honestly and affectionately made . . . your goodwill for mine."

Jacob had looked at her long and hard, without speaking, then slowly nodded acceptance of her bargain . . .

"Ma'am . . . ?" his voice was hesitant. "Then we will seal it with a gift from me . . ." He had delved into his pocket, and produced the fox-head pin from its wrapped cloth within its pouch.

"But it was an outright gift to you, Jacob! Yours by right . . ."

"No, ma'am . . . A loan . . . I held it only in safekeeping . . ." His weather beaten face grew ruddier, and creased with embarrassment as he struggled to find the words . . . "You gave it to me as something you valued; a remembrance of your brother, you confided, long missing in the wars . . . I beg you will receive it now, for his sake, and your own . . ."

"Then you may give it to him yourself, Jacob. He is within the carriage, and safe . . ."

David and Mary had descended from the coach in eager haste upon Sarah's murmured explanation and entreaty . . . Sarah had fastened the fox-head pin into David's silken cravat, and there had been a silence between them, too deeply binding for the need of words . . .

Jacob had watched the coach departing, David's and Mary's gratitude for his care of Sarah a warmth and kindness within him. The gold coins for himself and Joe Fowles were within his coat, and his fist closed comfortingly about them . . . They would lighten many a cold winter's day, and provide warmth and sustenance.

"'Tis not fitting that a carter should own so elegant a thing, sir . . ." he had said to David Tudor of the fox-head pin. "'tis best in the care of a gentleman like yourself . . . I could have no use for it . . . begging your pardon and indulgence . . ."

Oh! but he would miss it sorely. It was the only thing of value and beauty he had ever owned. A rare and lovely thing, and none would ever know the deep hurt of parting with it . . . But it had been returned to its home, like the carrier's lad . . . It was a strange old life, but the only one we had . . . 'twas best to make the best of it, while it lasted.

CHAPTER 27

Luc had experienced less elation than he had expected at helping to secure Saint Lo's confession. For the duke himself he had felt neither pity nor understanding, merely contempt. He was a murderer and a traitor, who had sold himself as cheaply as a whore sells flesh . . . Hasquencort, aware of Luc's exhaustion and discontent, knew that it sprang, not from any physical cause, but from conviction that his work in espionage was ended . . . The chain of escape and repatriation was severed, and could never be repaired. Had de Valanndré perhaps hoped that he would be returned to France, as Luc Nolais, escaped prisoner-of-war? It would seem so, and that his success in breaking Saint Lo had led, as surely, to the breaking of his own ambition.

Hasquencort wondered if, after all, Luc's return to his old regiment would be the best course. His restless energies might make him defiantly careless of the risks he took, unmindful of his own safety . . . As Luc's direct superior, Hasquencort decided, he would make strong recommendation that de Valandré be sent directly into France, as an agent of espionage . . . His field experience, and knowledge of the language, would hold him in good stead, and his loyalty could be as little in doubt as his will to succeed . . . Yes, that would be the best course, Hasquencort assured himself. He must work sedulously, but in secret, to influence those in command . . . Were he to succeed, it would be Luc's salvation.

There would, inevitably, be more interviews, more obstacles to overcome, before Saint Lo and his collaborators were finally brought to justice . . . Meanwhile, there was the meeting with Spencer Perceval and the Home Secretary which they had been, not requested, but commanded to attend . . . Hasquencort could not doubt that it would prove acrimonious and abrasive . . . Saint Lo, despite his present disgrace, had been a man of immense wealth and power, an influence upon politicians and those in authority . . . Surely there would be those among them still in his debt?

Spencer Perceval, however, had remained aloof from such involvement. He was a cold man; reserved in manner and sparing of speech. His questions to Luc and Hasquencort had been pertinent but brief, his grasp of the affair tenacious . . . Saint Lo, he declared unequivocally, was a traitor to his own country and that which had given him refuge. He had been the architect of his own fate . . . Death, for treason, was a punishment well deserved.

He had commended both Luc and Hasquencort for duty well done . . . reminding them stiffly that it was no more than was demanded and expected of those who served. He had put forward their names to "a higher authority", Spencer Perceval had declared in conclusion, "where their application to their task would be suitably acknowledged, and recognised . . ." Then, with a brisk handshake, he had dismissed them both.

When they were safely without the prime minister's room, Hasquencort had smiled wrily at Luc, saying, "Well, it is ended safely, and with as few heroics as I had hoped . . ."

"Indeed . . ." Luc's response had been amused, "and I am grateful, for that interview had held more terrors and pitfalls for me than the whole escapade . . ."

He had regretfully declined Hasquencort's offer to return with him to his house, asking that they defer their celebration. He must return to Salisbury Square to see General Loosely, Luc explained, and to learn news of David Tudor's progress, and his friend's expected return to his regiment.

They had parted cordially, and with agreement to meet soon, and so it was that Luc had hired a carriage and been driven, exalted, and shamefully eager to blurt out his good news to any who would listen. Saint Lo's arrest and trial on a charge of treason would be common knowledge within the hour. There would be no further need for silence.

It was General Loosely, engrossed in penning business letters at his desk, who had first heard the sound of carriage wheels halting beneath his window, and had arisen to investigate whom the visitor might be. David Tudor, too, had heard the arrival, and from his chair beside the window of the drawing room had glanced out in curiosity . . . Upon seeing Luc's descent, Sir Frederick had given an involuntary cry, and hurried to greet him, brushing quill and paper to the floor in his eager excitement. David had hurried without, cursing that stiffness in his leg which so hampered him. They had arrived at the door at the same moment, and David had stood aside that Sir Frederick might greet Luc first. The embrace between the two had been one of delighted relief, and as affectionate as that of father and son, and David's handclasp had been no less sincere . . . Both men were aware from Luc's mood of ill-suppressed excitement that he had news of importance to impart.

"Mary?" he had demanded urgently. "Is Mary here?"

Sir Frederick's warning glance had kept David from blurting that she was away upon some outing in the carriage, and Sarah beside her.

"Mary is expected to return soon . . ." he amended obediently. "She will be truly overjoyed to see you . . ."

Sir Frederick, nodding approval, had ushered them into his library, that they might more freely talk and imbibe.

Luc's concise exposition of Saint Lo's arrest, and the events which had led to it, was listened to in silence, and with incredulous amazement. Then the babble of excited questioning and congratulation had begun, only to be renewed with Luc's confession of his meeting with Spencer Perceval, and its promised outcome. David's praise had been as generously offered as the Madeira they had drunk, and Sir Frederick's vicarious pride had been touchingly evident in his every gesture and glance. His spoken words, however, had been as spare and restrained as he, for by habit, and nature, he was a man not given to easy emotion . . .

How strange, Sir Frederick thought, that path which had led from Valandré to this . . . a destiny near to fulfilment . . . And would he live to see its completion? He feared not, for he was already an old man, and the wars with the French cruelly unresolved . . . Yet, he thought with humility, I have played a part in Luc's growing to maturity . . . Perhaps I have helped in some small measure to give, not only home, but example, as my dear friend, Armand de Valandré, might have done . . . His hand strayed towards the calf-bound volume upon his desk, his immediate inclination to replace it neatly upon the shelf.

Something had stayed his hand, and the words of Alexander Pope which he had earlier read seemed, now, etched upon his mind, as deeply as upon the page, "A brave man struggling in the storms of fate." Yes, that was what Luc de Valandré truly was, and although General Loosely would never speak the words openly, he would hope that Luc knew he loved him as gratefully and wholeheartedly as if he were the child of his own flesh . . .

Sir Frederick had raised his glass high, eyes bright, and Luc had smiled his understanding . . . Diversion had come in the sound of the coach halting without, and, with a swift glance towards General Loosely, David had taken Luc's arm, and forced him hurriedly through the doorway, urging,

"Make haste, Luc! Let us be there when Mary alights from the coach. It will give her surprise and pleasure . . ." Luc had nodded and, amidst the laughter and bustling encouragement of Sir Frederick and David, had all but cleared the steps at a leap, to fling open the door of the coach.

It was not Mary who found herself in his arms and swung smilingly to the cobbles, but Sarah. Her delighted astonishment had been equalled only by Luc's, as, instead of releasing her as he ought, he held her as if he hoped never to set her free . . . Sarah had been as loath to lose the protection of his arms, and had clung to him fiercely, wetting his elegant jacket with her joyful tears, unaware of any save Luc, and his nearness . . . He had kissed her with lingering tenderness, and they might have remained locked possessively in each other's arms, had not Mary been forced to finally seek egress from the coach . . . The exclamations, questioning, and excited congratulations had begun anew, and the spirited joy of their celebrations bound them as securely as if they had never been forced apart.

Yet, all the while, Luc's deepest yearning was to be alone with Sarah, for he did not wish to share her, even with those he loved . . . He was jealous of every moment they had spent apart, and wanted to hold her, so fiercely that it was an ache within him . . . His gaze kept straying towards her, and often he was unaware of what was spoken, for his thoughts were wholly upon how beautiful she was, and how elegant in her dress and pelisse of palest gold, which gave depth to the warm amber and green of her slanting eyes . . .

When, at last, they were alone, and undisturbed, Sarah said quietly,

"And do you find me too much changed, Luc? I am not yet . . . wholly at ease in my splendid new clothes . . ."

"No, I do not find you changed, Sarah . . . you are beautiful, certainly, and as elegant a gentlewoman as any could wish . . . but I loved you no less as a drovers' maid, or with the poor shorn head of a carrier's lad . . ." She could not doubt his sincerity, nor the gentleness, then growing passion, with which he held and kissed her . . . Then, with startling suddenness, he had said gravely, "There are things which, until now, I have been unable to say to you; things about my past, and what the future might hold."

She had made to say that they were of no consequence to her, what was past was ended, and the future was not theirs to shape. Yet, seeing how strangely disturbed he was and eager to explain, she sat quietly, as he begged, and listened to the story of Valandré and all that had since transpired . . . When it was ended, and nothing spared, Sarah might have wept for pity and tenderness for him, but knew she must not. His own tears had long been shed, and it was her courage and faith in the future Luc had most need of now. He had knelt beside her chair, face upturned in question. His eyes were uncertain, and Sarah saw that, like a supplicant, his hands were clasped tightly, as if he hoped, yet dreaded, what the answer might be . . .

"And . . . will you marry me, Sarah Tudor, whatever the future holds?" he asked, at last.

"Yes, for I will have no love without you, Luc. No future. No life of my own . . ."

"And if, when war is ended, and, God willing, I return . . . will you come to Valandré with me, and make it your life?"

"You are my life, Luc." She said with simple honesty, "and wherever you are, that will be my home . . ."

"And if I do not return . . .?"

"Then I will go to Valandré in your stead. I will try to make it what you would have wished . . ."

He had kissed her then, with the love and longing he had felt for Valandré. And in his embrace was deliverance from grief and loss and the restless loneliness of the exiled years. With Sarah beside him, Jean-Luc, le Comte de Valandré, would be no longer an outcast and stranger, but a gentleman of France, returning to his home.

Epilogue

1816

EPILOGUE

The wars with the French had ended. Tens of thousands of men had been killed in battle, and as many more crippled in flesh and spirit . . . Napoleon and his armies were broken, and the self-styled emperor safely exiled to Elba . . . It had been a famous victory. Britain was at peace. Yet the shadows of war still lingered to darken the lives of the living, as they had rendered to darkness the dead.

Among the dead was Major David Tudor, promoted upon the field of battle, only to die there, grievously, of his wounds . . . His widow, Mary, survived to mourn him. Some, not actively engaged in the conflict, had prospered . . . Jed Perkins no longer trod the drovers' roads. He was a successful stock breeder and farmer, his advice valued, and respected. Becky, his devoted wife, was mother of two fine sons, with a daughter stillborn, and another who did not survive infancy . . . It was a brave new life for Jed and Becky, a life beyond their wildest imagining. Yet their friendship with those who had walked beside them upon the roads remained deep and lasting, and none was turned, neglected, from their door.

General Loosely had died peacefully in the last weeks of the war. Mary and Sarah, who had nursed him devotedly, were there beside him, to give him comfort and ease . . . It had been a gentle passing; as quiet and bravely resigned as his living. No more than the stirring of a breeze upon a desiccated leaf, and a gradual, inevitable return to earth.

There were others whose lives in war and peace showed no change. The paupers existed and endured, untroubled by victory, living always in defeat . . . Jane Grey had escaped. Her death from a fever untreated had freed her, but tightened the bonds upon others who had loved her . . . She was missed and mourned.

285

Luc had secretly returned to France, his mission, espionage
. . . His work ended with the ending of the war, he had returned
to Salisbury Square to his wife, Sarah, and the house they had
inherited. Mary had found isolation from grief in the house
upon the estate in Cornwall, which General Loosely had left in
her keeping . . . In the time of Luc's sojourn in France, he had
confined himself to his tasks in Paris . . . He had deliberately
steeled himself not to return to Riberac or Valandré; as much
from fear of discovery as fear of what he might discover . . .
He would set neither his work, nor himself, in jeopardy. When
the time was right, he would return.

The old man within the coach house was as spare and austere
as his frugal surroundings . . . He walked with the jerkiness of
the aged, that shuffling awkwardness of those whose sight grows
dim . . . He had been a large man, powerful and strong-boned.
Yet, now, the flesh was shrunken upon his frame, skin as loose
and ill-fitting as the poor clothing he wore . . . Yet, shrunken
and bowed as he was, the clothes were those of a seneschal,
and his features remained as strong as his will to survive.

He had heard the creaking of a coach as it trundled along
the carriageway, then halted upon the cobblestones of the yard,
and he roused himself to venture without . . . Some passing
stranger, he thought, who had glimpsed the chateau through
the trees which had been spared the woodman's axe, and come
to gaze with curiosity upon past greatness . . . Despite the ache
in his bones, he would walk beside them, every step of the way,
seeing that they stole nothing, destroyed nothing . . . Although,
God alone knew, there was little enough of worth remaining
. . . save those treasures in the dungeons, unseen.

He had tried to invest himself with his old authority, face
sternly autocratic, head held proud . . . The postillion had
already alighted and let down the steps of the coach, and
the old man was not close enough to see who it was who
descended from within, for his eyes were clouded, veiled by
some membrane . . . As he approached, he cleared his throat,
the better to caution them, for his voice, like all else, seemed as
awkwardly weakened by age as his limbs, and as determined to
betray him . . .

The nobleman who descended held a child in his arms, a boy

286

of some four or five years, and the slender gentlewoman cradled a babe, a girl child.

"Raoul . . .?"

The old seneschal had stiffened, and begun to tremble, and he scarcely dared to breathe the words, "Monsieur le Comte de Valandré?"

His voice had indeed betrayed him, for it was thickened, scarce audible.

"Yes, Raoul. I have returned . . ."

He had set the boy to the ground, and taken Raoul in affectionate embrace, and the old man had held him with the warmth and vigour of the past, as if he held the child, Jean-Luc. "Madame la Comtesse . . ." He had recollected himself, and bowed, stiffly, and Sarah had set the babe into his frail arms, kissing his cheek, and saying.

"You hold our daughter, Hélène, sir, and all my affectionate gratitude for . . . what is past."

Raoul had settled the babe with awkward tenderness, and she had gazed up at him with curiosity, inspecting the creased lines of his face, and the opaque eyes, heavy now with tears . . . She had gravely watched them overflow the furrowed skin, to drop silently from his mouth and chin. The boy had taken Raoul's hand, and gazed up at him in concern.

"Why are you crying?" he asked. "Are you not happy that I am here?"

Raoul looked above the head of Armand, Vicomte de Saint Hilaire, to where Jean-Luc de Valandré stood.

"I weep from joy . . ." he said simply. "I weep from joy . . ."